ACT

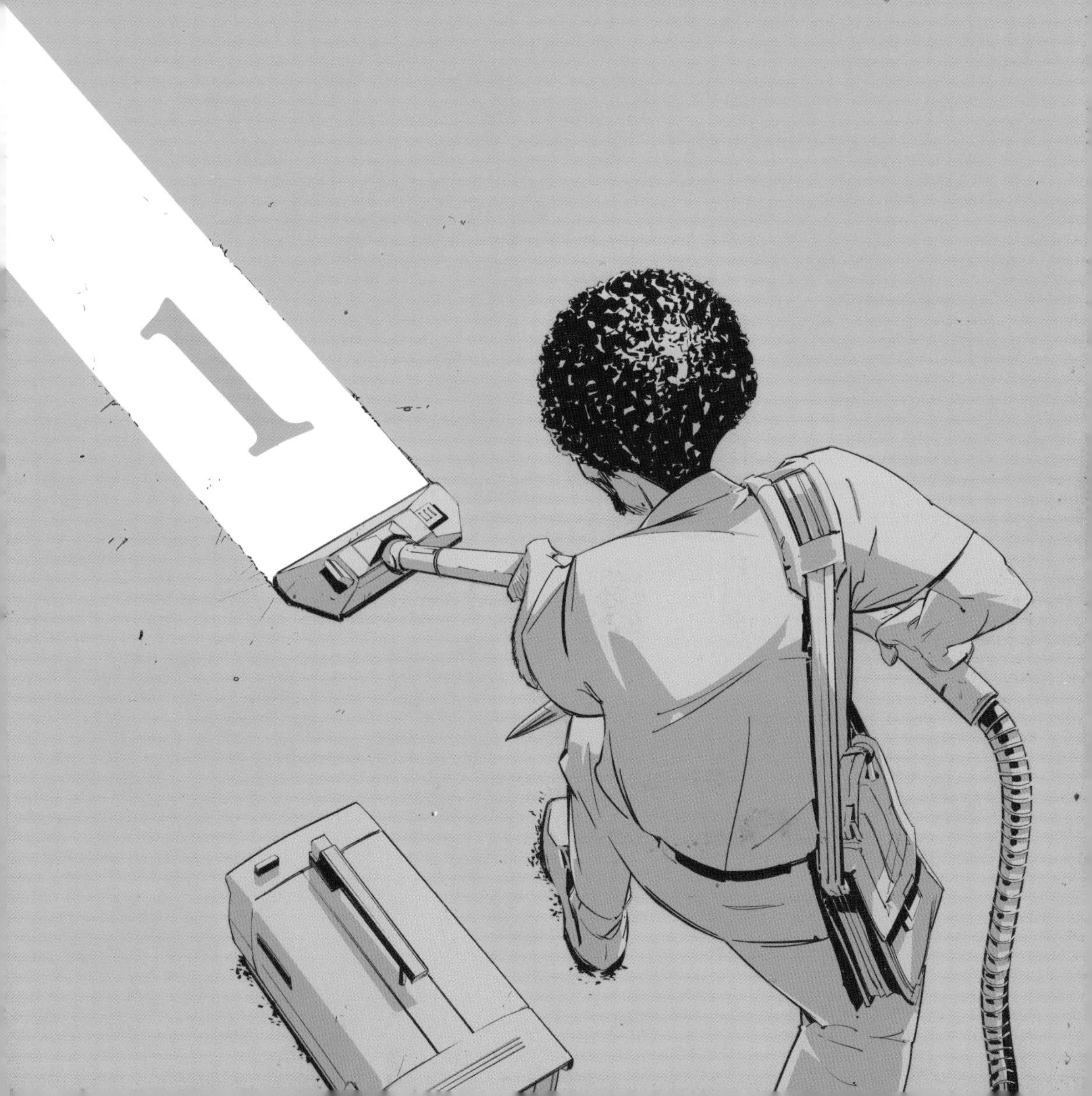
1

To my sister Anne, who motivated me to enroll in the comics workshop at the Maison des Arts d'Evreux. Today, you hold in your hands, the product of a journey you started me on. Thank you so much!

...And to my mom, I apologize in advance for all the bad words I wrote into this story.

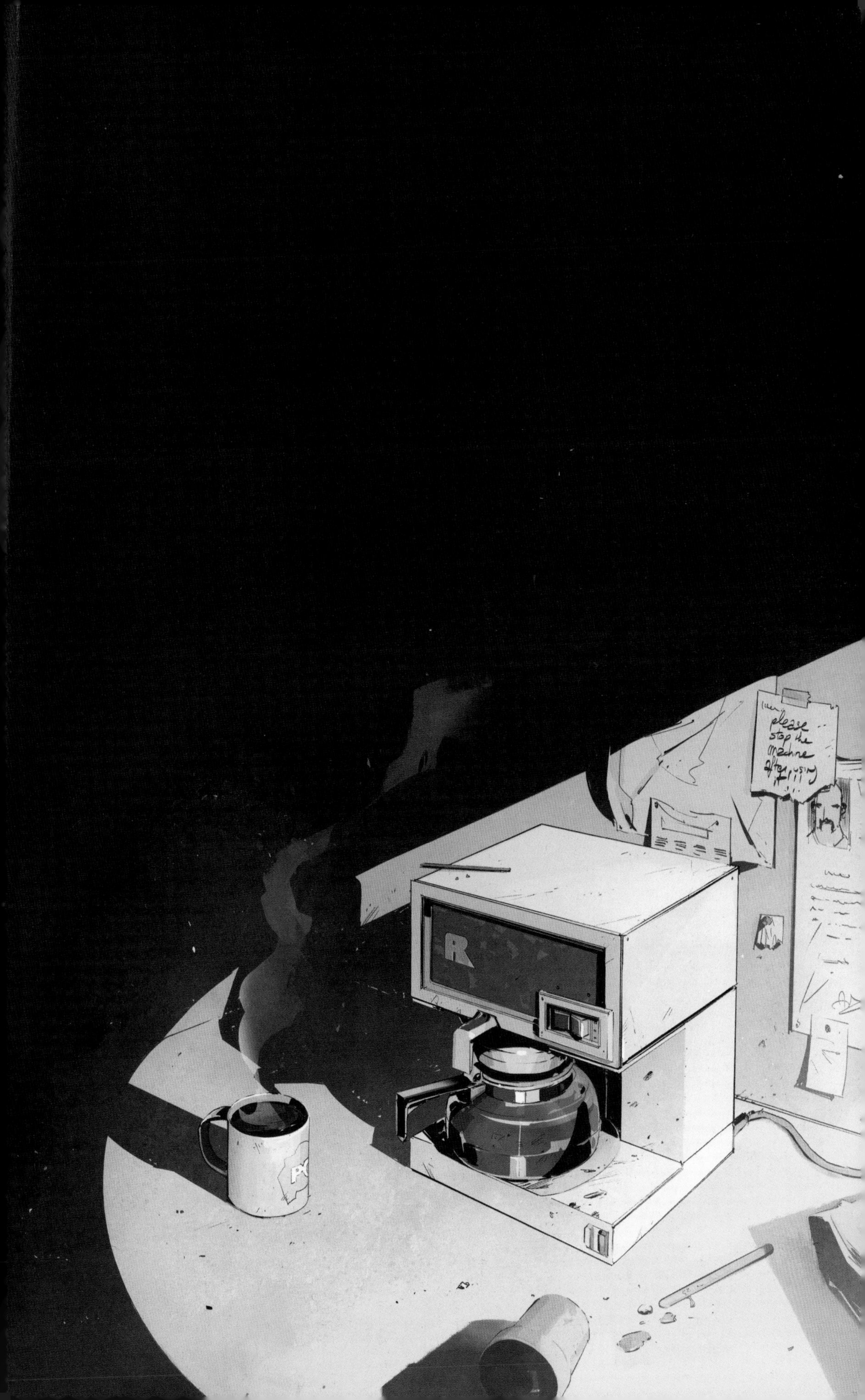
please stop the machine after using it!!!

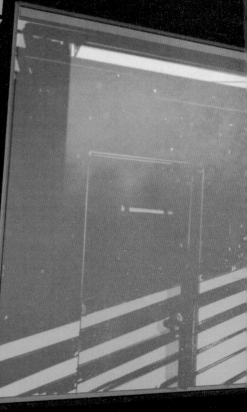

INTERROGATION ROOM
FALCON CITY
ARIZONA
OCTOBER 1981

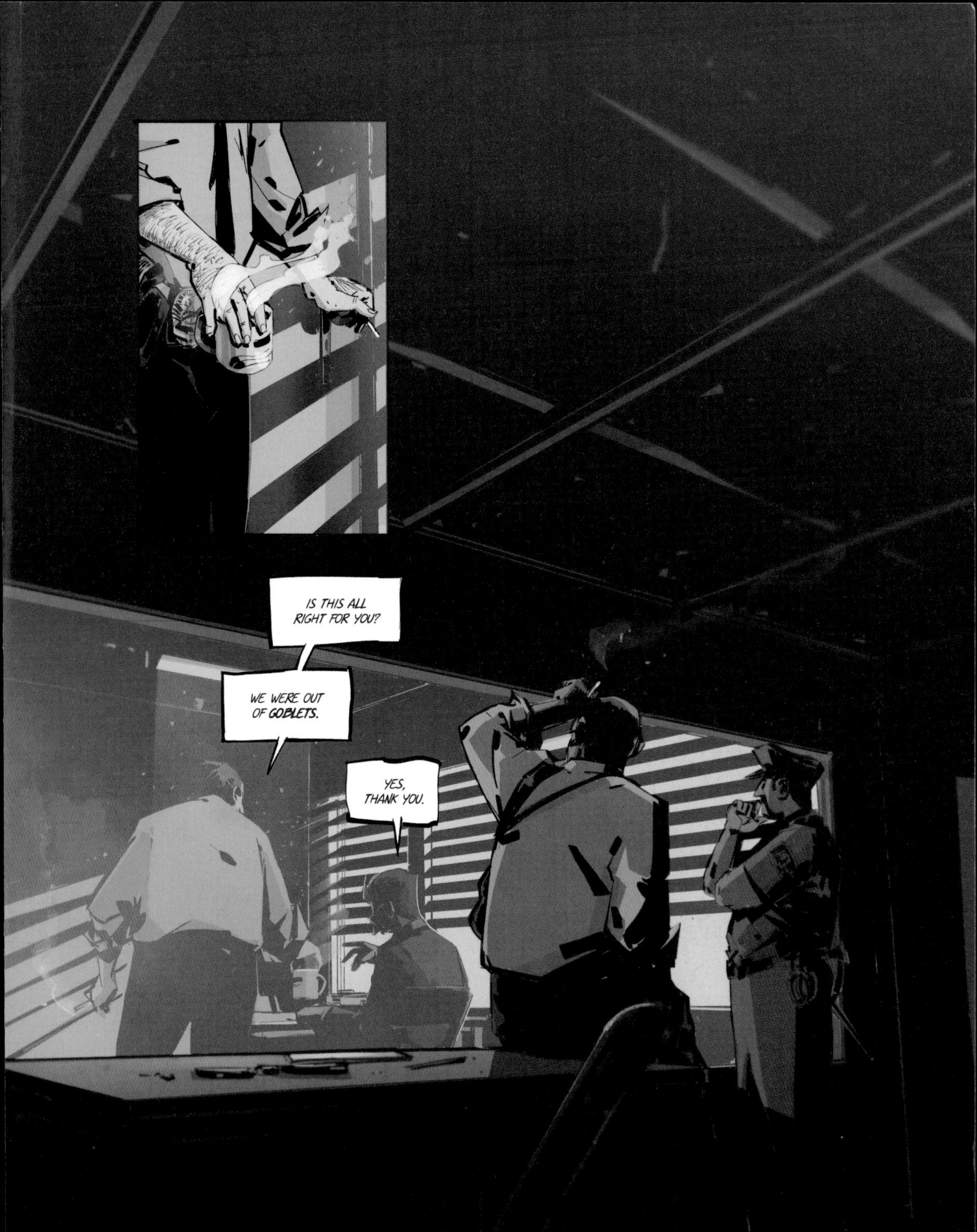
IS THIS ALL RIGHT FOR YOU?
WE WERE OUT OF GOBLETS.
YES, THANK YOU.

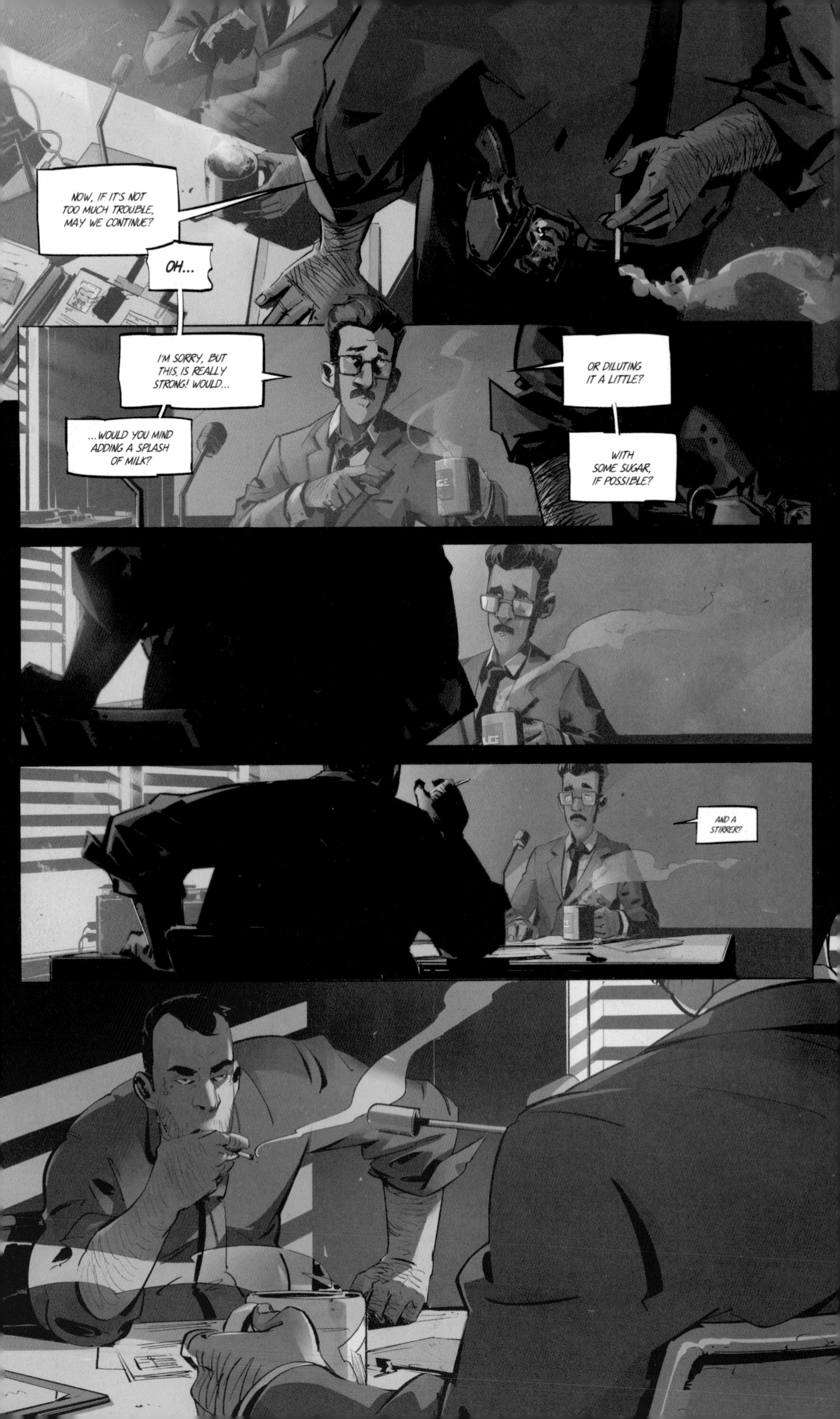
NOW, IF IT'S NOT TOO MUCH TROUBLE, MAY WE CONTINUE?
OH...
I'M SORRY, BUT THIS IS REALLY STRONG! WOULD...
...WOULD YOU MIND ADDING A SPLASH OF MILK?
OR DILUTING IT A LITTLE?
WITH SOME SUGAR, IF POSSIBLE?
AND A STIRRER?

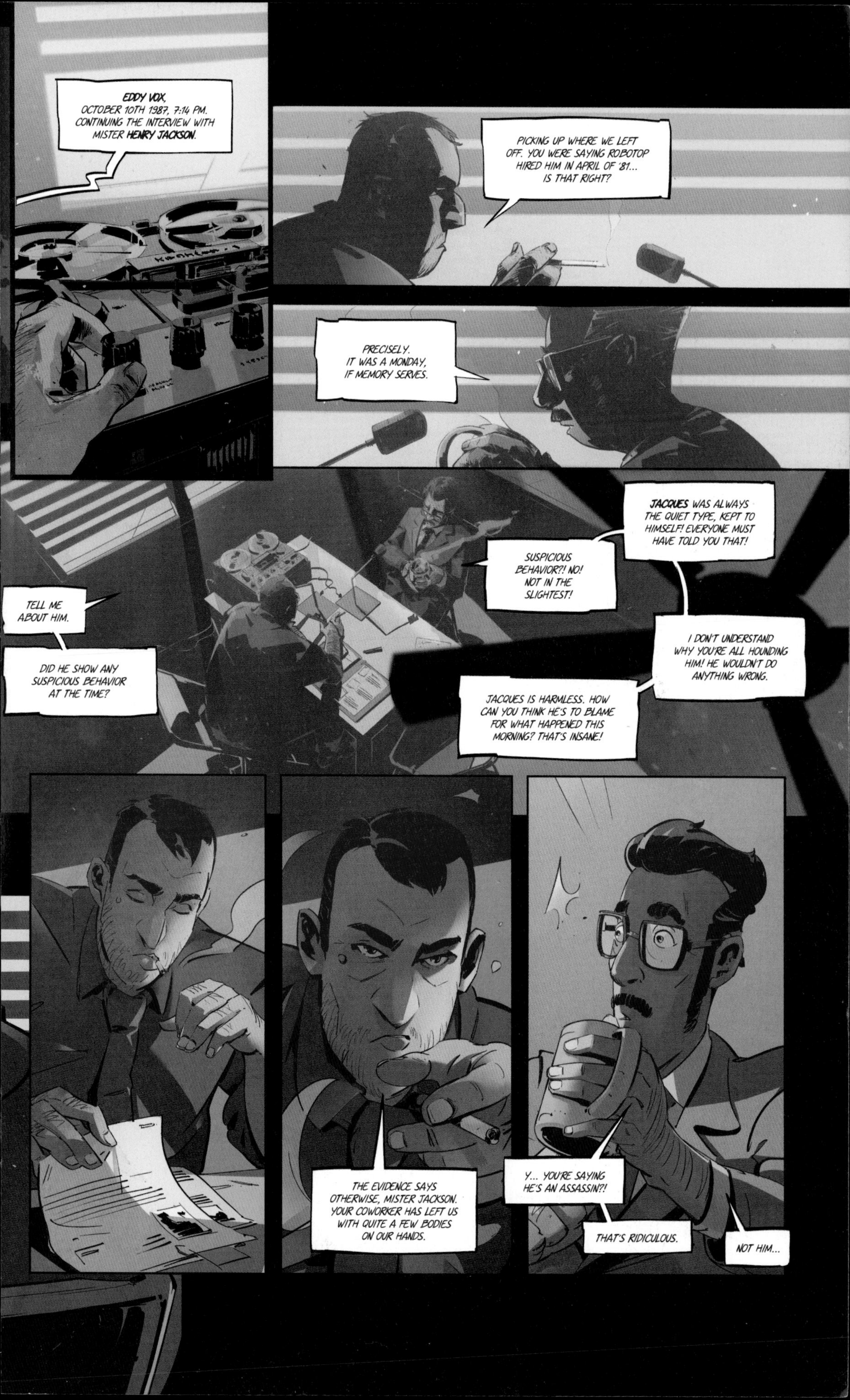
EDDY VOX,
OCTOBER 10TH 1987, 7:14 PM.
CONTINUING THE INTERVIEW WITH
MISTER HENRY JACKSON.
PICKING UP WHERE WE LEFT OFF. YOU WERE SAYING ROBOTOP HIRED HIM IN APRIL OF '81... IS THAT RIGHT?
PRECISELY. IT WAS A MONDAY, IF MEMORY SERVES.
TELL ME ABOUT HIM.
DID HE SHOW ANY SUSPICIOUS BEHAVIOR AT THE TIME?
SUSPICIOUS BEHAVIOR?! NO! NOT IN THE SLIGHTEST!
JACQUES WAS ALWAYS THE QUIET TYPE, KEPT TO HIMSELF! EVERYONE MUST HAVE TOLD YOU THAT!
I DON'T UNDERSTAND WHY YOU'RE ALL HOUNDING HIM! HE WOULDN'T DO ANYTHING WRONG.
JACQUES IS HARMLESS. HOW CAN YOU THINK HE'S TO BLAME FOR WHAT HAPPENED THIS MORNING? THAT'S INSANE!
THE EVIDENCE SAYS OTHERWISE, MISTER JACKSON. YOUR COWORKER HAS LEFT US WITH QUITE A FEW BODIES ON OUR HANDS.
Y... YOU'RE SAYING HE'S AN ASSASSIN?!
THAT'S RIDICULOUS.
NOT HIM...

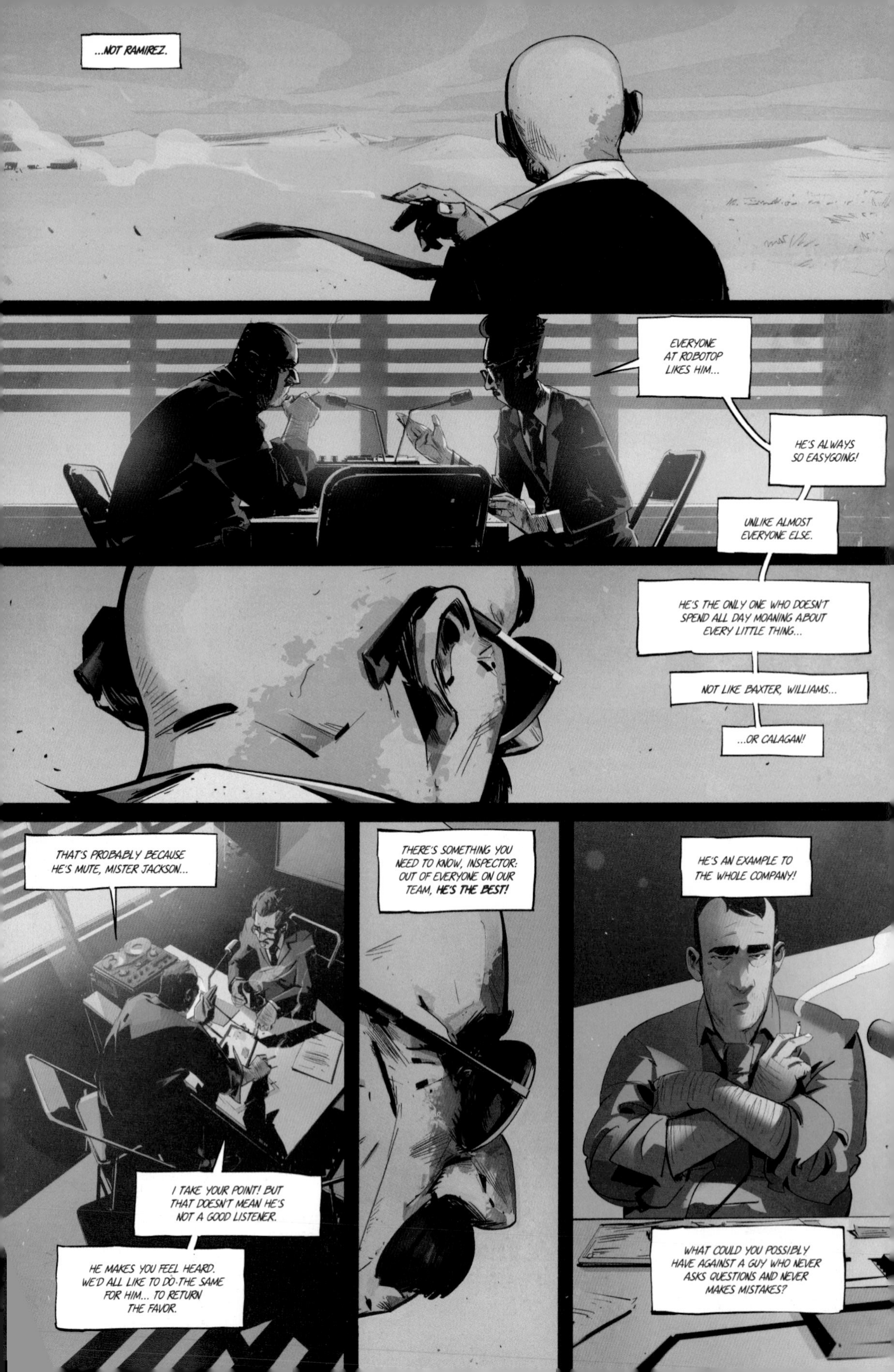
...NOT RAMIREZ.
EVERYONE AT ROBOTOP LIKES HIM...
HE'S ALWAYS SO EASYGOING!
UNLIKE ALMOST EVERYONE ELSE.
HE'S THE ONLY ONE WHO DOESN'T SPEND ALL DAY MOANING ABOUT EVERY LITTLE THING...
NOT LIKE BAXTER, WILLIAMS...
...OR CALAGAN!
THAT'S PROBABLY BECAUSE HE'S MUTE, MISTER JACKSON...
I TAKE YOUR POINT! BUT THAT DOESN'T MEAN HE'S NOT A GOOD LISTENER.
HE MAKES YOU FEEL HEARD. WE'D ALL LIKE TO DO THE SAME FOR HIM... TO RETURN THE FAVOR.
THERE'S SOMETHING YOU NEED TO KNOW, INSPECTOR: OUT OF EVERYONE ON OUR TEAM, HE'S THE BEST!
HE'S AN EXAMPLE TO THE WHOLE COMPANY!
WHAT COULD YOU POSSIBLY HAVE AGAINST A GUY WHO NEVER ASKS QUESTIONS AND NEVER MAKES MISTAKES?

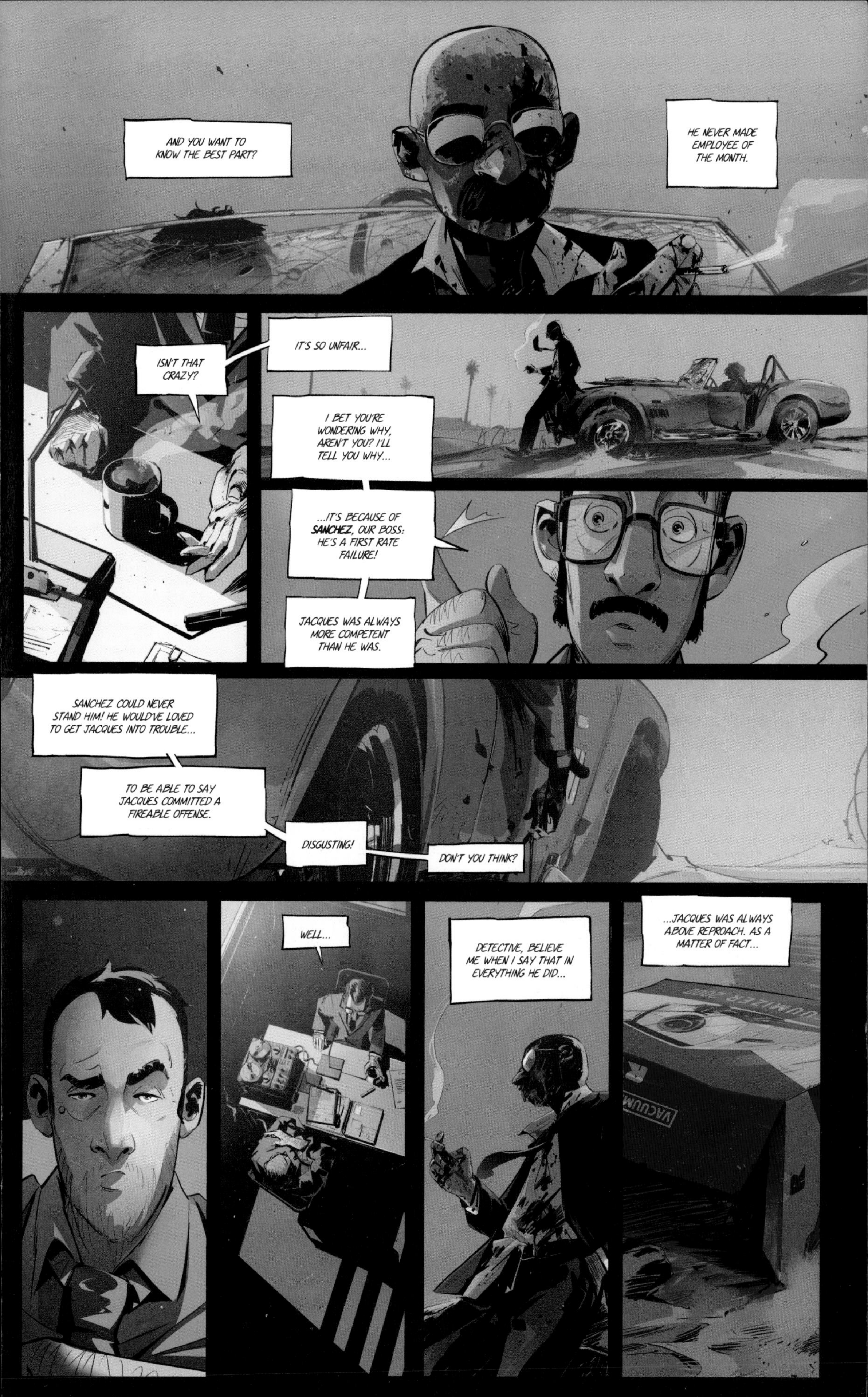
AND YOU WANT TO KNOW THE BEST PART?
HE NEVER MADE EMPLOYEE OF THE MONTH.
ISN'T THAT CRAZY?
IT'S SO UNFAIR...
I BET YOU'RE WONDERING WHY, AREN'T YOU? I'LL TELL YOU WHY...
...IT'S BECAUSE OF **SANCHEZ**, OUR BOSS: HE'S A FIRST RATE FAILURE!
JACQUES WAS ALWAYS MORE COMPETENT THAN HE WAS.
SANCHEZ COULD NEVER STAND HIM! HE WOULD'VE LOVED TO GET JACQUES INTO TROUBLE...
TO BE ABLE TO SAY JACQUES COMMITTED A FIREABLE OFFENSE.
DISGUSTING!
DON'T YOU THINK?
WELL...
DETECTIVE, BELIEVE ME WHEN I SAY THAT IN EVERYTHING HE DID...
...JACQUES WAS ALWAYS ABOVE REPROACH. AS A MATTER OF FACT...

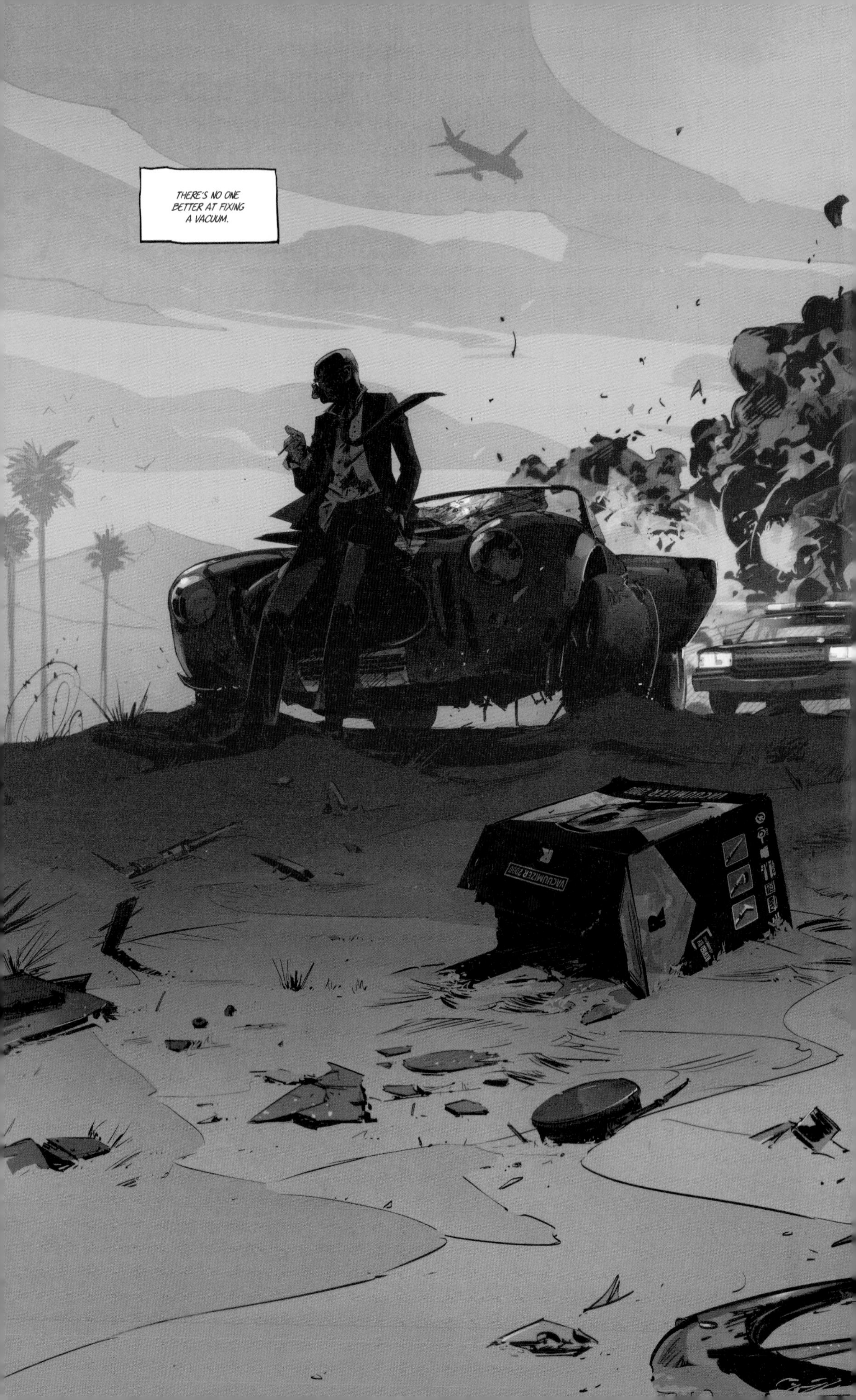
THERE'S NO ONE BETTER AT FIXING A VACUUM.
VACUUMIZER 2000

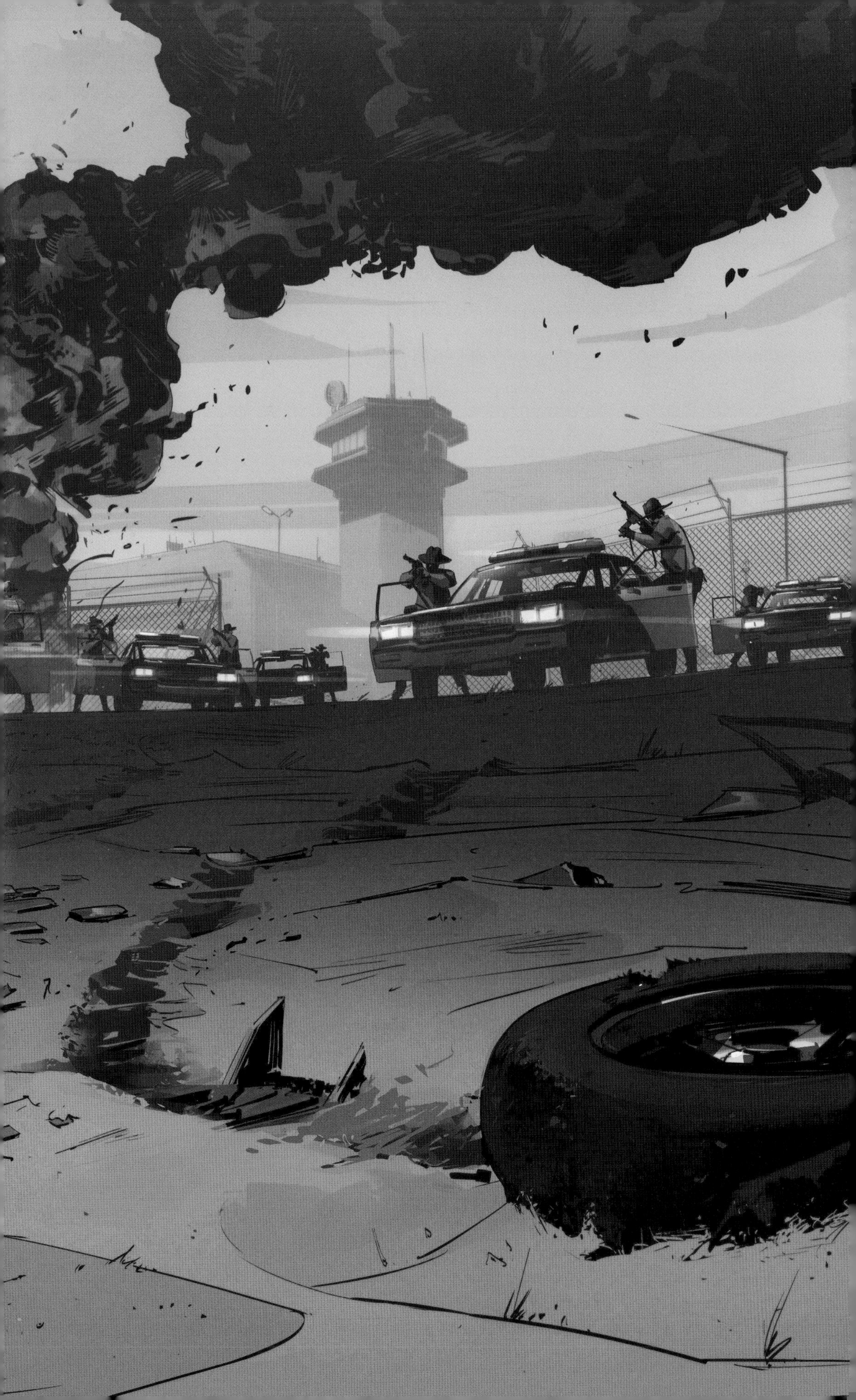

RUNNING FOR RAMIREZ

WRITTEN & DRAWN BY
NICOLAS PETRIMAUX

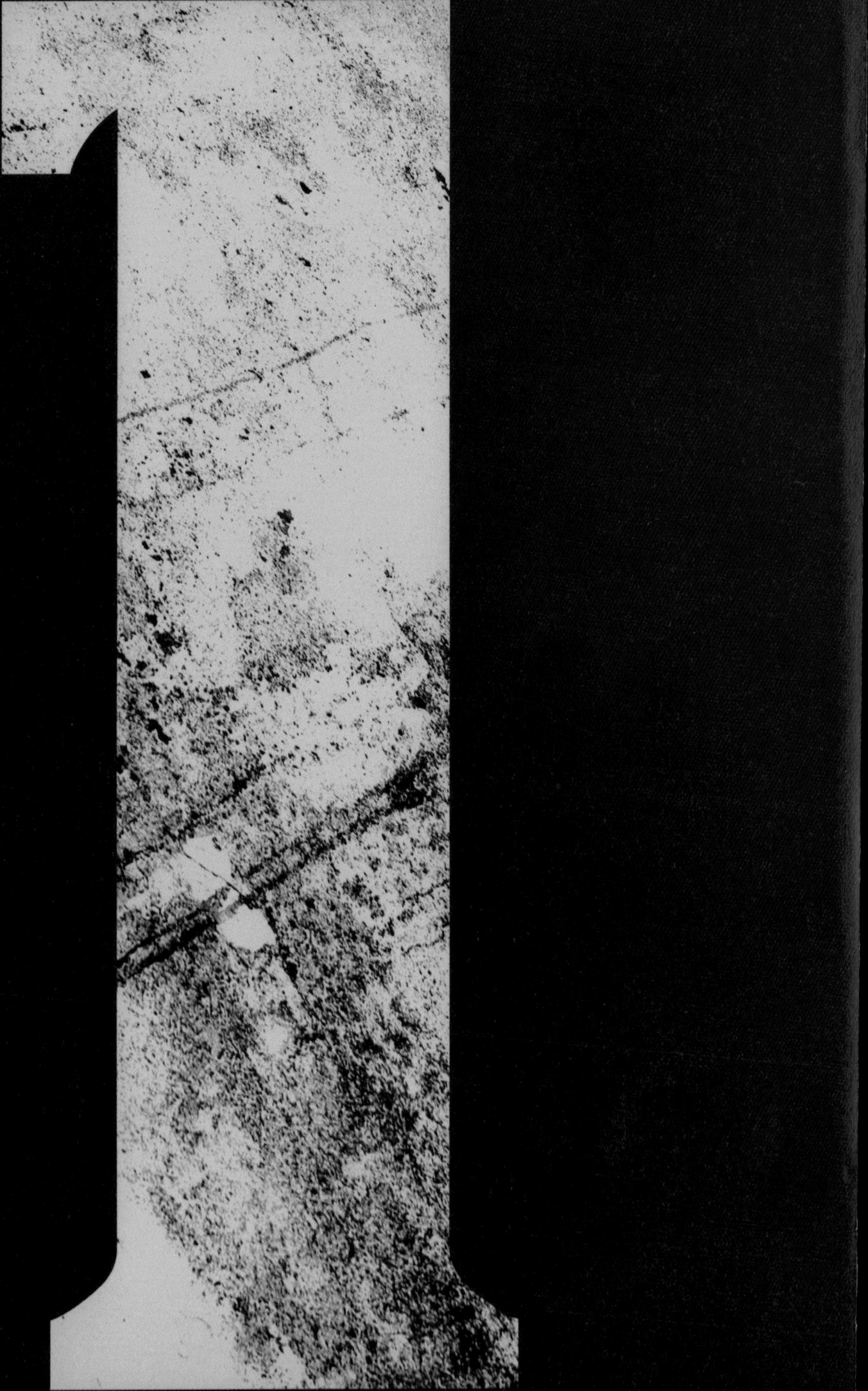

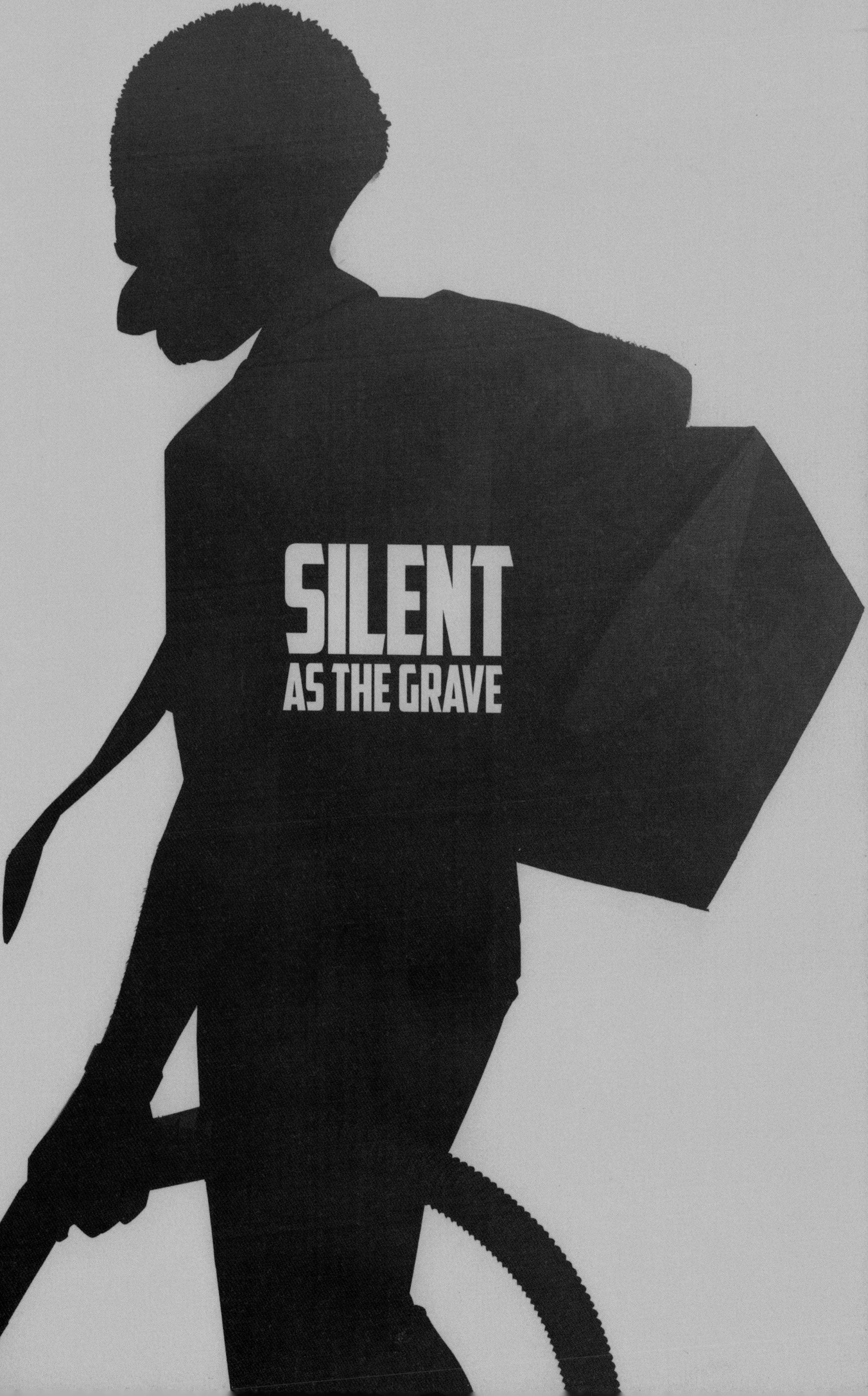
SILENT
AS THE GRAVE

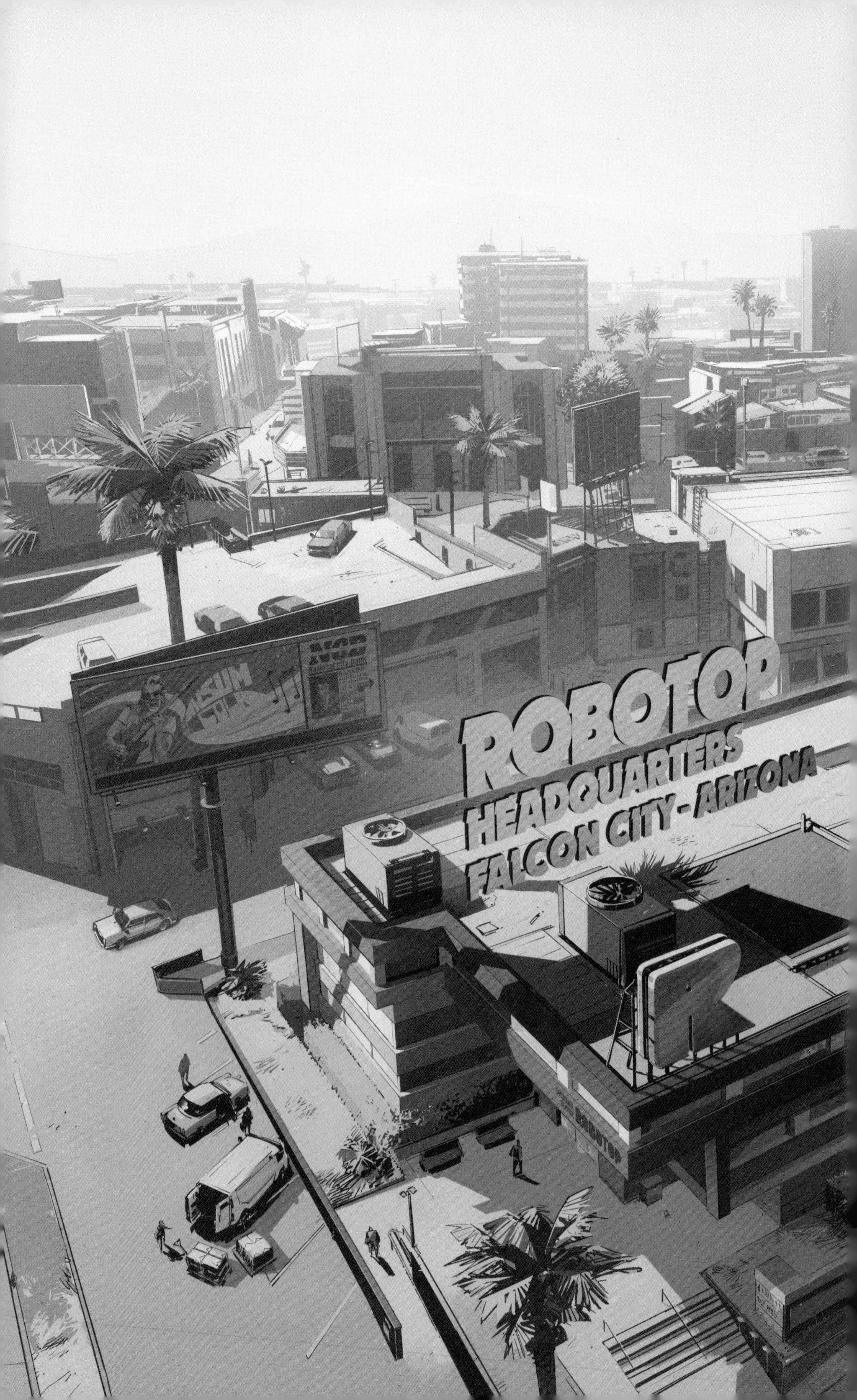

ROBOTOP
HEADQUARTERS
FALCON CITY - ARIZONA
National city bank
ROBOTOP

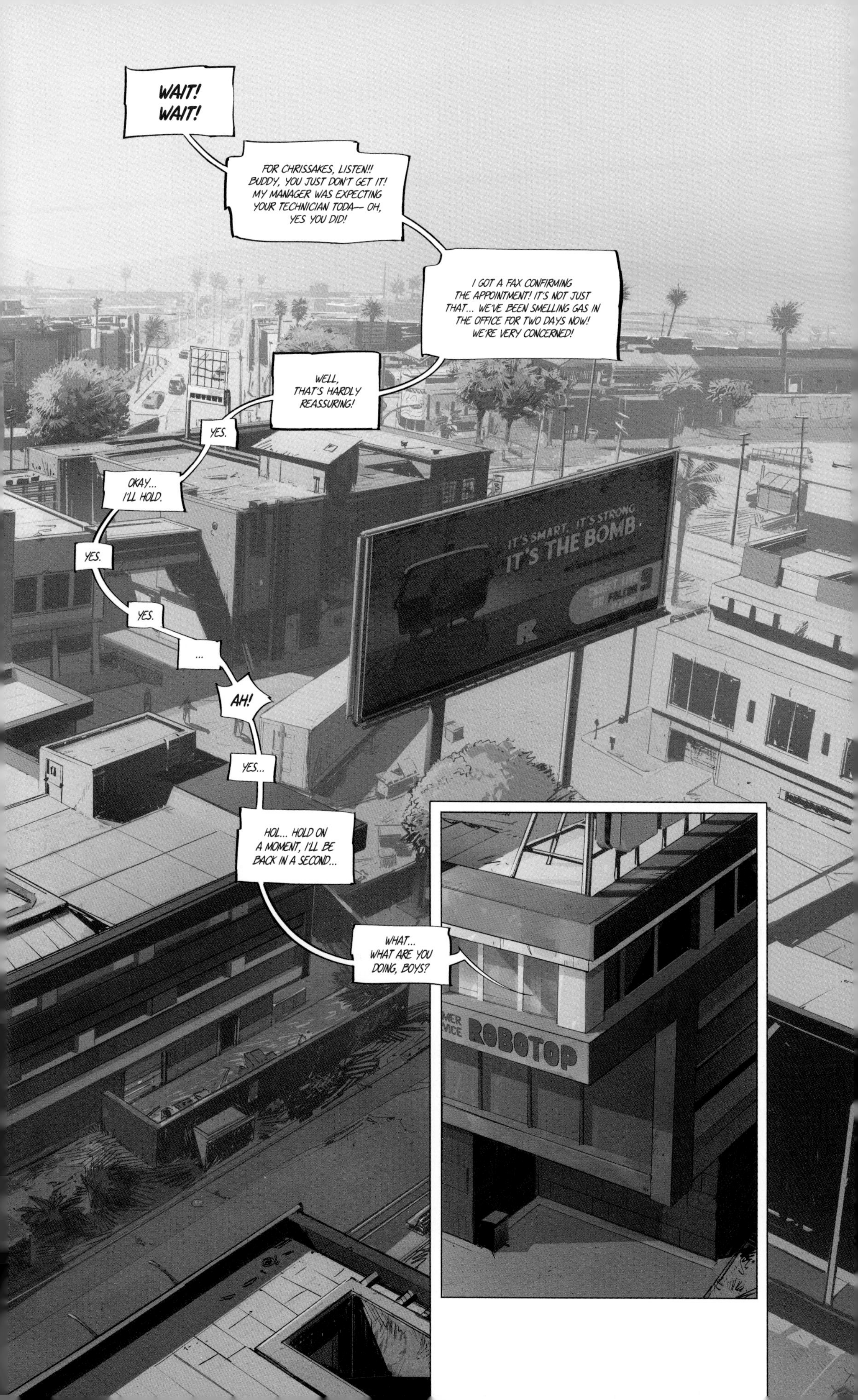
WAIT! WAIT!
FOR CHRISSAKES, LISTEN!! BUDDY, YOU JUST DON'T GET IT! MY MANAGER WAS EXPECTING YOUR TECHNICIAN TODA— OH, YES YOU DID!
I GOT A FAX CONFIRMING THE APPOINTMENT! IT'S NOT JUST THAT... WE'VE BEEN SMELLING GAS IN THE OFFICE FOR TWO DAYS NOW! WE'RE VERY CONCERNED!
WELL, THAT'S HARDLY REASSURING!
YES.
OKAY... I'LL HOLD.
YES.
YES.
...
AH!
YES...
HOL... HOLD ON A MOMENT, I'LL BE BACK IN A SECOND...
WHAT... WHAT ARE YOU DOING, BOYS?
IT'S SMART. IT'S STRONG.
IT'S THE BOMB.
ROBOTOP

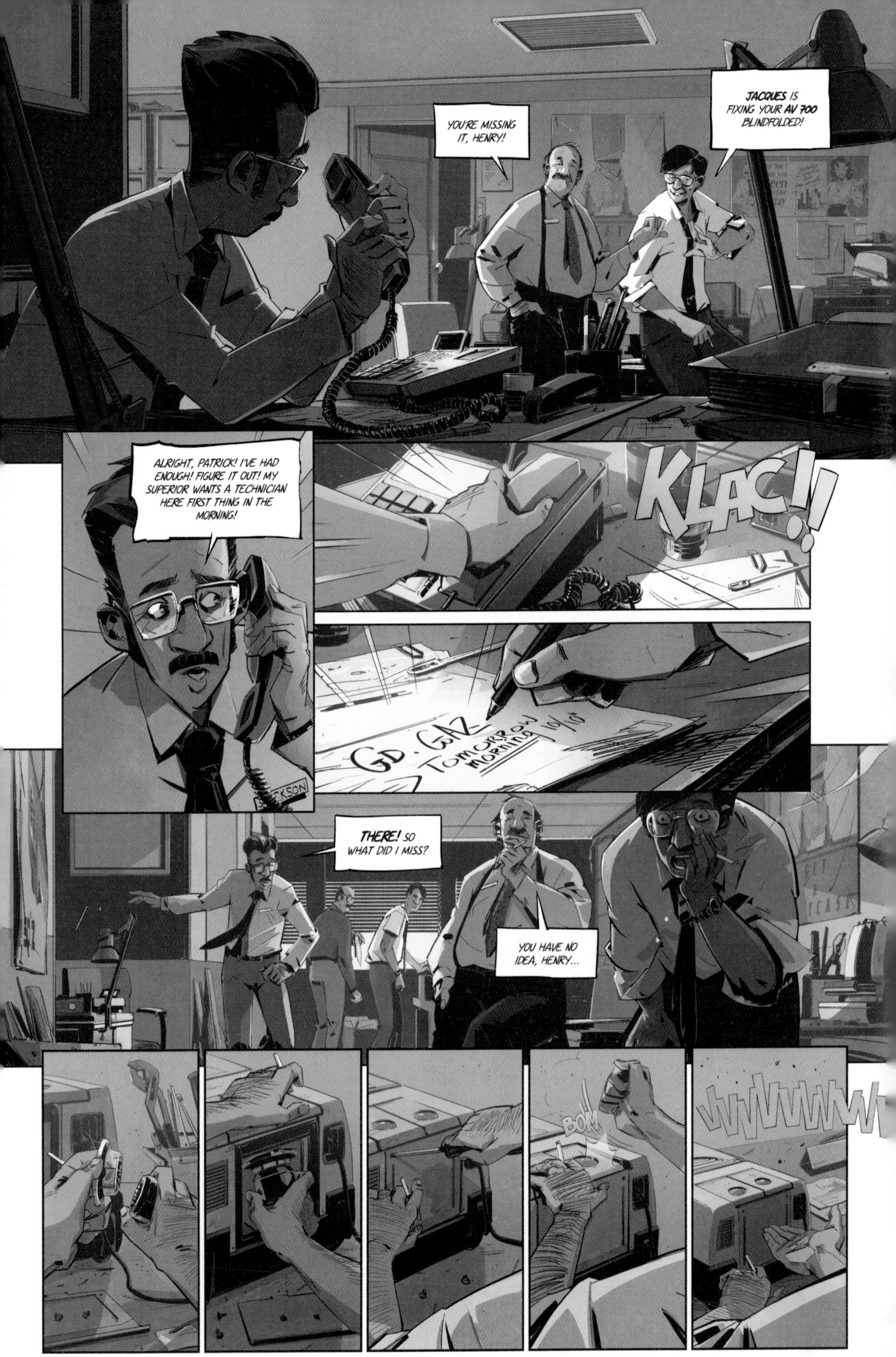
YOU'RE MISSING IT, HENRY!
JACQUES IS FIXING YOUR AV 700 BLINDFOLDED!
ALRIGHT, PATRICK! I'VE HAD ENOUGH! FIGURE IT OUT! MY SUPERIOR WANTS A TECHNICIAN HERE FIRST THING IN THE MORNING!
KLAC!!
GD. GAZ
TOMORROW
morning
10/10
THERE! SO WHAT DID I MISS?
YOU HAVE NO IDEA, HENRY...

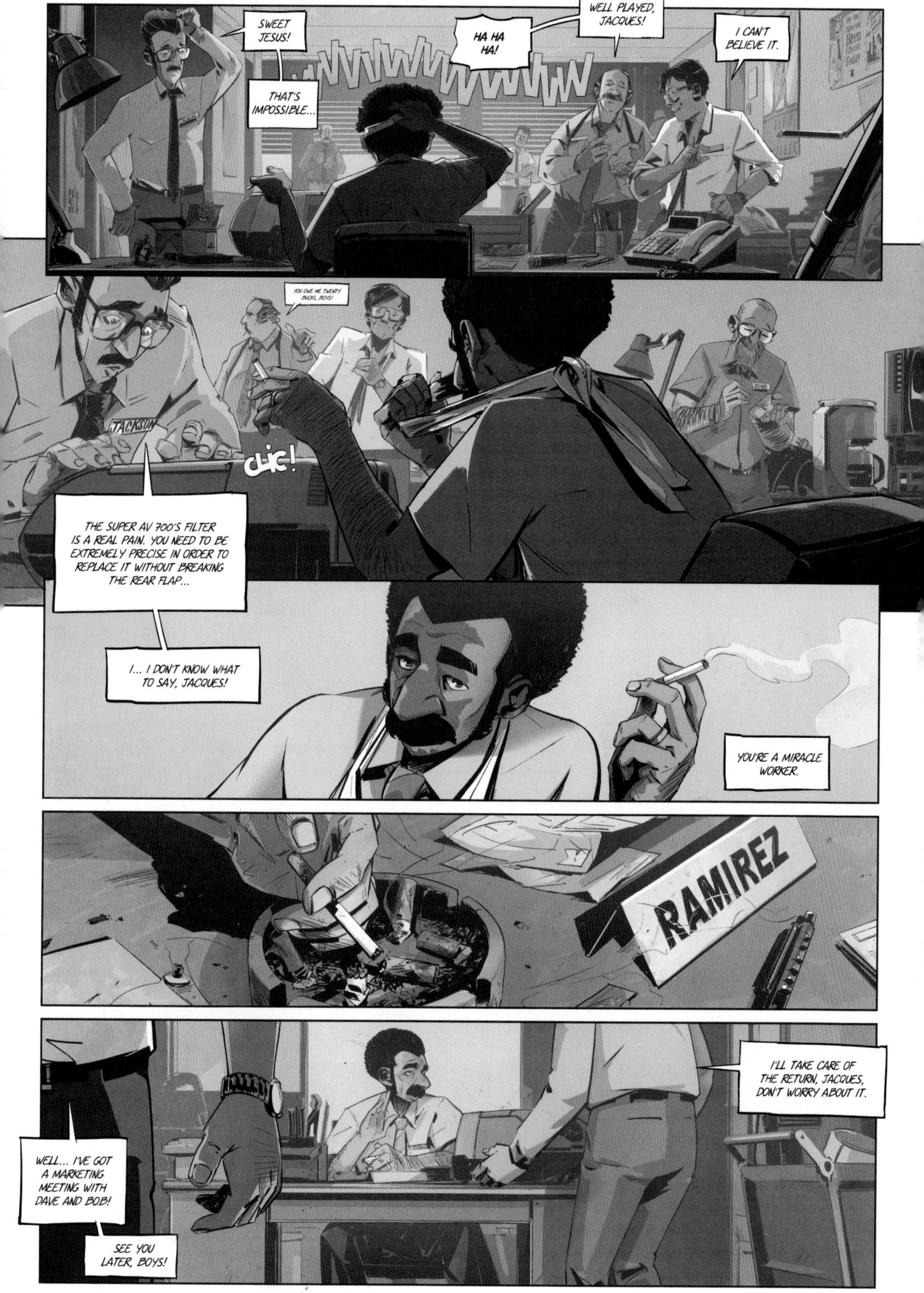
SWEET JESUS!
THAT'S IMPOSSIBLE...
HA HA HA!
WELL PLAYED, JACQUES!
I CAN'T BELIEVE IT.
YOU OWE ME TWENTY BUCKS, BOYS!
JACKSON
CLIC!
THE SUPER AV 700'S FILTER IS A REAL PAIN. YOU NEED TO BE EXTREMELY PRECISE IN ORDER TO REPLACE IT WITHOUT BREAKING THE REAR FLAP...
I... I DON'T KNOW WHAT TO SAY, JACQUES!
YOU'RE A MIRACLE WORKER.
RAMIREZ
I'LL TAKE CARE OF THE RETURN, JACQUES, DON'T WORRY ABOUT IT.
WELL... I'VE GOT A MARKETING MEETING WITH DAVE AND BOB!
SEE YOU LATER, BOYS!

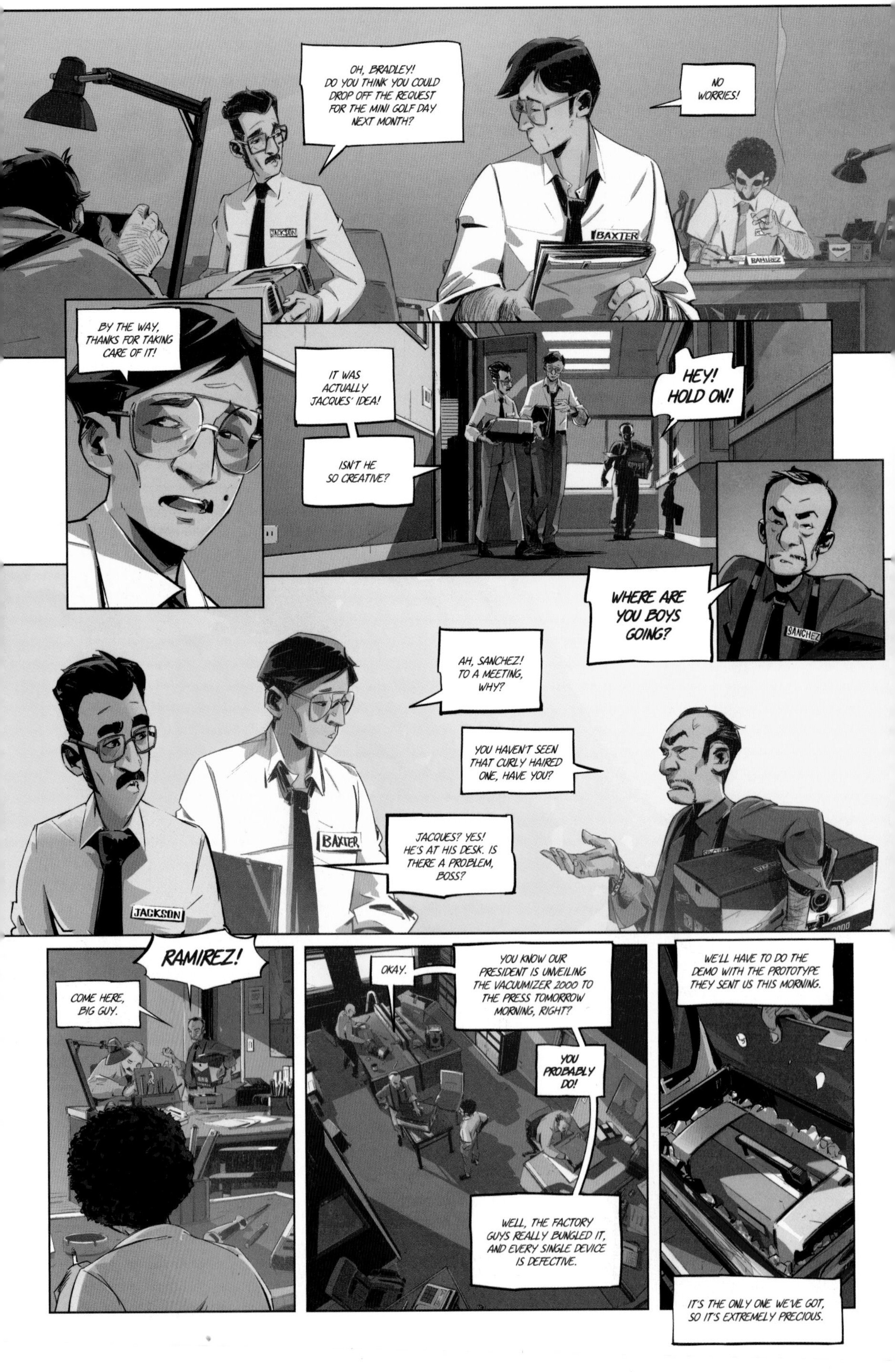
OH, BRADLEY! DO YOU THINK YOU COULD DROP OFF THE REQUEST FOR THE MINI GOLF DAY NEXT MONTH?
NO WORRIES!
JACKSON
BAXTER
BY THE WAY, THANKS FOR TAKING CARE OF IT!
IT WAS ACTUALLY JACQUES' IDEA!
ISN'T HE SO CREATIVE?
HEY! HOLD ON!
WHERE ARE YOU BOYS GOING?
SANCHEZ
AH, SANCHEZ! TO A MEETING, WHY?
YOU HAVEN'T SEEN THAT CURLY HAIRED ONE, HAVE YOU?
JACQUES? YES! HE'S AT HIS DESK. IS THERE A PROBLEM, BOSS?
BAXTER
JACKSON
RAMIREZ!
COME HERE, BIG GUY.
OKAY.
YOU KNOW OUR PRESIDENT IS UNVEILING THE VACUUMIZER 2000 TO THE PRESS TOMORROW MORNING, RIGHT?
YOU PROBABLY DO!
WELL, THE FACTORY GUYS REALLY BUNGLED IT, AND EVERY SINGLE DEVICE IS DEFECTIVE.
WE'LL HAVE TO DO THE DEMO WITH THE PROTOTYPE THEY SENT US THIS MORNING.
IT'S THE ONLY ONE WE'VE GOT, SO IT'S EXTREMELY PRECIOUS.

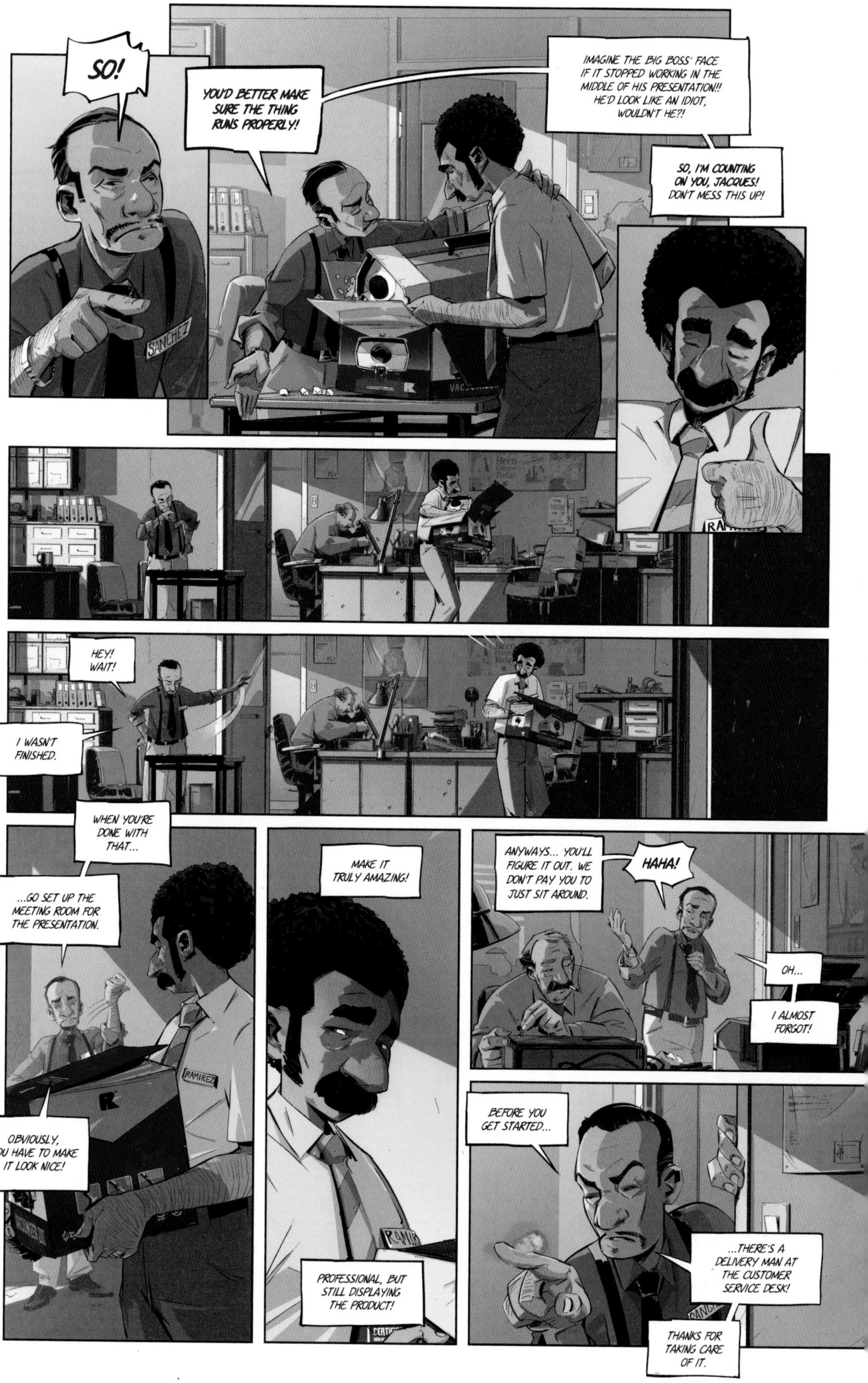
SO!
YOU'D BETTER MAKE SURE THE THING RUNS PROPERLY!
IMAGINE THE BIG BOSS' FACE IF IT STOPPED WORKING IN THE MIDDLE OF HIS PRESENTATION!! HE'D LOOK LIKE AN IDIOT, WOULDN'T HE?!
SO, I'M COUNTING ON YOU, JACQUES! DON'T MESS THIS UP!
SANCHEZ
HEY! WAIT!
I WASN'T FINISHED.
WHEN YOU'RE DONE WITH THAT...
...GO SET UP THE MEETING ROOM FOR THE PRESENTATION.
OBVIOUSLY, YOU HAVE TO MAKE IT LOOK NICE!
RAMIREZ
MAKE IT TRULY AMAZING!
PROFESSIONAL, BUT STILL DISPLAYING THE PRODUCT!
ANYWAYS... YOU'LL FIGURE IT OUT. WE DON'T PAY YOU TO JUST SIT AROUND.
HAHA!
OH...
I ALMOST FORGOT!
BEFORE YOU GET STARTED...
...THERE'S A DELIVERY MAN AT THE CUSTOMER SERVICE DESK!
THANKS FOR TAKING CARE OF IT.

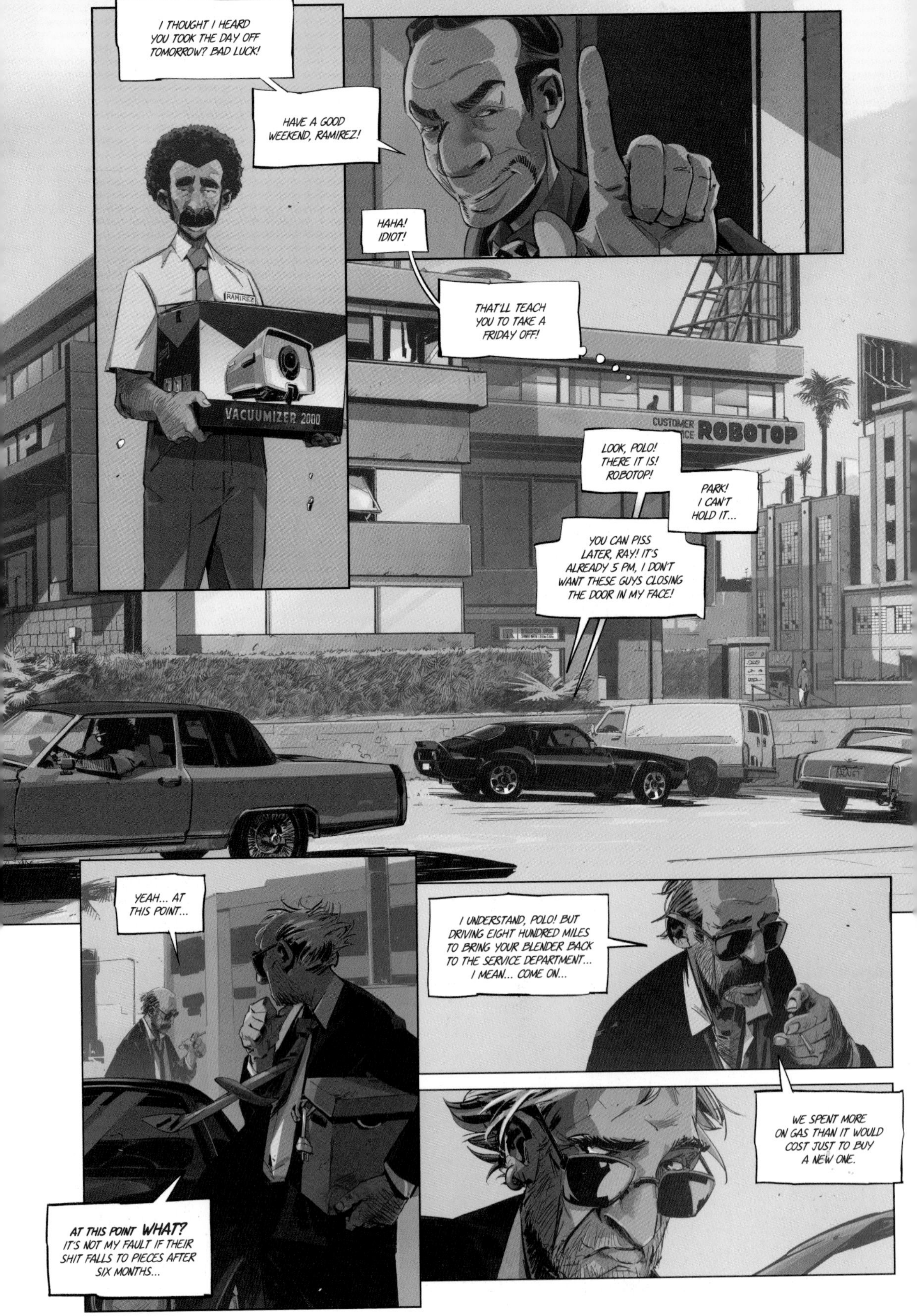
I THOUGHT I HEARD YOU TOOK THE DAY OFF TOMORROW? BAD LUCK!
HAVE A GOOD WEEKEND, RAMIREZ!
RAMIREZ
VACUUMIZER 2000
HAHA! IDIOT!
THAT'LL TEACH YOU TO TAKE A FRIDAY OFF!
ROBOTOP
LOOK, POLO! THERE IT IS! ROBOTOP!
PARK! I CAN'T HOLD IT...
YOU CAN PISS LATER, RAY! IT'S ALREADY 5 PM, I DON'T WANT THESE GUYS CLOSING THE DOOR IN MY FACE!
YEAH... AT THIS POINT...
AT THIS POINT WHAT? IT'S NOT MY FAULT IF THEIR SHIT FALLS TO PIECES AFTER SIX MONTHS...
I UNDERSTAND, POLO! BUT DRIVING EIGHT HUNDRED MILES TO BRING YOUR BLENDER BACK TO THE SERVICE DEPARTMENT... I MEAN... COME ON...
WE SPENT MORE ON GAS THAN IT WOULD COST JUST TO BUY A NEW ONE.

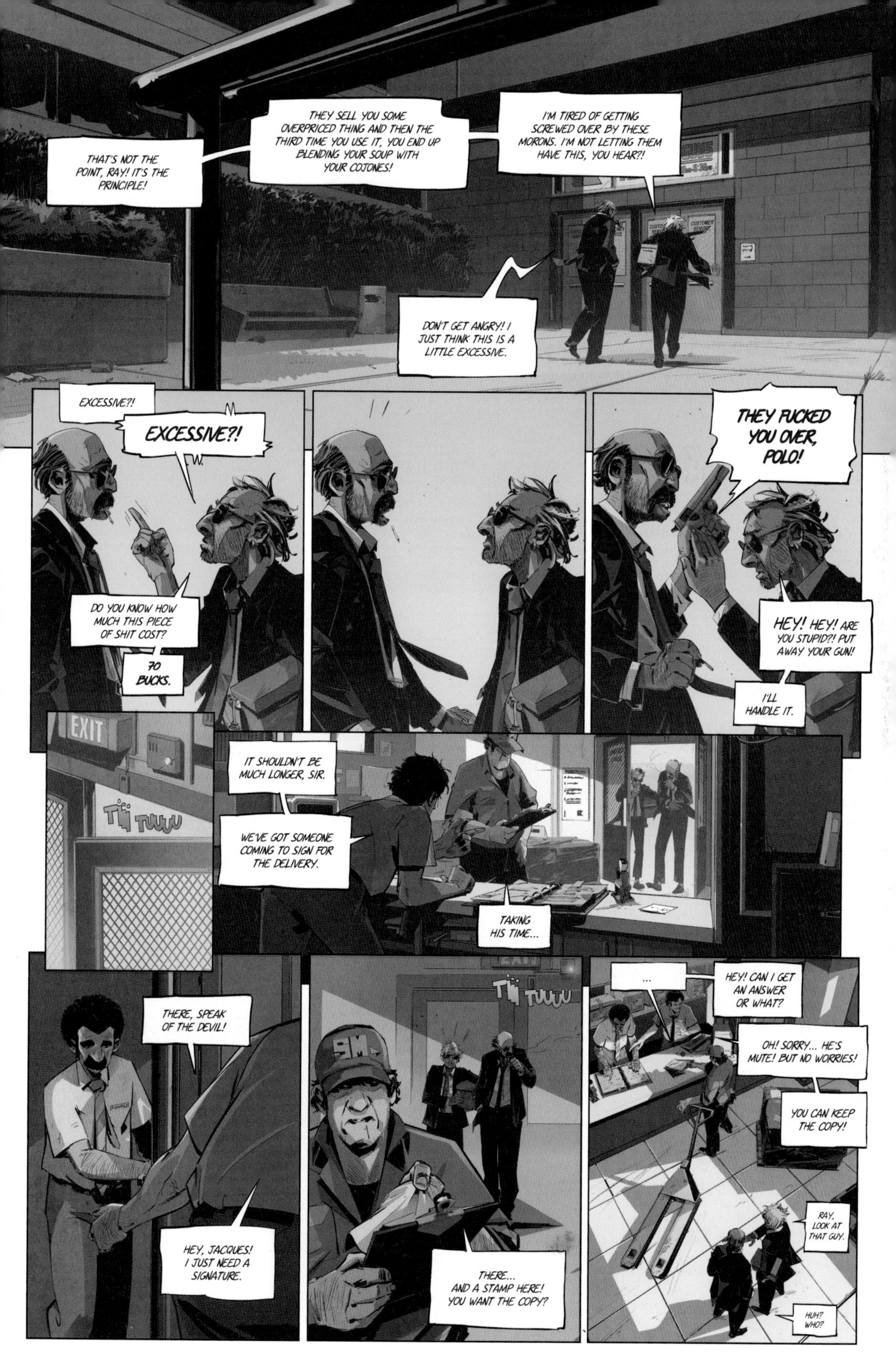
THAT'S NOT THE POINT, RAY! IT'S THE PRINCIPLE!
THEY SELL YOU SOME OVERPRICED THING AND THEN THE THIRD TIME YOU USE IT, YOU END UP BLENDING YOUR SOUP WITH YOUR COJONES!
I'M TIRED OF GETTING SCREWED OVER BY THESE MORONS. I'M NOT LETTING THEM HAVE THIS, YOU HEAR?!
DON'T GET ANGRY! I JUST THINK THIS IS A LITTLE EXCESSIVE.
EXCESSIVE?!
EXCESSIVE?!
DO YOU KNOW HOW MUCH THIS PIECE OF SHIT COST?
70 BUCKS.
THEY FUCKED YOU OVER, POLO!
HEY! HEY! ARE YOU STUPID?! PUT AWAY YOUR GUN!
I'LL HANDLE IT.
EXIT
TIII TUUUU
IT SHOULDN'T BE MUCH LONGER, SIR.
WE'VE GOT SOMEONE COMING TO SIGN FOR THE DELIVERY.
TAKING HIS TIME...
THERE, SPEAK OF THE DEVIL!
HEY, JACQUES! I JUST NEED A SIGNATURE.
TIII TUUUU
THERE... AND A STAMP HERE! YOU WANT THE COPY?
...
HEY! CAN I GET AN ANSWER OR WHAT?
OH! SORRY... HE'S MUTE! BUT NO WORRIES!
YOU CAN KEEP THE COPY!
RAY, LOOK AT THAT GUY.
HUH? WHO?

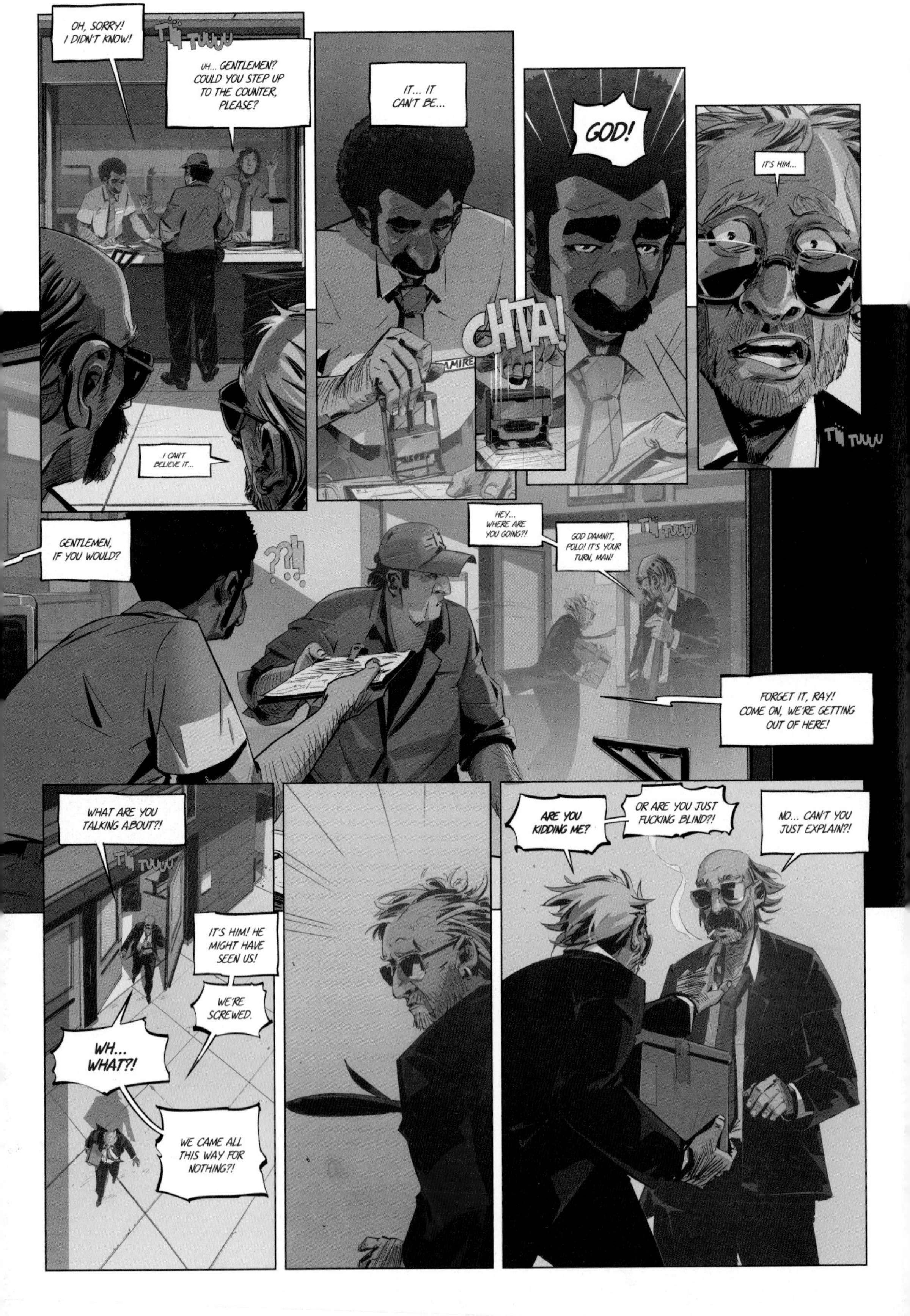
OH, SORRY! I DIDN'T KNOW!
TÏÏ TUUUU
UH... GENTLEMEN? COULD YOU STEP UP TO THE COUNTER, PLEASE?
I CAN'T BELIEVE IT...
IT... IT CAN'T BE...
GOD!
CHTA!
IT'S HIM...
TÏÏ TUUUU
GENTLEMEN, IF YOU WOULD?
?!!
HEY... WHERE ARE YOU GOING?!
GOD DAMNIT, POLO! IT'S YOUR TURN, MAN!
TÏÏ TUUUU
FORGET IT, RAY! COME ON, WE'RE GETTING OUT OF HERE!
WHAT ARE YOU TALKING ABOUT?!
TÏÏ TUUUU
IT'S HIM! HE MIGHT HAVE SEEN US!
WE'RE SCREWED.
WH... WHAT?!
WE CAME ALL THIS WAY FOR NOTHING?!
ARE YOU KIDDING ME?
OR ARE YOU JUST FUCKING BLIND?!
NO... CAN'T YOU JUST EXPLAIN?!

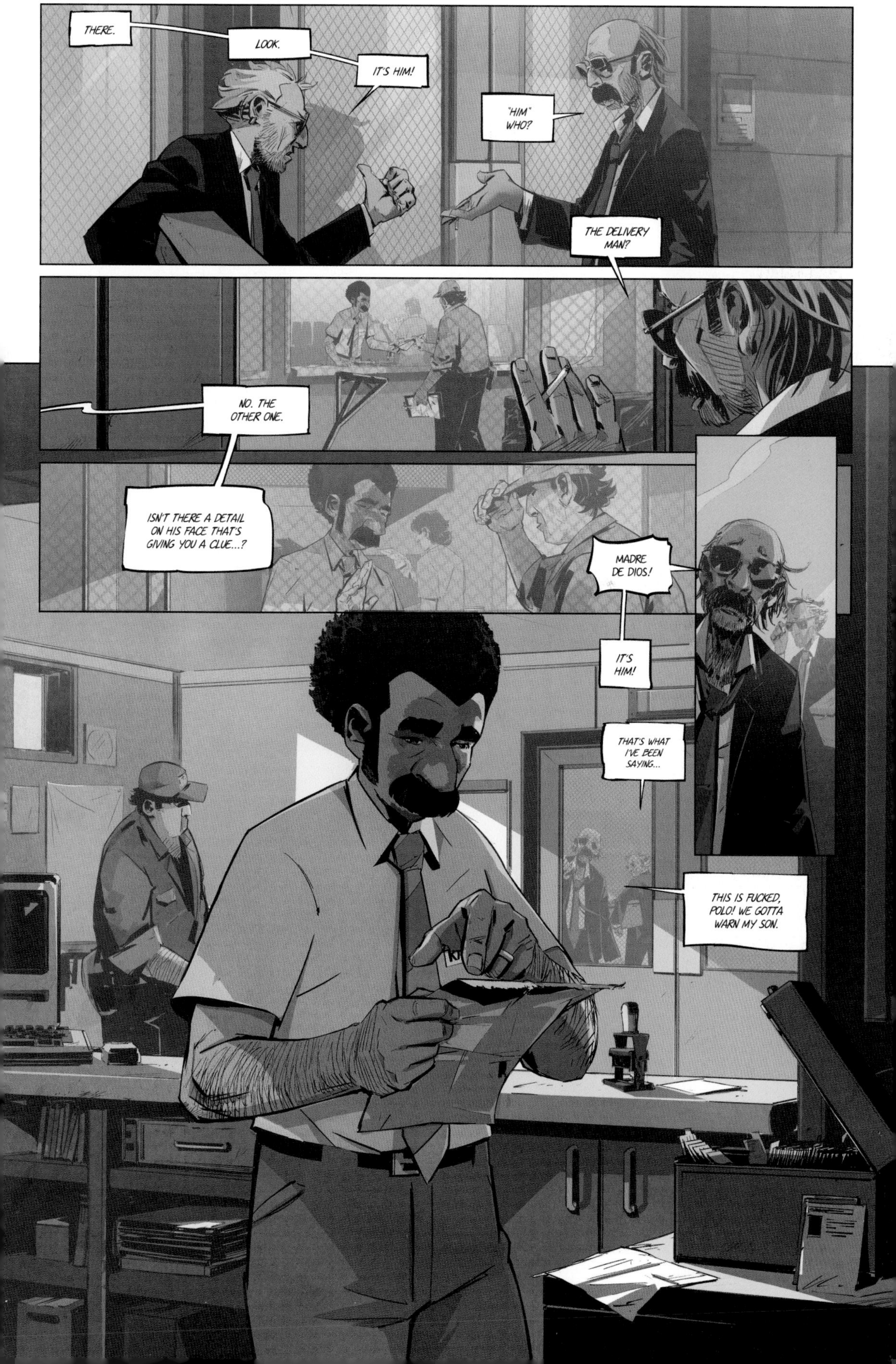
THERE.
LOOK.
IT'S HIM!
"HIM" WHO?
THE DELIVERY MAN?
NO. THE OTHER ONE.
ISN'T THERE A DETAIL ON HIS FACE THAT'S GIVING YOU A CLUE...?
MADRE DE DIOS!
IT'S HIM!
THAT'S WHAT I'VE BEEN SAYING...
THIS IS FUCKED, POLO! WE GOTTA WARN MY SON.

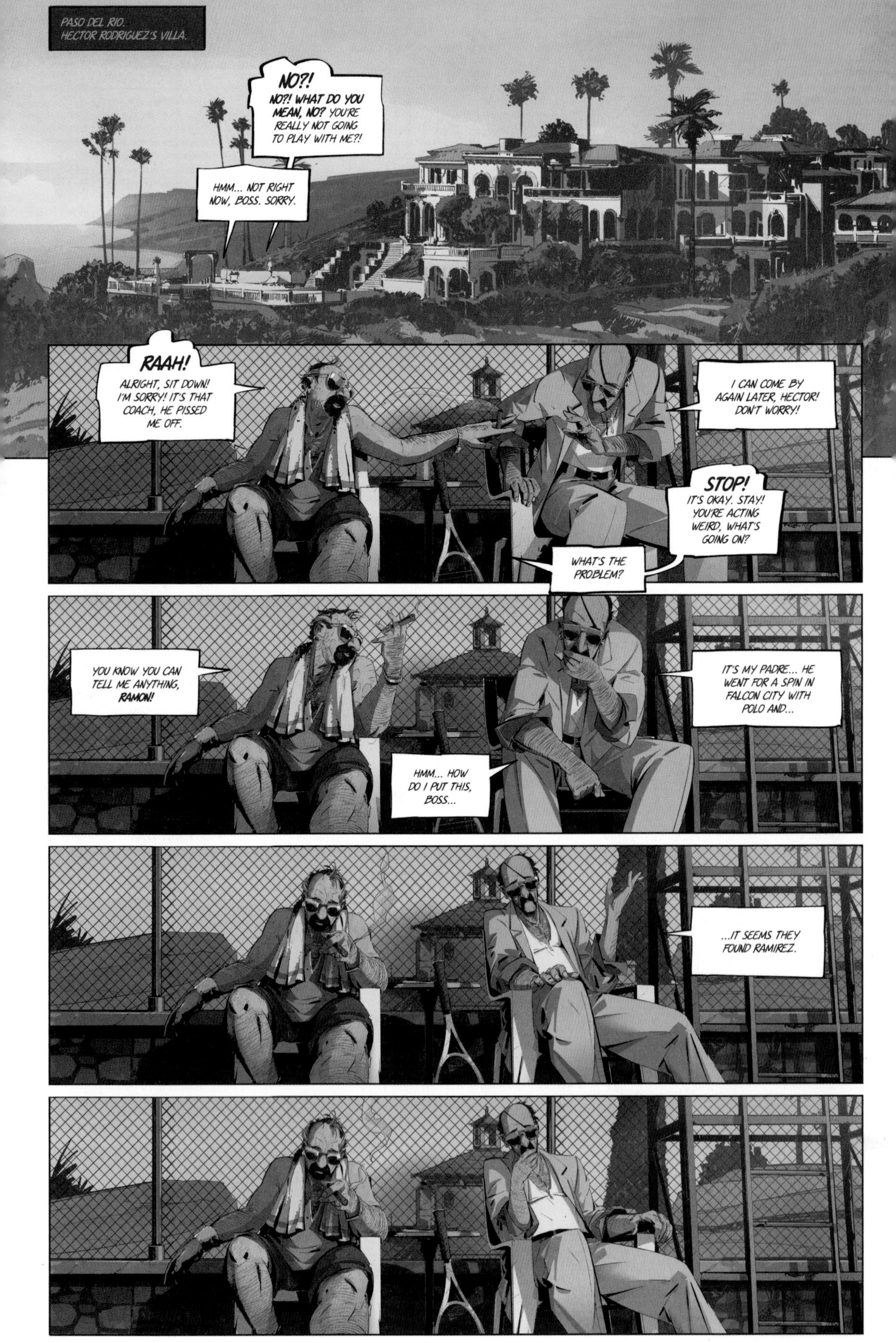
PASO DEL RIO.
HECTOR RODRIGUEZ'S VILLA.
NO?!
NO?! WHAT DO YOU MEAN, NO? YOU'RE REALLY NOT GOING TO PLAY WITH ME?!
HMM... NOT RIGHT NOW, BOSS. SORRY.
RAAH!
ALRIGHT, SIT DOWN! I'M SORRY! IT'S THAT COACH, HE PISSED ME OFF.
I CAN COME BY AGAIN LATER, HECTOR! DON'T WORRY!
STOP!
IT'S OKAY. STAY! YOU'RE ACTING WEIRD, WHAT'S GOING ON?
WHAT'S THE PROBLEM?
YOU KNOW YOU CAN TELL ME ANYTHING, RAMON!
HMM... HOW DO I PUT THIS, BOSS...
IT'S MY PADRE... HE WENT FOR A SPIN IN FALCON CITY WITH POLO AND...
...IT SEEMS THEY FOUND RAMIREZ.

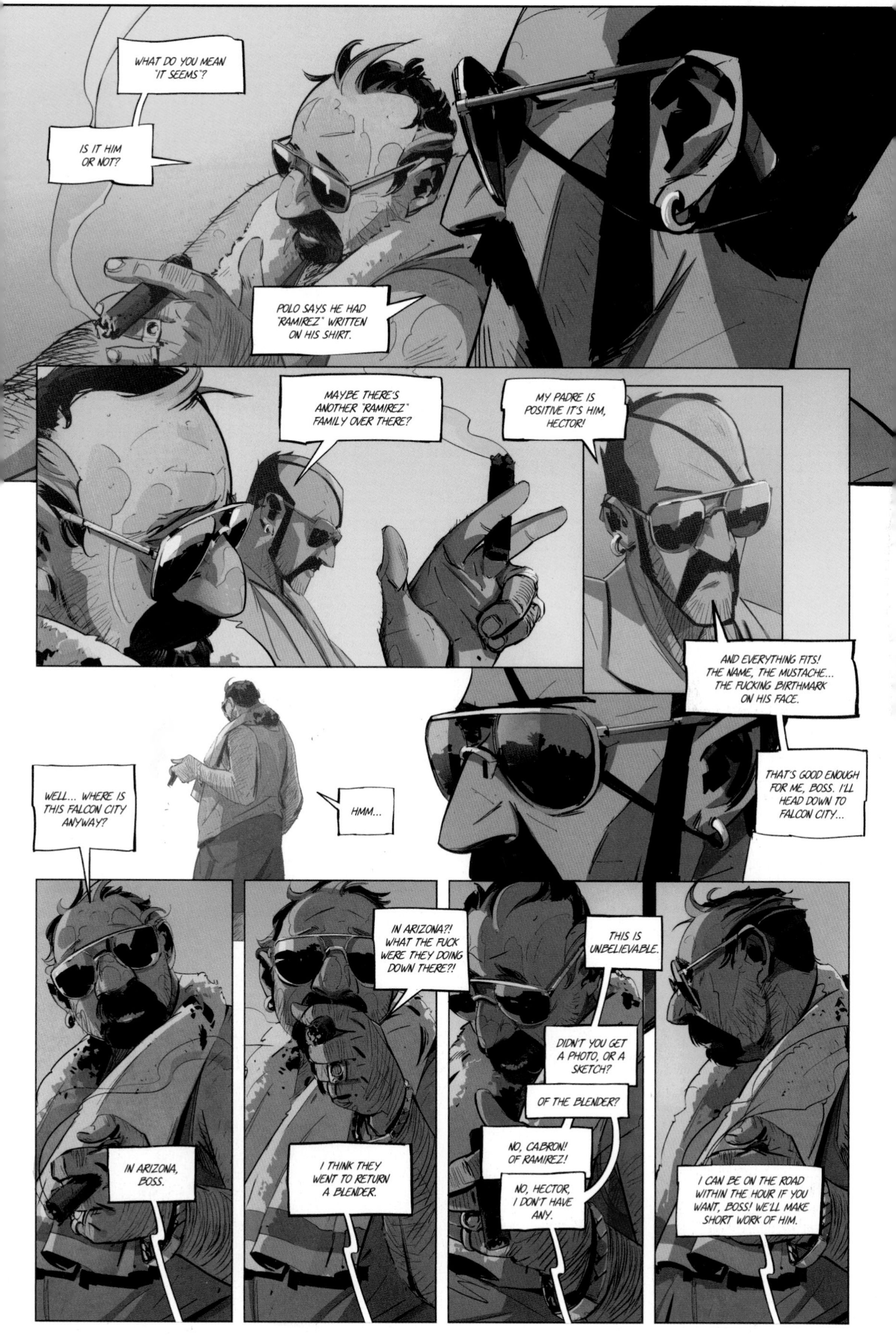
WHAT DO YOU MEAN "IT SEEMS"?
IS IT HIM OR NOT?
POLO SAYS HE HAD "RAMIREZ" WRITTEN ON HIS SHIRT.
MAYBE THERE'S ANOTHER "RAMIREZ" FAMILY OVER THERE?
MY PADRE IS POSITIVE IT'S HIM, HECTOR!
AND EVERYTHING FITS! THE NAME, THE MUSTACHE... THE FUCKING BIRTHMARK ON HIS FACE.
THAT'S GOOD ENOUGH FOR ME, BOSS. I'LL HEAD DOWN TO FALCON CITY...
HMM...
WELL... WHERE IS THIS FALCON CITY ANYWAY?
IN ARIZONA, BOSS.
IN ARIZONA?! WHAT THE FUCK WERE THEY DOING DOWN THERE?!
I THINK THEY WENT TO RETURN A BLENDER.
THIS IS UNBELIEVABLE.
DIDN'T YOU GET A PHOTO, OR A SKETCH?
OF THE BLENDER?
NO, CABRON! OF RAMIREZ!
NO, HECTOR, I DON'T HAVE ANY.
I CAN BE ON THE ROAD WITHIN THE HOUR IF YOU WANT, BOSS! WE'LL MAKE SHORT WORK OF HIM.

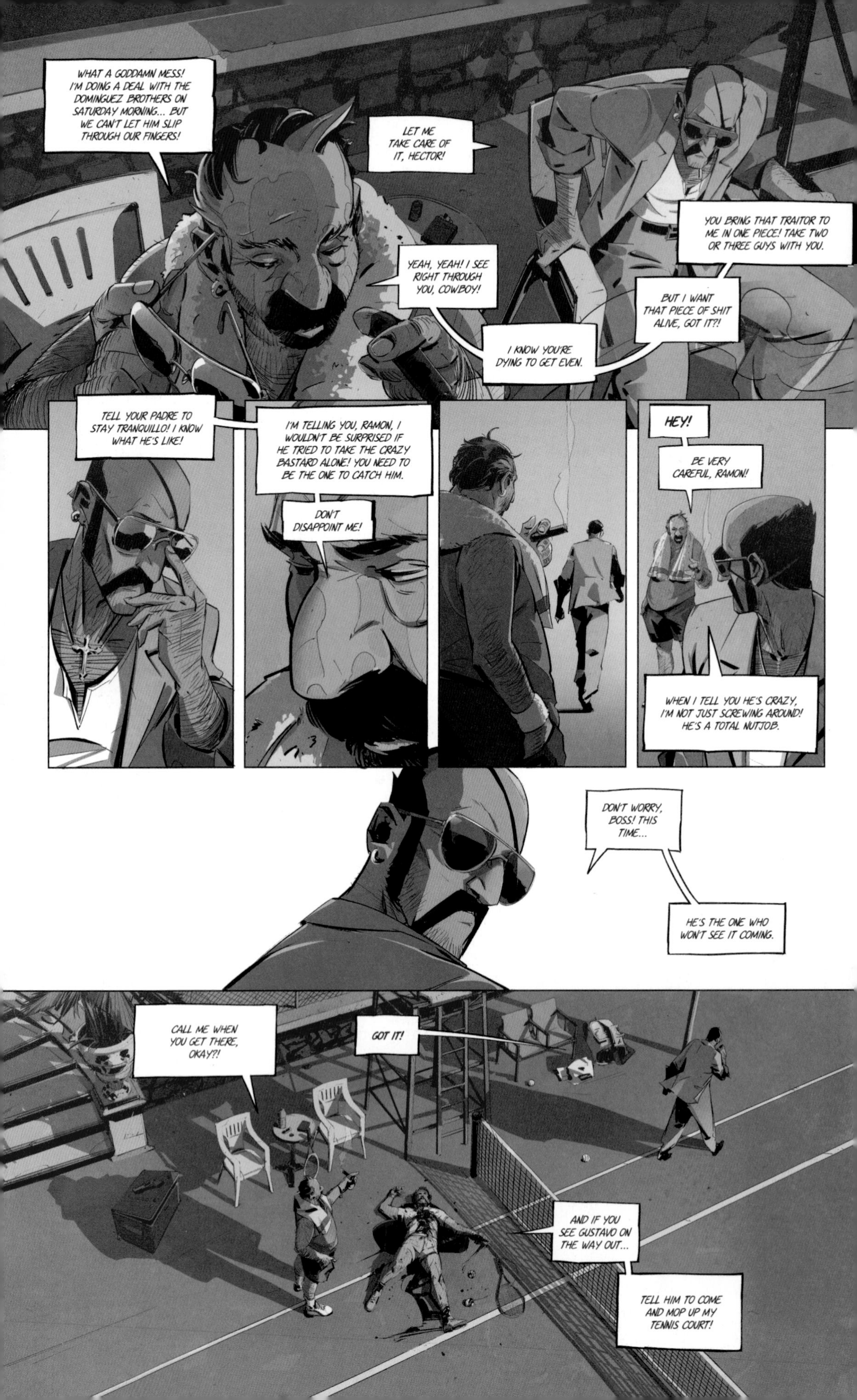
WHAT A GODDAMN MESS! I'M DOING A DEAL WITH THE DOMINGUEZ BROTHERS ON SATURDAY MORNING... BUT WE CAN'T LET HIM SLIP THROUGH OUR FINGERS!
LET ME TAKE CARE OF IT, HECTOR!
YEAH, YEAH! I SEE RIGHT THROUGH YOU, COWBOY!
I KNOW YOU'RE DYING TO GET EVEN.
YOU BRING THAT TRAITOR TO ME IN ONE PIECE! TAKE TWO OR THREE GUYS WITH YOU.
BUT I WANT THAT PIECE OF SHIT ALIVE, GOT IT?!
TELL YOUR PADRE TO STAY TRANQUILLO! I KNOW WHAT HE'S LIKE!
I'M TELLING YOU, RAMON, I WOULDN'T BE SURPRISED IF HE TRIED TO TAKE THE CRAZY BASTARD ALONE! YOU NEED TO BE THE ONE TO CATCH HIM.
DON'T DISAPPOINT ME!
HEY!
BE VERY CAREFUL, RAMON!
WHEN I TELL YOU HE'S CRAZY, I'M NOT JUST SCREWING AROUND! HE'S A TOTAL NUTJOB.
DON'T WORRY, BOSS! THIS TIME...
HE'S THE ONE WHO WON'T SEE IT COMING.
CALL ME WHEN YOU GET THERE, OKAY?!
GOT IT!
AND IF YOU SEE GUSTAVO ON THE WAY OUT...
TELL HIM TO COME AND MOP UP MY TENNIS COURT!

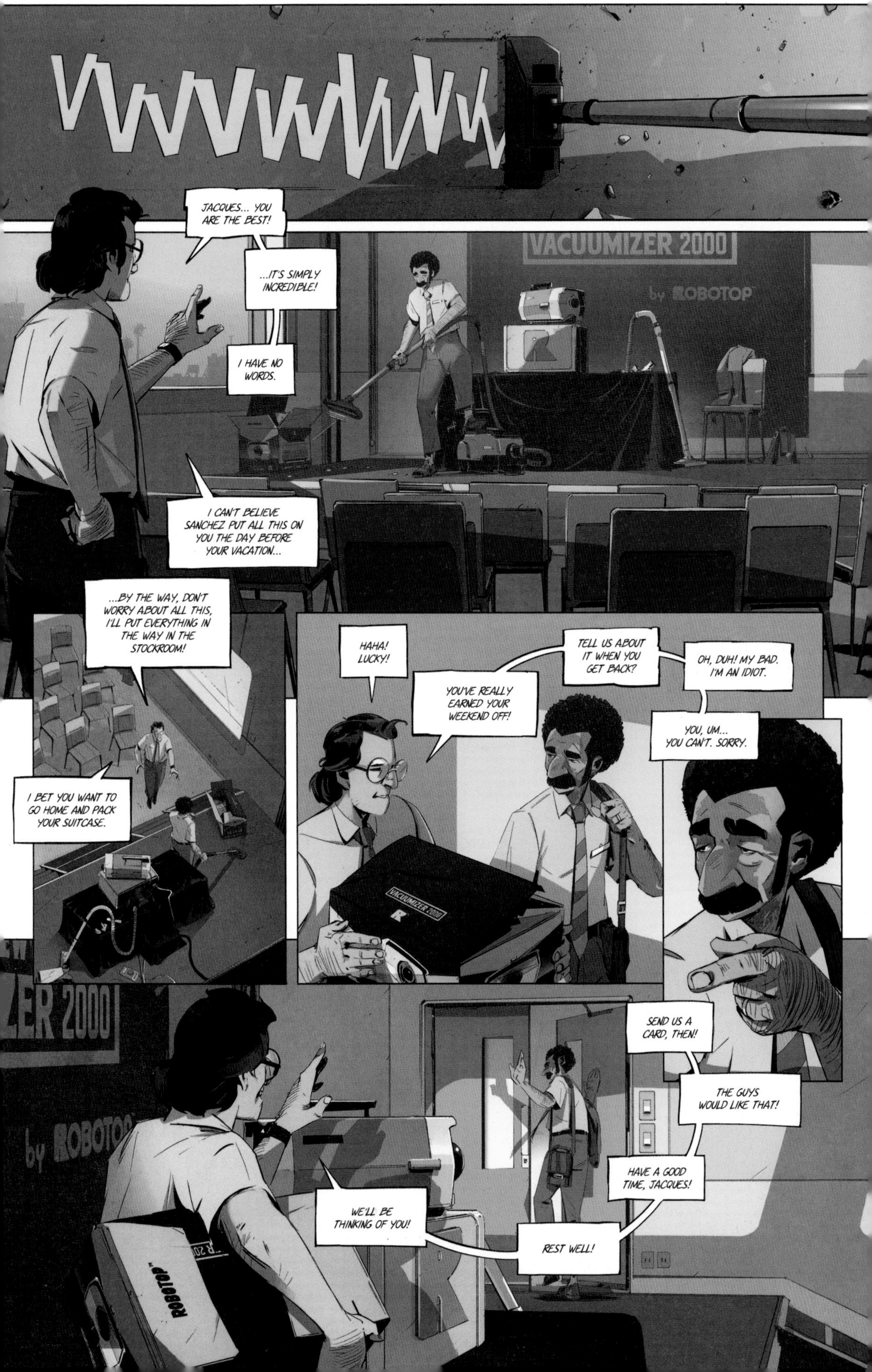
VVVVVVVVVVV
JACQUES... YOU ARE THE BEST!
...IT'S SIMPLY INCREDIBLE!
I HAVE NO WORDS.
VACUUMIZER 2000
by ROBOTOP
I CAN'T BELIEVE SANCHEZ PUT ALL THIS ON YOU THE DAY BEFORE YOUR VACATION...
...BY THE WAY, DON'T WORRY ABOUT ALL THIS, I'LL PUT EVERYTHING IN THE WAY IN THE STOCKROOM!
I BET YOU WANT TO GO HOME AND PACK YOUR SUITCASE.
HAHA! LUCKY!
YOU'VE REALLY EARNED YOUR WEEKEND OFF!
TELL US ABOUT IT WHEN YOU GET BACK?
OH, DUH! MY BAD. I'M AN IDIOT.
YOU, UM... YOU CAN'T. SORRY.
VACUUMIZER 2000
SEND US A CARD, THEN!
THE GUYS WOULD LIKE THAT!
HAVE A GOOD TIME, JACQUES!
REST WELL!
WE'LL BE THINKING OF YOU!
ROBOTOP

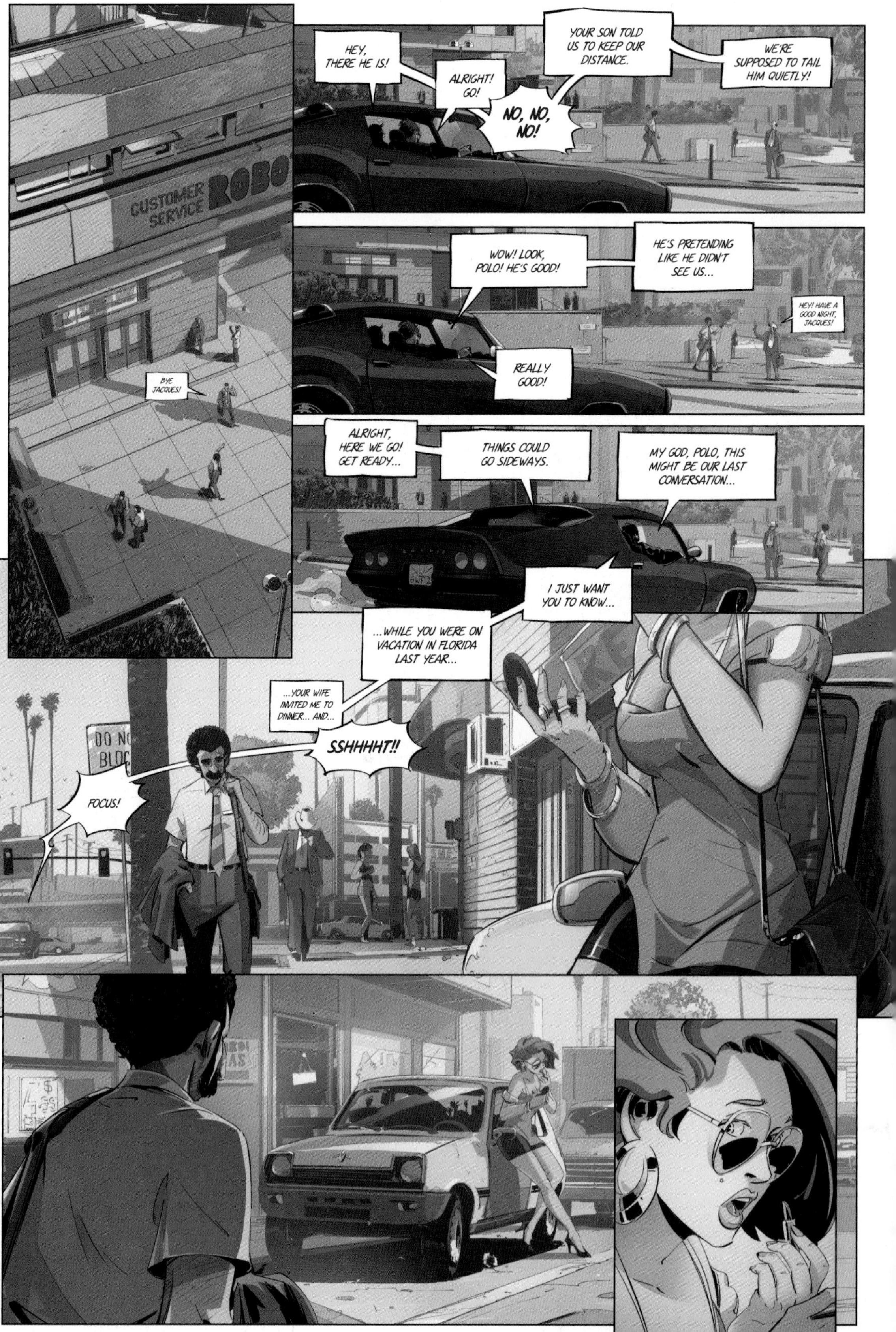
CUSTOMER SERVICE
BYE JACQUES!
HEY, THERE HE IS!
ALRIGHT! GO!
NO, NO, NO!
YOUR SON TOLD US TO KEEP OUR DISTANCE.
WE'RE SUPPOSED TO TAIL HIM QUIETLY!
WOW! LOOK, POLO! HE'S GOOD!
HE'S PRETENDING LIKE HE DIDN'T SEE US...
HEY! HAVE A GOOD NIGHT, JACQUES!
REALLY GOOD!
ALRIGHT, HERE WE GO! GET READY...
THINGS COULD GO SIDEWAYS.
MY GOD, POLO, THIS MIGHT BE OUR LAST CONVERSATION...
I JUST WANT YOU TO KNOW...
...WHILE YOU WERE ON VACATION IN FLORIDA LAST YEAR...
...YOUR WIFE INVITED ME TO DINNER... AND...
SSHHHHT!!
FOCUS!

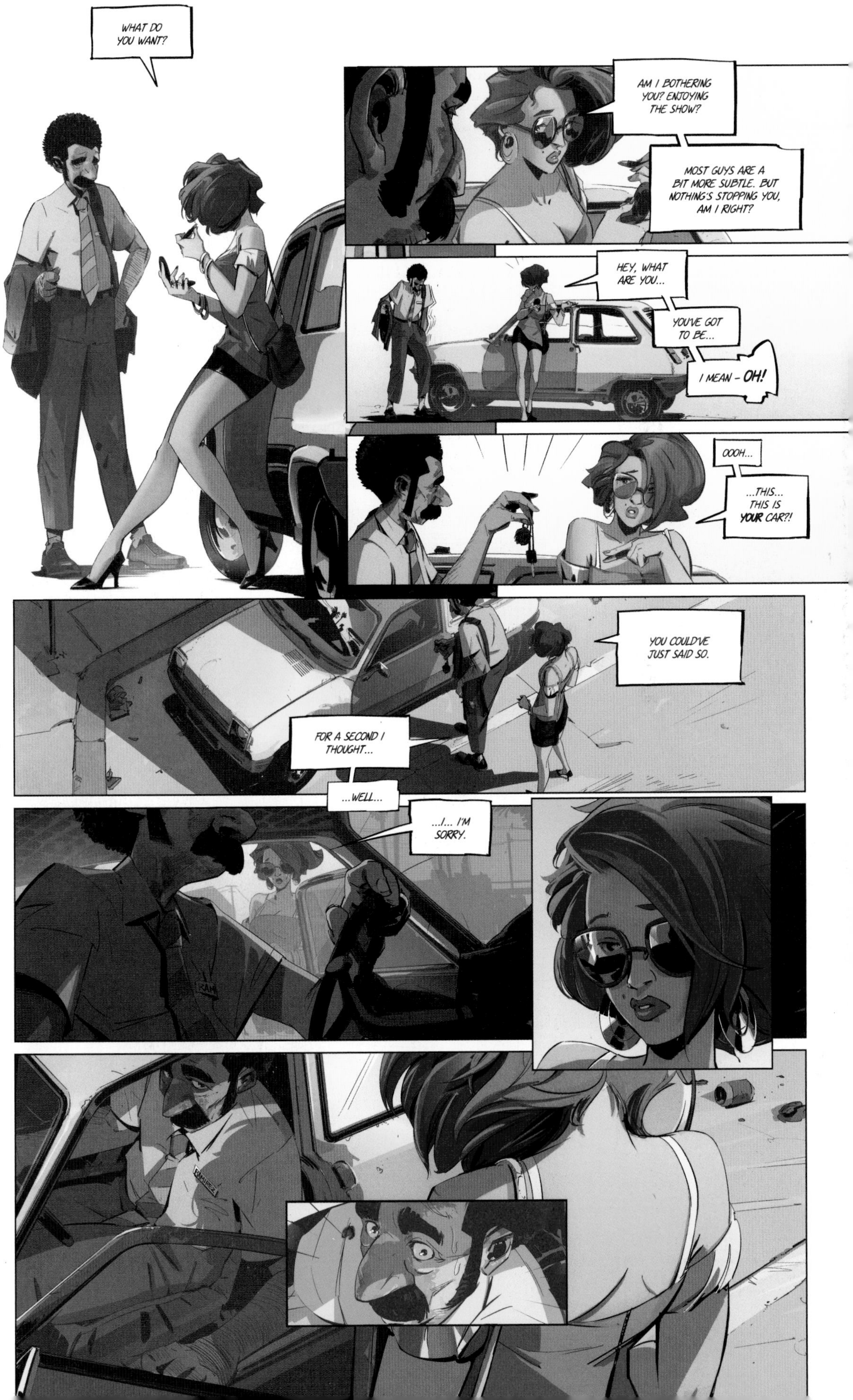
WHAT DO YOU WANT?
AM I BOTHERING YOU? ENJOYING THE SHOW?
MOST GUYS ARE A BIT MORE SUBTLE. BUT NOTHING'S STOPPING YOU, AM I RIGHT?
HEY, WHAT ARE YOU...
YOU'VE GOT TO BE...
I MEAN – OH!
OOOH...
...THIS... THIS IS YOUR CAR?!
YOU COULD'VE JUST SAID SO.
FOR A SECOND I THOUGHT...
...WELL...
...I... I'M SORRY.
RAMIREZ

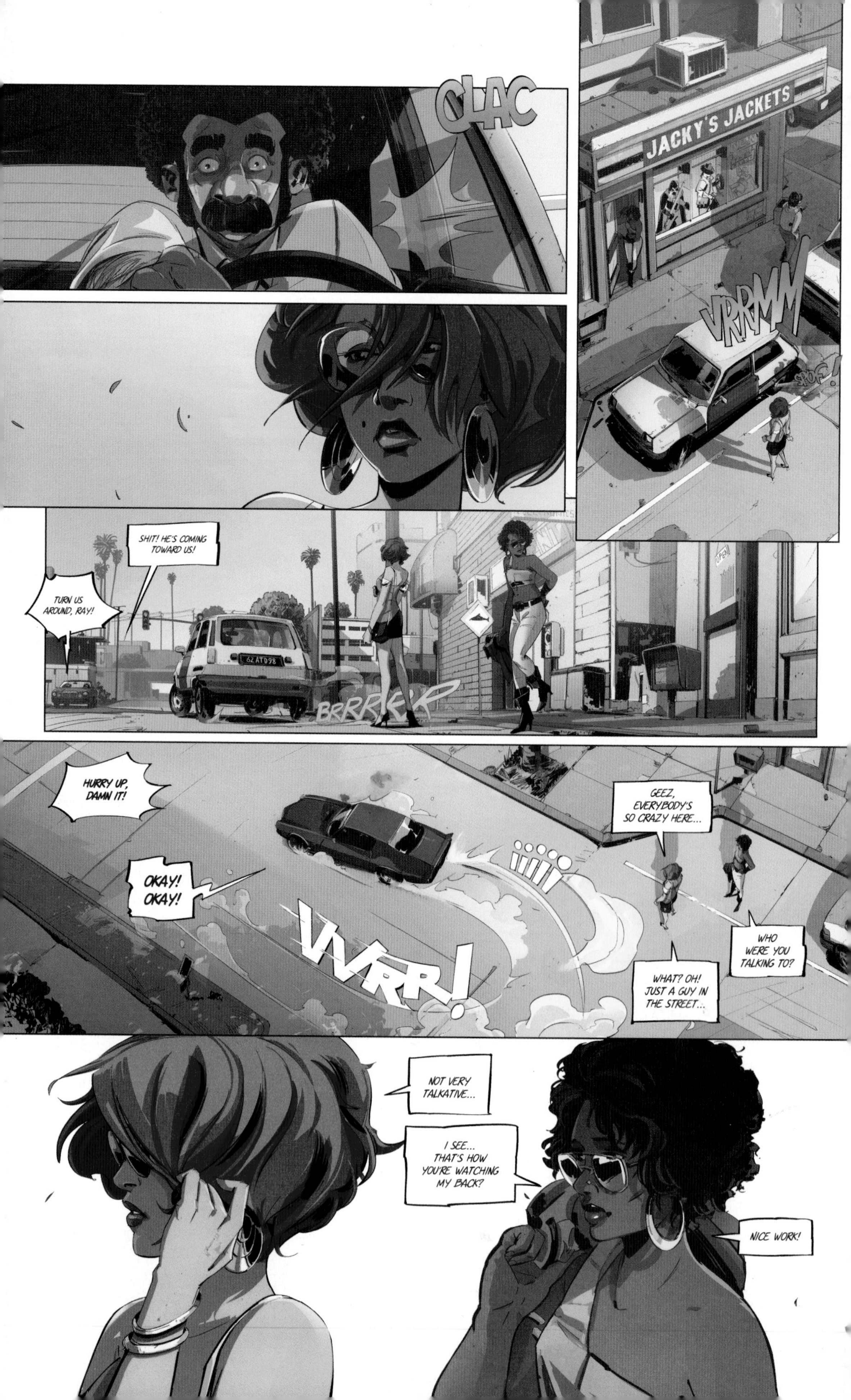
CLAC
JACKY'S JACKETS
VRRMM
SPOF!
SHIT! HE'S COMING TOWARD US!
TURN US AROUND, RAY!
6ZATD98
BRRRRRR
OPEN
HURRY UP, DAMN IT!
OKAY! OKAY!
VVRR!
GEEZ, EVERYBODY'S SO CRAZY HERE...
WHO WERE YOU TALKING TO?
WHAT? OH! JUST A GUY IN THE STREET...
NOT VERY TALKATIVE...
I SEE... THAT'S HOW YOU'RE WATCHING MY BACK?
NICE WORK!

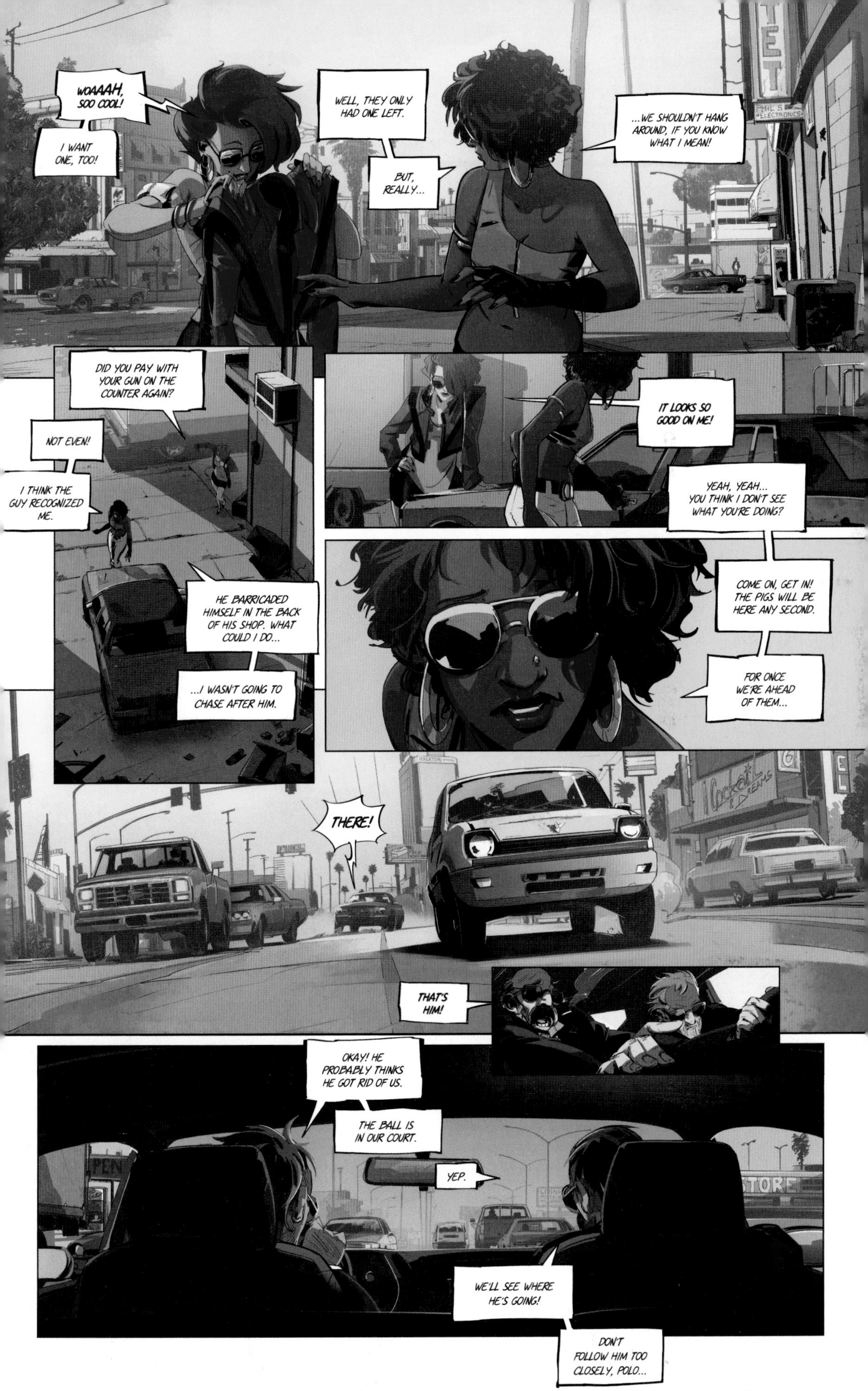
WOAAAH, SOO COOL!
I WANT ONE, TOO!
WELL, THEY ONLY HAD ONE LEFT.
BUT, REALLY...
...WE SHOULDN'T HANG AROUND, IF YOU KNOW WHAT I MEAN!
TET
PHIL'S ELECTRONICS
DID YOU PAY WITH YOUR GUN ON THE COUNTER AGAIN?
NOT EVEN!
I THINK THE GUY RECOGNIZED ME.
HE BARRICADED HIMSELF IN THE BACK OF HIS SHOP. WHAT COULD I DO...
...I WASN'T GOING TO CHASE AFTER HIM.
IT LOOKS SO GOOD ON ME!
YEAH, YEAH... YOU THINK I DON'T SEE WHAT YOU'RE DOING?
COME ON, GET IN! THE PIGS WILL BE HERE ANY SECOND.
FOR ONCE WE'RE AHEAD OF THEM...
THERE!
Cocktail & Dreams
THAT'S HIM!
OKAY! HE PROBABLY THINKS HE GOT RID OF US.
THE BALL IS IN OUR COURT.
YEP.
STORE
WE'LL SEE WHERE HE'S GOING!
DON'T FOLLOW HIM TOO CLOSELY, POLO...

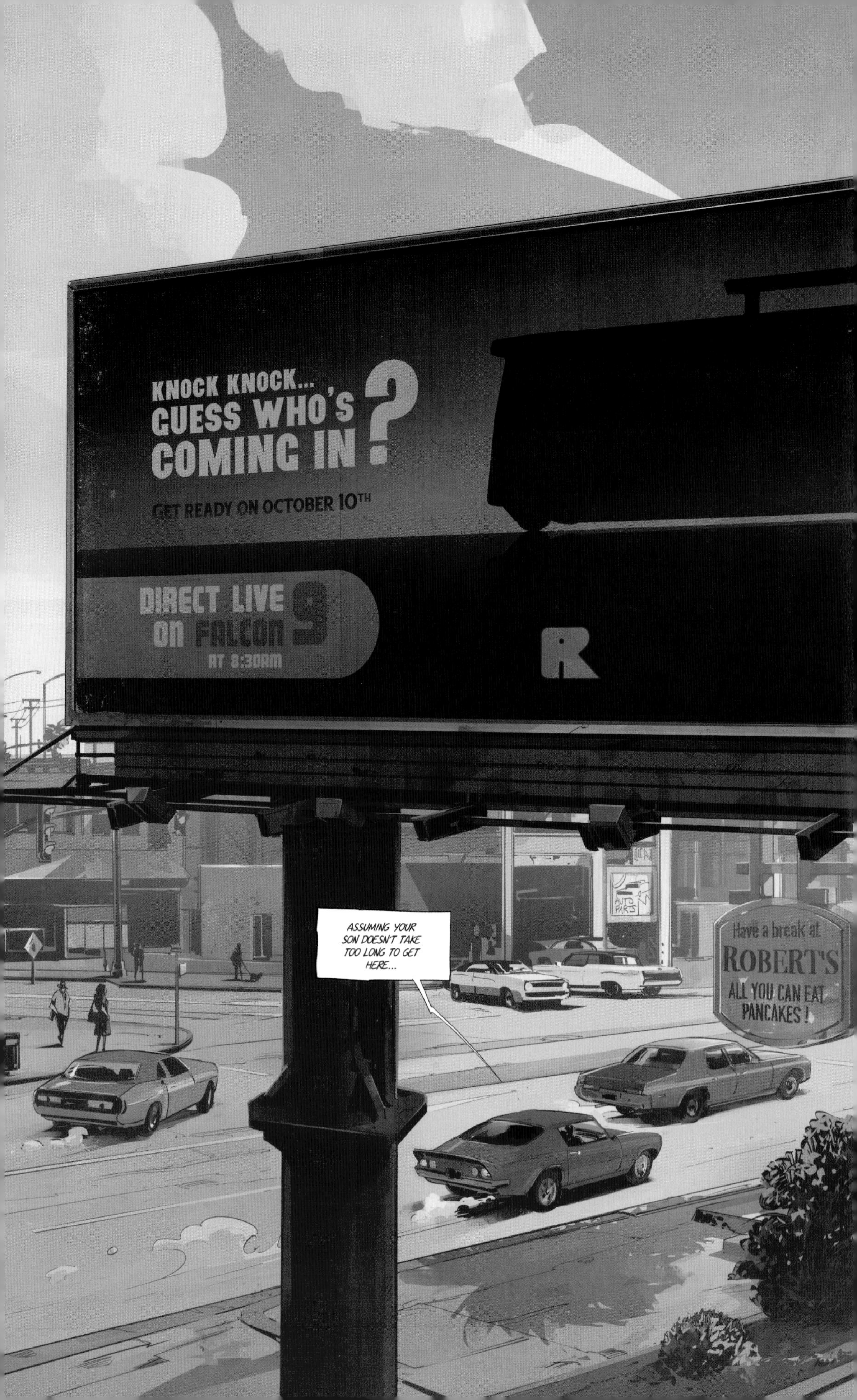
KNOCK KNOCK...
GUESS WHO'S
COMING IN?
GET READY ON OCTOBER 10TH
DIRECT LIVE ON FALCON 9
AT 8:30AM
R
AUTO PARTS
Have a break at
ROBERT'S
ALL YOU CAN EAT
PANCAKES!
ASSUMING YOUR SON DOESN'T TAKE TOO LONG TO GET HERE...

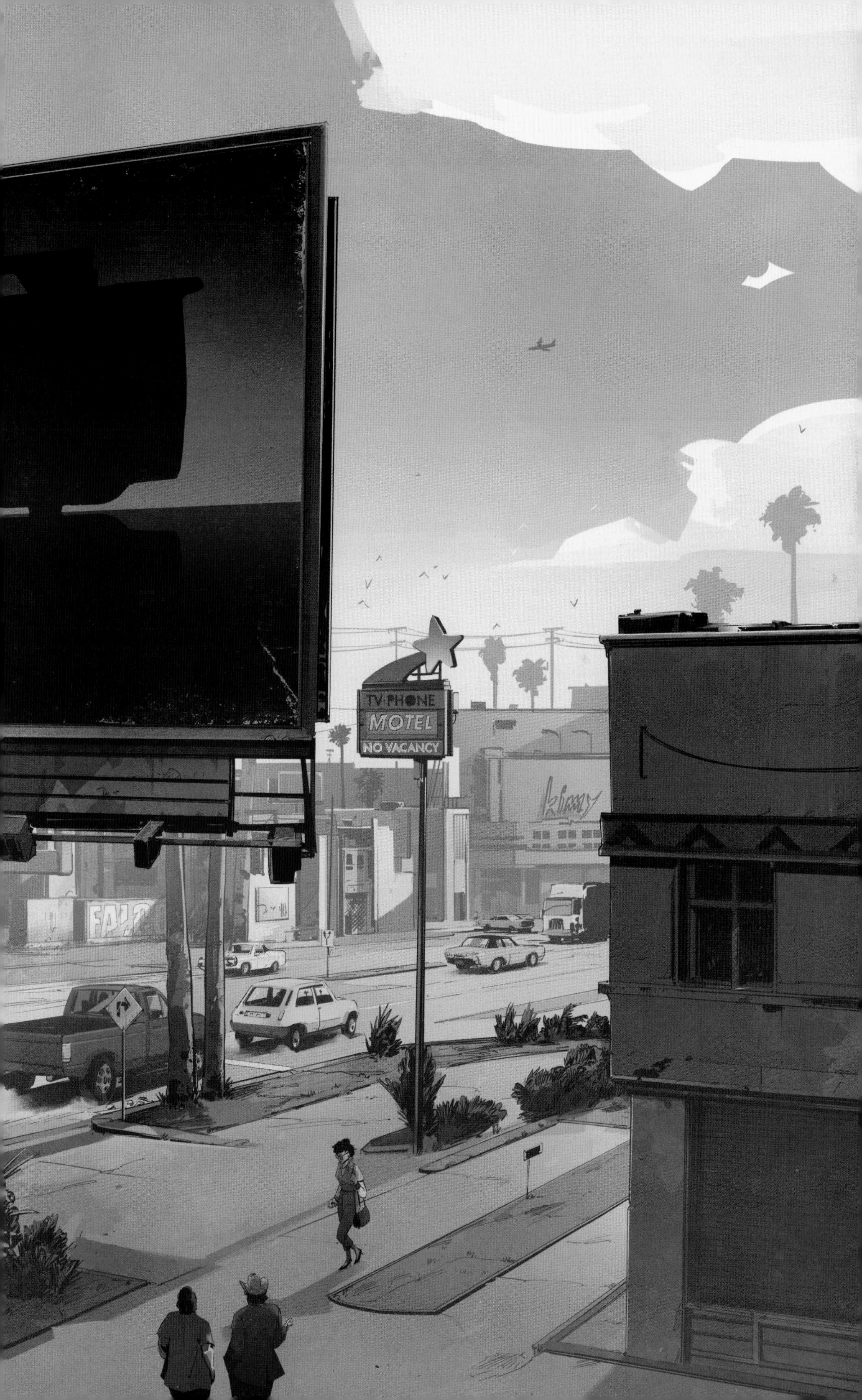
TV·PHONE
MOTEL
NO VACANCY

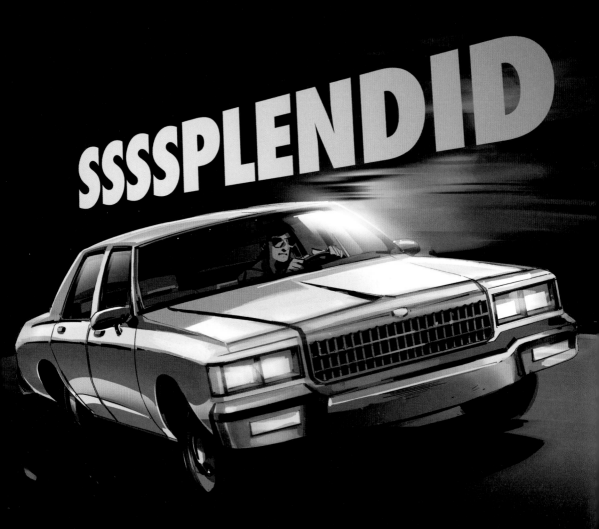

SSSSPLENDID

AS ROBUST AS THE AMERICAN SPIRIT!

You're not dreaming, the new Splendid is here! With its 4-cylinder engine and legendary automatic transmission, Harrison's newest model is the one you've been waiting for!

- New design
- New engine
- Auto-reverse audio cassette shit
- Absolutely incredible

Thanks to the new KLAXON FORCE 7 system, you'll be the new sheriff in town!

New: TURBO-powered 5-speed transmission
Now for the craziest part! From now on, you'll be racing along the highway in all 5 gears simultaneously. That's 507% more speed!

HARRISON SPLENDID

37 | Metallic colors available

Kx-7

"LA RED BLOUSE"
From JACK'S SONS

C «La Red Blouse»
~~$259.99~~

$430.20

C - Gwen Parker wears *La Red Blouse*.
Red jacket with long sleeves
high quality, top of the style!
weight. 60 cm approx.

Scarlet Red	744.2189
Sunshine Red	744.2190
Simply Red	744.2191
34/36, 38/40	

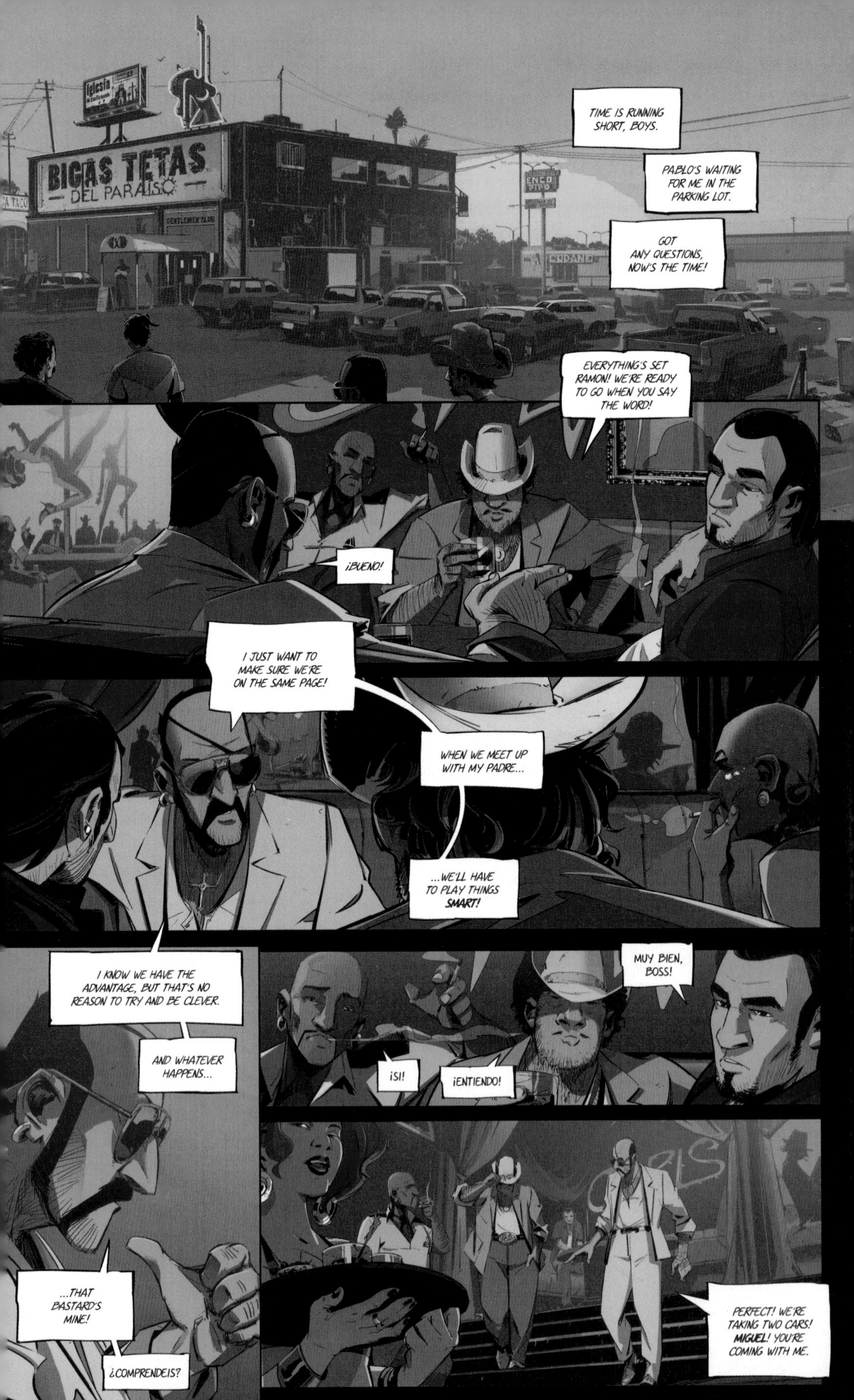
BIGAS TETAS
DEL PARAISO
TIME IS RUNNING SHORT, BOYS.
PABLO'S WAITING FOR ME IN THE PARKING LOT.
GOT ANY QUESTIONS, NOW'S THE TIME!
EVERYTHING'S SET RAMON! WE'RE READY TO GO WHEN YOU SAY THE WORD!
¡BUENO!
I JUST WANT TO MAKE SURE WE'RE ON THE SAME PAGE!
WHEN WE MEET UP WITH MY PADRE...
...WE'LL HAVE TO PLAY THINGS **SMART!**
I KNOW WE HAVE THE ADVANTAGE, BUT THAT'S NO REASON TO TRY AND BE CLEVER.
AND WHATEVER HAPPENS...
...THAT BASTARD'S MINE!
¿COMPRENDEIS?
MUY BIEN, BOSS!
¡SI!
¡ENTIENDO!
PERFECT! WE'RE TAKING TWO CARS! **MIGUEL!** YOU'RE COMING WITH ME.

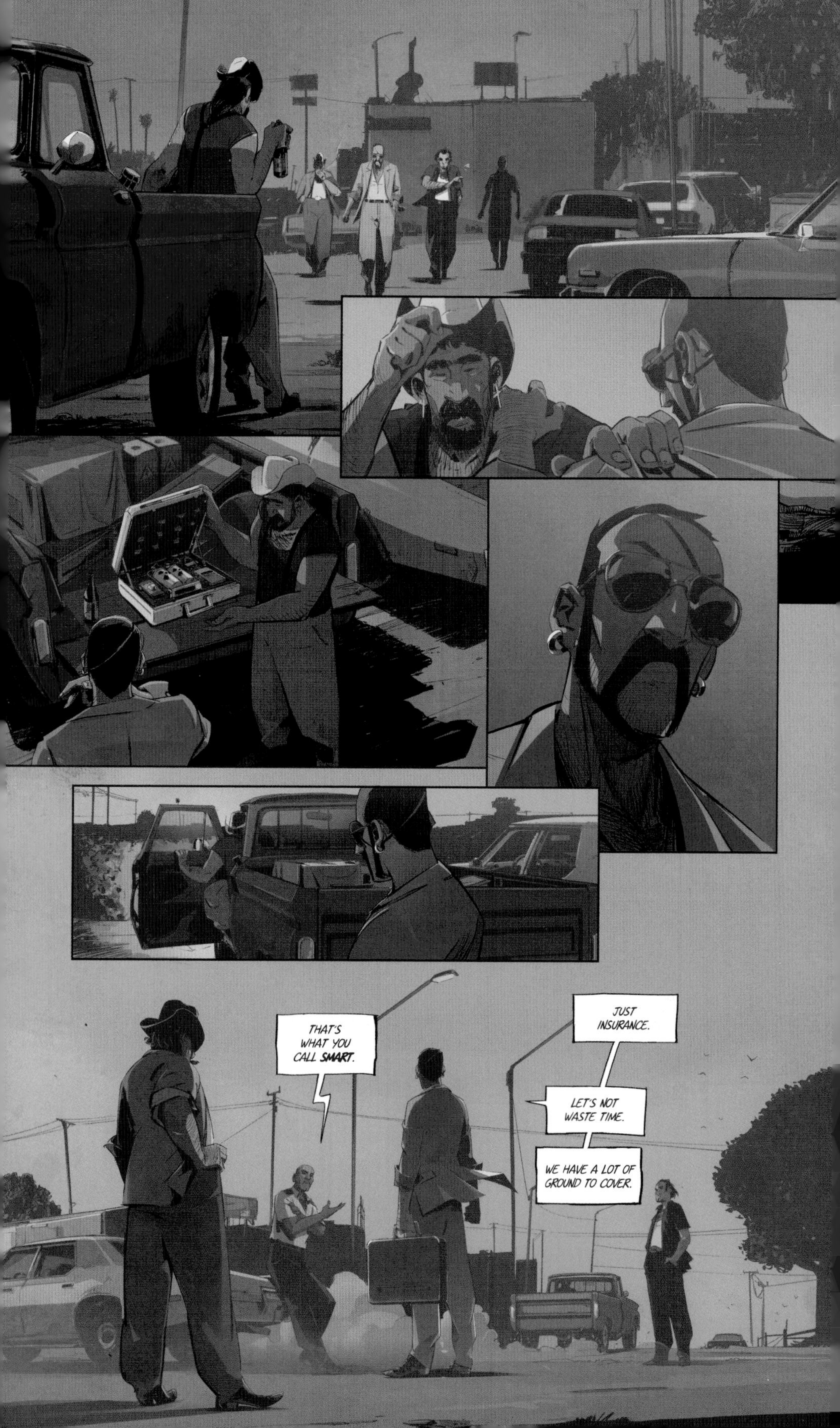
THAT'S WHAT YOU CALL SMART.
JUST INSURANCE.
LET'S NOT WASTE TIME.
WE HAVE A LOT OF GROUND TO COVER.

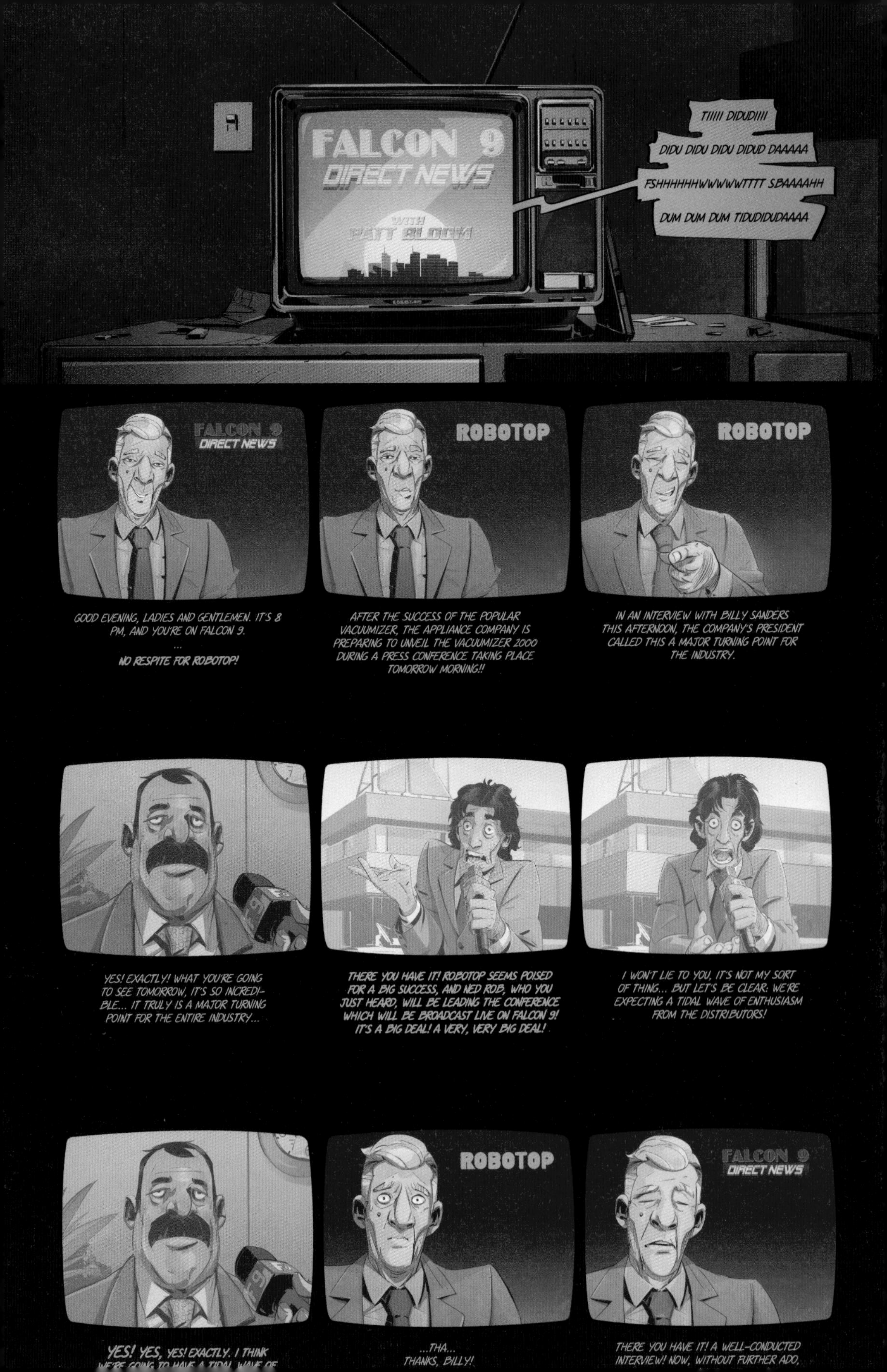
FALCON 9
DIRECT NEWS
WITH
PATT BLOOM
TIIIII DIDUDIIII
DIDU DIDU DIDU DIDUD DAAAAA
FSHHHHHHWWWWWTTTT S.BAAAAHH
DUM DUM DUM TIDUDIDUDAAAA
FALCON 9
DIRECT NEWS
GOOD EVENING, LADIES AND GENTLEMEN. IT'S 8 PM, AND YOU'RE ON FALCON 9.
...
NO RESPITE FOR ROBOTOP!
ROBOTOP
AFTER THE SUCCESS OF THE POPULAR VACUUMIZER, THE APPLIANCE COMPANY IS PREPARING TO UNVEIL THE VACUUMIZER 2000 DURING A PRESS CONFERENCE TAKING PLACE TOMORROW MORNING!!
ROBOTOP
IN AN INTERVIEW WITH BILLY SANDERS THIS AFTERNOON, THE COMPANY'S PRESIDENT CALLED THIS A MAJOR TURNING POINT FOR THE INDUSTRY.
YES! EXACTLY! WHAT YOU'RE GOING TO SEE TOMORROW, IT'S SO INCREDIBLE... IT TRULY IS A MAJOR TURNING POINT FOR THE ENTIRE INDUSTRY...
THERE YOU HAVE IT! ROBOTOP SEEMS POISED FOR A BIG SUCCESS, AND NED ROB, WHO YOU JUST HEARD, WILL BE LEADING THE CONFERENCE WHICH WILL BE BROADCAST LIVE ON FALCON 9! IT'S A BIG DEAL! A VERY, VERY BIG DEAL!
I WON'T LIE TO YOU, IT'S NOT MY SORT OF THING... BUT LET'S BE CLEAR: WE'RE EXPECTING A TIDAL WAVE OF ENTHUSIASM FROM THE DISTRIBUTORS!
YES! YES, YES! EXACTLY. I THINK
ROBOTOP
...THA...
THANKS, BILLY!
FALCON 9
DIRECT NEWS
THERE YOU HAVE IT! A WELL-CONDUCTED INTERVIEW! NOW, WITHOUT FURTHER ADO,

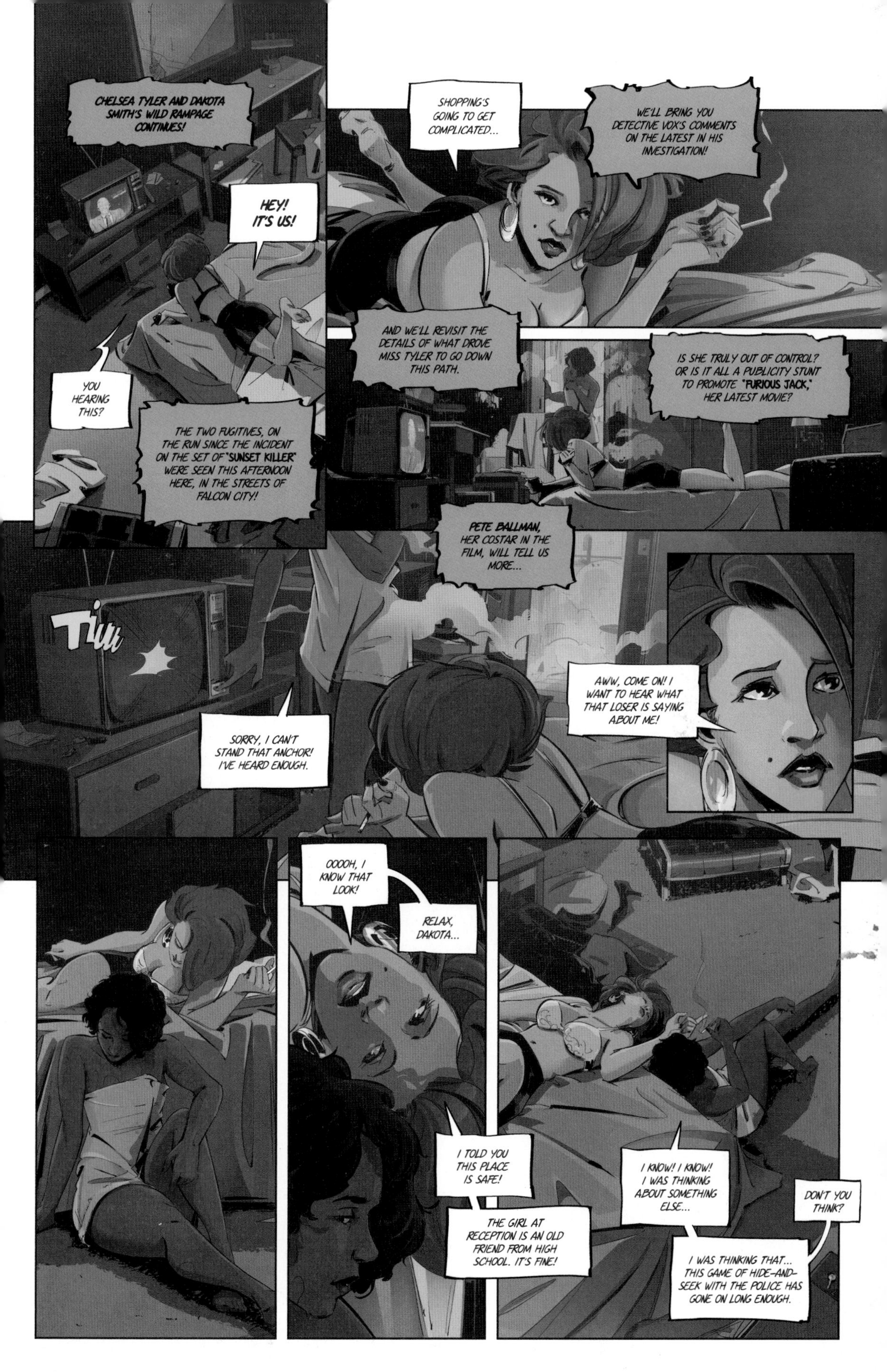
CHELSEA TYLER AND DAKOTA SMITH'S WILD RAMPAGE CONTINUES!
SHOPPING'S GOING TO GET COMPLICATED...
WE'LL BRING YOU DETECTIVE VOX'S COMMENTS ON THE LATEST IN HIS INVESTIGATION!
HEY! IT'S US!
YOU HEARING THIS?
THE TWO FUGITIVES, ON THE RUN SINCE THE INCIDENT ON THE SET OF "SUNSET KILLER" WERE SEEN THIS AFTERNOON HERE, IN THE STREETS OF FALCON CITY!
AND WE'LL REVISIT THE DETAILS OF WHAT DROVE MISS TYLER TO GO DOWN THIS PATH.
IS SHE TRULY OUT OF CONTROL? OR IS IT ALL A PUBLICITY STUNT TO PROMOTE "FURIOUS JACK," HER LATEST MOVIE?
PETE BALLMAN, HER COSTAR IN THE FILM, WILL TELL US MORE...
TIU
SORRY, I CAN'T STAND THAT ANCHOR! I'VE HEARD ENOUGH.
AWW, COME ON! I WANT TO HEAR WHAT THAT LOSER IS SAYING ABOUT ME!
OOOOH, I KNOW THAT LOOK!
RELAX, DAKOTA...
I TOLD YOU THIS PLACE IS SAFE!
THE GIRL AT RECEPTION IS AN OLD FRIEND FROM HIGH SCHOOL. IT'S FINE!
I KNOW! I KNOW! I WAS THINKING ABOUT SOMETHING ELSE...
I WAS THINKING THAT... THIS GAME OF HIDE-AND-SEEK WITH THE POLICE HAS GONE ON LONG ENOUGH.
DON'T YOU THINK?

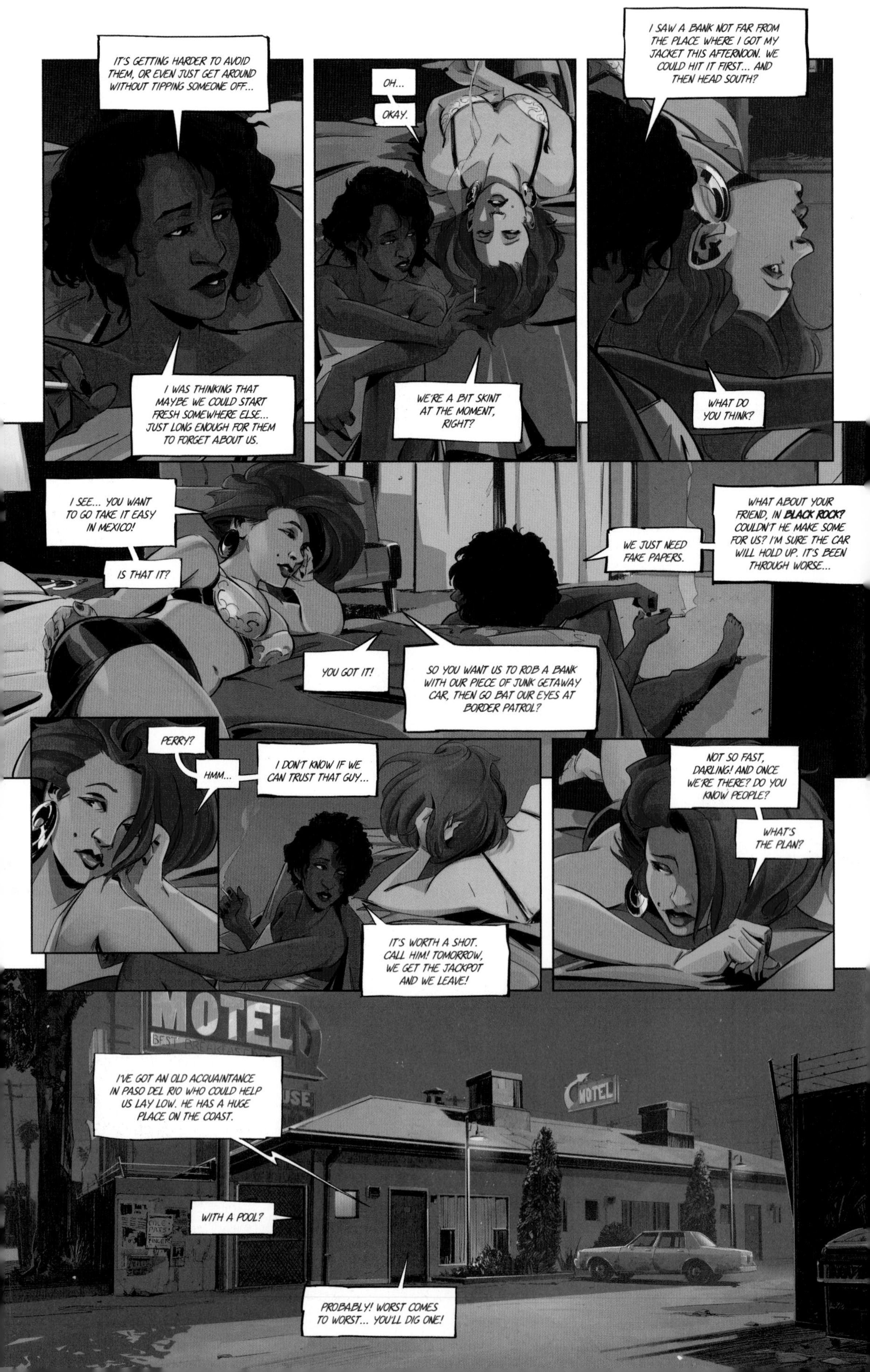

IT'S GETTING HARDER TO AVOID THEM, OR EVEN JUST GET AROUND WITHOUT TIPPING SOMEONE OFF...
I WAS THINKING THAT MAYBE WE COULD START FRESH SOMEWHERE ELSE... JUST LONG ENOUGH FOR THEM TO FORGET ABOUT US.
OH...
OKAY.
WE'RE A BIT SKINT AT THE MOMENT, RIGHT?
I SAW A BANK NOT FAR FROM THE PLACE WHERE I GOT MY JACKET THIS AFTERNOON. WE COULD HIT IT FIRST... AND THEN HEAD SOUTH?
WHAT DO YOU THINK?
I SEE... YOU WANT TO GO TAKE IT EASY IN MEXICO!
IS THAT IT?
YOU GOT IT!
SO YOU WANT US TO ROB A BANK WITH OUR PIECE OF JUNK GETAWAY CAR, THEN GO BAT OUR EYES AT BORDER PATROL?
WE JUST NEED FAKE PAPERS.
WHAT ABOUT YOUR FRIEND, IN BLACK ROCK? COULDN'T HE MAKE SOME FOR US? I'M SURE THE CAR WILL HOLD UP. IT'S BEEN THROUGH WORSE...
PERRY?
HMM...
I DON'T KNOW IF WE CAN TRUST THAT GUY...
IT'S WORTH A SHOT. CALL HIM! TOMORROW, WE GET THE JACKPOT AND WE LEAVE!
NOT SO FAST, DARLING! AND ONCE WE'RE THERE? DO YOU KNOW PEOPLE?
WHAT'S THE PLAN?
MOTEL
I'VE GOT AN OLD ACQUAINTANCE IN PASO DEL RIO WHO COULD HELP US LAY LOW. HE HAS A HUGE PLACE ON THE COAST.
MOTEL
WITH A POOL?
PROBABLY! WORST COMES TO WORST... YOU'LL DIG ONE!

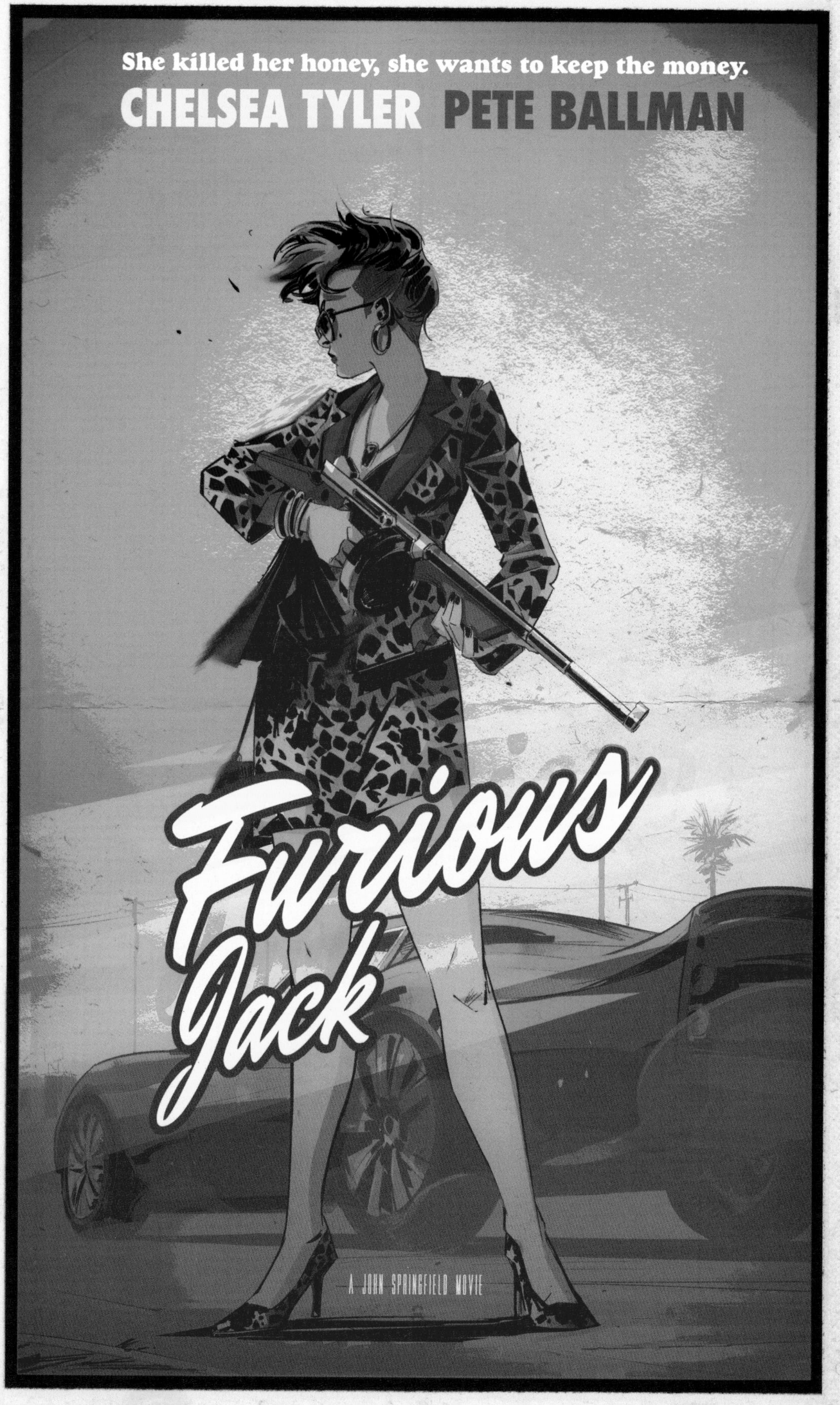
She killed her honey, she wants to keep the money.
CHELSEA TYLER PETE BALLMAN
Furious Jack
A JOHN SPRINGFIELD MOVIE

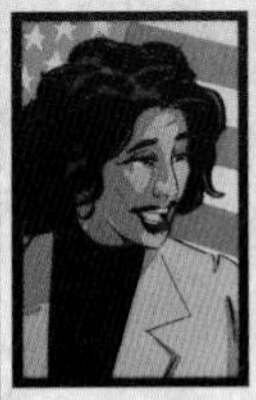

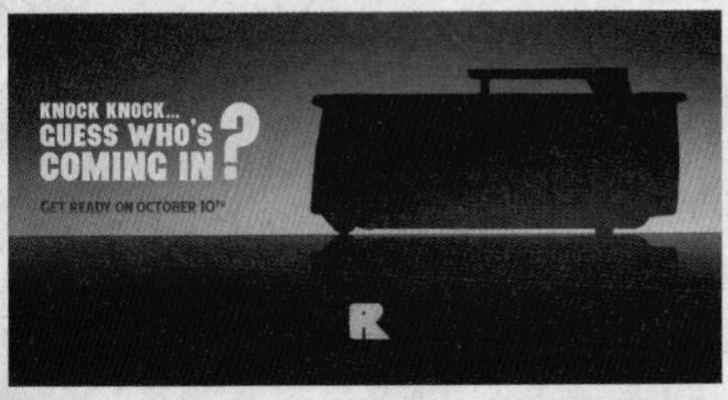

FALCON TODAY

Almost N°1 in Arizona

THURSDAY,

OCTOBER 9, 1987

HEADLINE IN BLACK

MAN KILLED IN SECOND MAN'S SUICIDE ATTEMPT
implicating third man whose life is in danger

ARON SPAYLING'S BIG RETURN
His new project: *SHANONA HILLS 666.*

EXPLOSION AT ELECTROGAS
Fourth time this week. Safety problems possible.

PRESIDENT: "OH, SHIT!"
American people awaiting clarification

FIRST LADY ANNOUNCES HER CANDIDACY White House in state of shock!

CANDIDATE LADY LIDIA TO VISIT DILLINGTOWN
Debate to be announced.

DOG RESCUES ITTY BITTY KITTY
An epic and touching tale.

LADY LIDIA NO LONGER TO VISIT DILLINGTOWN
The debate has been canceled.

SERIES OF DEATHS AT STAR SLICER 3000 :
The informercial host is a prime suspect.

DOLOREAN SUED FOR NUMEROUS DISAPPEARANCES OF ITS VEHICLES
at high speeds.

A MAN PLAYS BANJO IN FRONT OF A CAR, YOU WON'T BELIEVE WHAT HE DOES NEXT !
Video available on VHS at local library, 3rd floor, left side, ask for Catherine

SHE EATS ONE NUT A DAY AND HER TRANSFORMATION WILL BLOW YOU AWAY...
To read the rest on page 9, send $1 to "SONS OF THE BEACH" - 1087 Skyroad avenue - FALCON CITY 90234, AZ".

CINEMA

PETE BALLMAN , HONORED

The famous Canadian actor, Pete Ballman, set a new record this week with eight films being released, seven of which feature him as the lead!

STATISTICS SECTION!

Question for October 2nd:
Do you agree that we should send back Indians to space?

I love you les Indians
but you need to go home.
8%
Passionately 3%
Wildly 12%
Yep... 8%
Very much 7%
62%
Somewhat

Next question:
Have you ever eaten a family member?

KNOCK KNOCK...
GUESS WHO'S COMING IN ?
GET READY ON OCTOBER 10TH
R

The Country's news
Straight from over 50 States!

Weather Forecast
Sun, clouds, and rain. But also wind, storms and snow.

News in Sports
MEXICAN GAYS victorious, 1009-1 "Olé!"

Panic in the city!

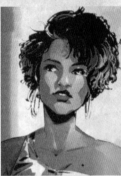

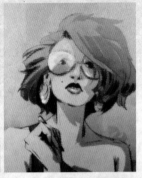

Dakota Smith & Chelsea Tyler spotted in Palmer Heights!!!

Police are apparently struggling to put an end to the two young women's crime spree, which shows no sign of stopping.
According to a Palmer Heights store owner, the pair were spotted late Wednesday night strolling near Park Avenue. According to the tipster, Miss Tyler appeared to be under the influence, as she did not hesitate to flaunt herself on the street. The search for the two women began two weeks ago, after their blunder on the set of "Sunset Killer." Although police have committed significant resources to finding and apprehending the fugitives, the women have already crossed two state lines, robbed a GoldBank branch in Coven Springs, and been involved in numerous deaths.

Continued on **p.2**

Eating 28 lbs of meat per day is very bad for Americans' health...

Other countries haven't had this issue, but a report delivered by the ASAME (Association of American Meat-Eaters) denounced a "alleged" claim that overconsumption of meat can cause health issues. Additional studies are underway.

Continued on **p.7**

Feature

NCB Bank branch Security under scrutiny

An NCB Bank of America employee criticizes security practices at the financial group's bank branches. He reveals behind-the-scenes details of security protocols NCB implemented in 1983, and gives tips on how to beat the system. But that's not all! Last week, the same employee expressed serious concerns about the reliability of the two-digit code that secures the main vault...

Feature **p.16**

ROBOTOP President ready to take on the FUTURE!

We are filling this really quite narrow space with a block of tiny text instead of leaving it blank so that you don't think we have nothing interesting to say. Do you see what we mean? For real? Ok, so...

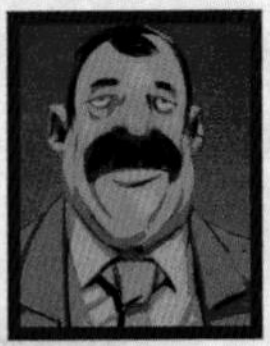

At 9:00 sharp tomorrow morning, ROBOTOP's newest revolutionary vacuum cleaner will be unveiled! As they have done every year since the memorable 1984 launch of the AV 700, the American appliance company continues to ride a tidal wave of success, which has lately transformed into a steamroller, crushing competitors as they attempt (as best they can) to match Robotop's unprecedented success. According to the latest sales figures, more than 700 million households are equipped with one of these famous vacuum cleaners. Some studies also show that a number of households have more than four Robotop vacuums...

Continued on **p.7**

Quality Label

The hard truth, or nothing at all!

Even at the risk of great danger, our journalists fight every day to get the truth, and nothing but the truth in front of your eyes so you can see how our society actually functiuns. We firmly believe that publishing factual information and crosschecking the often-sensationalized is detrimental to juicier and more profitable news for our newspaper. That's why we do our best to address as many of the rumors and other whispers. Our readers have a right to know what's going on in THEIR country, for christ's sake!

John MacNews

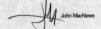

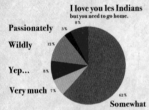

THE TERROR OF THE CARTELS

Prostitution, money, drugs... An exclusive, breathtaking report from the heart of the MEXICAN cartels.

Feature **p.11**

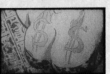

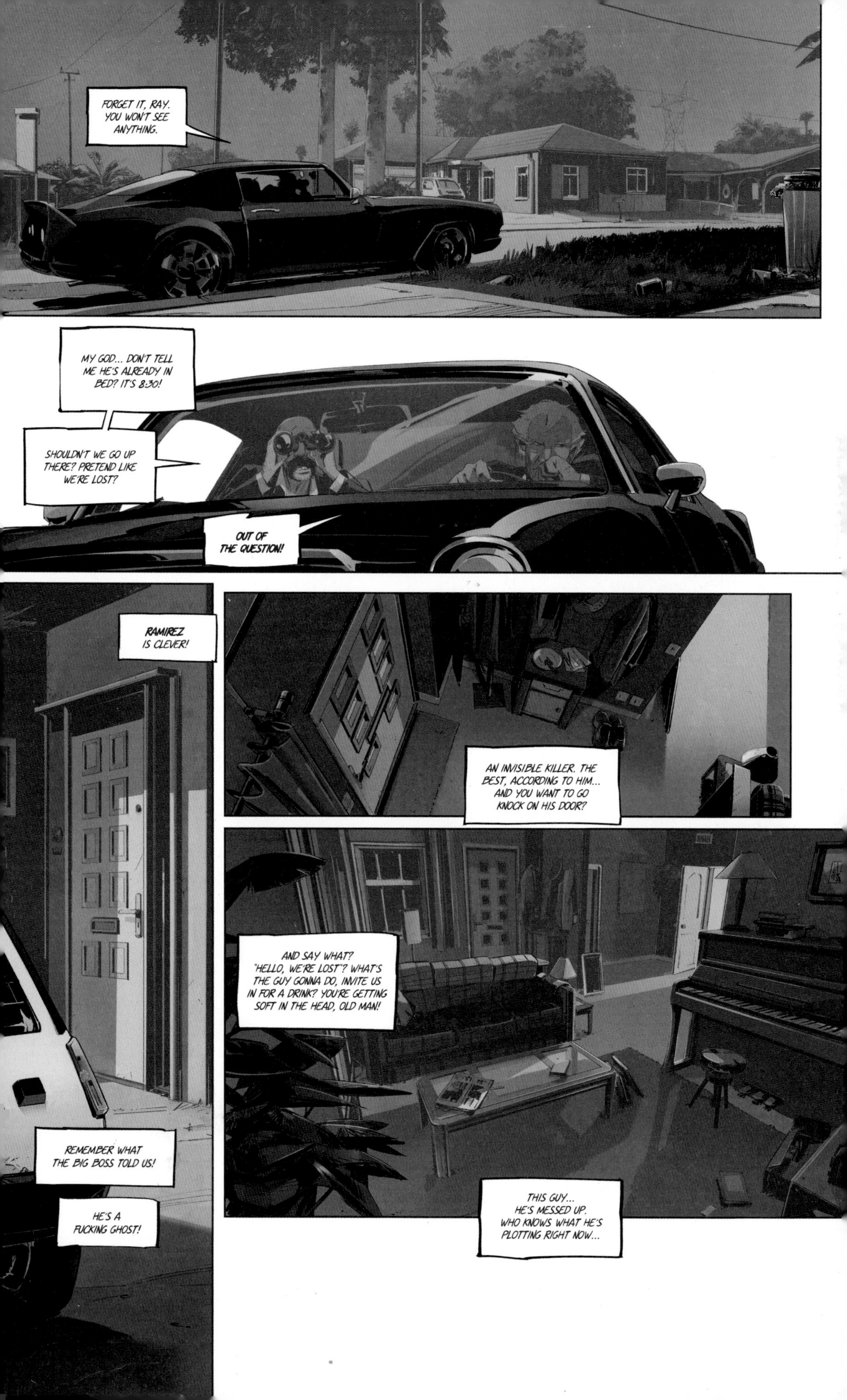
FORGET IT, RAY. YOU WON'T SEE ANYTHING.
MY GOD... DON'T TELL ME HE'S ALREADY IN BED? IT'S 8:30!
SHOULDN'T WE GO UP THERE? PRETEND LIKE WE'RE LOST?
OUT OF THE QUESTION!
RAMIREZ IS CLEVER!
REMEMBER WHAT THE BIG BOSS TOLD US!
HE'S A FUCKING GHOST!
AN INVISIBLE KILLER. THE BEST, ACCORDING TO HIM... AND YOU WANT TO GO KNOCK ON HIS DOOR?
AND SAY WHAT? "HELLO, WE'RE LOST"? WHAT'S THE GUY GONNA DO, INVITE US IN FOR A DRINK? YOU'RE GETTING SOFT IN THE HEAD, OLD MAN!
THIS GUY... HE'S MESSED UP. WHO KNOWS WHAT HE'S PLOTTING RIGHT NOW...

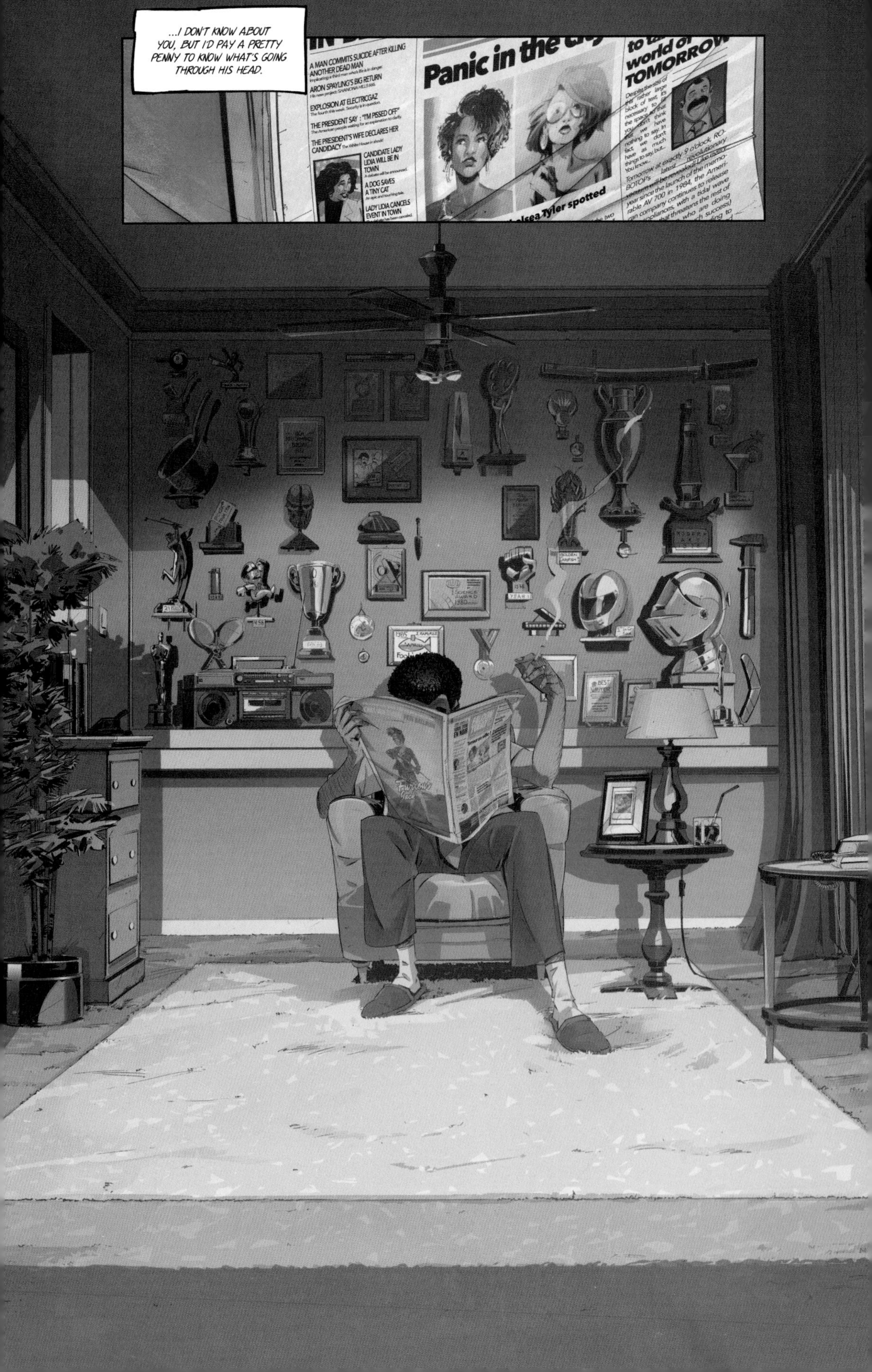
...I DON'T KNOW ABOUT YOU, BUT I'D PAY A PRETTY PENNY TO KNOW WHAT'S GOING THROUGH HIS HEAD.
A MAN COMMITS SUICIDE AFTER KILLING ANOTHER DEAD MAN
ARON SPAYLING'S BIG RETURN
EXPLOSION AT ELECTRIGAZ
THE PRESIDENT SAY : "I'M PISSED OFF"
THE PRESIDENT'S WIFE DECLARES HER CANDIDACY
CANDIDATE LADY LIDIA WILL BE IN TOWN
A DOG SAVES A TINY CAT
LADY LIDIA CANCELS EVENT IN TOWN
Panic in the
world of TOMORROW

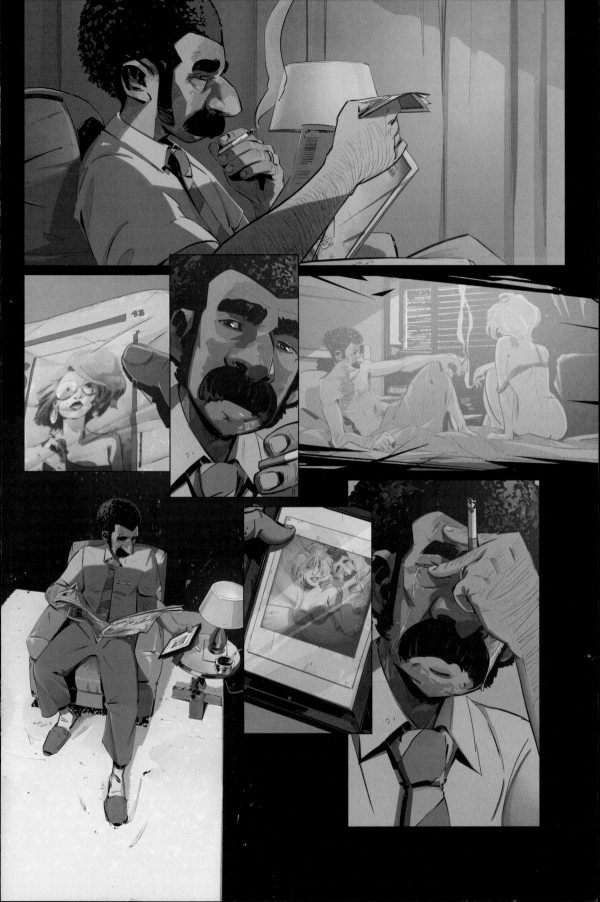

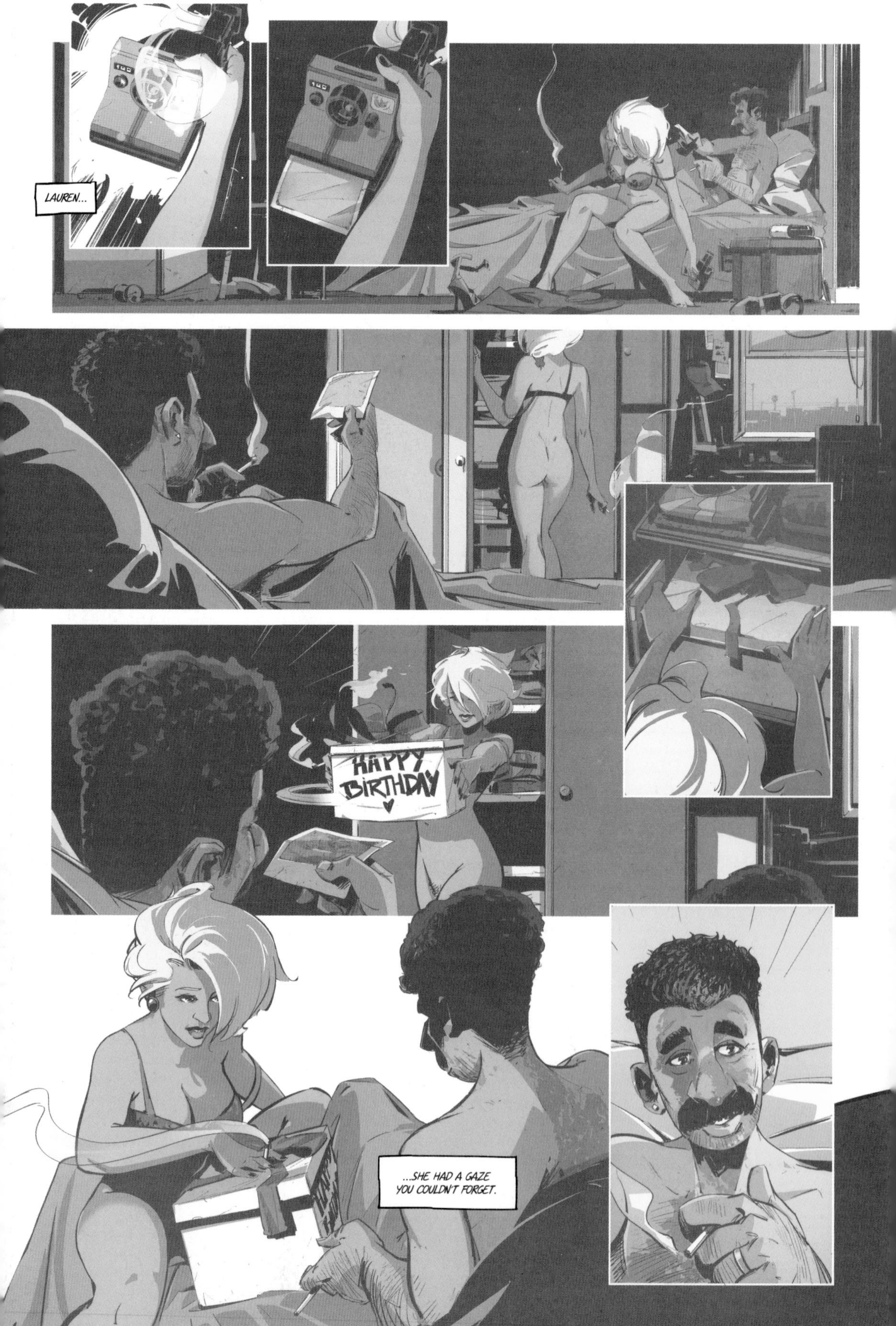
LAUREN...
HAPPY BIRTHDAY
...SHE HAD A GAZE YOU COULDN'T FORGET.

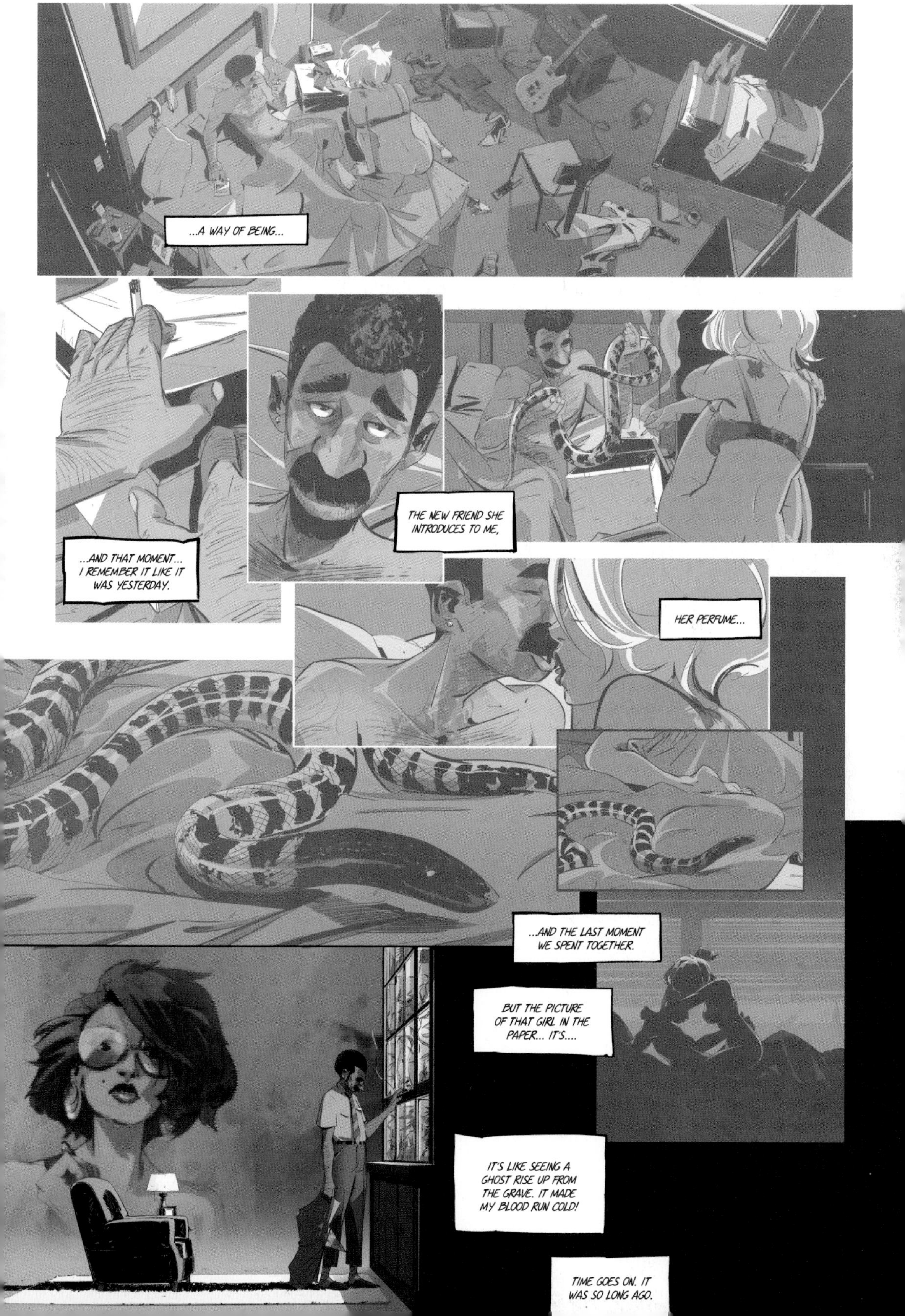
...A WAY OF BEING...
...AND THAT MOMENT... I REMEMBER IT LIKE IT WAS YESTERDAY.
THE NEW FRIEND SHE INTRODUCES TO ME,
HER PERFUME...
...AND THE LAST MOMENT WE SPENT TOGETHER.
BUT THE PICTURE OF THAT GIRL IN THE PAPER... IT'S....
IT'S LIKE SEEING A GHOST RISE UP FROM THE GRAVE. IT MADE MY BLOOD RUN COLD!
TIME GOES ON. IT WAS SO LONG AGO.

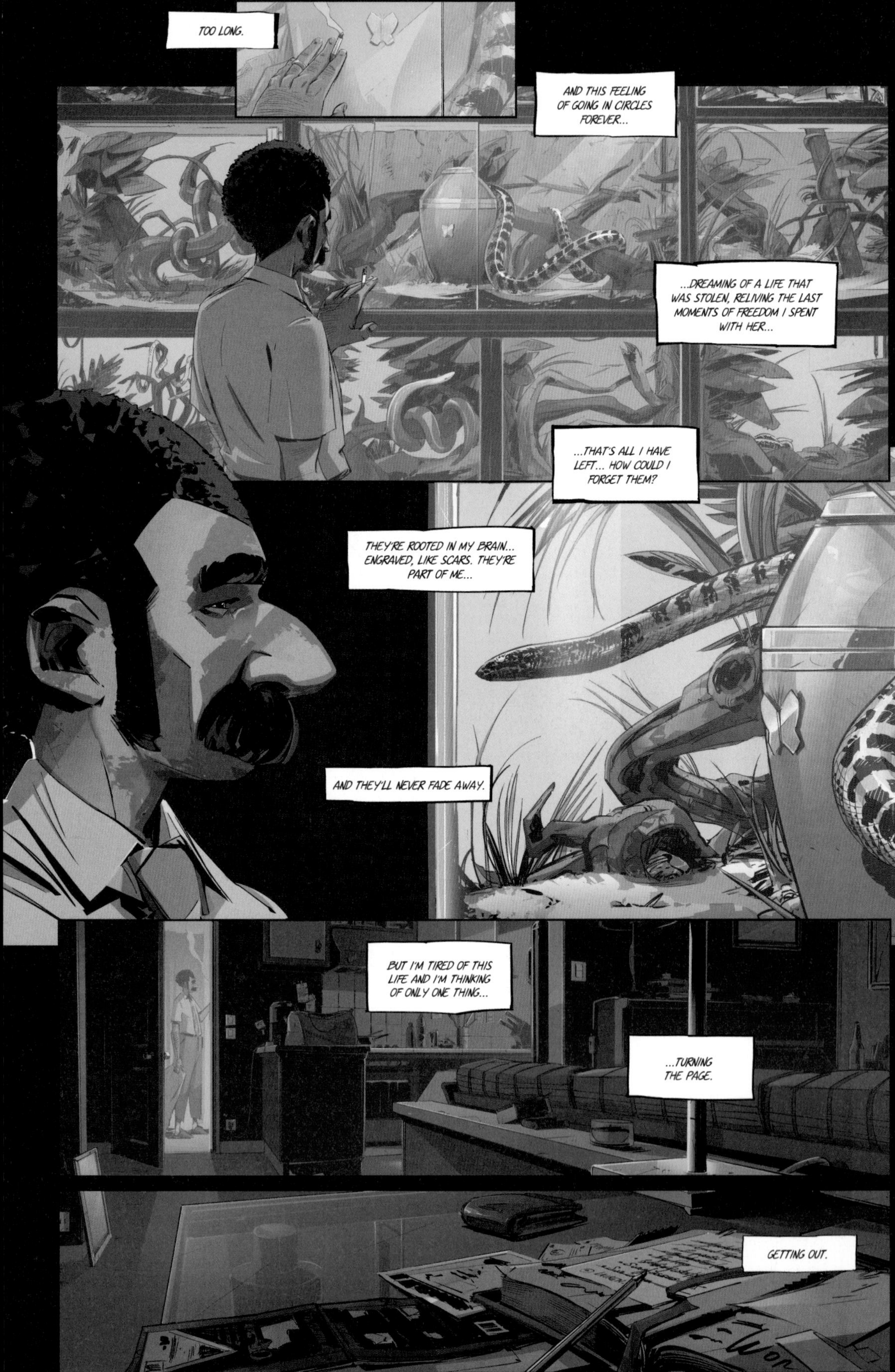
TOO LONG.
AND THIS FEELING OF GOING IN CIRCLES FOREVER...
...DREAMING OF A LIFE THAT WAS STOLEN, RELIVING THE LAST MOMENTS OF FREEDOM I SPENT WITH HER...
...THAT'S ALL I HAVE LEFT... HOW COULD I FORGET THEM?
THEY'RE ROOTED IN MY BRAIN... ENGRAVED, LIKE SCARS. THEY'RE PART OF ME...
AND THEY'LL NEVER FADE AWAY.
BUT I'M TIRED OF THIS LIFE AND I'M THINKING OF ONLY ONE THING...
...TURNING THE PAGE.
GETTING OUT.

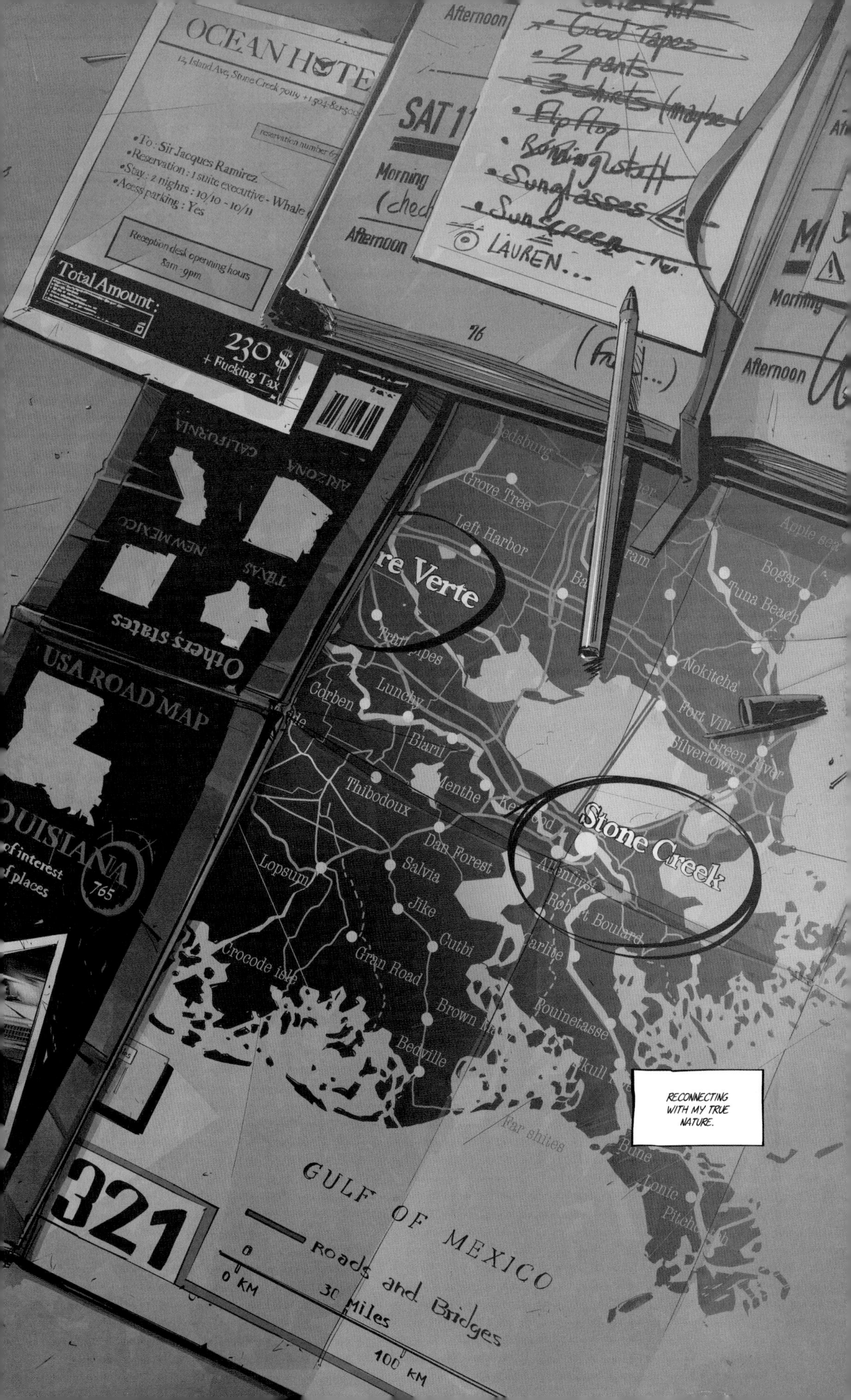

OCEAN HOTE
•To : Sir Jacques Ramirez
•Reservation : 1 suite executive - Whale
•Stay : 2 nights : 10/10 - 10/11
•Acess parking : Yes
Reception desk openning hours 8am - 9pm
Total Amount :
230 $
+ Fucking Tax
Afternoon
SAT 11
Morning
Afternoon
• Good Tapes
• 2 pants
• Flip Flop
• Sunglasses
LAUREN...
76
Morning
Afternoon
USA ROAD MAP
CALIFORNIA
ARIZONA
NEW MEXICO
TEXAS
Others-states
765
321
Grove Tree
Left Harbor
re Verte
Corben
Lunchy
Blaril
Menthe
Thibodoux
Dan Forest
Salvia
Lopsum
Jike
Cutbi
Gran Road
Crocode isle
Bedville
Stone Creek
Robert Boulard
Carlite
Rouinetasse
Apple sea
Boggy
Tuna Beach
Nokitcha
Silvertown
Green River
Far shites
Bune
GULF OF MEXICO
Roads and Bridges
0
0 KM
30 Miles
100 KM
RECONNECTING WITH MY TRUE NATURE.

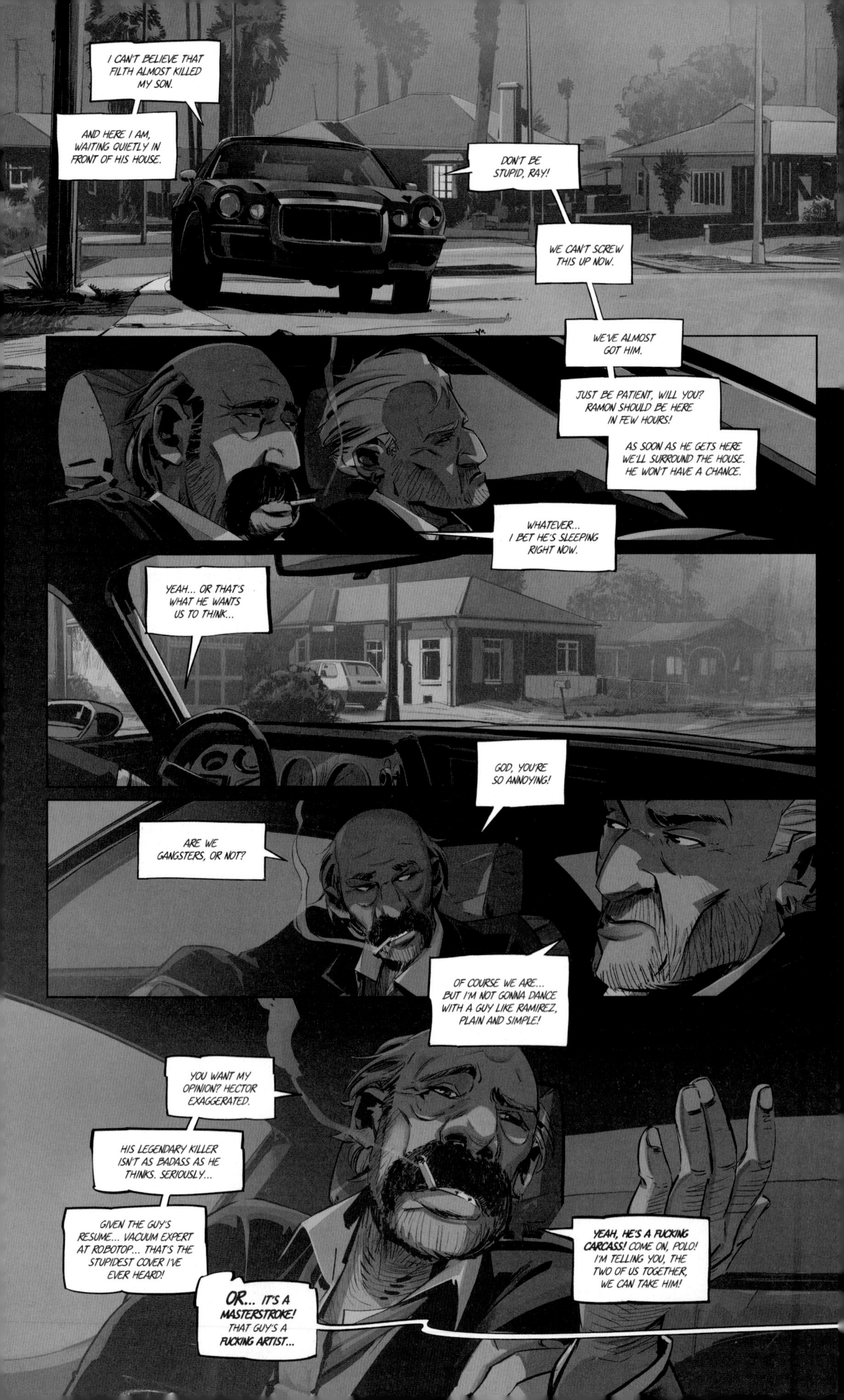
I CAN'T BELIEVE THAT FILTH ALMOST KILLED MY SON.
AND HERE I AM, WAITING QUIETLY IN FRONT OF HIS HOUSE.
DON'T BE STUPID, RAY!
WE CAN'T SCREW THIS UP NOW.
WE'VE ALMOST GOT HIM.
JUST BE PATIENT, WILL YOU? RAMON SHOULD BE HERE IN FEW HOURS!
AS SOON AS HE GETS HERE WE'LL SURROUND THE HOUSE. HE WON'T HAVE A CHANCE.
WHATEVER... I BET HE'S SLEEPING RIGHT NOW.
YEAH... OR THAT'S WHAT HE WANTS US TO THINK...
GOD, YOU'RE SO ANNOYING!
ARE WE GANGSTERS, OR NOT?
OF COURSE WE ARE... BUT I'M NOT GONNA DANCE WITH A GUY LIKE RAMIREZ, PLAIN AND SIMPLE!
YOU WANT MY OPINION? HECTOR EXAGGERATED.
HIS LEGENDARY KILLER ISN'T AS BADASS AS HE THINKS. SERIOUSLY...
GIVEN THE GUY'S RESUME... VACUUM EXPERT AT ROBOTOP... THAT'S THE STUPIDEST COVER I'VE EVER HEARD!
YEAH, HE'S A FUCKING CARCASS! COME ON, POLO! I'M TELLING YOU, THE TWO OF US TOGETHER, WE CAN TAKE HIM!
OR... IT'S A MASTERSTROKE! THAT GUY'S A FUCKING ARTIST...

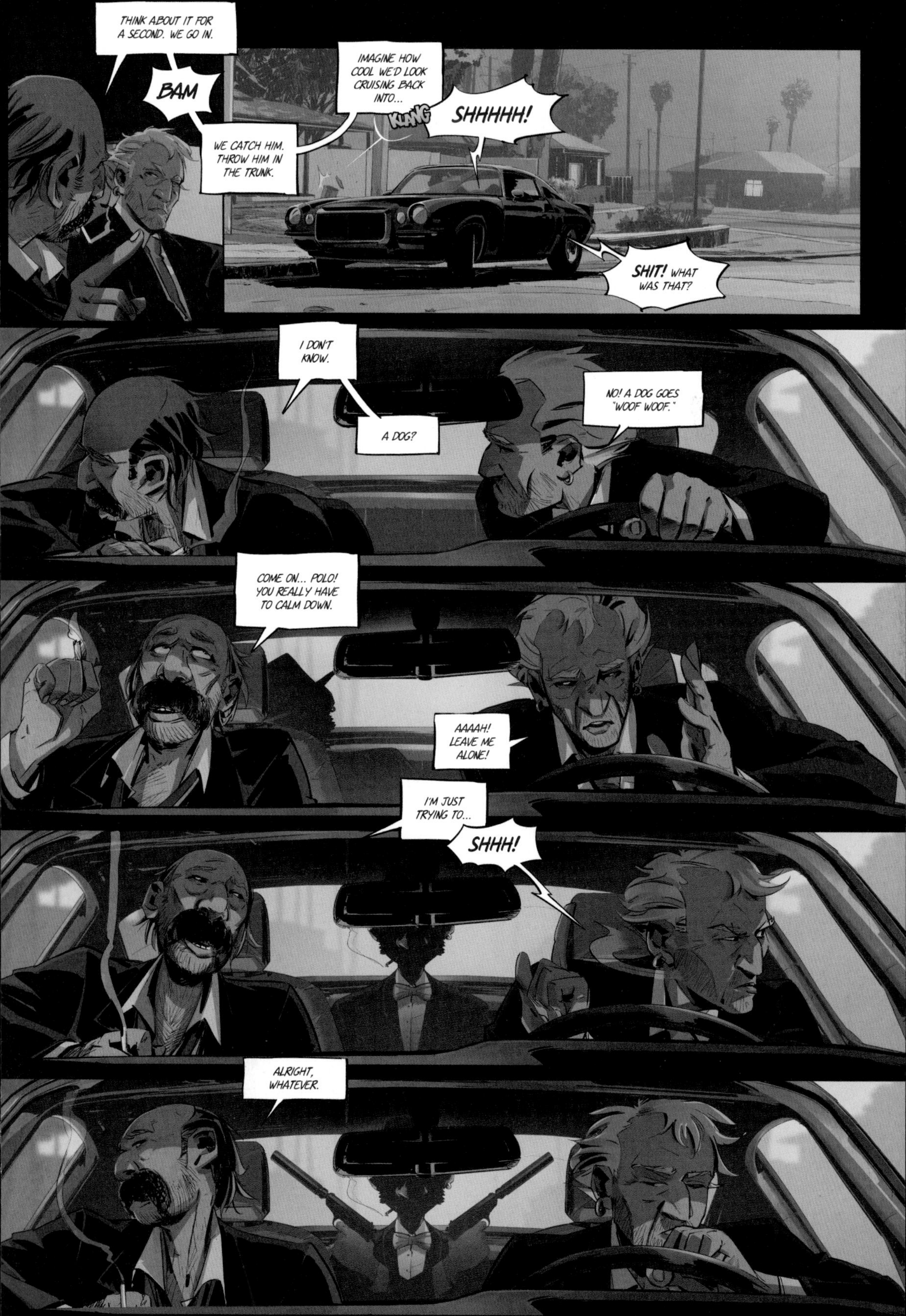
THINK ABOUT IT FOR A SECOND. WE GO IN.
BAM
WE CATCH HIM. THROW HIM IN THE TRUNK.
IMAGINE HOW COOL WE'D LOOK CRUISING BACK INTO...
KLANG
SHHHHH!
SHIT! WHAT WAS THAT?
I DON'T KNOW.
A DOG?
NO! A DOG GOES "WOOF WOOF."
COME ON... POLO! YOU REALLY HAVE TO CALM DOWN.
AAAAH! LEAVE ME ALONE!
I'M JUST TRYING TO...
SHHH!
ALRIGHT, WHATEVER.

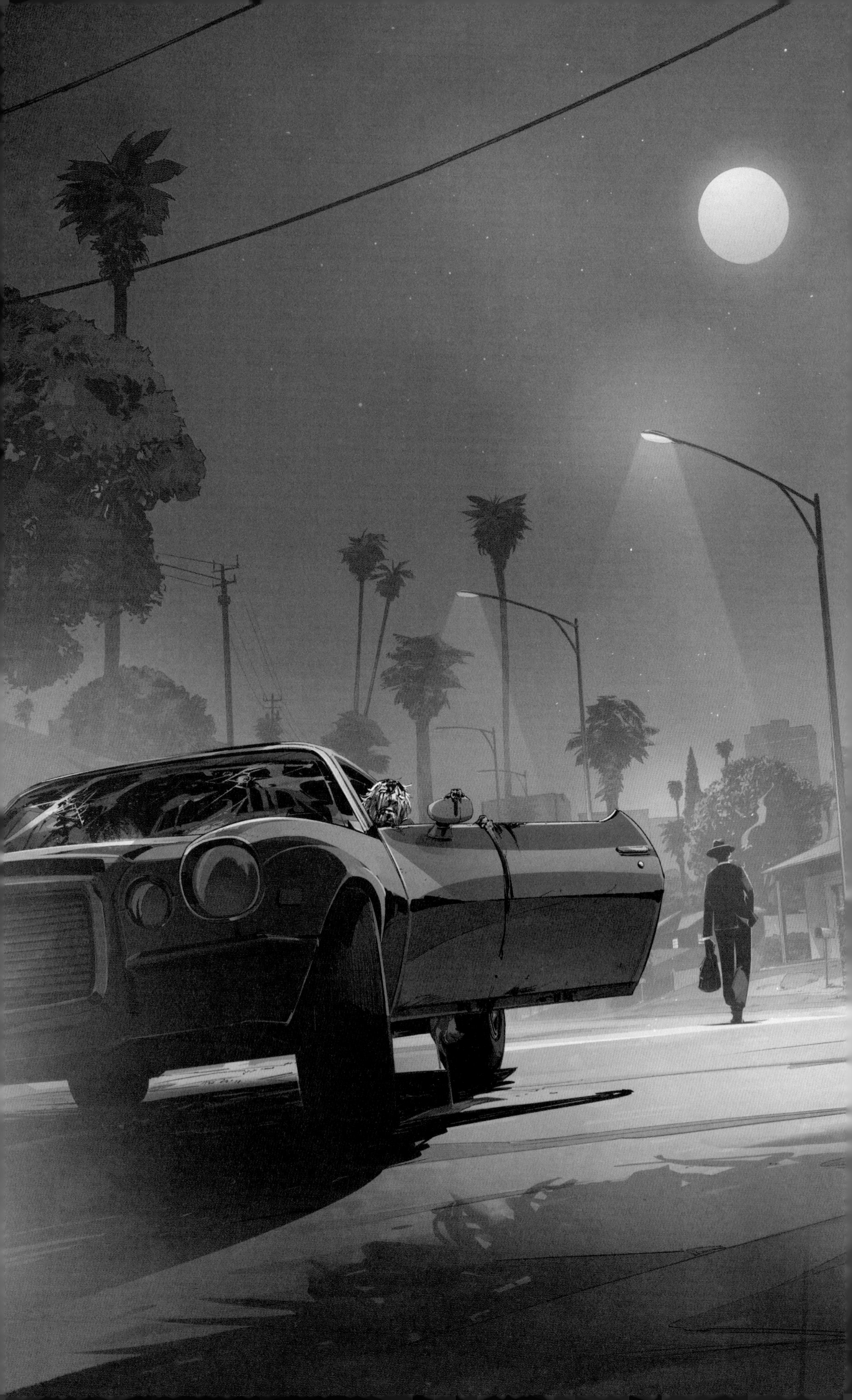

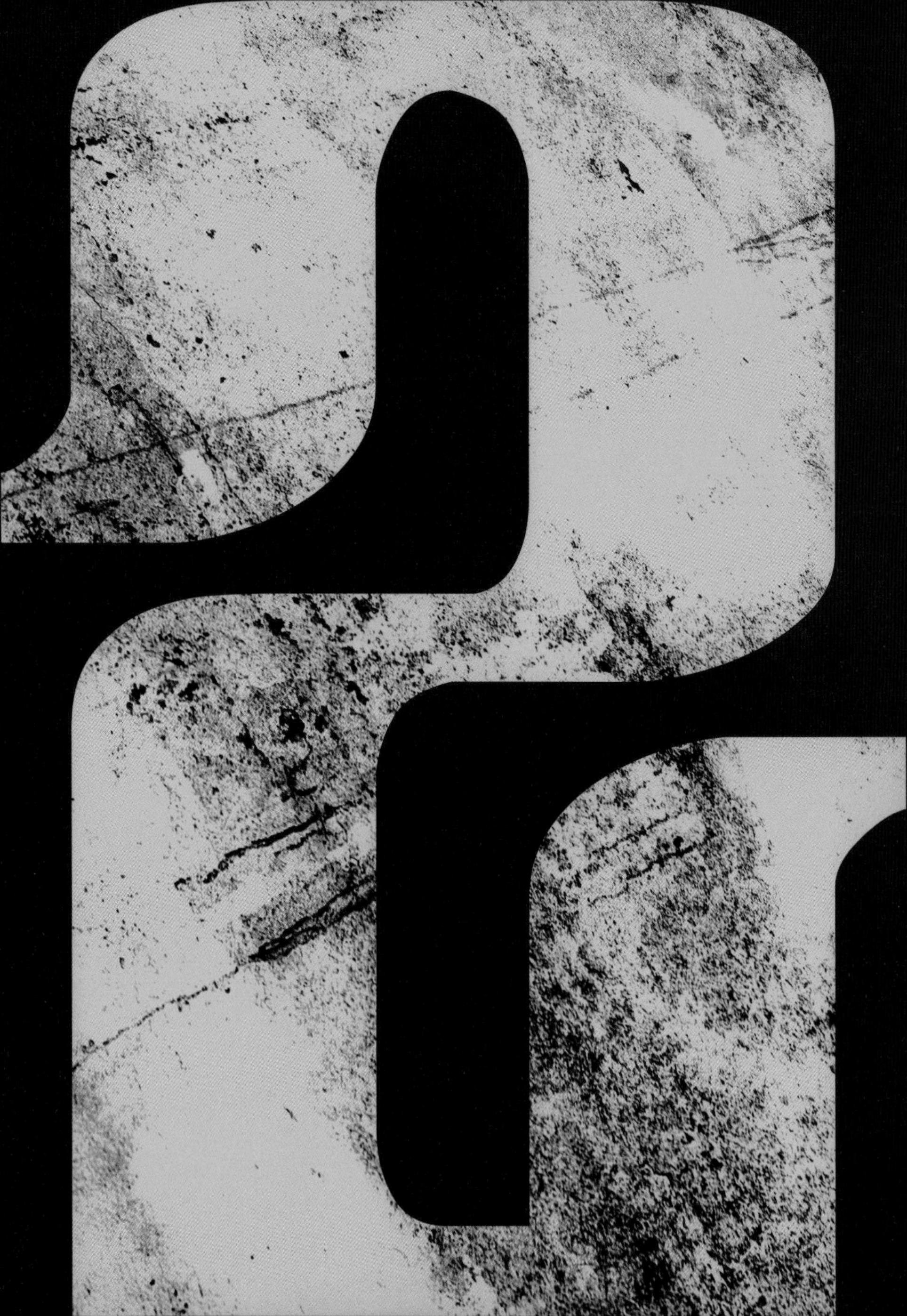

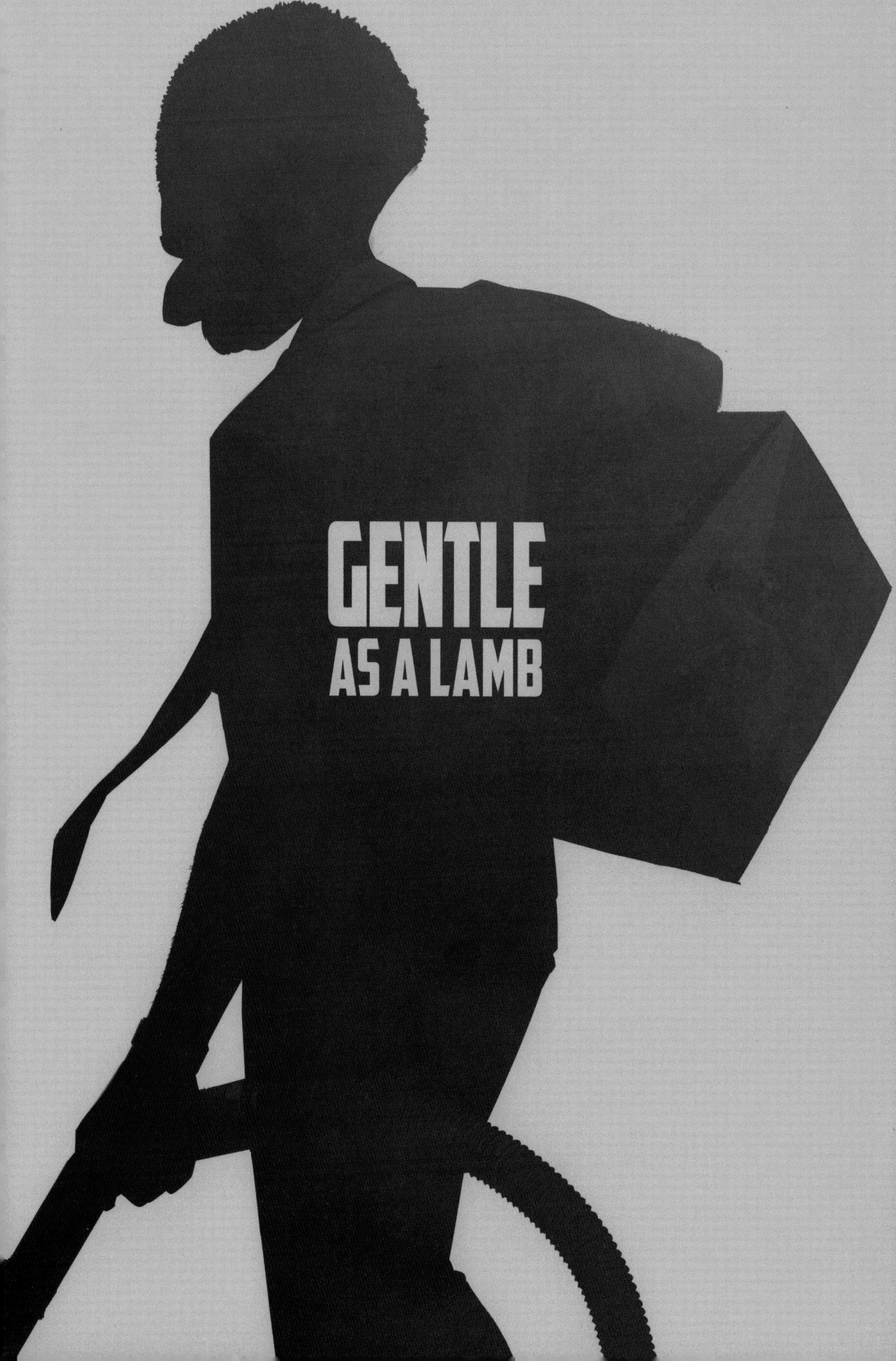
GENTLE
AS A LAMB

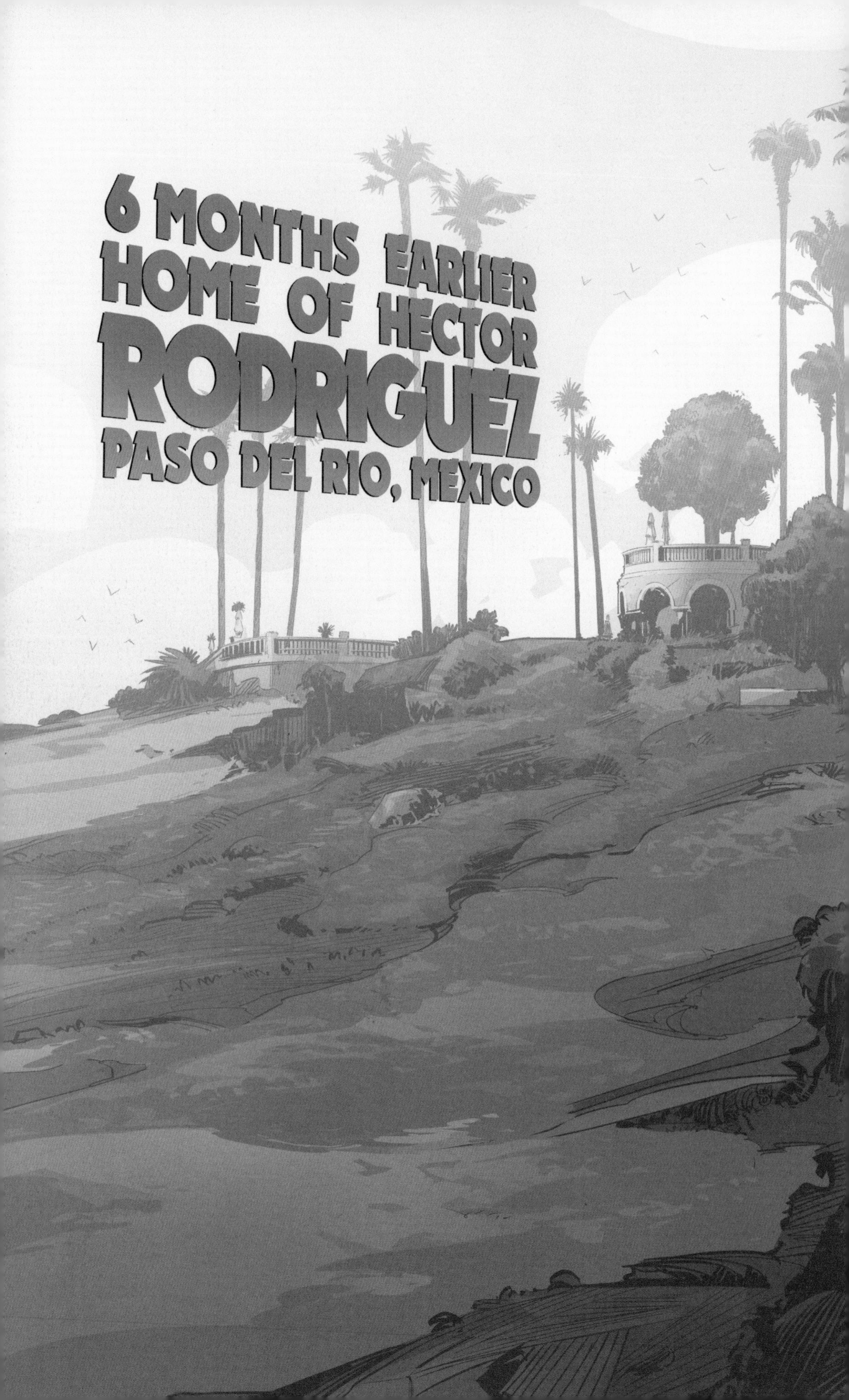
6 MONTHS EARLIER
HOME OF HECTOR
RODRIGUEZ
PASO DEL RIO, MEXICO

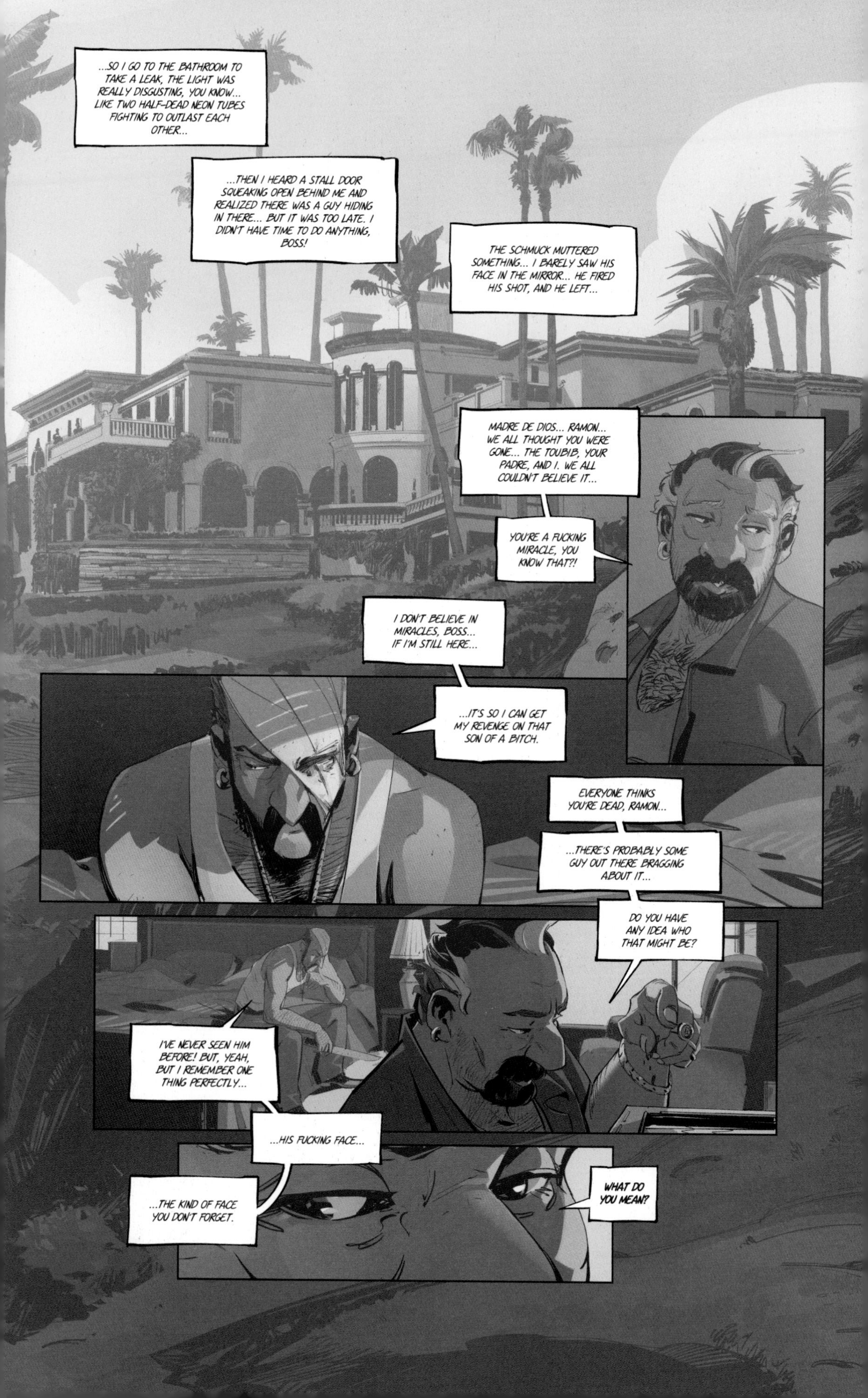
...SO I GO TO THE BATHROOM TO TAKE A LEAK, THE LIGHT WAS REALLY DISGUSTING, YOU KNOW... LIKE TWO HALF-DEAD NEON TUBES FIGHTING TO OUTLAST EACH OTHER...
...THEN I HEARD A STALL DOOR SQUEAKING OPEN BEHIND ME AND REALIZED THERE WAS A GUY HIDING IN THERE... BUT IT WAS TOO LATE. I DIDN'T HAVE TIME TO DO ANYTHING, BOSS!
THE SCHMUCK MUTTERED SOMETHING... I BARELY SAW HIS FACE IN THE MIRROR... HE FIRED HIS SHOT, AND HE LEFT...
MADRE DE DIOS... RAMON... WE ALL THOUGHT YOU WERE GONE... THE TOUBIB, YOUR PADRE, AND I. WE ALL COULDN'T BELIEVE IT...
YOU'RE A FUCKING MIRACLE, YOU KNOW THAT?!
I DON'T BELIEVE IN MIRACLES, BOSS... IF I'M STILL HERE...
...IT'S SO I CAN GET MY REVENGE ON THAT SON OF A BITCH.
EVERYONE THINKS YOU'RE DEAD, RAMON...
...THERE'S PROBABLY SOME GUY OUT THERE BRAGGING ABOUT IT...
DO YOU HAVE ANY IDEA WHO THAT MIGHT BE?
I'VE NEVER SEEN HIM BEFORE! BUT, YEAH, BUT I REMEMBER ONE THING PERFECTLY...
...HIS FUCKING FACE...
...THE KIND OF FACE YOU DON'T FORGET.
WHAT DO YOU MEAN?

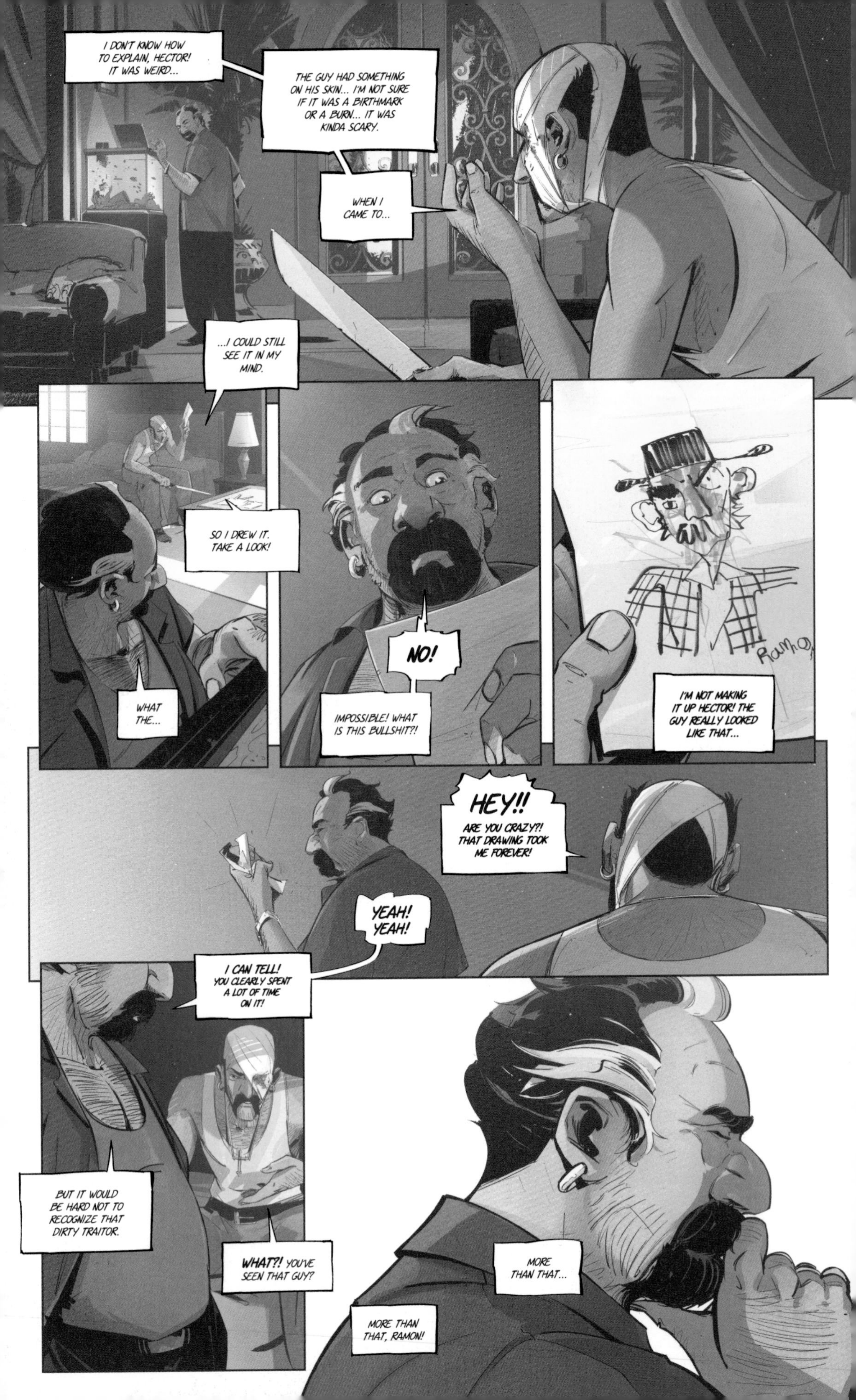

I DON'T KNOW HOW TO EXPLAIN, HECTOR! IT WAS WEIRD...
THE GUY HAD SOMETHING ON HIS SKIN... I'M NOT SURE IF IT WAS A BIRTHMARK OR A BURN... IT WAS KINDA SCARY.
WHEN I CAME TO...
...I COULD STILL SEE IT IN MY MIND.
SO I DREW IT. TAKE A LOOK!
WHAT THE...
NO!
IMPOSSIBLE! WHAT IS THIS BULLSHIT?!
Ramon
I'M NOT MAKING IT UP HECTOR! THE GUY REALLY LOOKED LIKE THAT...
HEY!!
ARE YOU CRAZY?! THAT DRAWING TOOK ME FOREVER!
YEAH! YEAH!
I CAN TELL! YOU CLEARLY SPENT A LOT OF TIME ON IT!
BUT IT WOULD BE HARD NOT TO RECOGNIZE THAT DIRTY TRAITOR.
WHAT?! YOU'VE SEEN THAT GUY?
MORE THAN THAT...
MORE THAN THAT, RAMON!

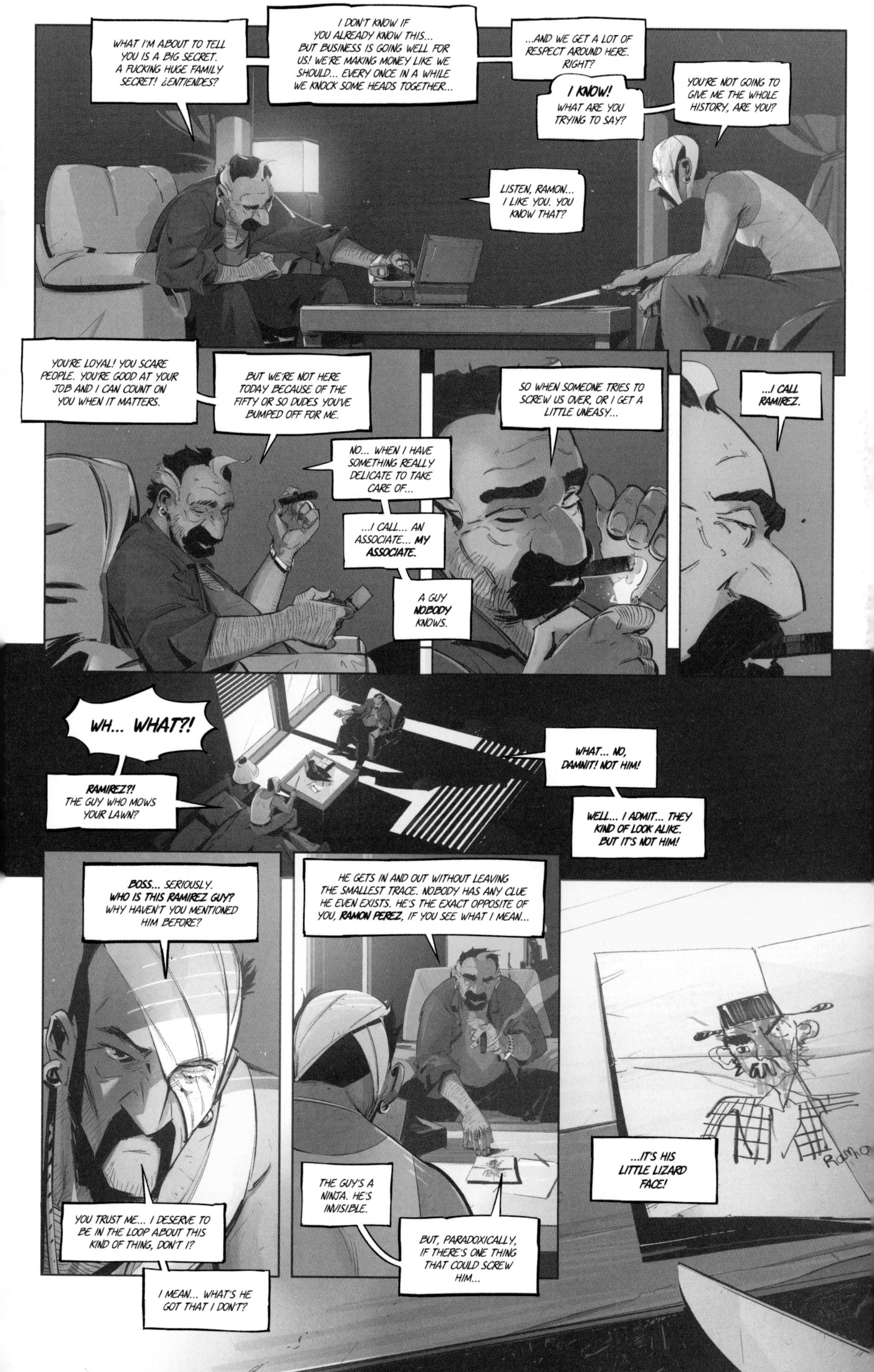
WHAT I'M ABOUT TO TELL YOU IS A BIG SECRET. A FUCKING HUGE FAMILY SECRET! ¿ENTIENDES?
I DON'T KNOW IF YOU ALREADY KNOW THIS... BUT BUSINESS IS GOING WELL FOR US! WE'RE MAKING MONEY LIKE WE SHOULD... EVERY ONCE IN A WHILE WE KNOCK SOME HEADS TOGETHER...
...AND WE GET A LOT OF RESPECT AROUND HERE. RIGHT?
I KNOW! WHAT ARE YOU TRYING TO SAY?
YOU'RE NOT GOING TO GIVE ME THE WHOLE HISTORY, ARE YOU?
LISTEN, RAMON... I LIKE YOU. YOU KNOW THAT?
YOU'RE LOYAL! YOU SCARE PEOPLE. YOU'RE GOOD AT YOUR JOB AND I CAN COUNT ON YOU WHEN IT MATTERS.
BUT WE'RE NOT HERE TODAY BECAUSE OF THE FIFTY OR SO DUDES YOU'VE BUMPED OFF FOR ME.
NO... WHEN I HAVE SOMETHING REALLY DELICATE TO TAKE CARE OF...
...I CALL... AN ASSOCIATE... **MY ASSOCIATE.**
A GUY **NOBODY** KNOWS.
SO WHEN SOMEONE TRIES TO SCREW US OVER, OR I GET A LITTLE UNEASY...
...I CALL RAMIREZ.
WH... WHAT?!
RAMIREZ?! THE GUY WHO MOWS YOUR LAWN?
WHAT... NO, DAMNIT! NOT HIM!
WELL... I ADMIT... THEY KIND OF LOOK ALIKE. BUT IT'S NOT HIM!
BOSS... SERIOUSLY. **WHO IS THIS RAMIREZ GUY?** WHY HAVEN'T YOU MENTIONED HIM BEFORE?
YOU TRUST ME... I DESERVE TO BE IN THE LOOP ABOUT THIS KIND OF THING, DON'T I?
I MEAN... WHAT'S HE GOT THAT I DON'T?
HE GETS IN AND OUT WITHOUT LEAVING THE SMALLEST TRACE. NOBODY HAS ANY CLUE HE EVEN EXISTS. HE'S THE EXACT OPPOSITE OF YOU, **RAMON PEREZ**, IF YOU SEE WHAT I MEAN...
THE GUY'S A NINJA. HE'S INVISIBLE.
BUT, PARADOXICALLY, IF THERE'S ONE THING THAT COULD SCREW HIM...
...IT'S HIS LITTLE LIZARD FACE!

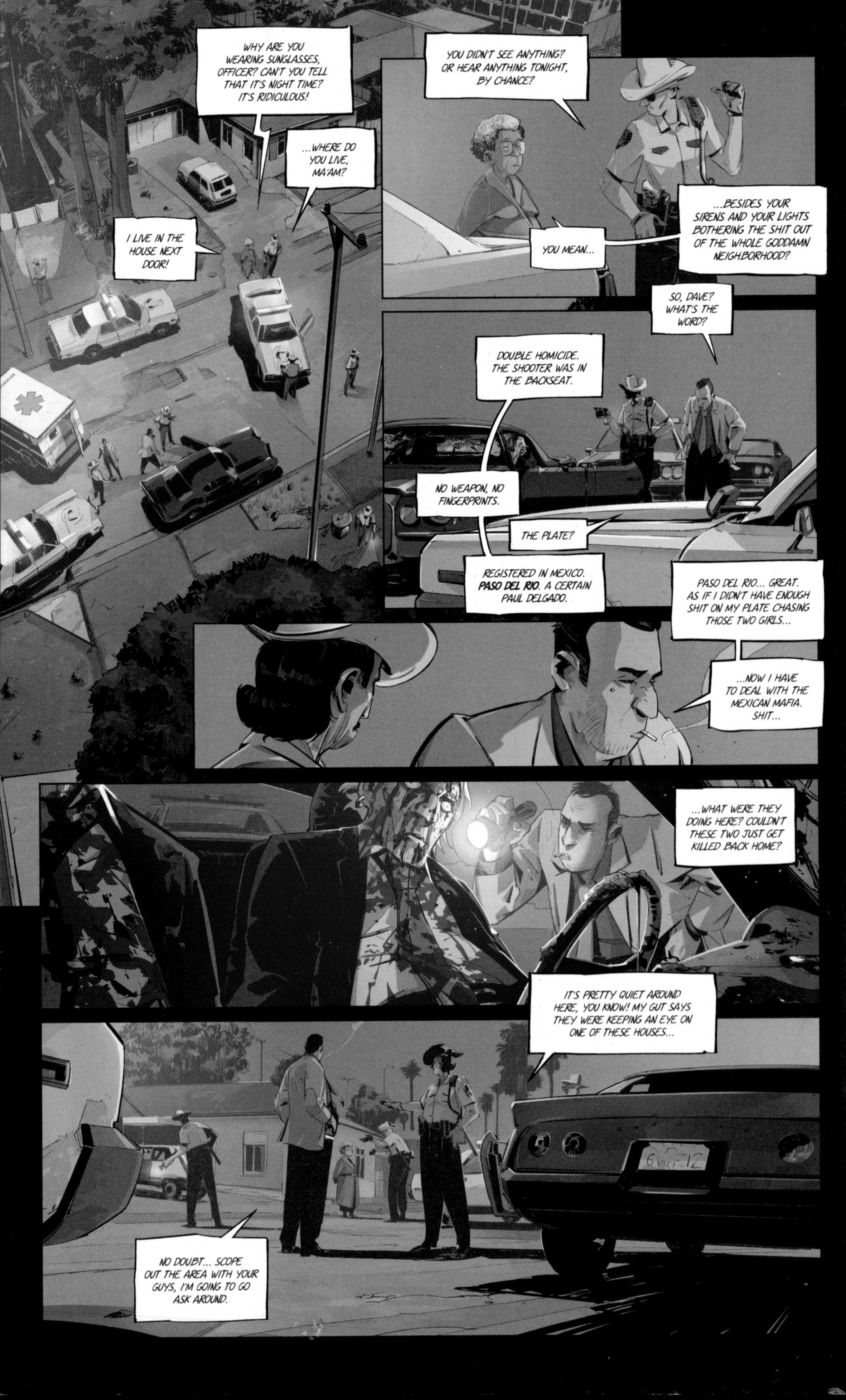
WHY ARE YOU WEARING SUNGLASSES, OFFICER? CAN'T YOU TELL THAT IT'S NIGHT TIME? IT'S RIDICULOUS!
...WHERE DO YOU LIVE, MA'AM?
I LIVE IN THE HOUSE NEXT DOOR!
YOU DIDN'T SEE ANYTHING? OR HEAR ANYTHING TONIGHT, BY CHANCE?
YOU MEAN...
...BESIDES YOUR SIRENS AND YOUR LIGHTS BOTHERING THE SHIT OUT OF THE WHOLE GODDAMN NEIGHBORHOOD?
SO, DAVE? WHAT'S THE WORD?
DOUBLE HOMICIDE. THE SHOOTER WAS IN THE BACKSEAT.
NO WEAPON, NO FINGERPRINTS.
THE PLATE?
REGISTERED IN MEXICO. PASO DEL RIO. A CERTAIN PAUL DELGADO.
PASO DEL RIO... GREAT. AS IF I DIDN'T HAVE ENOUGH SHIT ON MY PLATE CHASING THOSE TWO GIRLS...
...NOW I HAVE TO DEAL WITH THE MEXICAN MAFIA. SHIT...
...WHAT WERE THEY DOING HERE? COULDN'T THESE TWO JUST GET KILLED BACK HOME?
IT'S PRETTY QUIET AROUND HERE, YOU KNOW! MY GUT SAYS THEY WERE KEEPING AN EYE ON ONE OF THESE HOUSES...
NO DOUBT... SCOPE OUT THE AREA WITH YOUR GUYS, I'M GOING TO GO ASK AROUND.

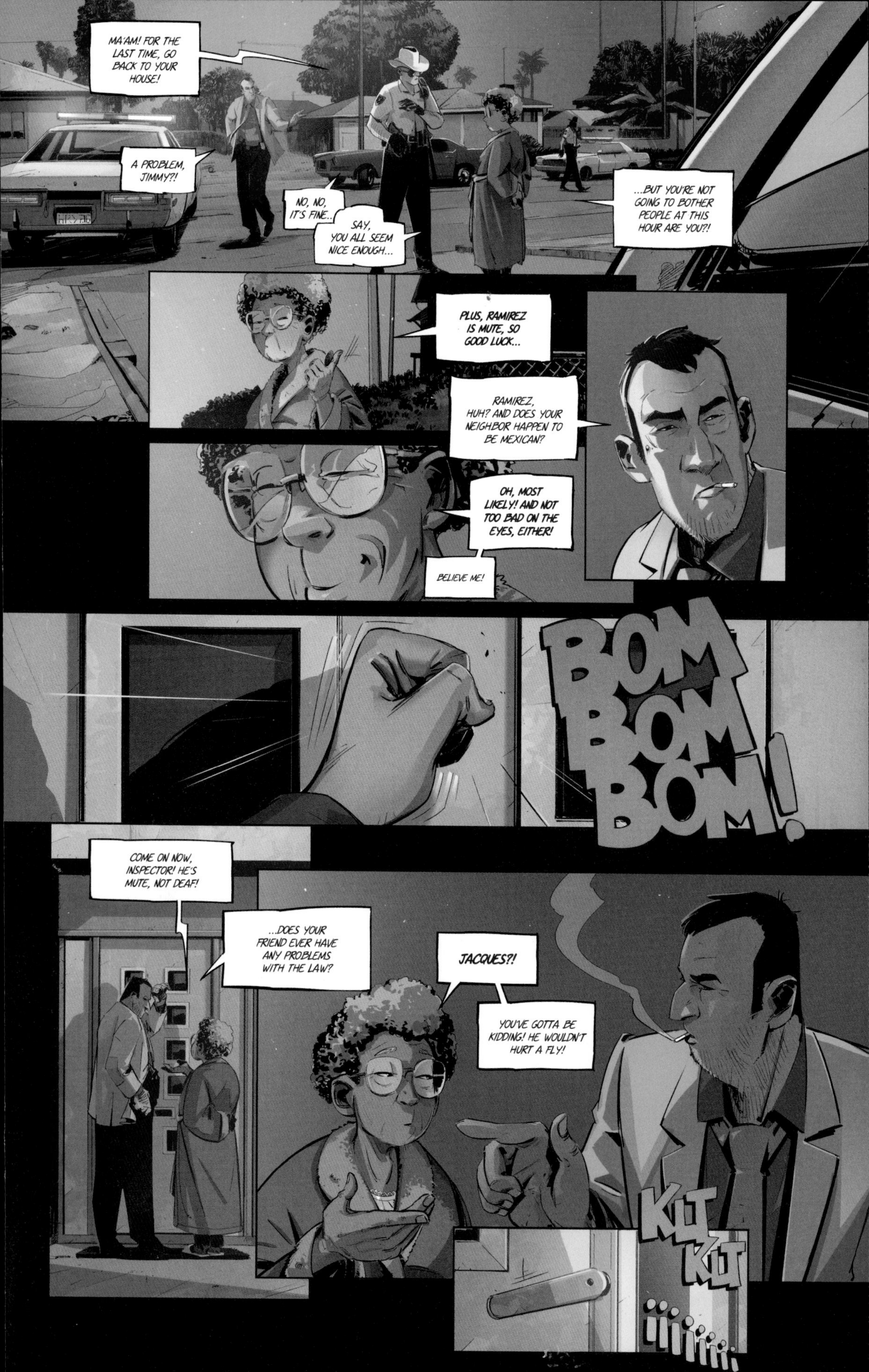

MA'AM! FOR THE LAST TIME, GO BACK TO YOUR HOUSE!
A PROBLEM, JIMMY?!
NO, NO, IT'S FINE...
SAY, YOU ALL SEEM NICE ENOUGH...
...BUT YOU'RE NOT GOING TO BOTHER PEOPLE AT THIS HOUR ARE YOU?!
PLUS, RAMIREZ IS MUTE, SO GOOD LUCK...
RAMIREZ, HUH? AND DOES YOUR NEIGHBOR HAPPEN TO BE MEXICAN?
OH, MOST LIKELY! AND NOT TOO BAD ON THE EYES, EITHER!
BELIEVE ME!
BOM BOM BOM!
COME ON NOW, INSPECTOR! HE'S MUTE, NOT DEAF!
...DOES YOUR FRIEND EVER HAVE ANY PROBLEMS WITH THE LAW?
JACQUES?!
YOU'VE GOTTA BE KIDDING! HE WOULDN'T HURT A FLY!
KLIT KLIT

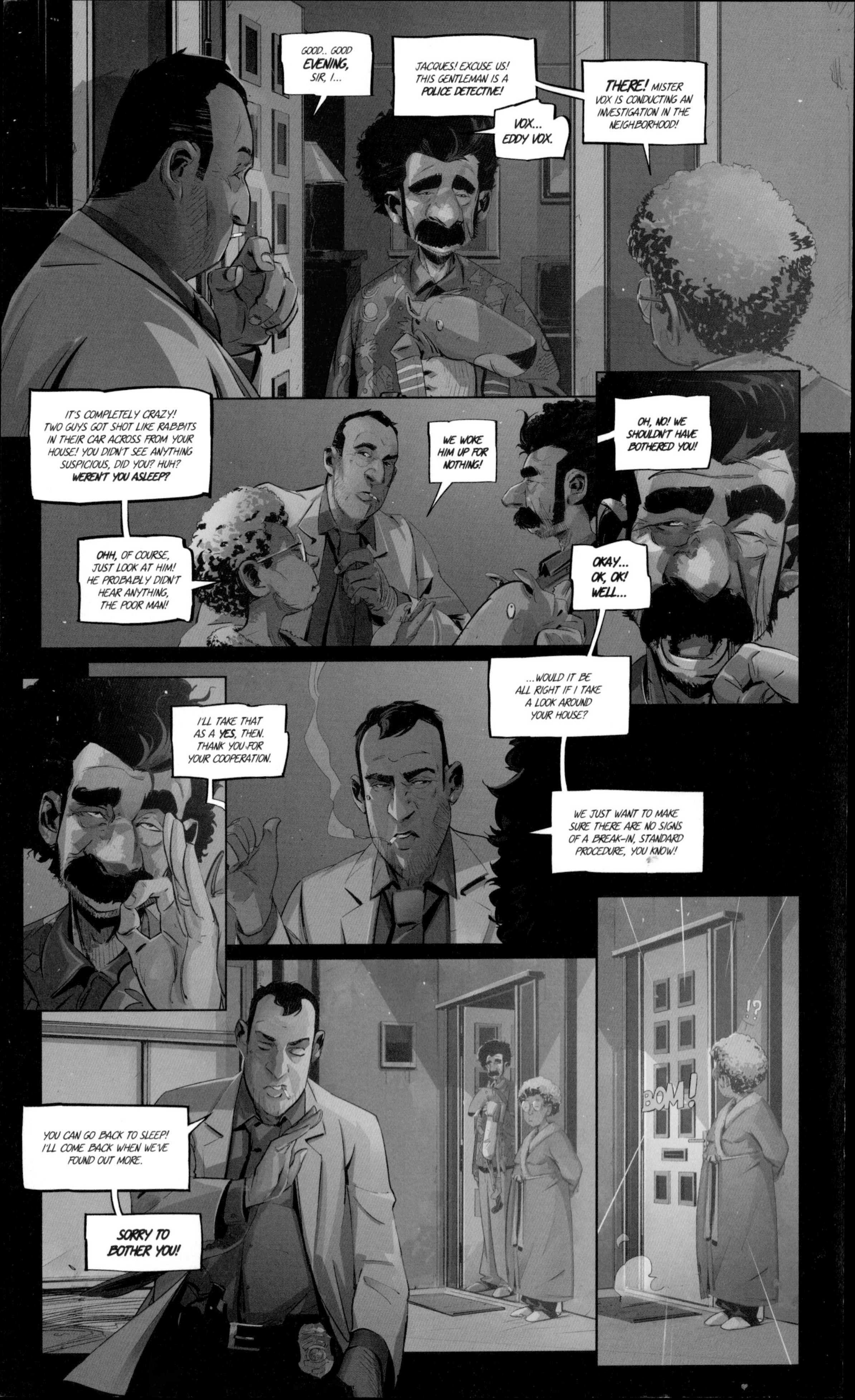
GOOD.. GOOD EVENING, SIR, I...
JACQUES! EXCUSE US! THIS GENTLEMAN IS A POLICE DETECTIVE!
VOX... EDDY VOX.
THERE! MISTER VOX IS CONDUCTING AN INVESTIGATION IN THE NEIGHBORHOOD!
IT'S COMPLETELY CRAZY! TWO GUYS GOT SHOT LIKE RABBITS IN THEIR CAR ACROSS FROM YOUR HOUSE! YOU DIDN'T SEE ANYTHING SUSPICIOUS, DID YOU? HUH? WEREN'T YOU ASLEEP?
OHH, OF COURSE, JUST LOOK AT HIM! HE PROBABLY DIDN'T HEAR ANYTHING, THE POOR MAN!
WE WOKE HIM UP FOR NOTHING!
OH, NO! WE SHOULDN'T HAVE BOTHERED YOU!
OKAY... OK, OK! WELL...
...WOULD IT BE ALL RIGHT IF I TAKE A LOOK AROUND YOUR HOUSE?
WE JUST WANT TO MAKE SURE THERE ARE NO SIGNS OF A BREAK-IN, STANDARD PROCEDURE, YOU KNOW!
I'LL TAKE THAT AS A YES, THEN. THANK YOU FOR YOUR COOPERATION.
YOU CAN GO BACK TO SLEEP! I'LL COME BACK WHEN WE'VE FOUND OUT MORE.
SORRY TO BOTHER YOU!
BOM!
!?

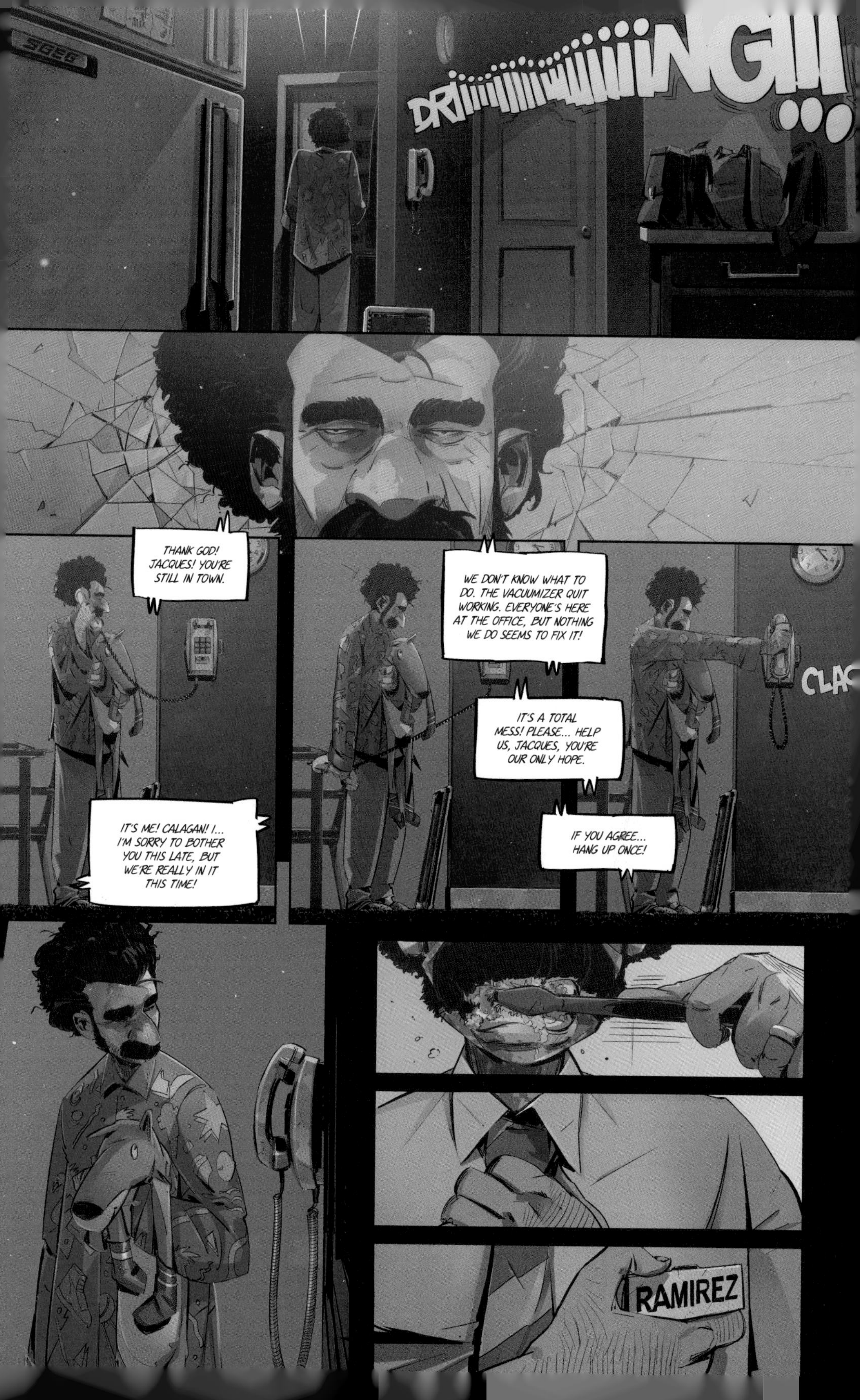
DRIIIIIIIIIIIIIIIIING!!!
THANK GOD! JACQUES! YOU'RE STILL IN TOWN.
IT'S ME! CALAGAN! I... I'M SORRY TO BOTHER YOU THIS LATE, BUT WE'RE REALLY IN IT THIS TIME!
WE DON'T KNOW WHAT TO DO. THE VACUUMIZER QUIT WORKING. EVERYONE'S HERE AT THE OFFICE, BUT NOTHING WE DO SEEMS TO FIX IT!
IT'S A TOTAL MESS! PLEASE... HELP US, JACQUES, YOU'RE OUR ONLY HOPE.
IF YOU AGREE... HANG UP ONCE!
CLAS
RAMIREZ

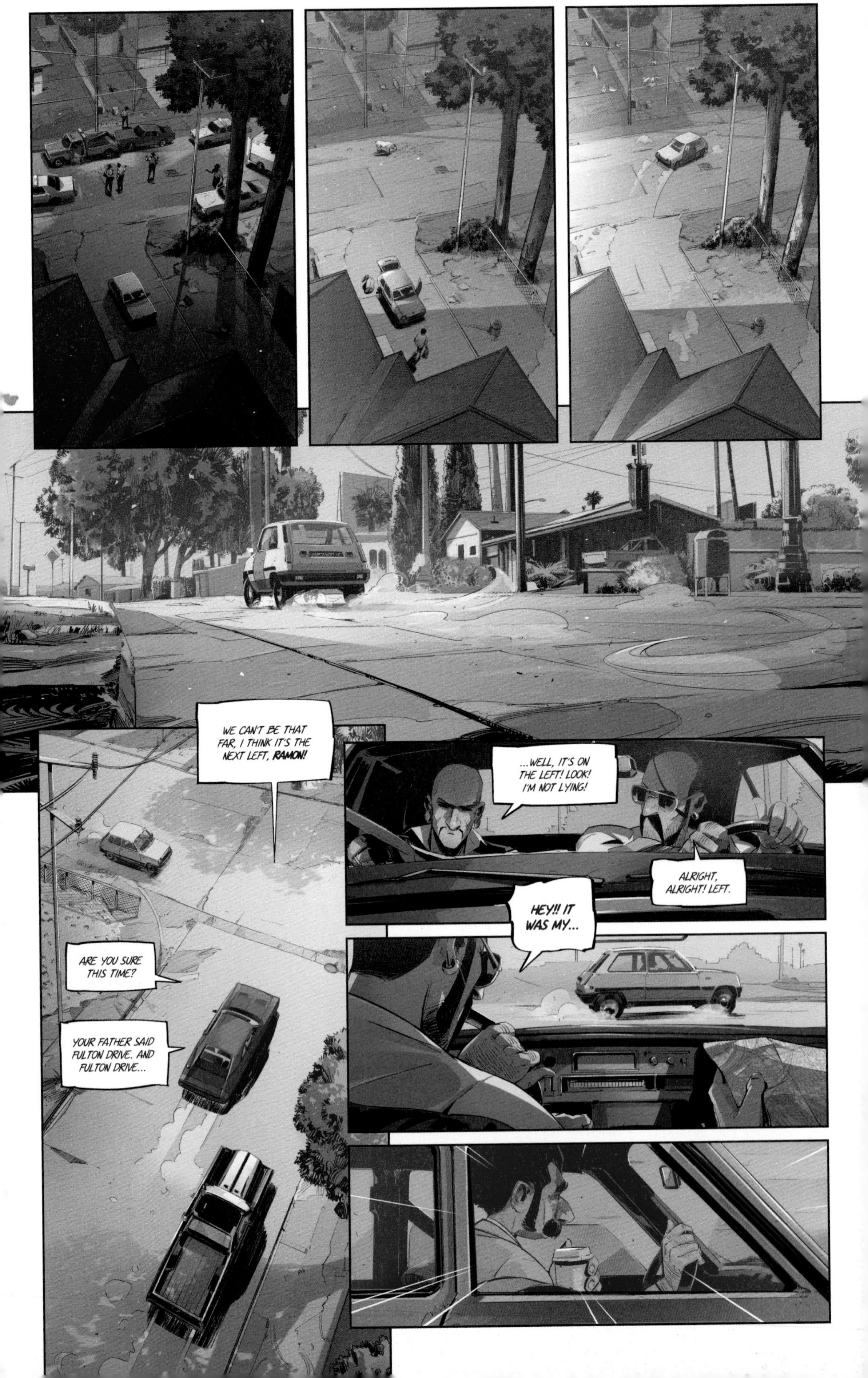
WE CAN'T BE THAT FAR, I THINK IT'S THE NEXT LEFT, RAMON!
ARE YOU SURE THIS TIME?
YOUR FATHER SAID FULTON DRIVE. AND FULTON DRIVE...
...WELL, IT'S ON THE LEFT! LOOK! I'M NOT LYING!
ALRIGHT, ALRIGHT! LEFT.
HEY!! IT WAS MY...

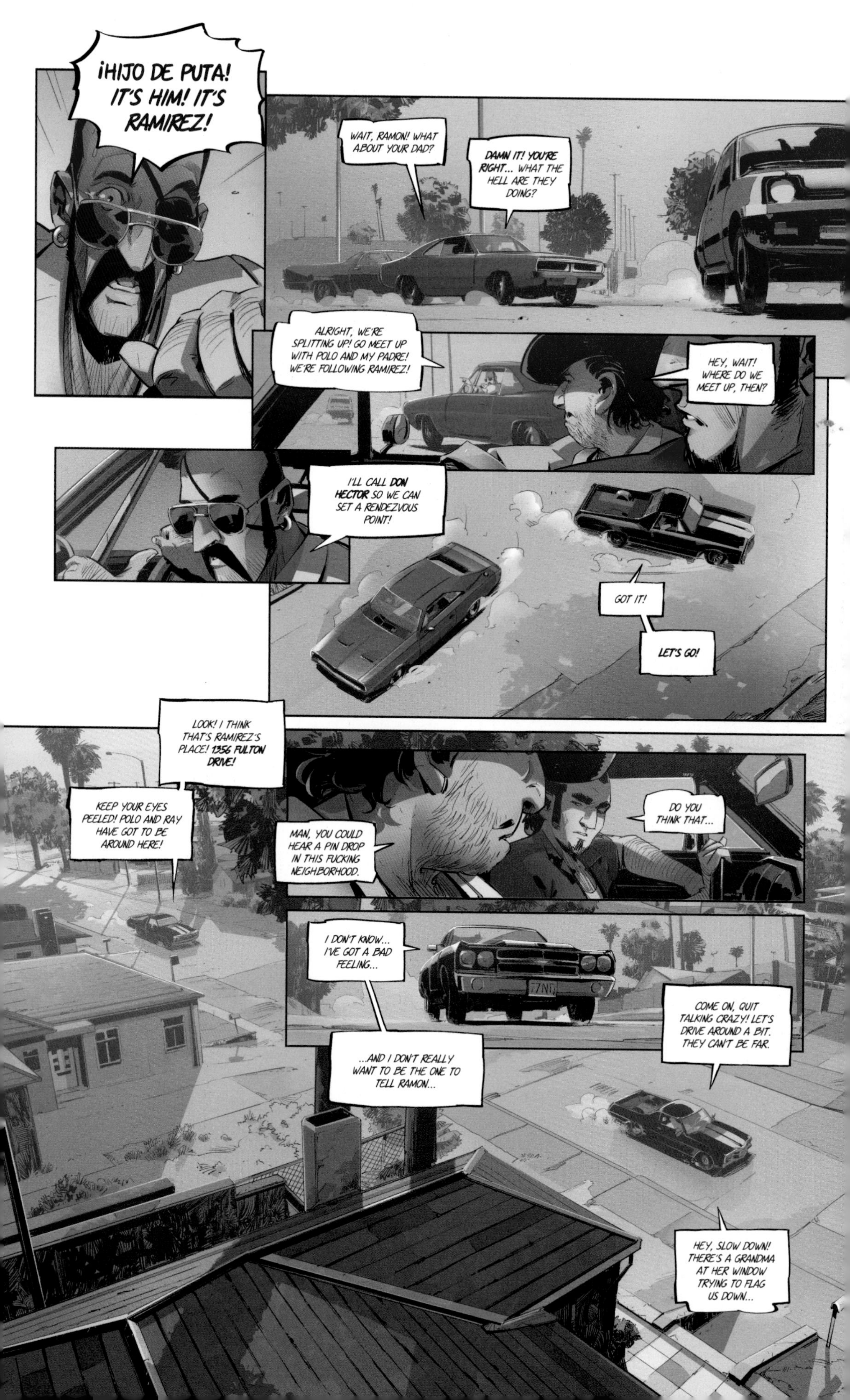
¡HIJO DE PUTA! IT'S HIM! IT'S RAMIREZ!
WAIT, RAMON! WHAT ABOUT YOUR DAD?
DAMN IT! YOU'RE RIGHT... WHAT THE HELL ARE THEY DOING?
ALRIGHT, WE'RE SPLITTING UP! GO MEET UP WITH POLO AND MY PADRE! WE'RE FOLLOWING RAMIREZ!
HEY, WAIT! WHERE DO WE MEET UP, THEN?
I'LL CALL DON HECTOR SO WE CAN SET A RENDEZVOUS POINT!
GOT IT!
LET'S GO!
LOOK! I THINK THAT'S RAMIREZ'S PLACE! 1356 FULTON DRIVE!
KEEP YOUR EYES PEELED! POLO AND RAY HAVE GOT TO BE AROUND HERE!
MAN, YOU COULD HEAR A PIN DROP IN THIS FUCKING NEIGHBORHOOD.
DO YOU THINK THAT...
I DON'T KNOW... I'VE GOT A BAD FEELING...
...AND I DON'T REALLY WANT TO BE THE ONE TO TELL RAMON...
COME ON, QUIT TALKING CRAZY! LET'S DRIVE AROUND A BIT. THEY CAN'T BE FAR.
HEY, SLOW DOWN! THERE'S A GRANDMA AT HER WINDOW TRYING TO FLAG US DOWN...

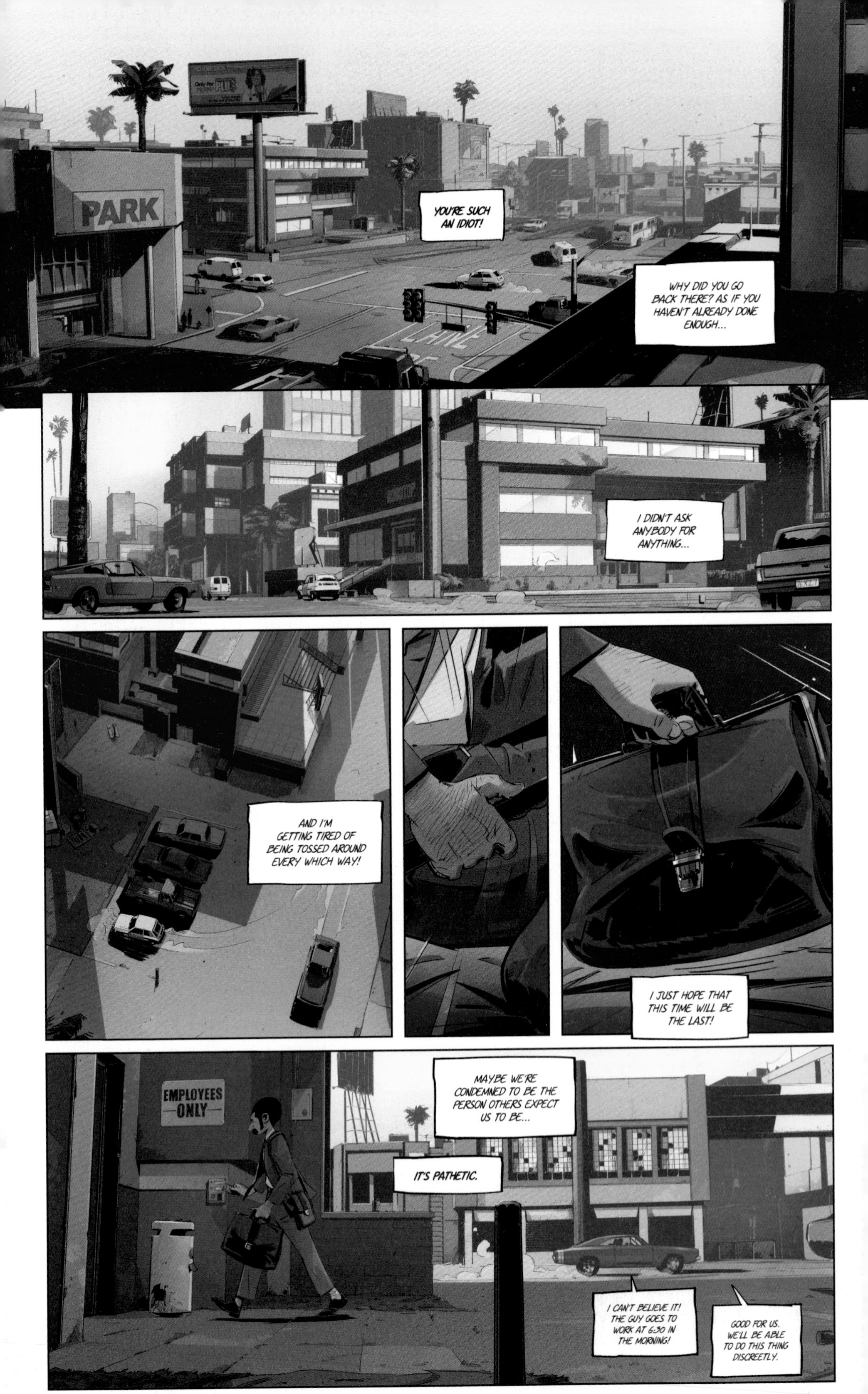
PARK
YOU'RE SUCH AN IDIOT!
WHY DID YOU GO BACK THERE? AS IF YOU HAVEN'T ALREADY DONE ENOUGH...
I DIDN'T ASK ANYBODY FOR ANYTHING...
AND I'M GETTING TIRED OF BEING TOSSED AROUND EVERY WHICH WAY!
I JUST HOPE THAT THIS TIME WILL BE THE LAST!
EMPLOYEES ONLY
MAYBE WE'RE CONDEMNED TO BE THE PERSON OTHERS EXPECT US TO BE...
IT'S PATHETIC.
I CAN'T BELIEVE IT! THE GUY GOES TO WORK AT 6:30 IN THE MORNING!
GOOD FOR US. WE'LL BE ABLE TO DO THIS THING DISCREETLY.

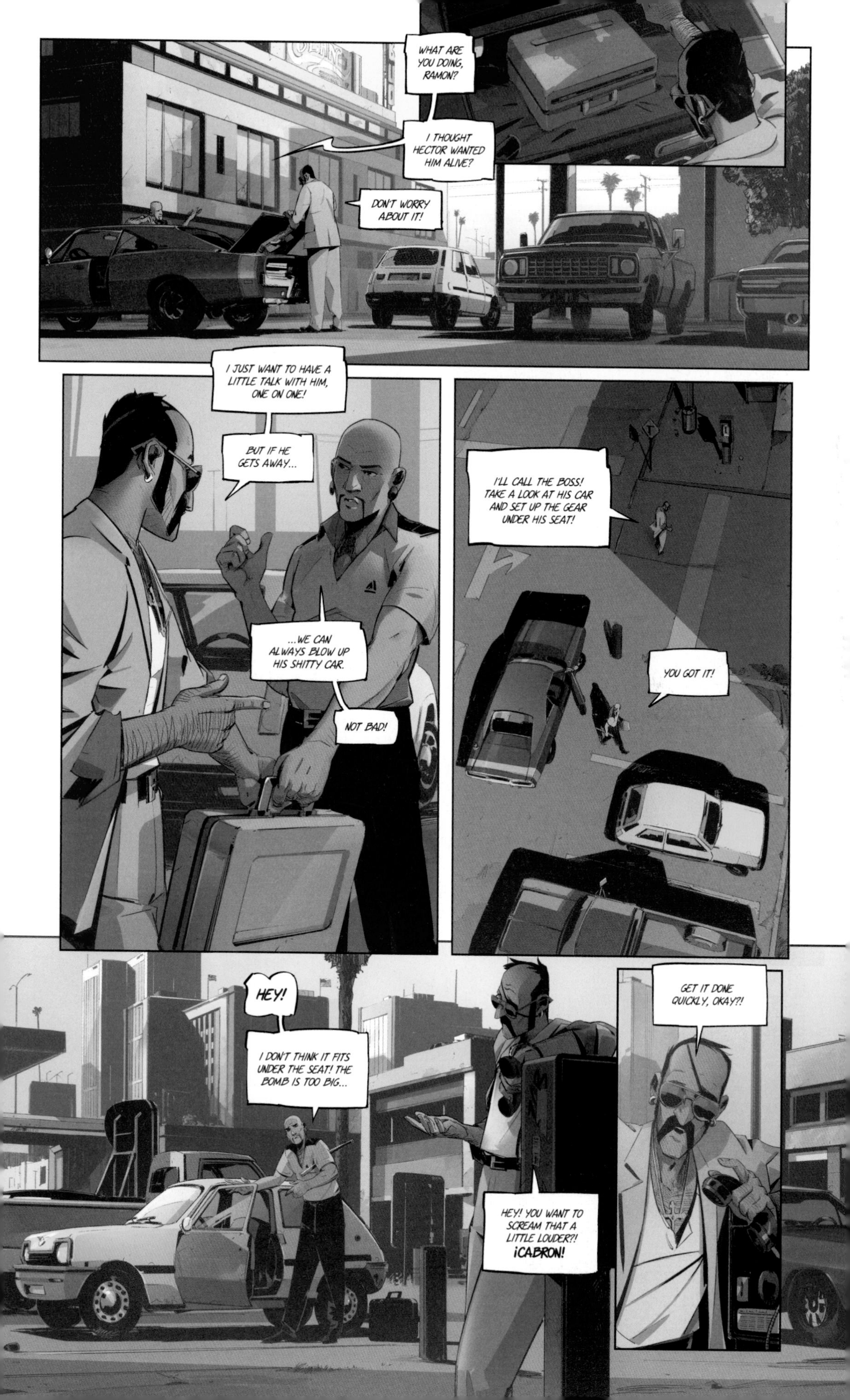
WHAT ARE YOU DOING, RAMON?
I THOUGHT HECTOR WANTED HIM ALIVE?
DON'T WORRY ABOUT IT!
I JUST WANT TO HAVE A LITTLE TALK WITH HIM, ONE ON ONE!
BUT IF HE GETS AWAY...
...WE CAN ALWAYS BLOW UP HIS SHITTY CAR.
NOT BAD!
I'LL CALL THE BOSS! TAKE A LOOK AT HIS CAR AND SET UP THE GEAR UNDER HIS SEAT!
YOU GOT IT!
HEY!
I DON'T THINK IT FITS UNDER THE SEAT! THE BOMB IS TOO BIG...
HEY! YOU WANT TO SCREAM THAT A LITTLE LOUDER?! ¡CABRON!
GET IT DONE QUICKLY, OKAY?!

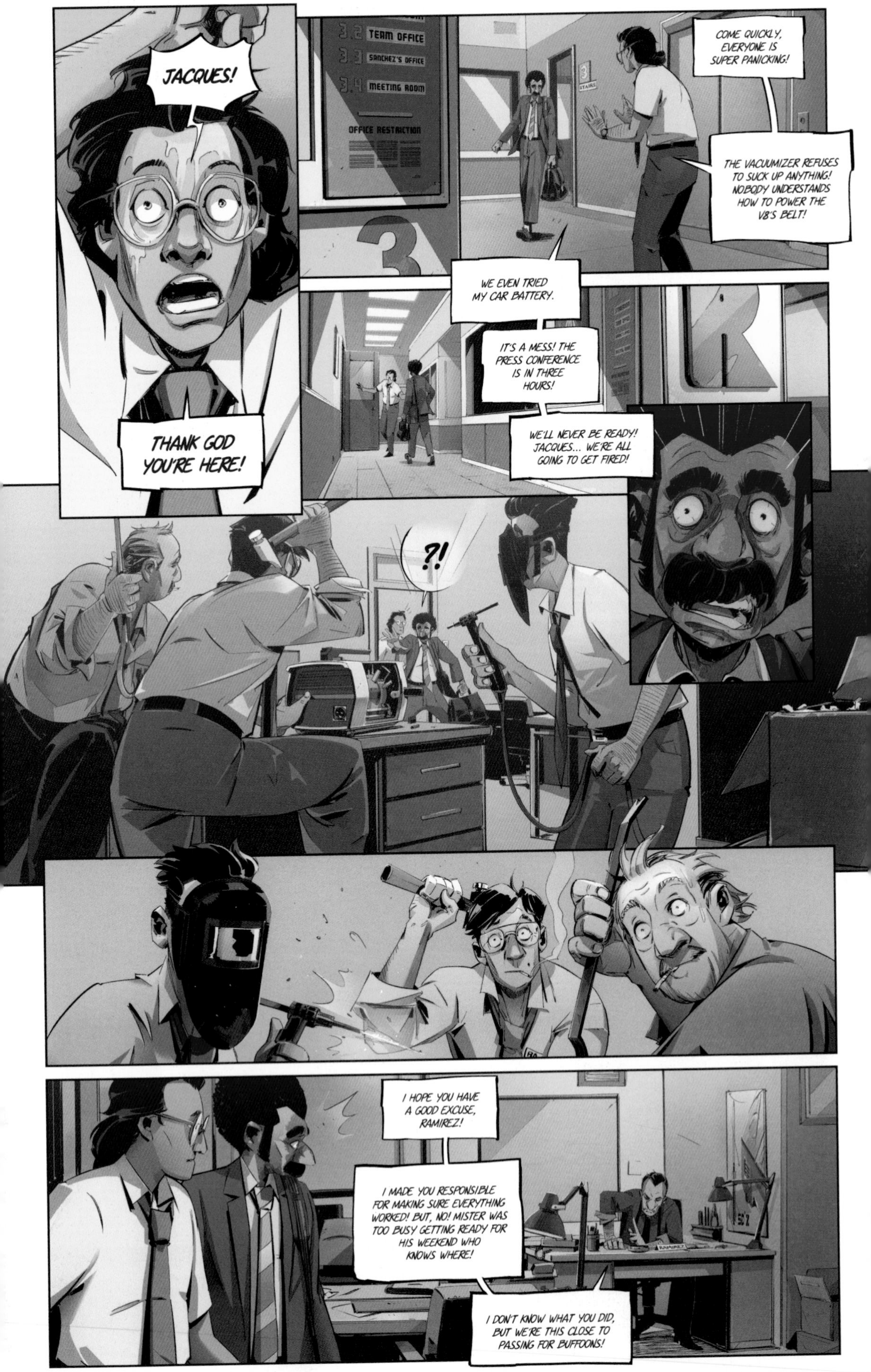
JACQUES!
THANK GOD YOU'RE HERE!
3.2 TEAM OFFICE
3.3 SANCHEZ'S OFFICE
3.4 MEETING ROOM
OFFICE RESTRICTION
COME QUICKLY, EVERYONE IS SUPER PANICKING!
THE VACUUMIZER REFUSES TO SUCK UP ANYTHING! NOBODY UNDERSTANDS HOW TO POWER THE V8'S BELT!
WE EVEN TRIED MY CAR BATTERY.
IT'S A MESS! THE PRESS CONFERENCE IS IN THREE HOURS!
WE'LL NEVER BE READY! JACQUES... WE'RE ALL GOING TO GET FIRED!
?!
I HOPE YOU HAVE A GOOD EXCUSE, RAMIREZ!
I MADE YOU RESPONSIBLE FOR MAKING SURE EVERYTHING WORKED! BUT, NO! MISTER WAS TOO BUSY GETTING READY FOR HIS WEEKEND WHO KNOWS WHERE!
I DON'T KNOW WHAT YOU DID, BUT WE'RE THIS CLOSE TO PASSING FOR BUFFOONS!

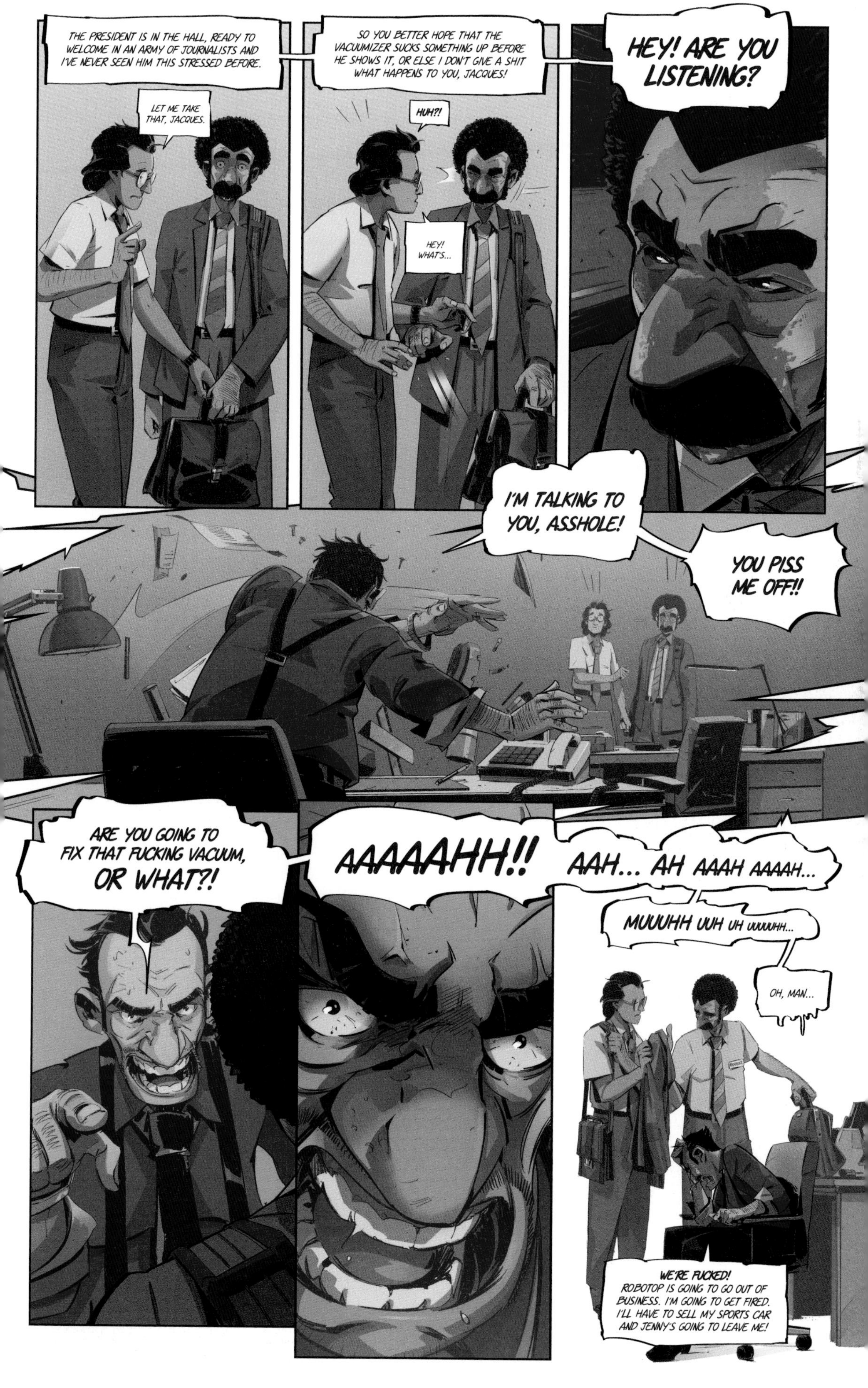
THE PRESIDENT IS IN THE HALL, READY TO WELCOME IN AN ARMY OF JOURNALISTS AND I'VE NEVER SEEN HIM THIS STRESSED BEFORE.
LET ME TAKE THAT, JACQUES.
SO YOU BETTER HOPE THAT THE VACUUMIZER SUCKS SOMETHING UP BEFORE HE SHOWS IT, OR ELSE I DON'T GIVE A SHIT WHAT HAPPENS TO YOU, JACQUES!
HUH?!
HEY! WHAT'S...
HEY! ARE YOU LISTENING?
I'M TALKING TO YOU, ASSHOLE!
YOU PISS ME OFF!!
ARE YOU GOING TO FIX THAT FUCKING VACUUM, OR WHAT?!
AAAAAHH!!
AAH... AH AAAH AAAAH...
MUUUHH UUH UH UUUUHH...
OH, MAN...
WE'RE FUCKED! ROBOTOP IS GOING TO GO OUT OF BUSINESS. I'M GOING TO GET FIRED. I'LL HAVE TO SELL MY SPORTS CAR AND JENNY'S GOING TO LEAVE ME!

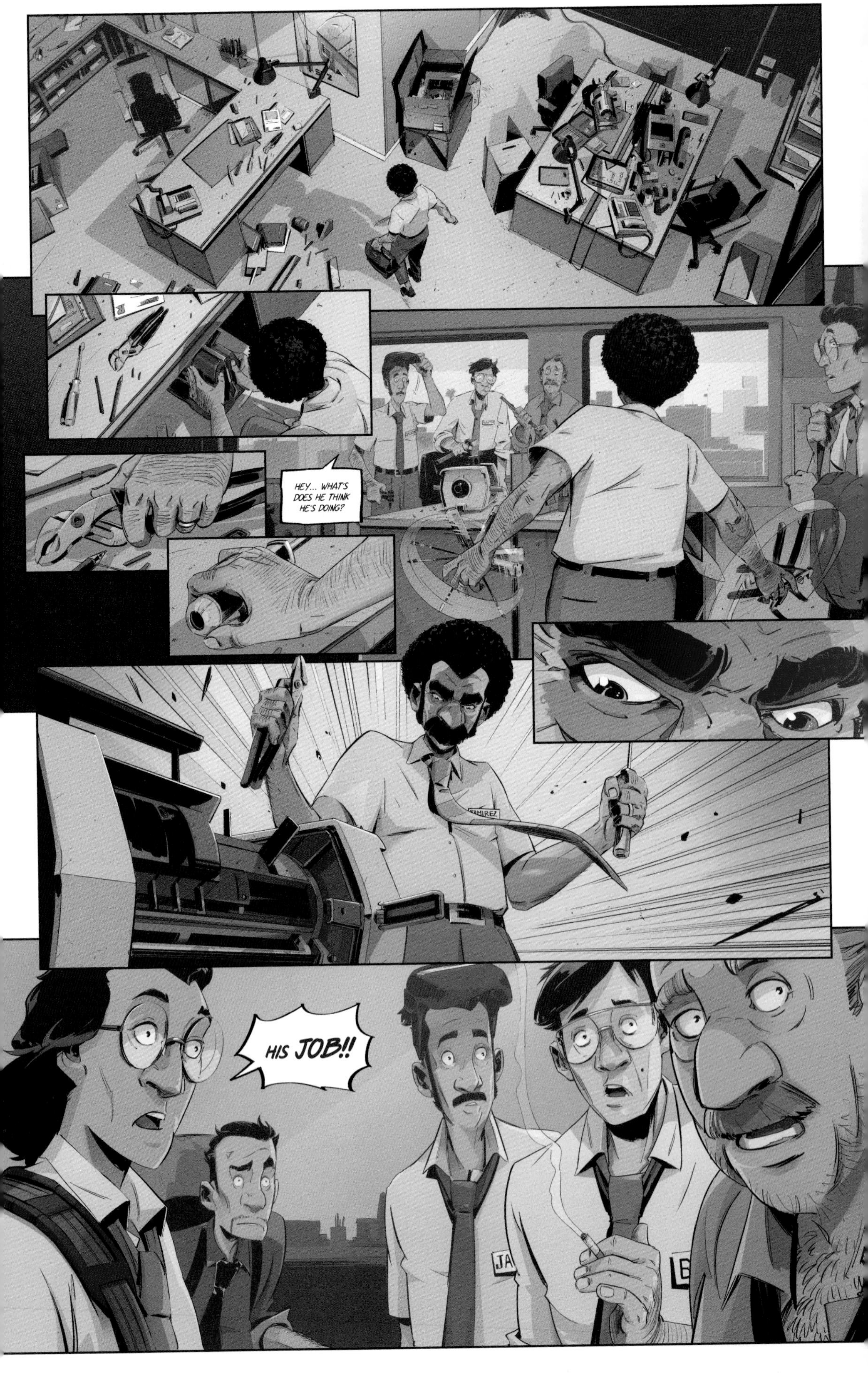
HEY... WHAT'S DOES HE THINK HE'S DOING?
RAMIREZ
HIS JOB!!

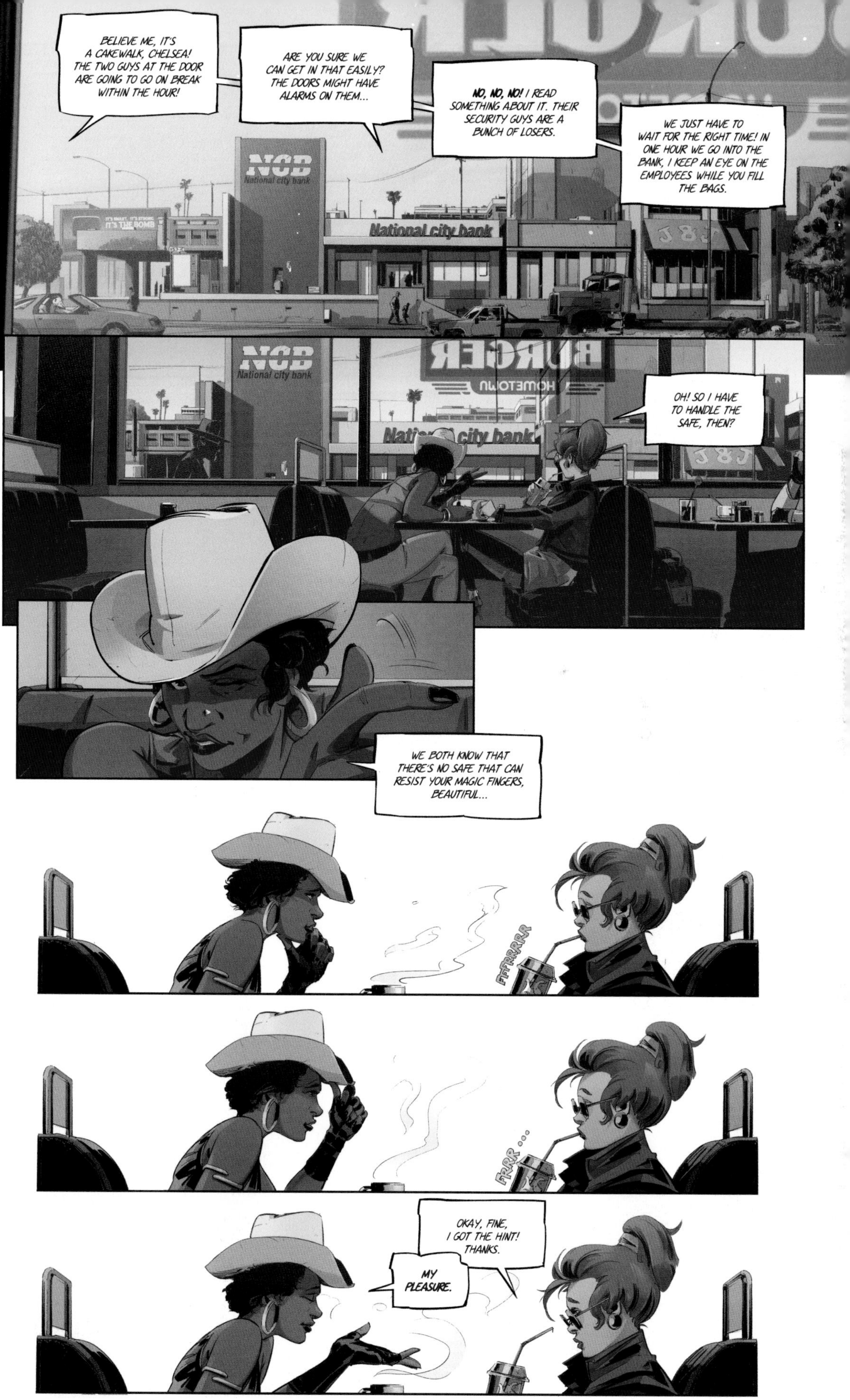
BELIEVE ME, IT'S A CAKEWALK, CHELSEA! THE TWO GUYS AT THE DOOR ARE GOING TO GO ON BREAK WITHIN THE HOUR!
ARE YOU SURE WE CAN GET IN THAT EASILY? THE DOORS MIGHT HAVE ALARMS ON THEM...
NO, NO, NO! I READ SOMETHING ABOUT IT. THEIR SECURITY GUYS ARE A BUNCH OF LOSERS.
WE JUST HAVE TO WAIT FOR THE RIGHT TIME! IN ONE HOUR WE GO INTO THE BANK, I KEEP AN EYE ON THE EMPLOYEES WHILE YOU FILL THE BAGS.
NCB
National city bank
National city bank
IT'S THE BOMB
J&J
BURGER
HOMETOWN
OH! SO I HAVE TO HANDLE THE SAFE, THEN?
WE BOTH KNOW THAT THERE'S NO SAFE THAT CAN RESIST YOUR MAGIC FINGERS, BEAUTIFUL...
FFFRRRRR
FRRR...
OKAY, FINE, I GOT THE HINT! THANKS.
MY PLEASURE.

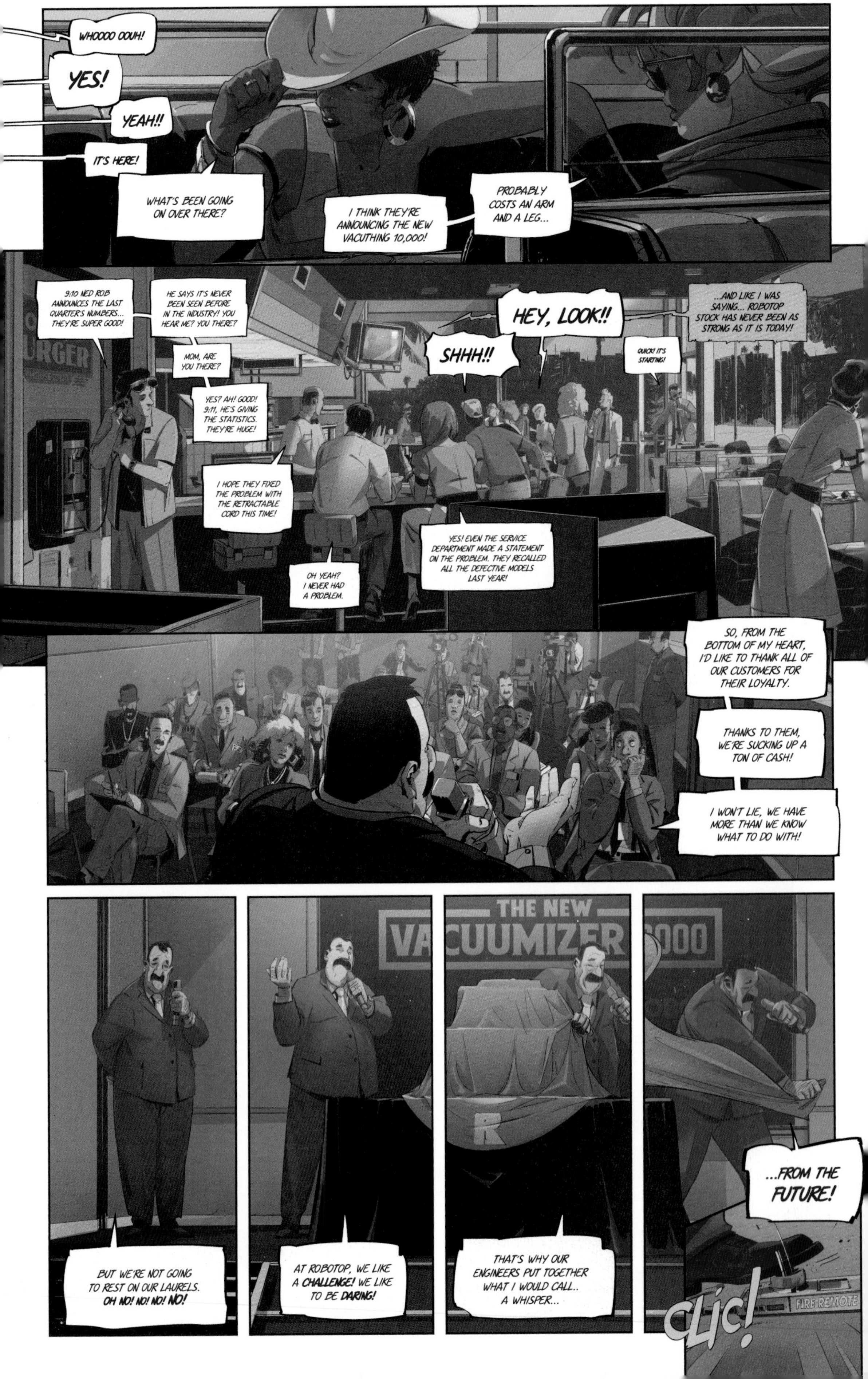
WHOOOO OOUH!
YES!
YEAH!!
IT'S HERE!
WHAT'S BEEN GOING ON OVER THERE?
I THINK THEY'RE ANNOUNCING THE NEW VACUTHING 10,000!
PROBABLY COSTS AN ARM AND A LEG...
9:10 NED ROB ANNOUNCES THE LAST QUARTER'S NUMBERS... THEY'RE SUPER GOOD!
HE SAYS IT'S NEVER BEEN SEEN BEFORE IN THE INDUSTRY! YOU HEAR ME? YOU THERE?
MOM, ARE YOU THERE?
YES? AH! GOOD! 9:11, HE'S GIVING THE STATISTICS. THEY'RE HUGE!
HEY, LOOK!!
SHHH!!
...AND LIKE I WAS SAYING... ROBOTOP STOCK HAS NEVER BEEN AS STRONG AS IT IS TODAY!
QUICK! IT'S STARTING!
I HOPE THEY FIXED THE PROBLEM WITH THE RETRACTABLE CORD THIS TIME!
OH YEAH? I NEVER HAD A PROBLEM.
YES! EVEN THE SERVICE DEPARTMENT MADE A STATEMENT ON THE PROBLEM. THEY RECALLED ALL THE DEFECTIVE MODELS LAST YEAR!
SO, FROM THE BOTTOM OF MY HEART, I'D LIKE TO THANK ALL OF OUR CUSTOMERS FOR THEIR LOYALTY.
THANKS TO THEM, WE'RE SUCKING UP A TON OF CASH!
I WON'T LIE, WE HAVE MORE THAN WE KNOW WHAT TO DO WITH!
THE NEW
VACUUMIZER
BUT WE'RE NOT GOING TO REST ON OUR LAURELS. OH NO! NO! NO! NO!
AT ROBOTOP, WE LIKE A CHALLENGE! WE LIKE TO BE DARING!
THAT'S WHY OUR ENGINEERS PUT TOGETHER WHAT I WOULD CALL.. A WHISPER...
...FROM THE FUTURE!
FIRE REMOTE
CLIC!

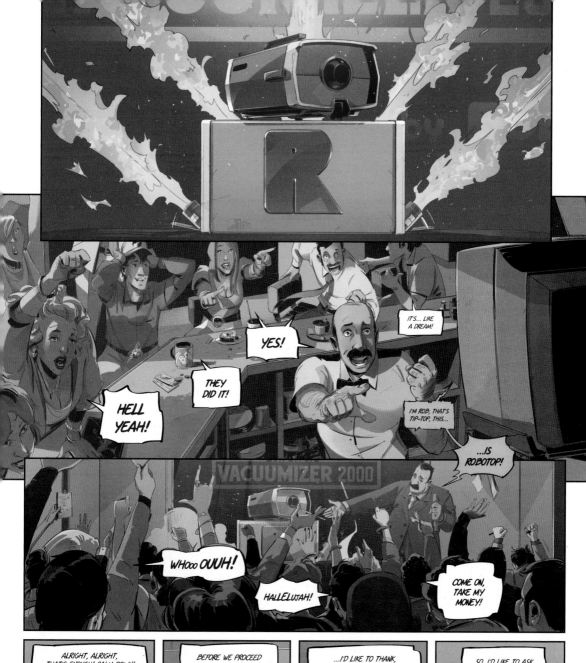

YES!

THEY DID IT!

HELL YEAH!

IT'S... LIKE A DREAM!

I'M ROB, THAT'S TIP-TOP, THIS...

...IS ROBOTOP!

WHOOO OUUH!

HALLELUJAH!

COME ON, TAKE MY MONEY!

VACUUMIZER 2000

ALRIGHT, ALRIGHT, THAT'S ENOUGH! CALM DOWN! YOU STILL HAVEN'T SEEN THE THING IN ACTION! IT'S GOING TO BE CRAZY!

BEFORE WE PROCEED WITH THE DEMONSTRATION OF THIS LITTLE MIRACLE...

...I'D LIKE TO THANK, BUT ESPECIALLY, TO REWARD, A DESERVING MEMBER OF ROBOTOP.

IF OUR AFTER-SALES SERVICE IS NUMBER ONE, IT'S THANKS TO HIM.

SO, I'D LIKE TO ASK FOR A HUGE ROUND OF APPLAUSE...

...FOR OUR BEST EMPLOYEE!

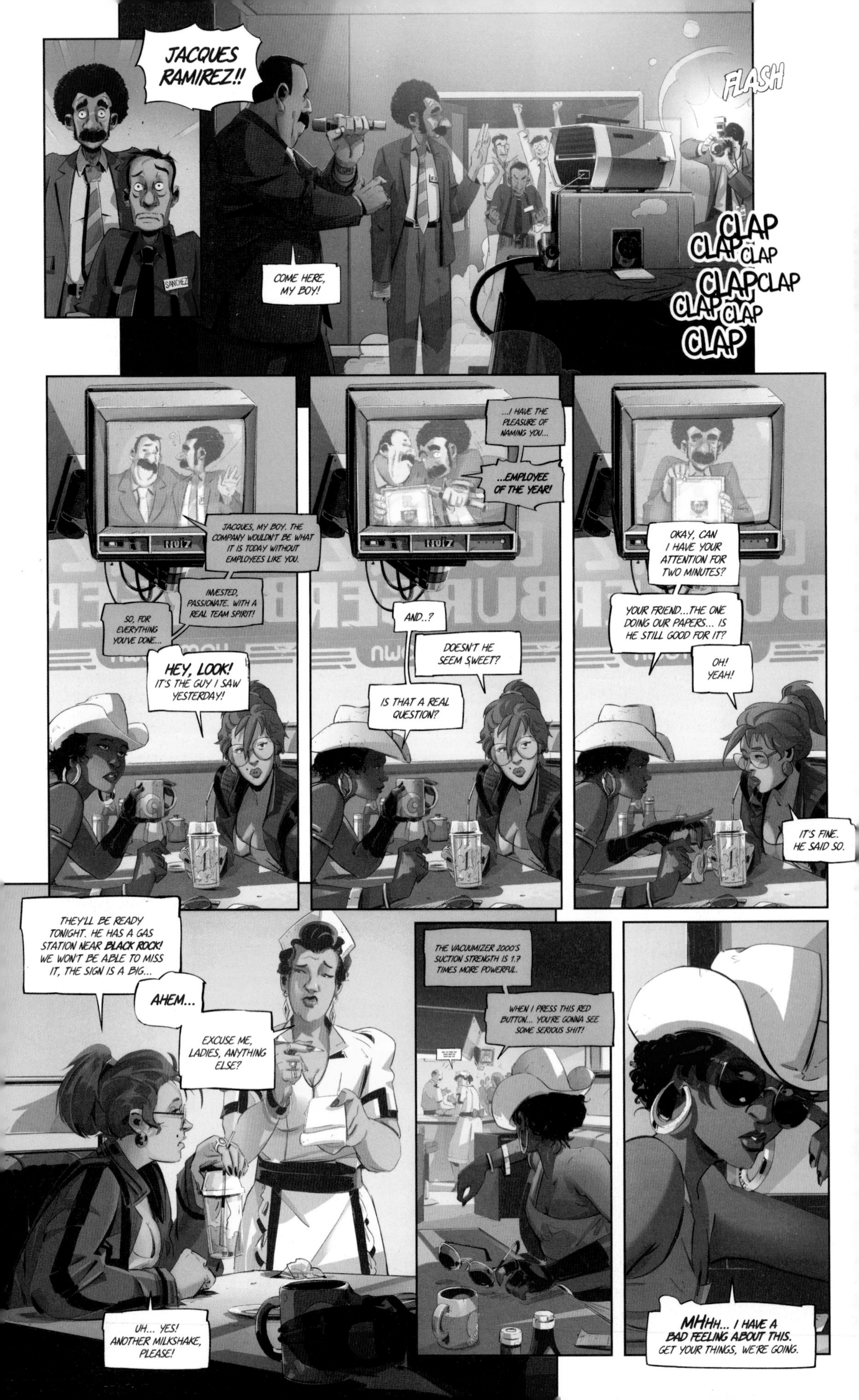

JACQUES RAMIREZ!!
FLASH
COME HERE, MY BOY!
CLAP CLAP CLAP CLAP CLAP CLAP CLAP CLAP
JACQUES, MY BOY. THE COMPANY WOULDN'T BE WHAT IT IS TODAY WITHOUT EMPLOYEES LIKE YOU.
INVESTED, PASSIONATE. WITH A REAL TEAM SPIRIT!
SO, FOR EVERYTHING YOU'VE DONE...
HEY, LOOK! IT'S THE GUY I SAW YESTERDAY!
...I HAVE THE PLEASURE OF NAMING YOU...
...EMPLOYEE OF THE YEAR!
AND..?
DOESN'T HE SEEM SWEET?
IS THAT A REAL QUESTION?
OKAY, CAN I HAVE YOUR ATTENTION FOR TWO MINUTES?
YOUR FRIEND...THE ONE DOING OUR PAPERS... IS HE STILL GOOD FOR IT?
OH! YEAH!
IT'S FINE. HE SAID SO.
THEY'LL BE READY TONIGHT. HE HAS A GAS STATION NEAR BLACK ROCK! WE WON'T BE ABLE TO MISS IT, THE SIGN IS A BIG...
AHEM...
EXCUSE ME, LADIES, ANYTHING ELSE?
UH... YES! ANOTHER MILKSHAKE, PLEASE!
THE VACUUMIZER 2000'S SUCTION STRENGTH IS 1.7 TIMES MORE POWERFUL.
WHEN I PRESS THIS RED BUTTON... YOU'RE GONNA SEE SOME SERIOUS SHIT!
MHHH... I HAVE A BAD FEELING ABOUT THIS. GET YOUR THINGS, WE'RE GOING.

R

VACUUMIZER 2000

FOR THE DUST? IT'S A MUST!

VACUUMIZER 2000

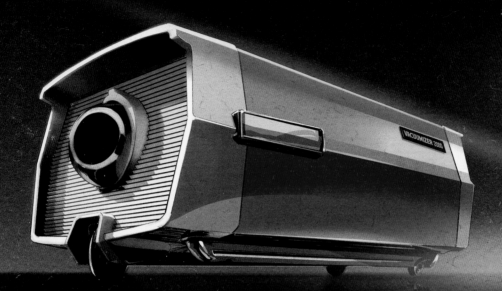

MORE THAN A VACUUM...

THIS LITTLE GUY LOVES YOUR LIVING ROOM!

The Vacumizer 2000 rethinks the world at its core and ushers in a new dust-less era, thanks to its remarkable sucking power, its ergonomic construction, and avant-garde design.

The new ASX technology searches for dust where no other device could before. Powered by a V8 thermoreactive impulsion engine, its poly-alloy carbon motor is unprecedented! And, for your comfort, you can count on its metal-reinforced gigatube.

Cleaning your house won't be a chore anymore, the Vacuumizer will reinspire you to keep your home pristine.

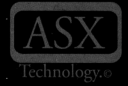

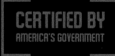

ASX Technology.©

130 DB

V8 TURBO▸▸▸

SYST

CERTIFIED BY AMERICA'S GOVERNMENT

ROBOTOP™

AS SEEN ON TV

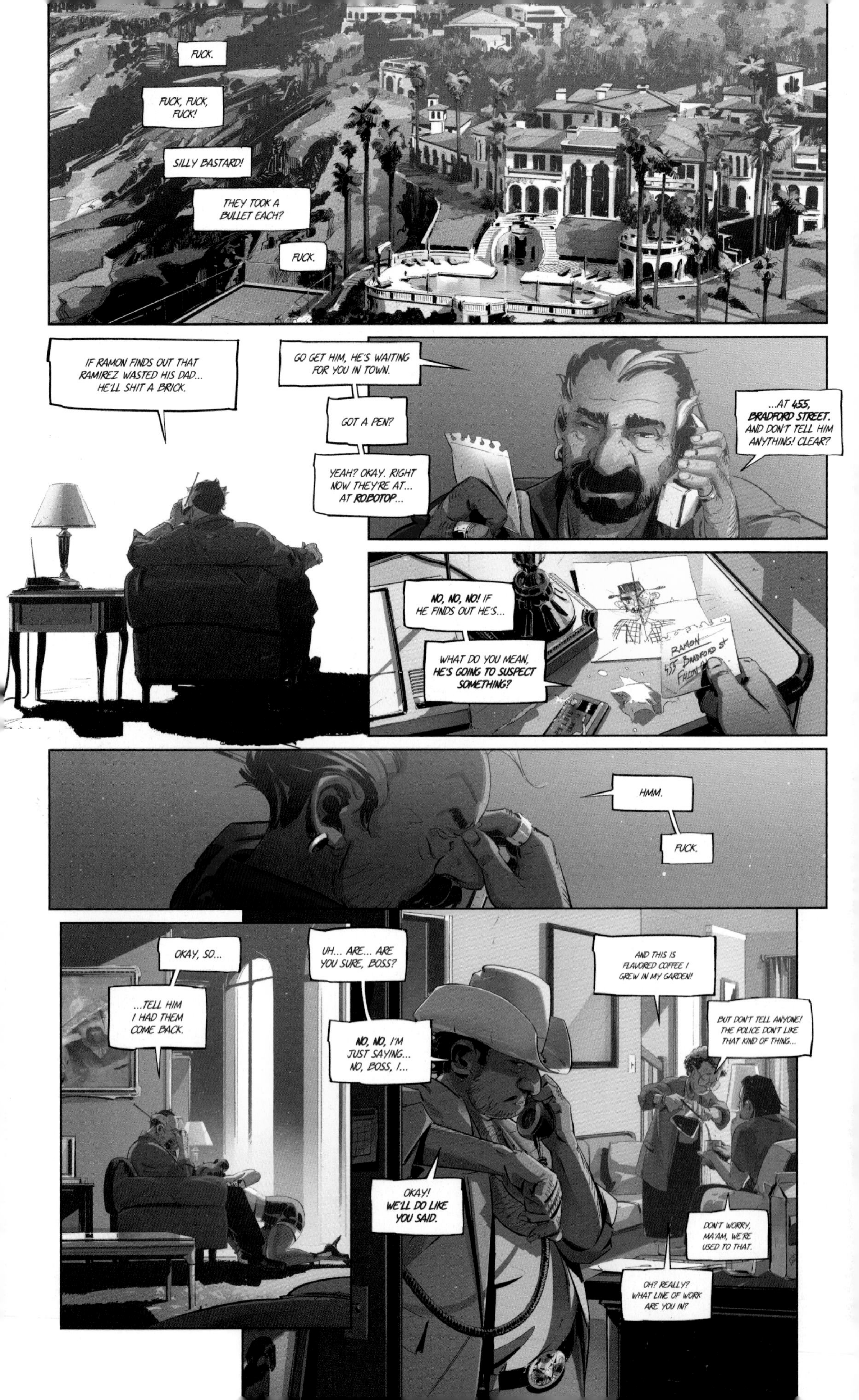
FUCK.
FUCK, FUCK, FUCK!
SILLY BASTARD!
THEY TOOK A BULLET EACH?
FUCK.
IF RAMON FINDS OUT THAT RAMIREZ WASTED HIS DAD... HE'LL SHIT A BRICK.
GO GET HIM, HE'S WAITING FOR YOU IN TOWN.
GOT A PEN?
YEAH? OKAY. RIGHT NOW THEY'RE AT... AT ROBOTOP...
...AT 455, BRADFORD STREET. AND DON'T TELL HIM ANYTHING! CLEAR?
NO, NO, NO! IF HE FINDS OUT HE'S...
WHAT DO YOU MEAN, HE'S GOING TO SUSPECT SOMETHING?
RAMON
455 Bradford st
HMM.
FUCK.
OKAY, SO...
...TELL HIM I HAD THEM COME BACK.
UH... ARE... ARE YOU SURE, BOSS?
NO, NO, I'M JUST SAYING... NO, BOSS, I...
AND THIS IS FLAVORED COFFEE I GREW IN MY GARDEN!
BUT DON'T TELL ANYONE! THE POLICE DON'T LIKE THAT KIND OF THING...
OKAY! WE'LL DO LIKE YOU SAID.
DON'T WORRY, MA'AM, WE'RE USED TO THAT.
OH? REALLY? WHAT LINE OF WORK ARE YOU IN?

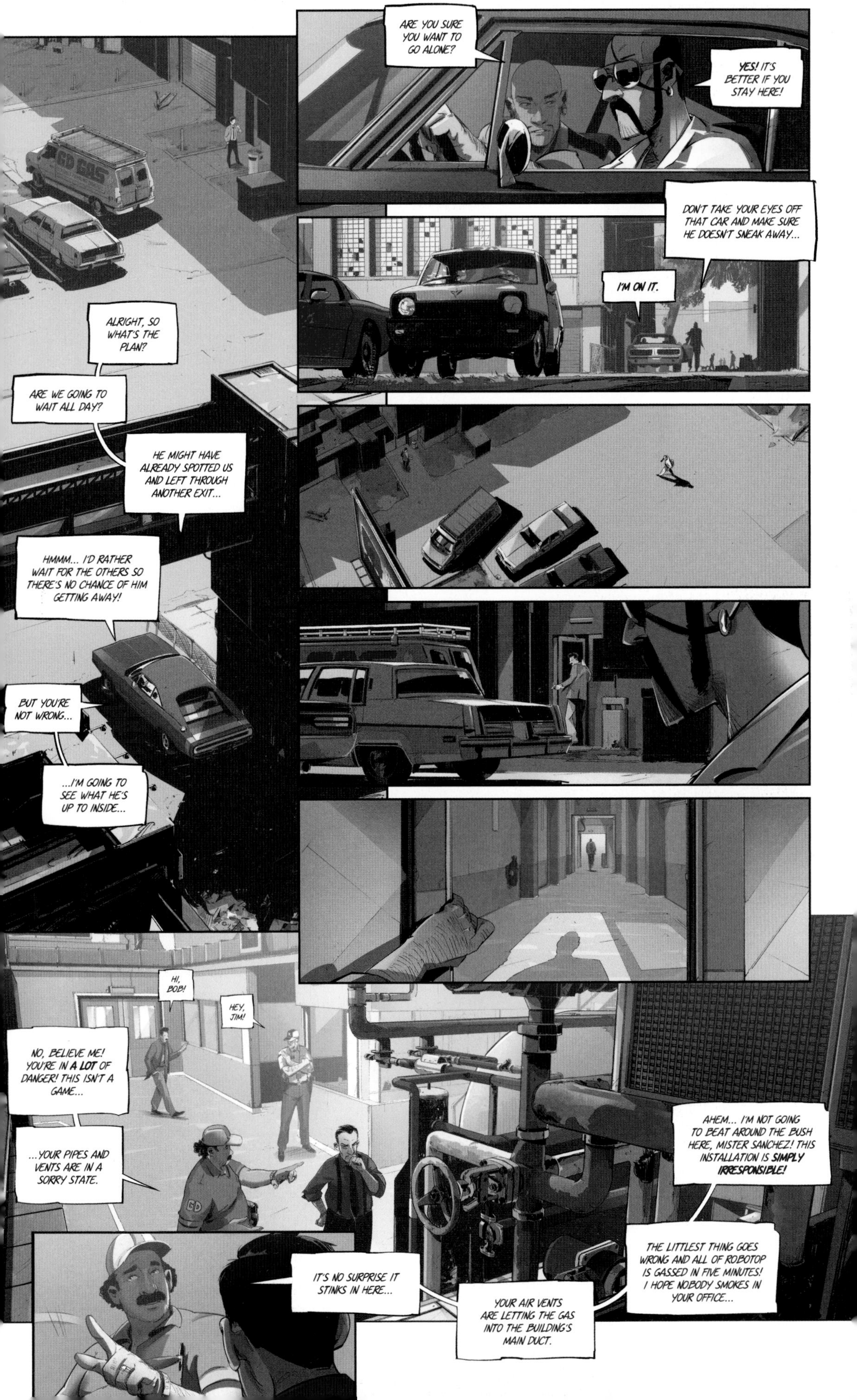

ALRIGHT, SO WHAT'S THE PLAN?
ARE WE GOING TO WAIT ALL DAY?
HE MIGHT HAVE ALREADY SPOTTED US AND LEFT THROUGH ANOTHER EXIT...
HMMM... I'D RATHER WAIT FOR THE OTHERS SO THERE'S NO CHANCE OF HIM GETTING AWAY!
BUT YOU'RE NOT WRONG...
...I'M GOING TO SEE WHAT HE'S UP TO INSIDE...
ARE YOU SURE YOU WANT TO GO ALONE?
YES! IT'S BETTER IF YOU STAY HERE!
DON'T TAKE YOUR EYES OFF THAT CAR AND MAKE SURE HE DOESN'T SNEAK AWAY...
I'M ON IT.
HI, BOB!
HEY, JIM!
NO, BELIEVE ME! YOU'RE IN **A LOT** OF DANGER! THIS ISN'T A GAME...
...YOUR PIPES AND VENTS ARE IN A SORRY STATE.
AHEM... I'M NOT GOING TO BEAT AROUND THE BUSH HERE, MISTER SANCHEZ! THIS INSTALLATION IS **SIMPLY IRRESPONSIBLE!**
THE LITTLEST THING GOES WRONG AND ALL OF ROBOTOP IS GASSED IN FIVE MINUTES! I HOPE NOBODY SMOKES IN YOUR OFFICE...
IT'S NO SURPRISE IT STINKS IN HERE...
YOUR AIR VENTS ARE LETTING THE GAS INTO THE BUILDING'S MAIN DUCT.

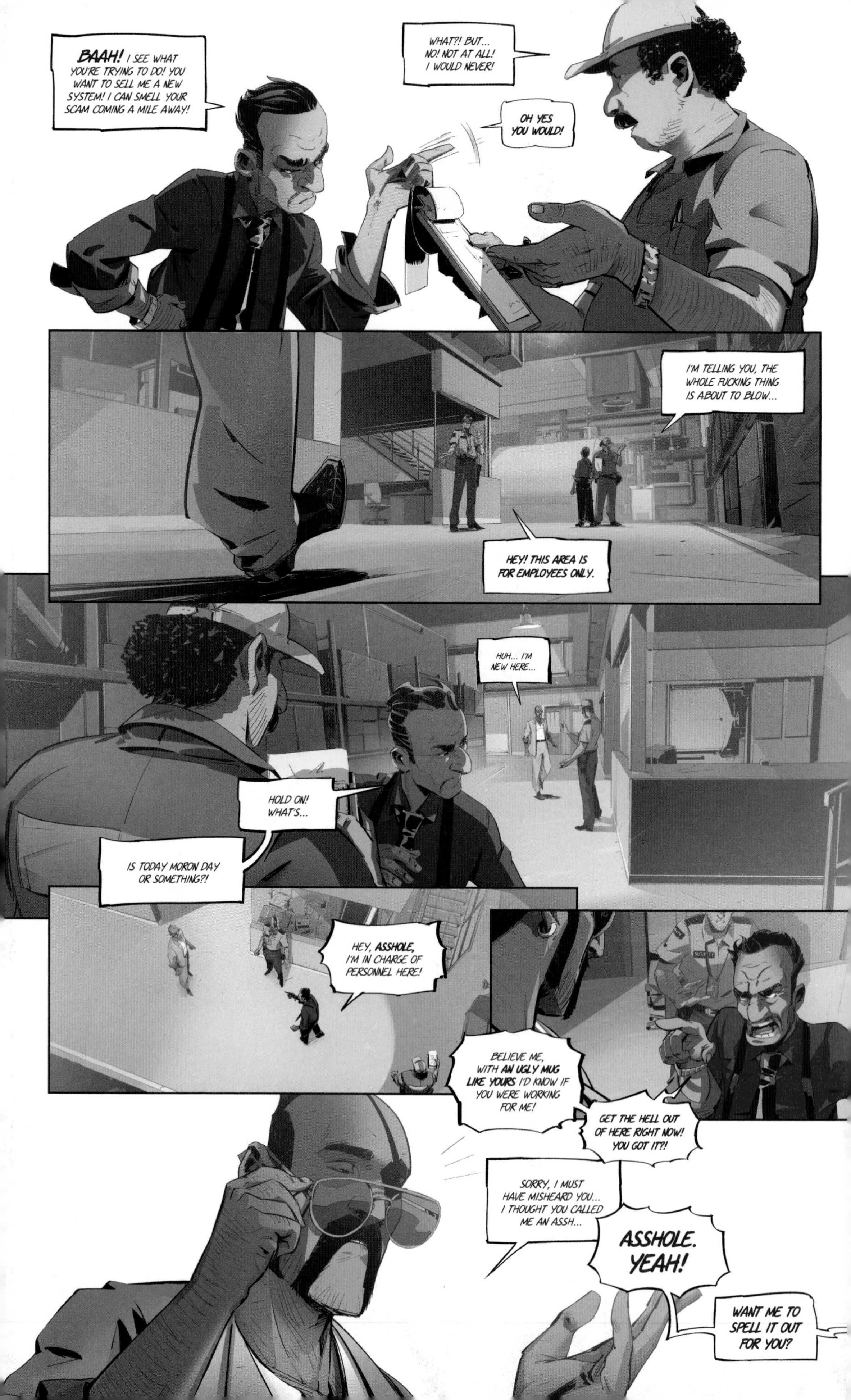
BAAH! I SEE WHAT YOU'RE TRYING TO DO! YOU WANT TO SELL ME A NEW SYSTEM! I CAN SMELL YOUR SCAM COMING A MILE AWAY!
WHAT?! BUT... NO! NOT AT ALL! I WOULD NEVER!
OH YES YOU WOULD!
I'M TELLING YOU, THE WHOLE FUCKING THING IS ABOUT TO BLOW...
HEY! THIS AREA IS FOR EMPLOYEES ONLY.
HUH... I'M NEW HERE...
HOLD ON! WHAT'S...
IS TODAY MORON DAY OR SOMETHING?!
HEY, ASSHOLE, I'M IN CHARGE OF PERSONNEL HERE!
BELIEVE ME, WITH AN UGLY MUG LIKE YOURS I'D KNOW IF YOU WERE WORKING FOR ME!
GET THE HELL OUT OF HERE RIGHT NOW! YOU GOT IT?!
SORRY, I MUST HAVE MISHEARD YOU... I THOUGHT YOU CALLED ME AN ASSH...
ASSHOLE. YEAH!
WANT ME TO SPELL IT OUT FOR YOU?

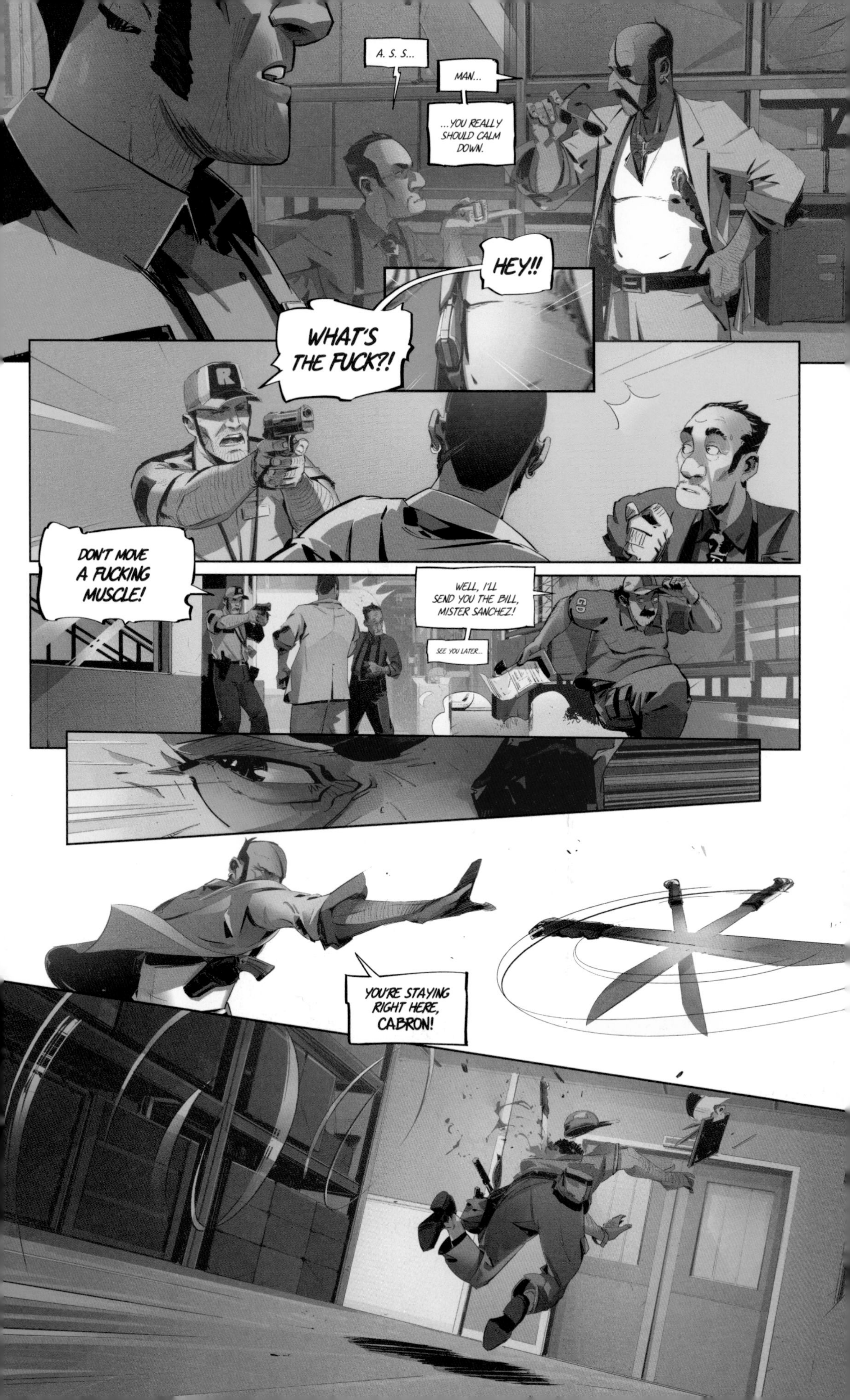

A. S. S...
MAN...
...YOU REALLY SHOULD CALM DOWN.
HEY!!
WHAT'S THE FUCK?!
DON'T MOVE A FUCKING MUSCLE!
WELL, I'LL SEND YOU THE BILL, MISTER SANCHEZ!
SEE YOU LATER...
YOU'RE STAYING RIGHT HERE, CABRON!

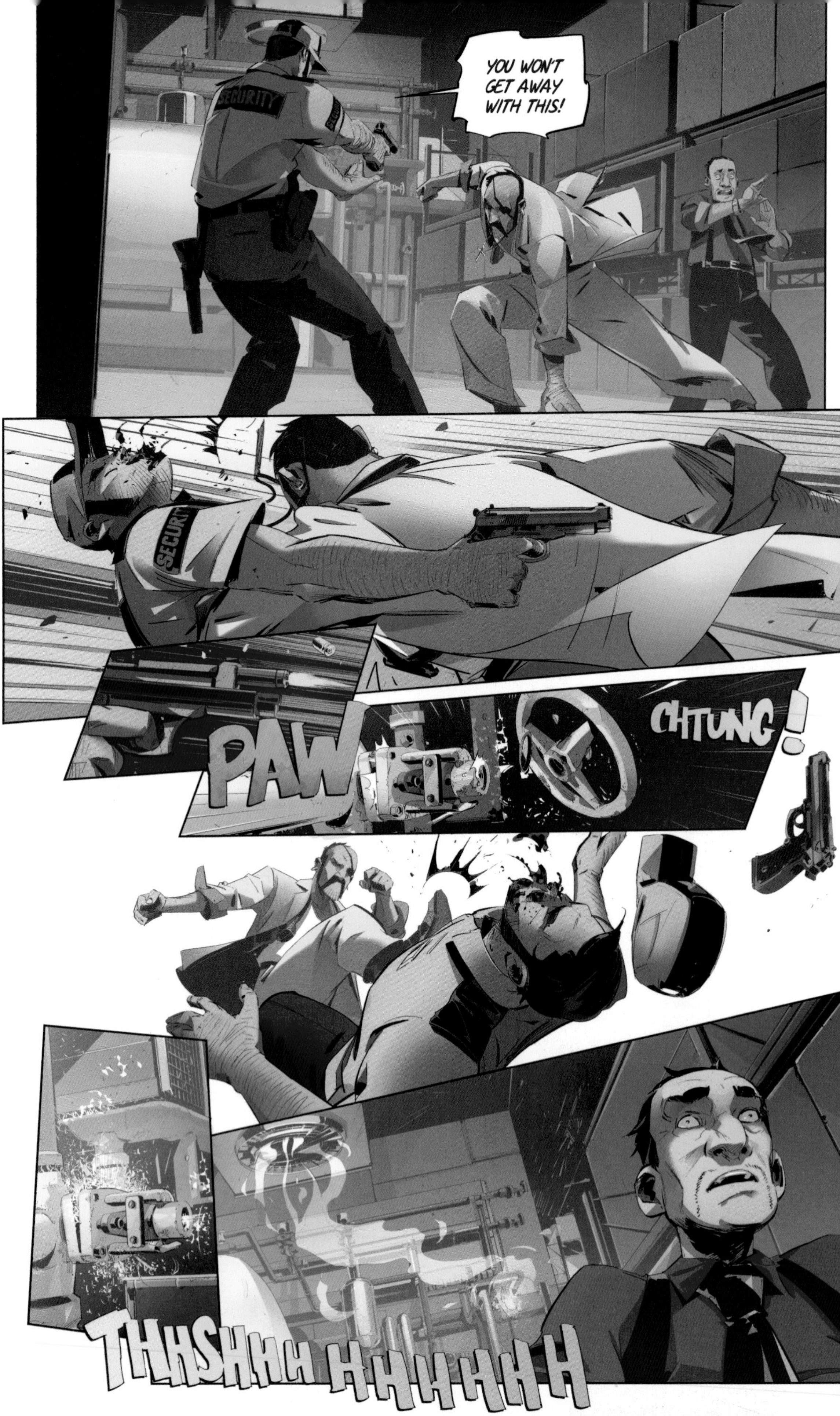
YOU WON'T GET AWAY WITH THIS!
PAW
CHTUNG!
THHSHHH HHHHHHH

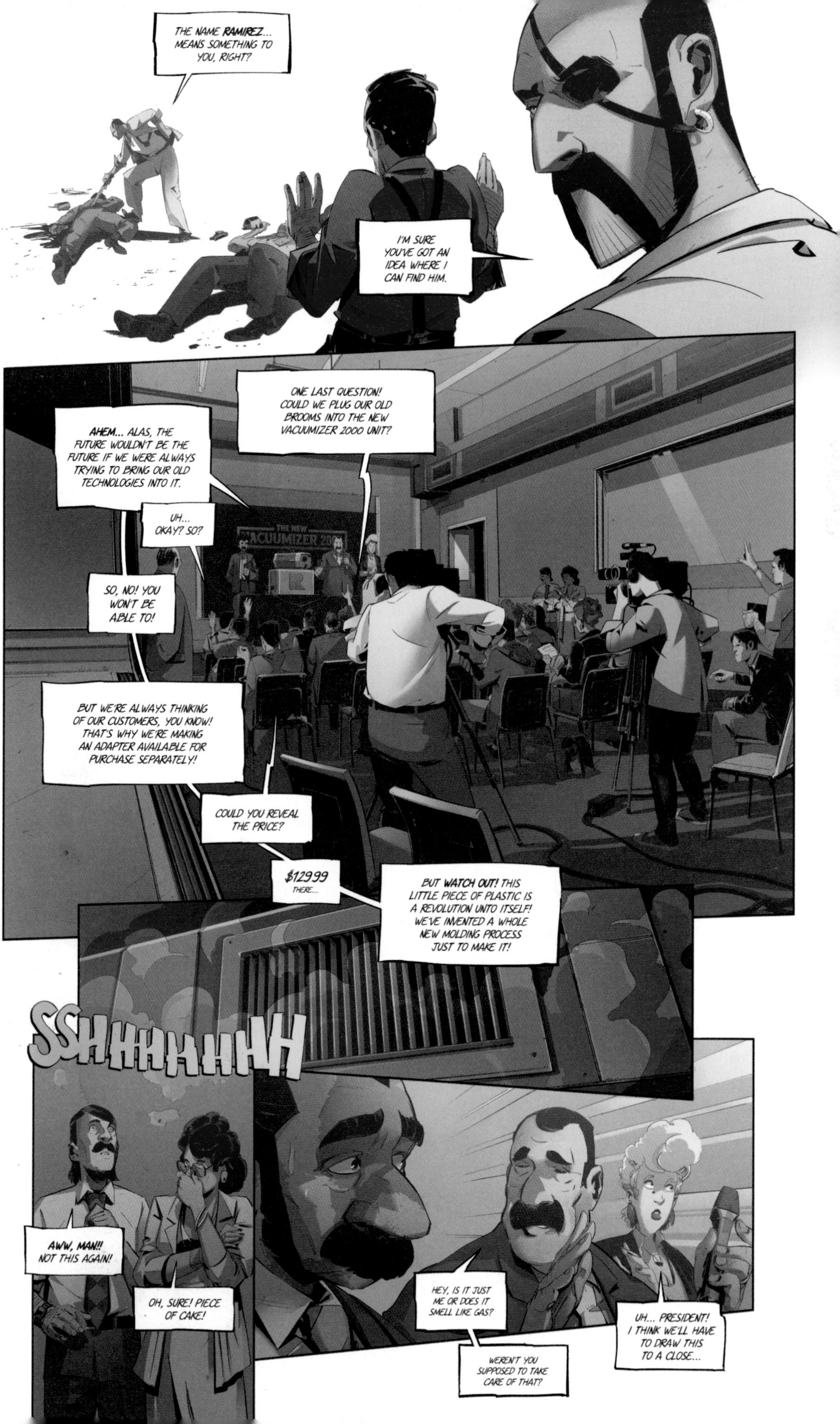
THE NAME RAMIREZ... MEANS SOMETHING TO YOU, RIGHT?
I'M SURE YOU'VE GOT AN IDEA WHERE I CAN FIND HIM.
ONE LAST QUESTION! COULD WE PLUG OUR OLD BROOMS INTO THE NEW VACUUMIZER 2000 UNIT?
AHEM... ALAS, THE FUTURE WOULDN'T BE THE FUTURE IF WE WERE ALWAYS TRYING TO BRING OUR OLD TECHNOLOGIES INTO IT.
UH... OKAY? SO?
SO, NO! YOU WON'T BE ABLE TO!
BUT WE'RE ALWAYS THINKING OF OUR CUSTOMERS, YOU KNOW! THAT'S WHY WE'RE MAKING AN ADAPTER AVAILABLE FOR PURCHASE SEPARATELY!
COULD YOU REVEAL THE PRICE?
$129.99 THERE...
BUT WATCH OUT! THIS LITTLE PIECE OF PLASTIC IS A REVOLUTION UNTO ITSELF! WE'VE INVENTED A WHOLE NEW MOLDING PROCESS JUST TO MAKE IT!
SSHHHHHHHH
AWW, MAN!! NOT THIS AGAIN!
OH, SURE! PIECE OF CAKE!
HEY, IS IT JUST ME OR DOES IT SMELL LIKE GAS?
WEREN'T YOU SUPPOSED TO TAKE CARE OF THAT?
UH... PRESIDENT! I THINK WE'LL HAVE TO DRAW THIS TO A CLOSE...

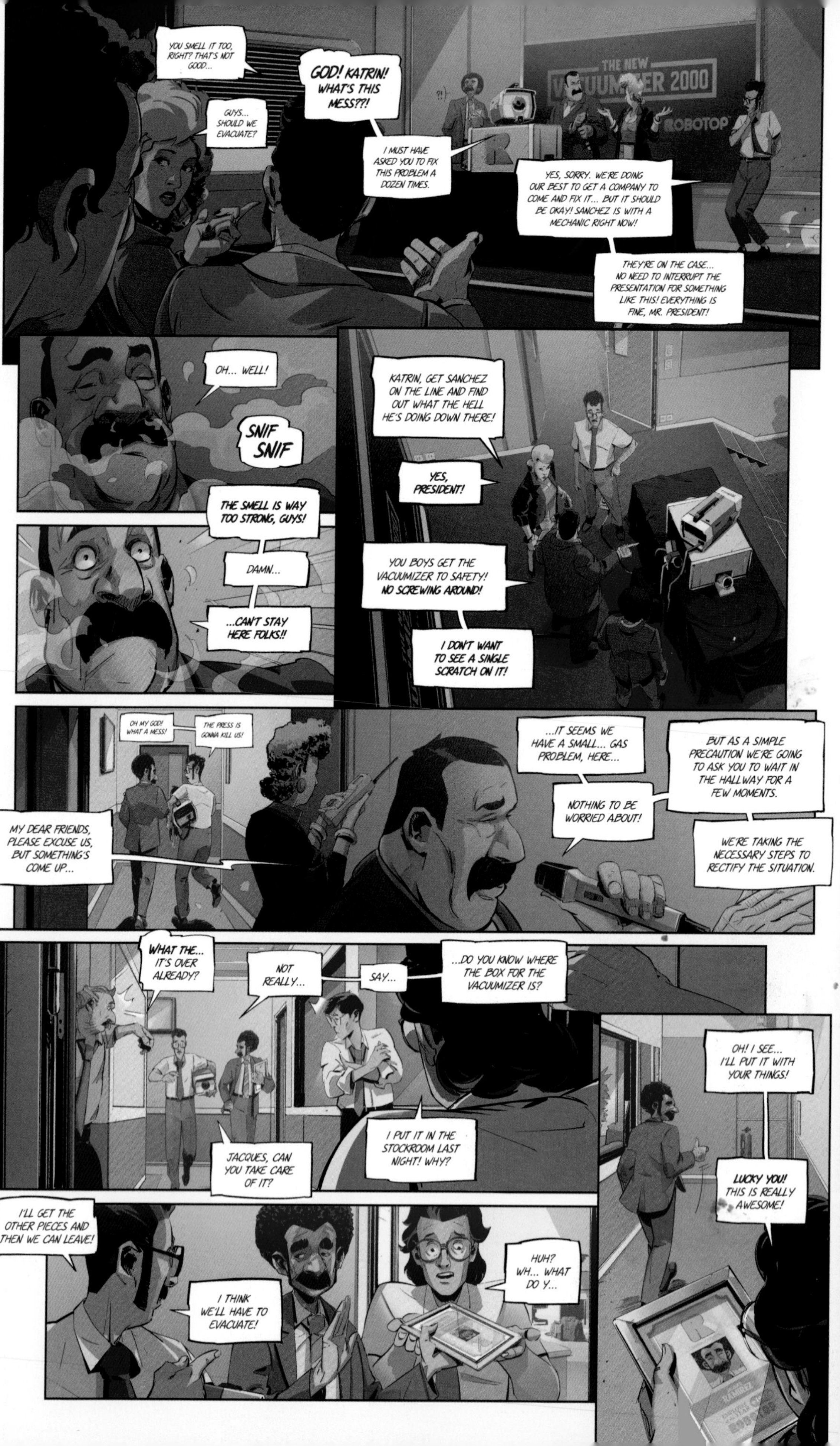
THE NEW
ROBOTOP
YOU SMELL IT TOO, RIGHT? THAT'S NOT GOOD...
GUYS... SHOULD WE EVACUATE?
GOD! KATRIN! WHAT'S THIS MESS??!
I MUST HAVE ASKED YOU TO FIX THIS PROBLEM A DOZEN TIMES.
YES, SORRY. WE'RE DOING OUR BEST TO GET A COMPANY TO COME AND FIX IT... BUT IT SHOULD BE OKAY! SANCHEZ IS WITH A MECHANIC RIGHT NOW!
THEY'RE ON THE CASE... NO NEED TO INTERRUPT THE PRESENTATION FOR SOMETHING LIKE THIS! EVERYTHING IS FINE, MR. PRESIDENT!
OH... WELL!
SNIF SNIF
THE SMELL IS WAY TOO STRONG, GUYS!
DAMN...
...CAN'T STAY HERE FOLKS!!
KATRIN, GET SANCHEZ ON THE LINE AND FIND OUT WHAT THE HELL HE'S DOING DOWN THERE!
YES, PRESIDENT!
YOU BOYS GET THE VACUUMIZER TO SAFETY! NO SCREWING AROUND!
I DON'T WANT TO SEE A SINGLE SCRATCH ON IT!
OH MY GOD! WHAT A MESS!
THE PRESS IS GONNA KILL US!
MY DEAR FRIENDS, PLEASE EXCUSE US, BUT SOMETHING'S COME UP...
...IT SEEMS WE HAVE A SMALL... GAS PROBLEM, HERE...
NOTHING TO BE WORRIED ABOUT!
BUT AS A SIMPLE PRECAUTION WE'RE GOING TO ASK YOU TO WAIT IN THE HALLWAY FOR A FEW MOMENTS.
WE'RE TAKING THE NECESSARY STEPS TO RECTIFY THE SITUATION.
WHAT THE... IT'S OVER ALREADY?
NOT REALLY...
SAY...
...DO YOU KNOW WHERE THE BOX FOR THE VACUUMIZER IS?
I PUT IT IN THE STOCKROOM LAST NIGHT! WHY?
JACQUES, CAN YOU TAKE CARE OF IT?
I'LL GET THE OTHER PIECES AND THEN WE CAN LEAVE!
I THINK WE'LL HAVE TO EVACUATE!
HUH? WH... WHAT DO Y...
OH! I SEE... I'LL PUT IT WITH YOUR THINGS!
LUCKY YOU! THIS IS REALLY AWESOME!
RAMIREZ
ROBOTOP

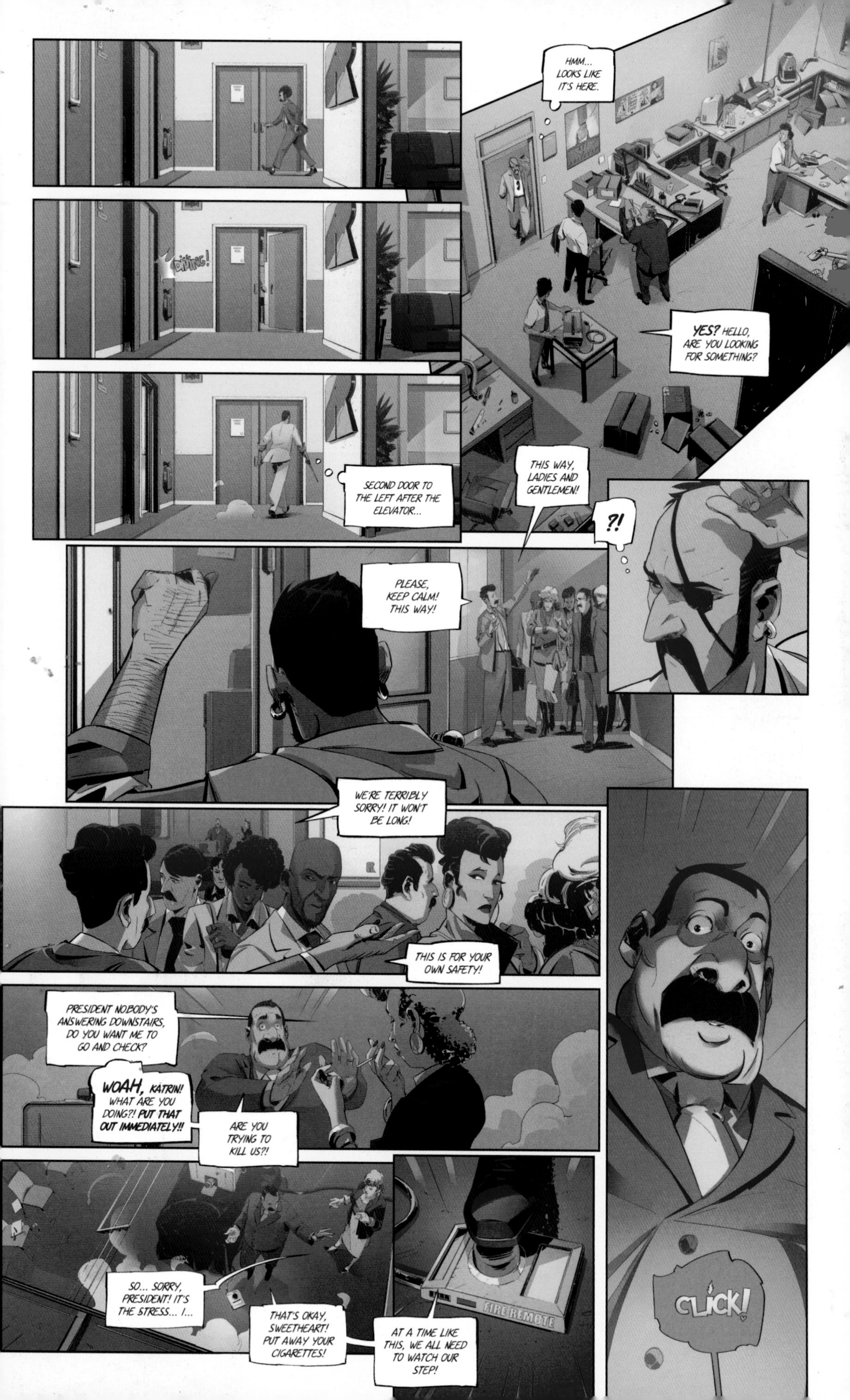
DIIING!
HMM... LOOKS LIKE IT'S HERE.
YES? HELLO, ARE YOU LOOKING FOR SOMETHING?
SECOND DOOR TO THE LEFT AFTER THE ELEVATOR...
THIS WAY, LADIES AND GENTLEMEN!
?!
PLEASE, KEEP CALM! THIS WAY!
WE'RE TERRIBLY SORRY! IT WON'T BE LONG!
THIS IS FOR YOUR OWN SAFETY!
PRESIDENT NOBODY'S ANSWERING DOWNSTAIRS, DO YOU WANT ME TO GO AND CHECK?
WOAH, KATRIN! WHAT ARE YOU DOING?! PUT THAT OUT IMMEDIATELY!!
ARE YOU TRYING TO KILL US?!
SO... SORRY, PRESIDENT! IT'S THE STRESS... I...
THAT'S OKAY, SWEETHEART! PUT AWAY YOUR CIGARETTES!
AT A TIME LIKE THIS, WE ALL NEED TO WATCH OUR STEP!
FIRE REMOTE
CLICK!

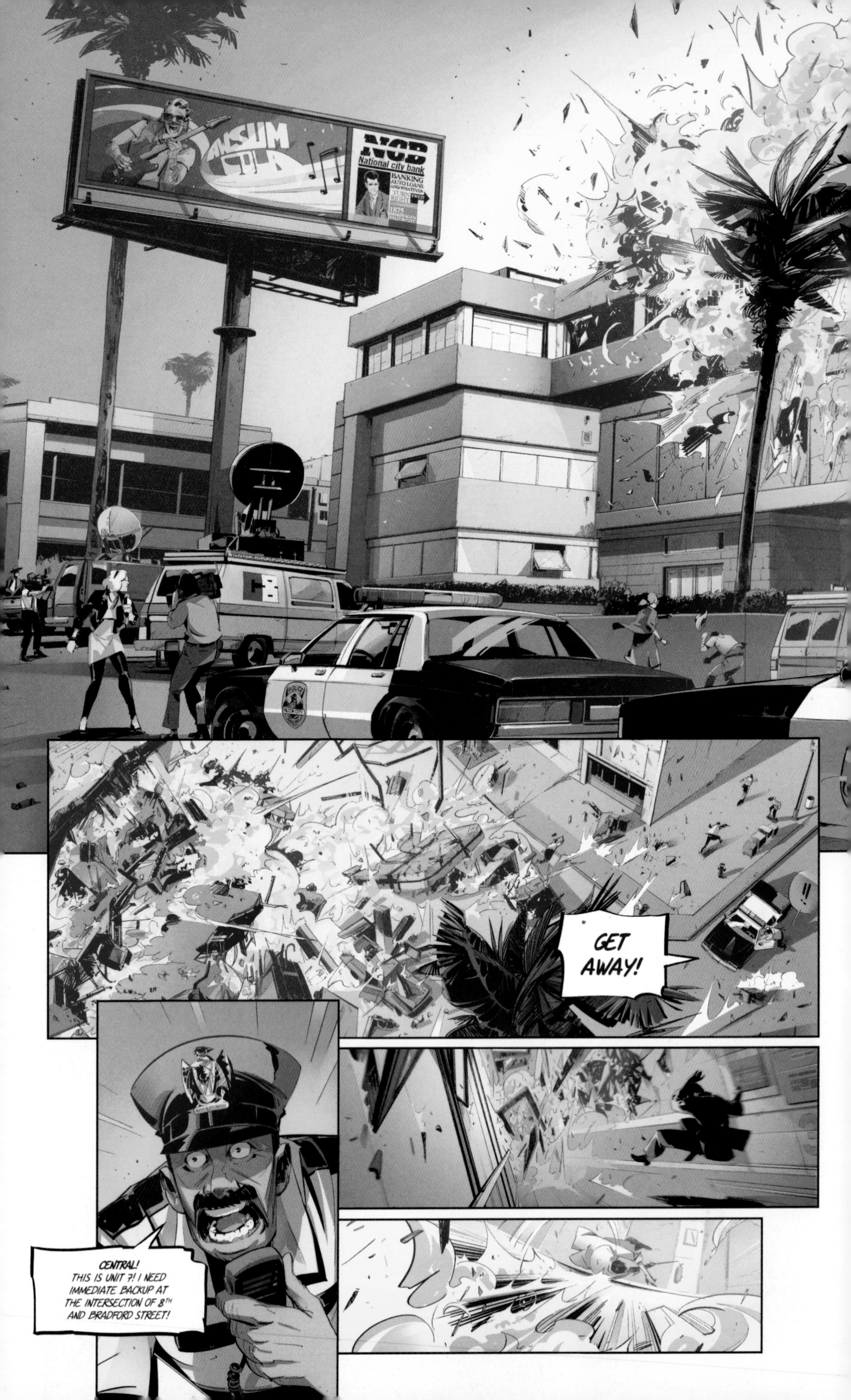
NCB
National city bank
BANKING
GET AWAY!
CENTRAL! THIS IS UNIT 7! I NEED IMMEDIATE BACKUP AT THE INTERSECTION OF 8TH AND BRADFORD STREET!

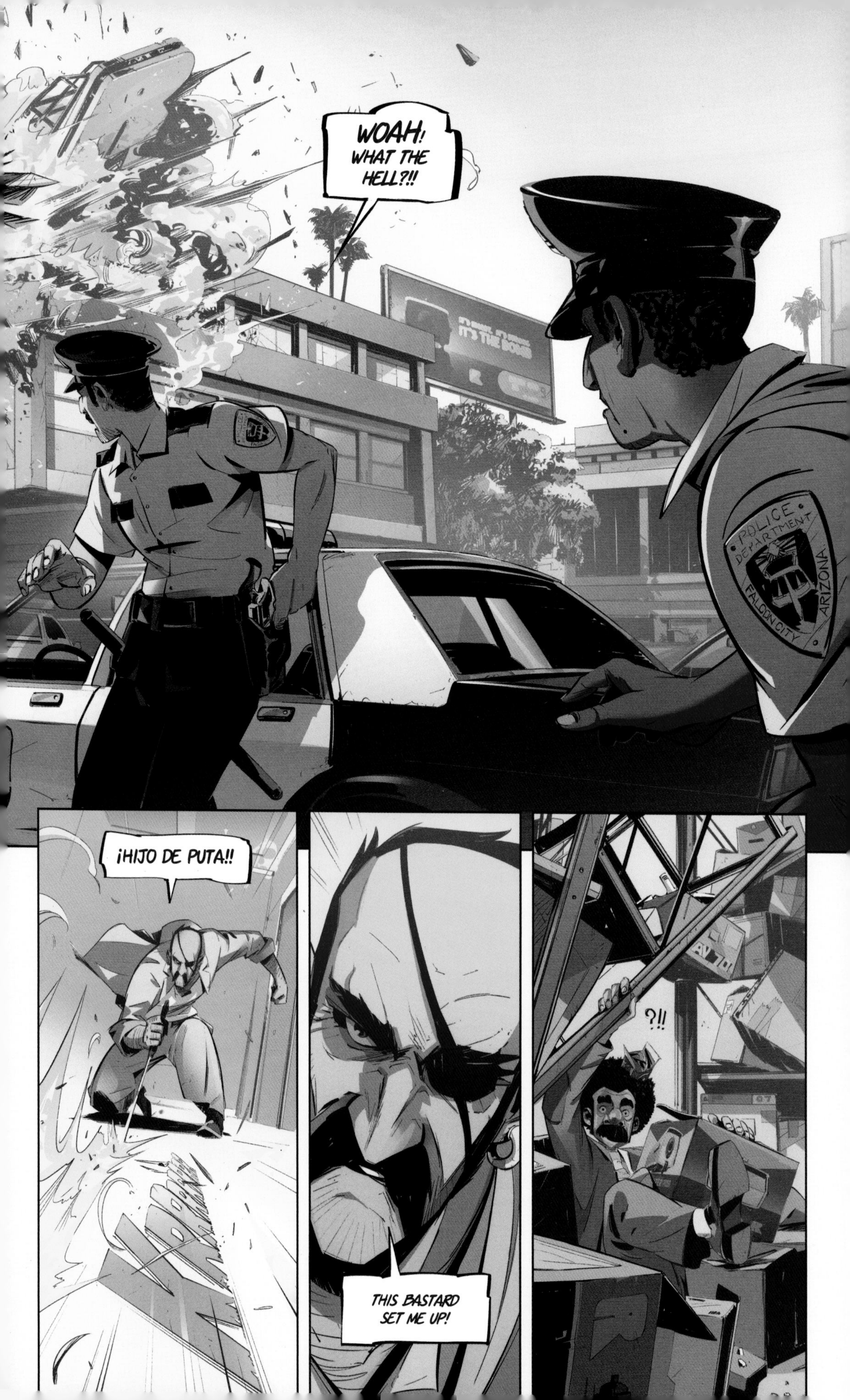
WOAH! WHAT THE HELL?!!
POLICE DEPARTMENT FALCON CITY ARIZONA
¡HIJO DE PUTA!!
THIS BASTARD SET ME UP!
?!!

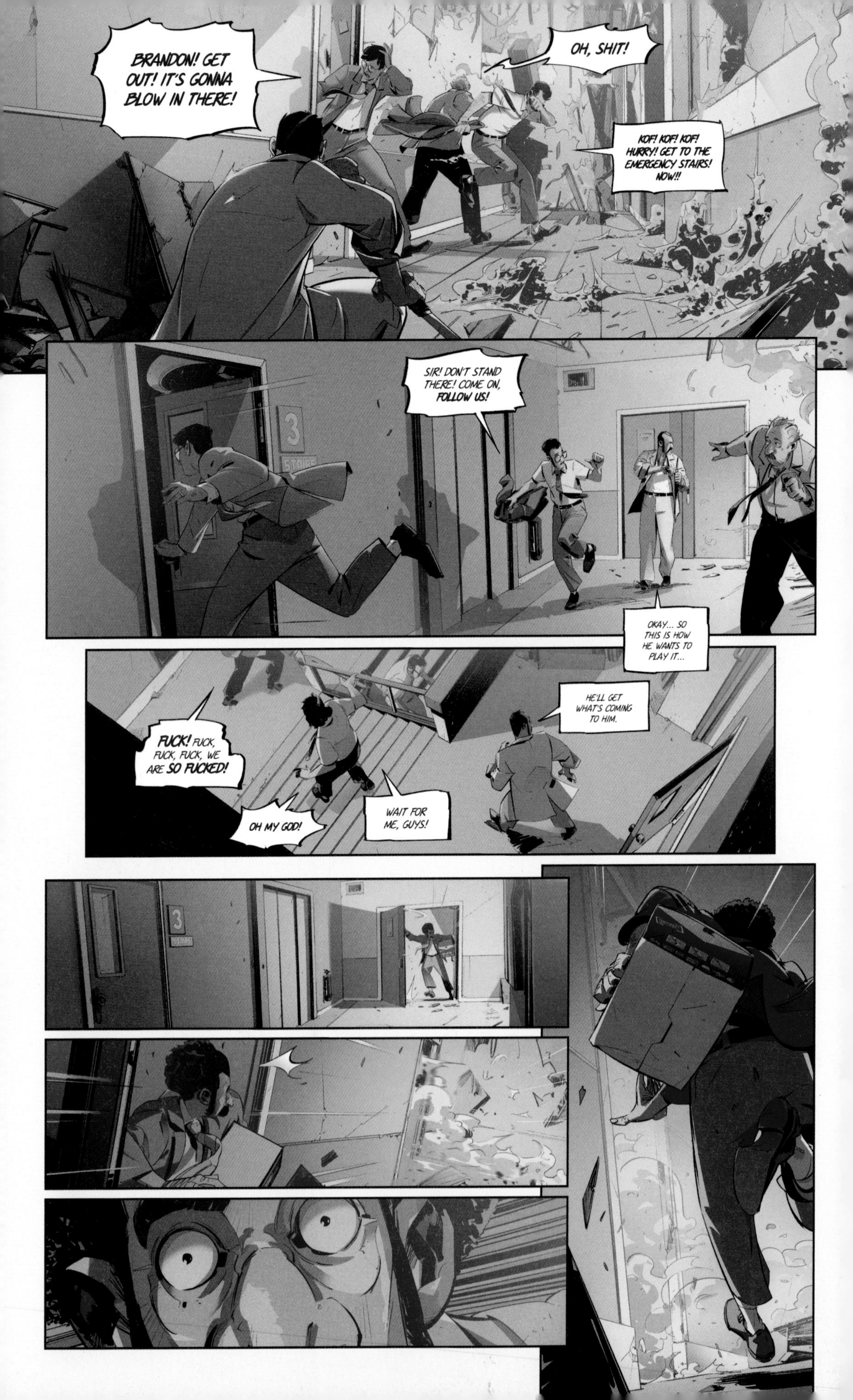
BRANDON! GET OUT! IT'S GONNA BLOW IN THERE!
OH, SHIT!
KOF! KOF! KOF! HURRY! GET TO THE EMERGENCY STAIRS! NOW!!
SIR! DON'T STAND THERE! COME ON, FOLLOW US!
OKAY... SO THIS IS HOW HE WANTS TO PLAY IT...
HE'LL GET WHAT'S COMING TO HIM.
FUCK! FUCK, FUCK, FUCK, WE ARE SO FUCKED!
OH MY GOD!
WAIT FOR ME, GUYS!

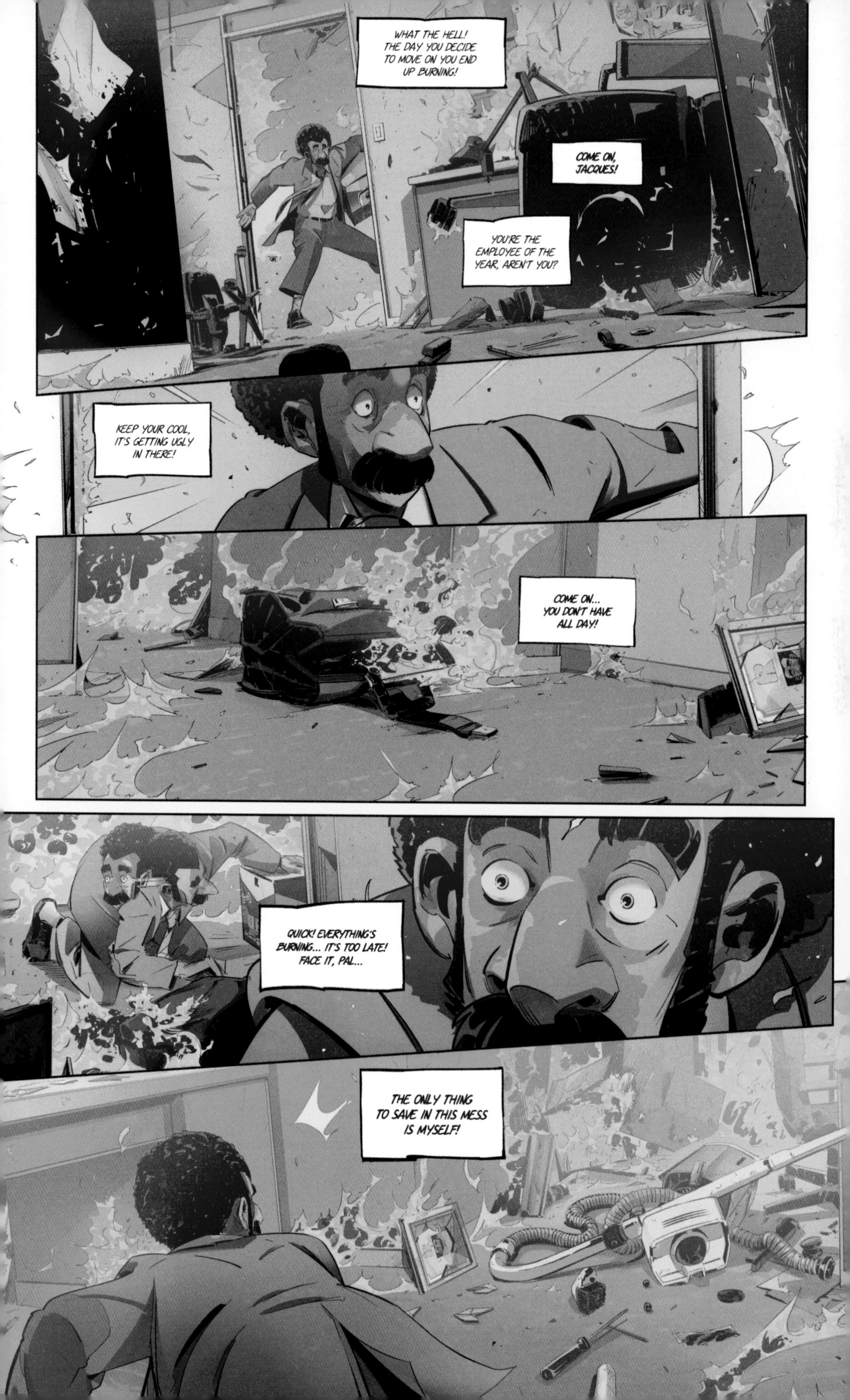
WHAT THE HELL! THE DAY YOU DECIDE TO MOVE ON YOU END UP BURNING!
COME ON, JACQUES!
YOU'RE THE EMPLOYEE OF THE YEAR, AREN'T YOU?
KEEP YOUR COOL, IT'S GETTING UGLY IN THERE!
COME ON... YOU DON'T HAVE ALL DAY!
QUICK! EVERYTHING'S BURNING... IT'S TOO LATE! FACE IT, PAL...
THE ONLY THING TO SAVE IN THIS MESS IS MYSELF!

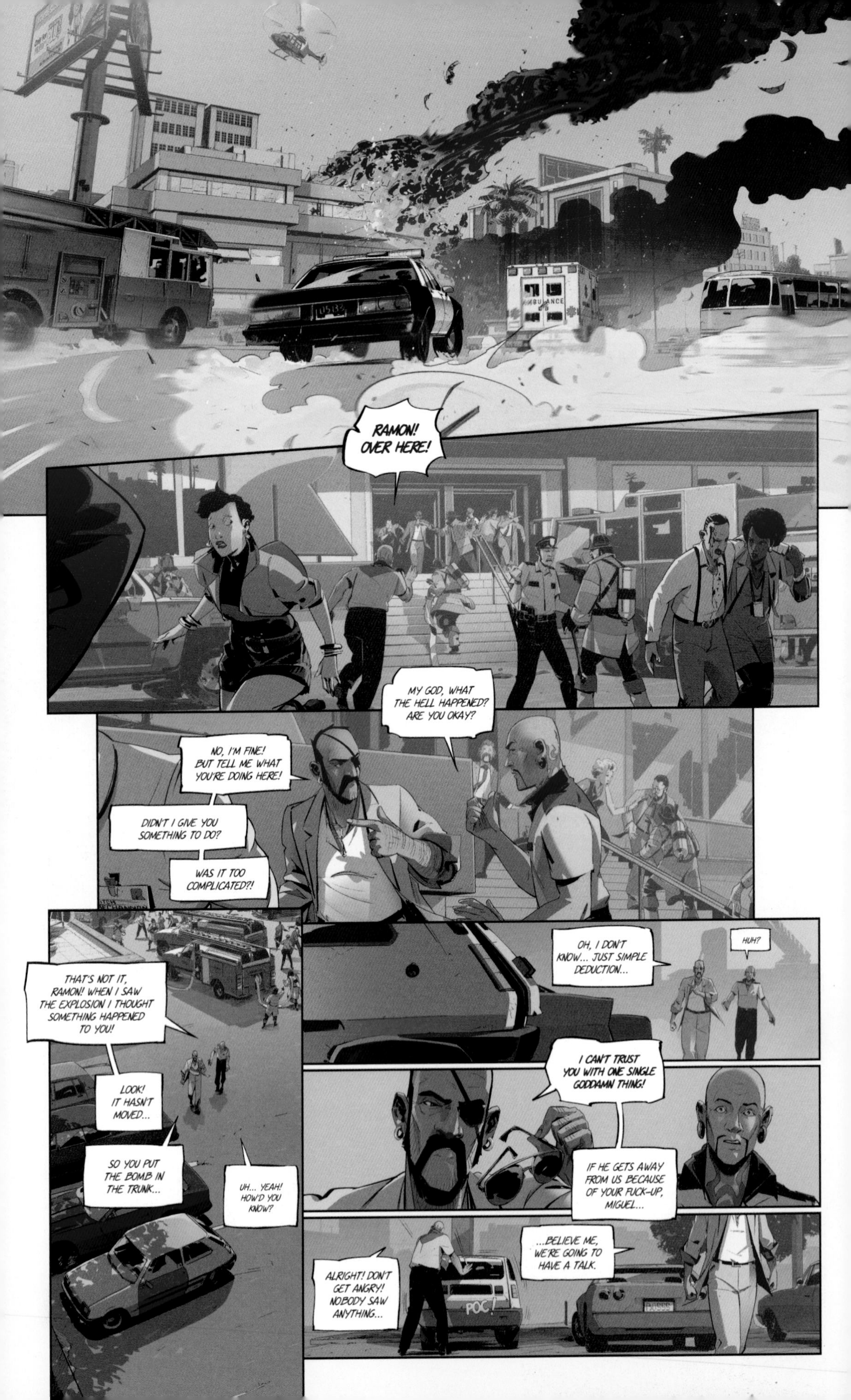
RAMON! OVER HERE!
MY GOD, WHAT THE HELL HAPPENED? ARE YOU OKAY?
NO, I'M FINE! BUT TELL ME WHAT YOU'RE DOING HERE!
DIDN'T I GIVE YOU SOMETHING TO DO?
WAS IT TOO COMPLICATED?!
THAT'S NOT IT, RAMON! WHEN I SAW THE EXPLOSION I THOUGHT SOMETHING HAPPENED TO YOU!
LOOK! IT HASN'T MOVED...
SO YOU PUT THE BOMB IN THE TRUNK...
UH... YEAH! HOW'D YOU KNOW?
OH, I DON'T KNOW... JUST SIMPLE DEDUCTION...
HUH?
I CAN'T TRUST YOU WITH ONE SINGLE GODDAMN THING!
IF HE GETS AWAY FROM US BECAUSE OF YOUR FUCK-UP, MIGUEL...
...BELIEVE ME, WE'RE GOING TO HAVE A TALK.
ALRIGHT! DON'T GET ANGRY! NOBODY SAW ANYTHING...
POC!

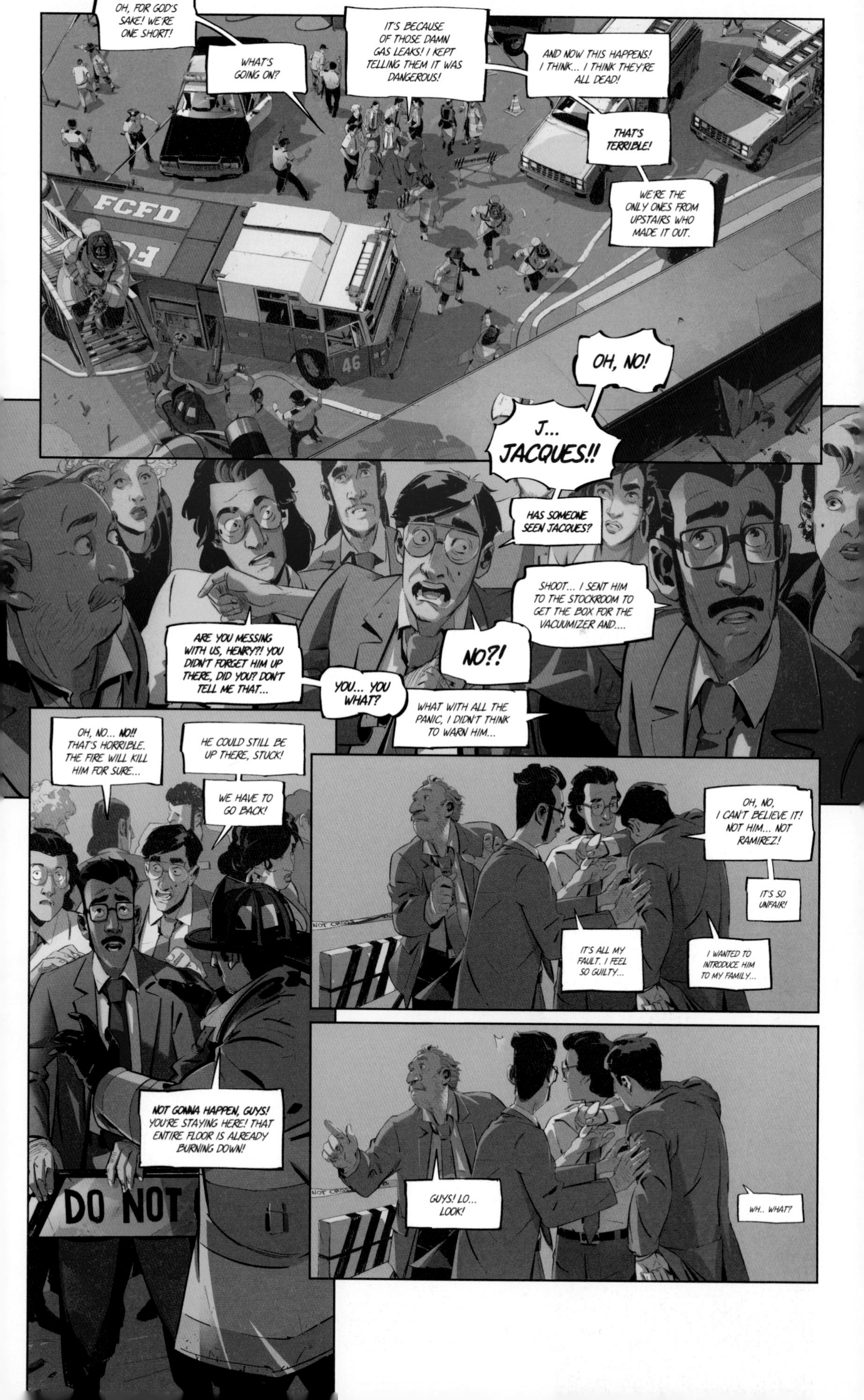
OH, FOR GOD'S SAKE! WE'RE ONE SHORT!
WHAT'S GOING ON?
IT'S BECAUSE OF THOSE DAMN GAS LEAKS! I KEPT TELLING THEM IT WAS DANGEROUS!
AND NOW THIS HAPPENS! I THINK... I THINK THEY'RE ALL DEAD!
THAT'S TERRIBLE!
WE'RE THE ONLY ONES FROM UPSTAIRS WHO MADE IT OUT.
FCFD
46
OH, NO!
J... JACQUES!!
HAS SOMEONE SEEN JACQUES?
SHOOT... I SENT HIM TO THE STOCKROOM TO GET THE BOX FOR THE VACUUMIZER AND....
NO?!
ARE YOU MESSING WITH US, HENRY?! YOU DIDN'T FORGET HIM UP THERE, DID YOU? DON'T TELL ME THAT...
YOU... YOU WHAT?
WHAT WITH ALL THE PANIC, I DIDN'T THINK TO WARN HIM...
OH, NO... NO!! THAT'S HORRIBLE. THE FIRE WILL KILL HIM FOR SURE...
HE COULD STILL BE UP THERE, STUCK!
WE HAVE TO GO BACK!
NOT GONNA HAPPEN, GUYS! YOU'RE STAYING HERE! THAT ENTIRE FLOOR IS ALREADY BURNING DOWN!
DO NOT
OH, NO, I CAN'T BELIEVE IT! NOT HIM... NOT RAMIREZ!
IT'S SO UNFAIR!
IT'S ALL MY FAULT. I FEEL SO GUILTY...
I WANTED TO INTRODUCE HIM TO MY FAMILY...
GUYS! LO... LOOK!
WH.. WHAT?

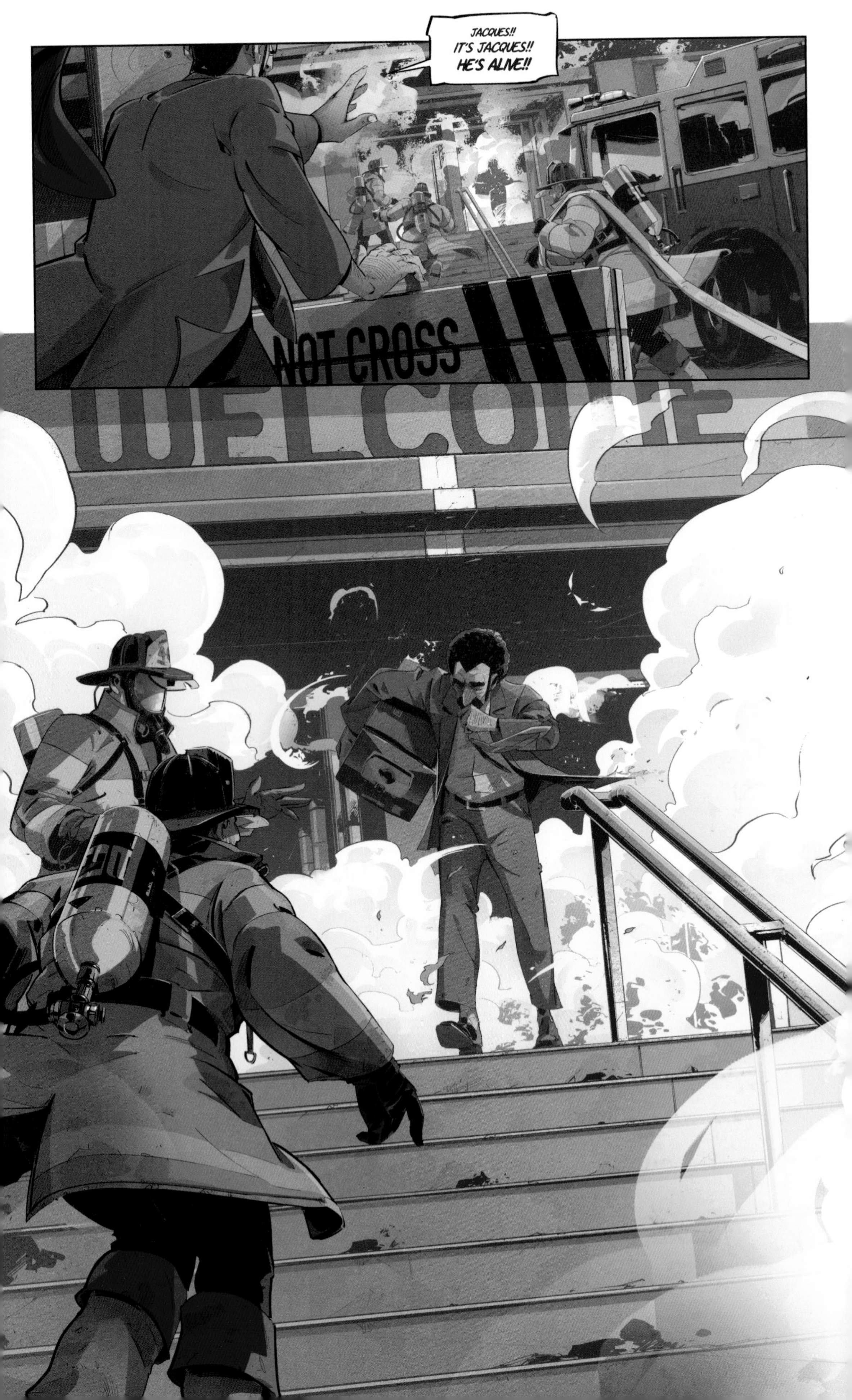
JACQUES!!
IT'S JACQUES!!
HE'S ALIVE!!
NOT CROSS
WELCO

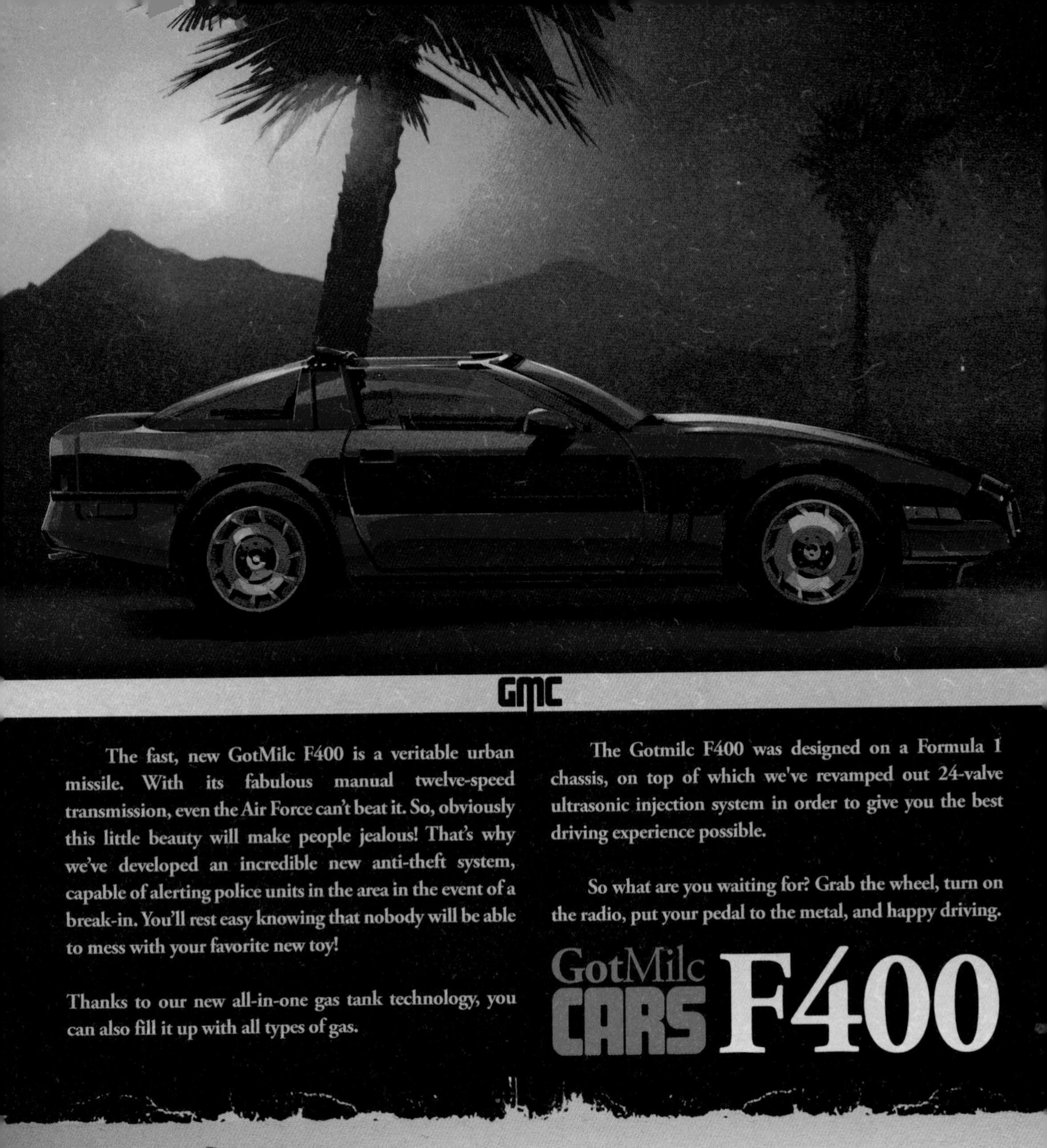

GMC

The fast, new GotMilc F400 is a veritable urban missile. With its fabulous manual twelve-speed transmission, even the Air Force can't beat it. So, obviously this little beauty will make people jealous! That's why we've developed an incredible new anti-theft system, capable of alerting police units in the area in the event of a break-in. You'll rest easy knowing that nobody will be able to mess with your favorite new toy!

Thanks to our new all-in-one gas tank technology, you can also fill it up with all types of gas.

The Gotmilc F400 was designed on a Formula 1 chassis, on top of which we've revamped out 24-valve ultrasonic injection system in order to give you the best driving experience possible.

So what are you waiting for? Grab the wheel, turn on the radio, put your pedal to the metal, and happy driving.

GotMilc CARS **F400**

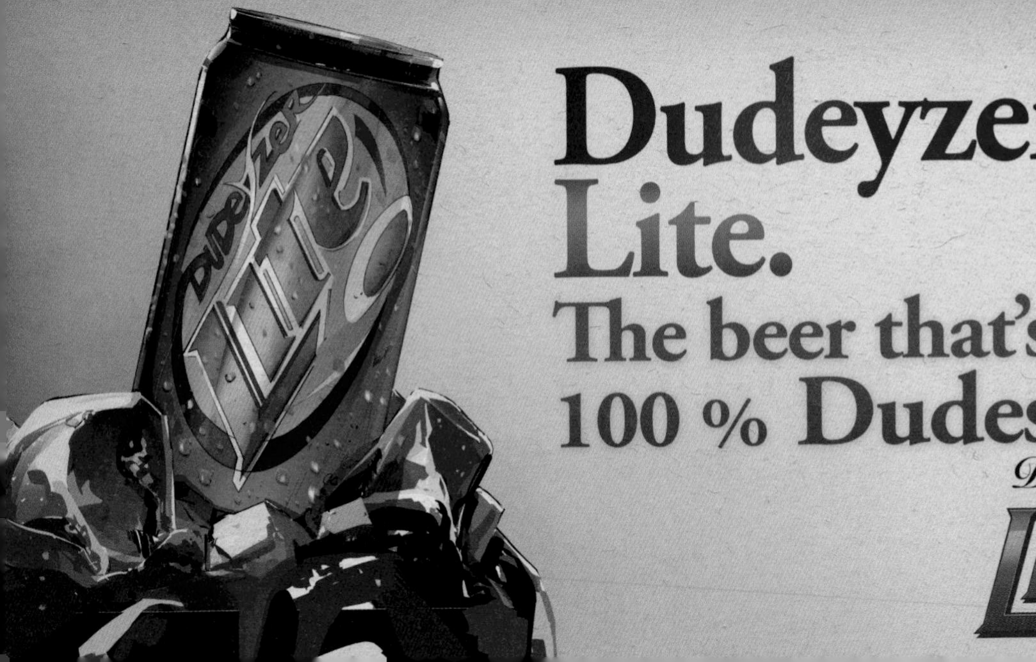

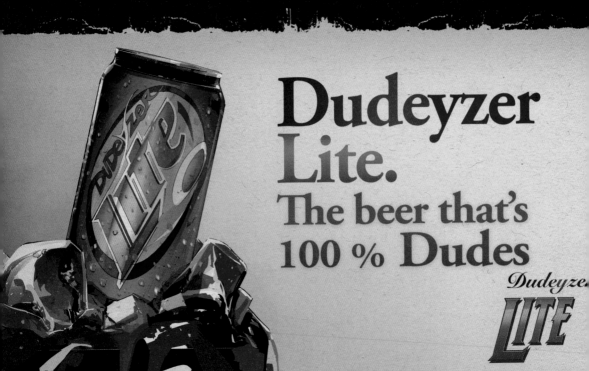

Dudeyzer Lite.

The beer that's 100 % Dudes

Dudeyze. LITE

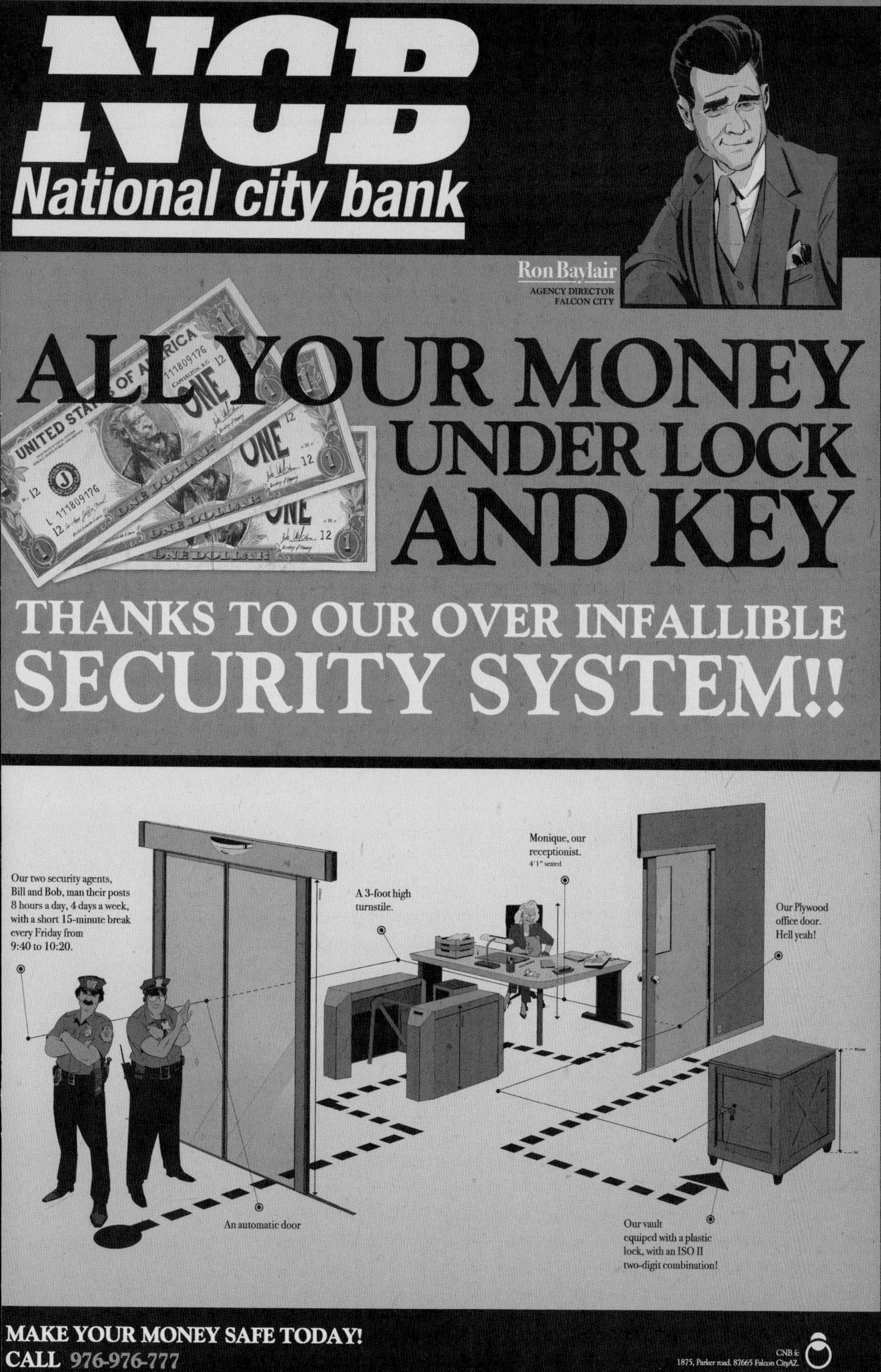
NCB
National city bank
Ron Baylair
AGENCY DIRECTOR
FALCON CITY
ALL YOUR MONEY
UNDER LOCK
AND KEY
THANKS TO OUR OVER INFALLIBLE
SECURITY SYSTEM!!
Our two security agents, Bill and Bob, man their posts 8 hours a day, 4 days a week, with a short 15-minute break every Friday from 9:40 to 10:20.
A 3-foot high turnstile.
Monique, our receptionist.
4′1″ seated
Our Plywood office door. Hell yeah!
An automatic door
Our vault equiped with a plastic lock, with an ISO II two-digit combination!
MAKE YOUR MONEY SAFE TODAY!
CALL 976-976-777
CNB fc
1875, Parker road. 87665 Falcon CityAZ.

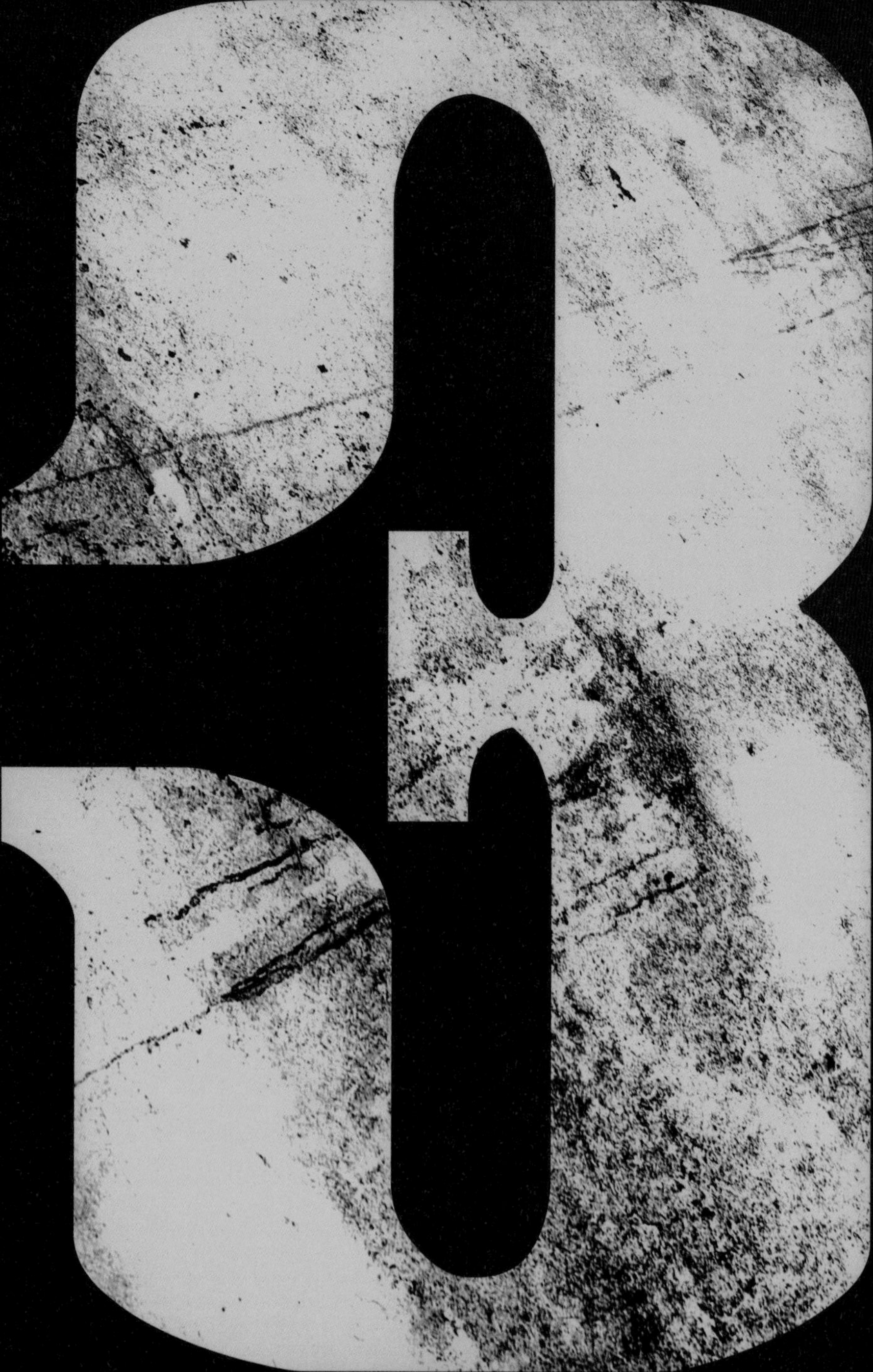

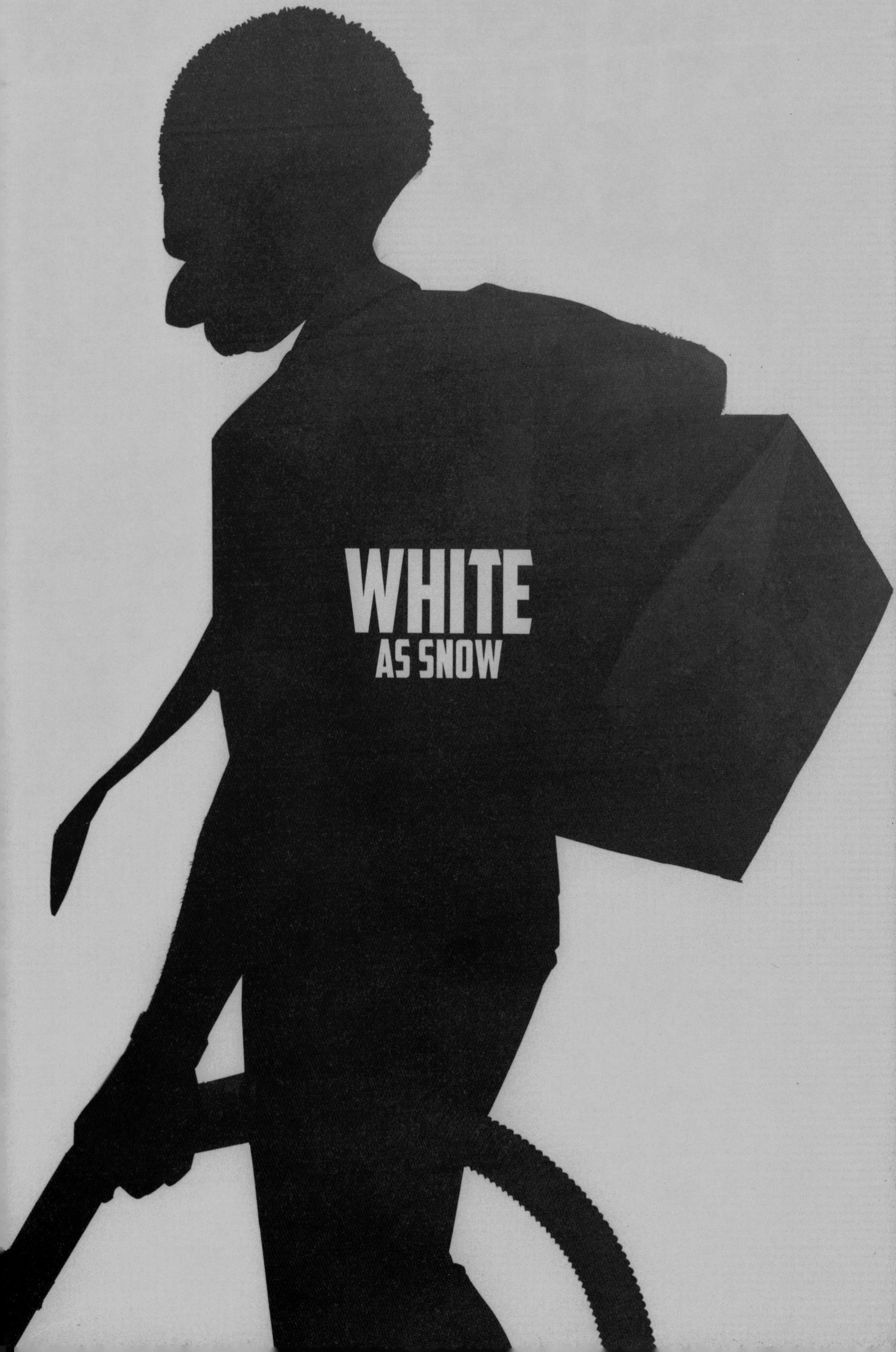
WHITE
AS SNOW

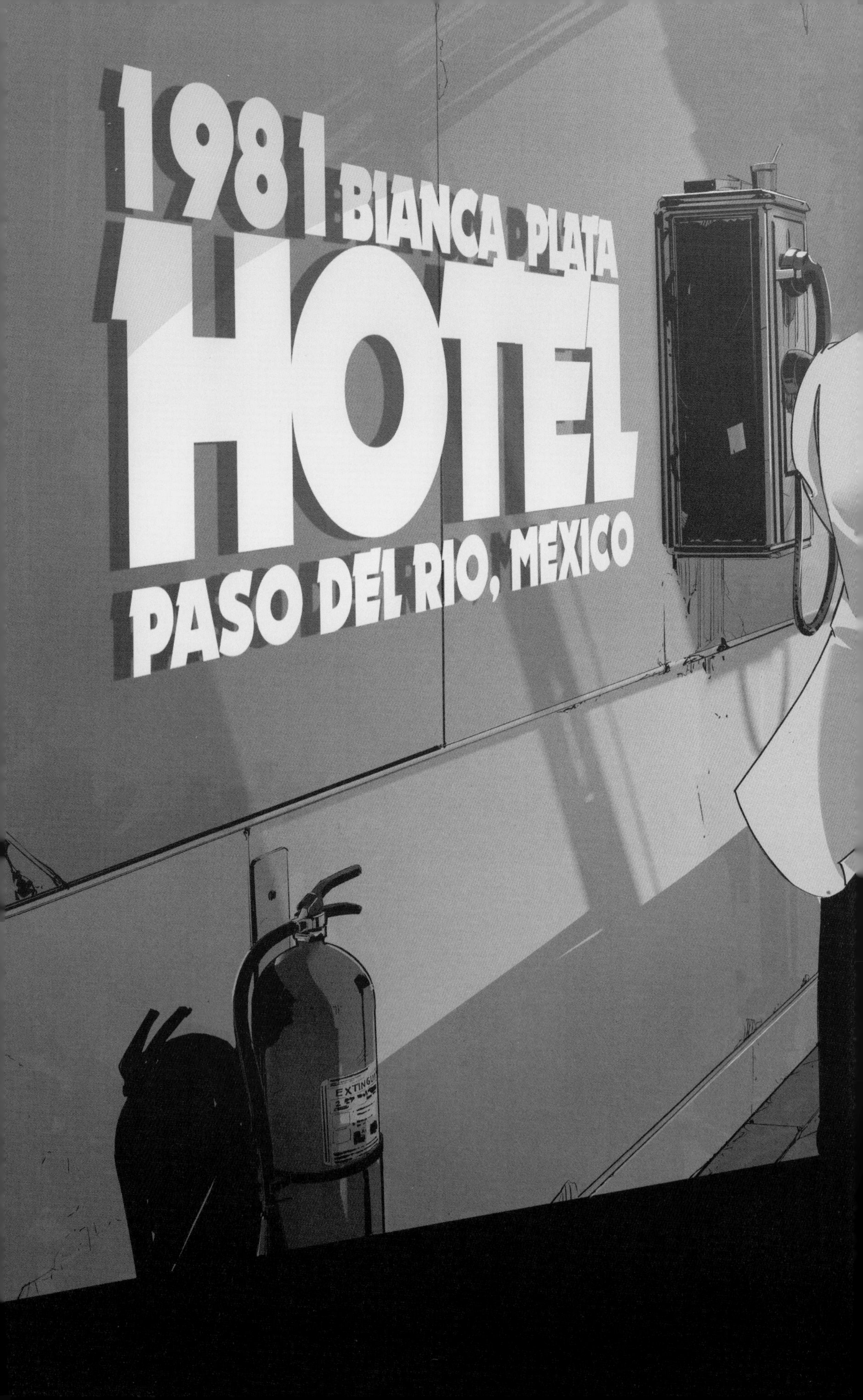
1981
BIANCA PLATA
HOTEL
PASO DEL RIO, MEXICO

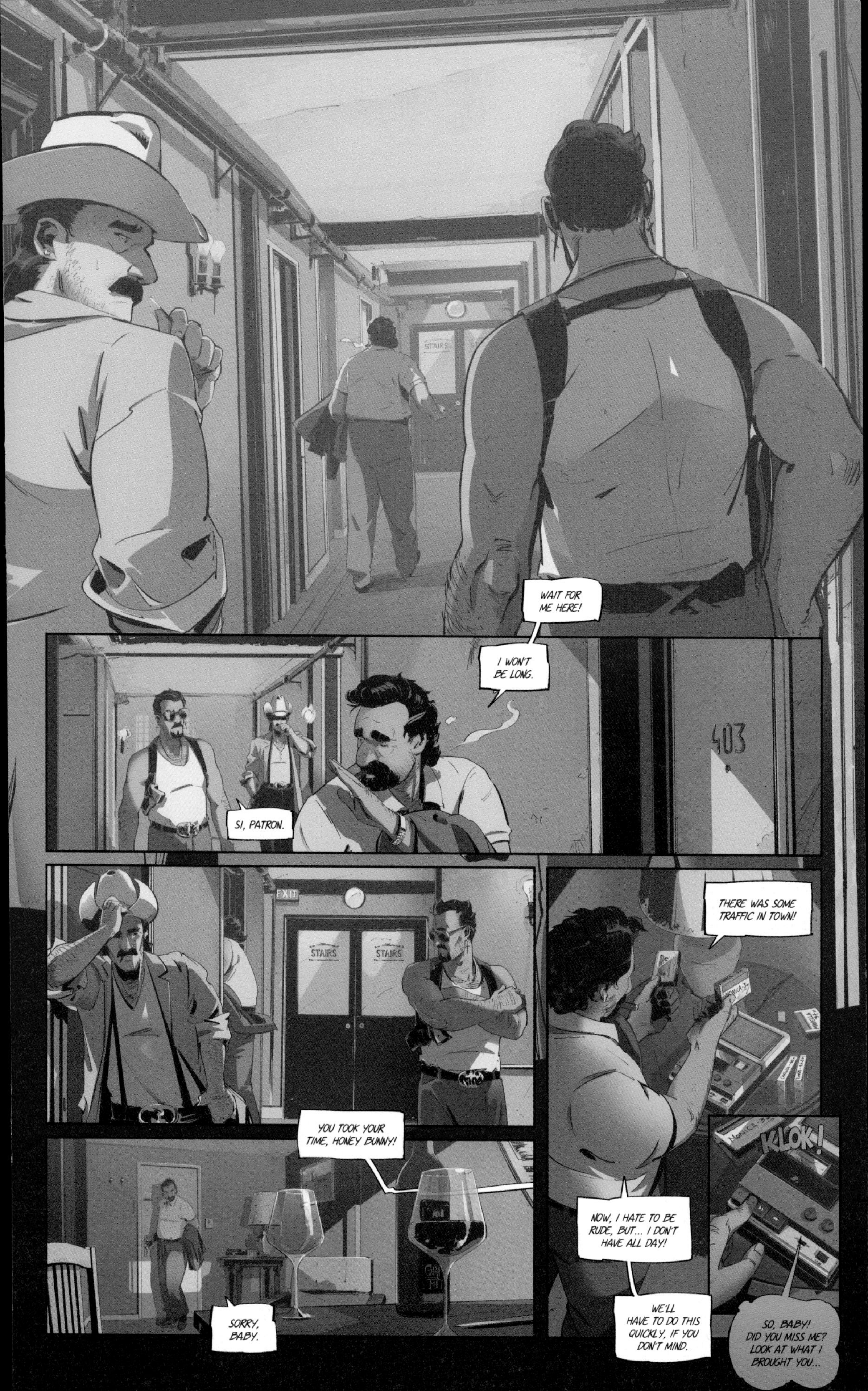
STAIRS
WAIT FOR ME HERE!
I WON'T BE LONG.
403
SI, PATRON.
EXIT
STAIRS
STAIRS
THERE WAS SOME TRAFFIC IN TOWN!
YOU TOOK YOUR TIME, HONEY BUNNY!
SORRY, BABY.
NOW, I HATE TO BE RUDE, BUT... I DON'T HAVE ALL DAY!
WE'LL HAVE TO DO THIS QUICKLY, IF YOU DON'T MIND.
KLOK!
SO, BABY! DID YOU MISS ME? LOOK AT WHAT I BROUGHT YOU...

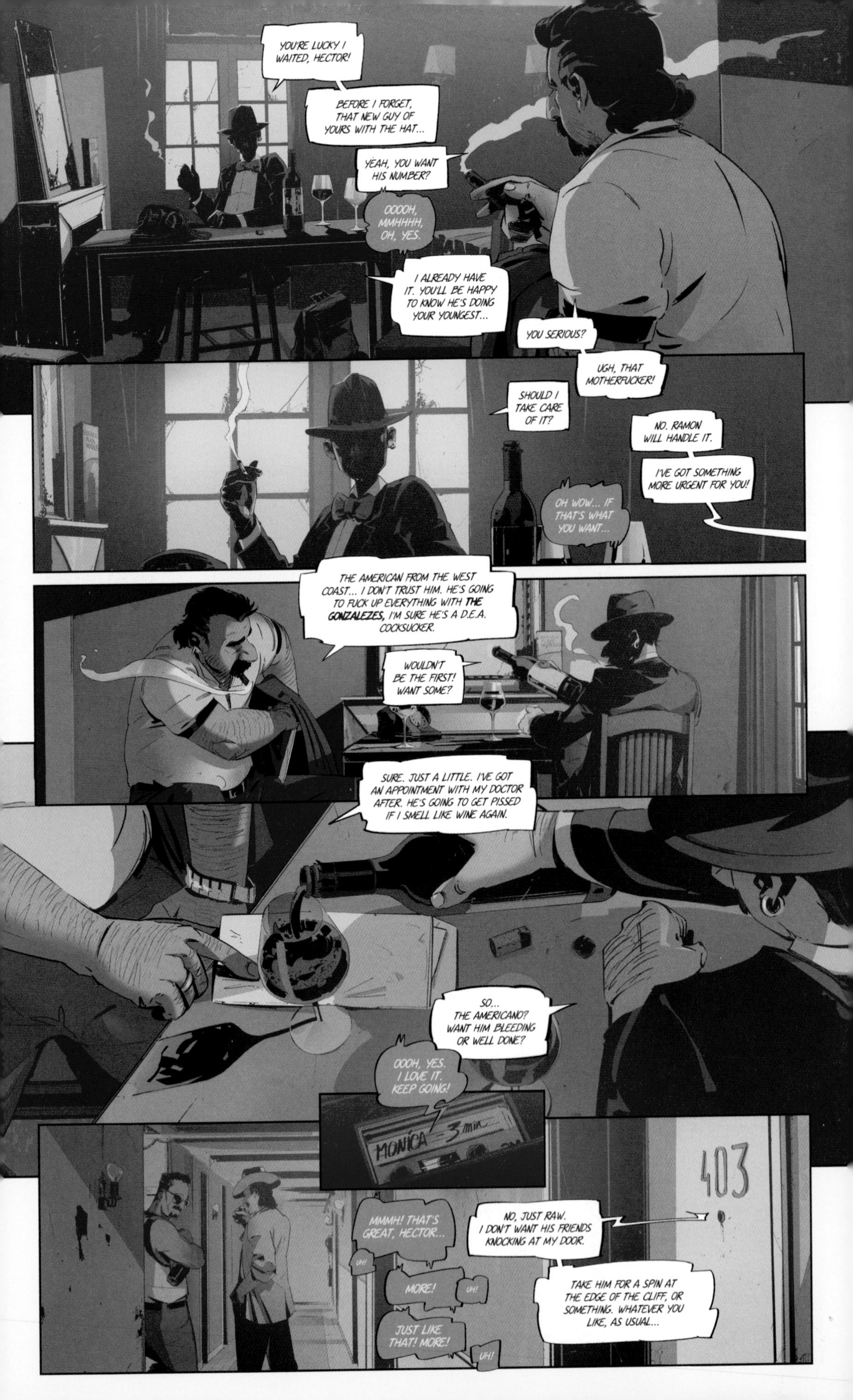
YOU'RE LUCKY I WAITED, HECTOR!
BEFORE I FORGET, THAT NEW GUY OF YOURS WITH THE HAT...
YEAH, YOU WANT HIS NUMBER?
OOOOH, MMHHHH, OH, YES.
I ALREADY HAVE IT. YOU'LL BE HAPPY TO KNOW HE'S DOING YOUR YOUNGEST...
YOU SERIOUS?
UGH, THAT MOTHERFUCKER!
SHOULD I TAKE CARE OF IT?
NO. RAMON WILL HANDLE IT.
I'VE GOT SOMETHING MORE URGENT FOR YOU!
OH WOW... IF THAT'S WHAT YOU WANT...
THE AMERICAN FROM THE WEST COAST... I DON'T TRUST HIM. HE'S GOING TO FUCK UP EVERYTHING WITH **THE GONZALEZES,** I'M SURE HE'S A D.E.A. COCKSUCKER.
WOULDN'T BE THE FIRST! WANT SOME?
SURE. JUST A LITTLE. I'VE GOT AN APPOINTMENT WITH MY DOCTOR AFTER. HE'S GOING TO GET PISSED IF I SMELL LIKE WINE AGAIN.
SO... THE AMERICANO? WANT HIM BLEEDING OR WELL DONE?
OOOH, YES. I LOVE IT. KEEP GOING!
MONICA 3 min
403
MMMH! THAT'S GREAT, HECTOR...
UH!
MORE!
UH!
JUST LIKE THAT! MORE!
UH!
NO, JUST RAW. I DON'T WANT HIS FRIENDS KNOCKING AT MY DOOR.
TAKE HIM FOR A SPIN AT THE EDGE OF THE CLIFF, OR SOMETHING. WHATEVER YOU LIKE, AS USUAL...

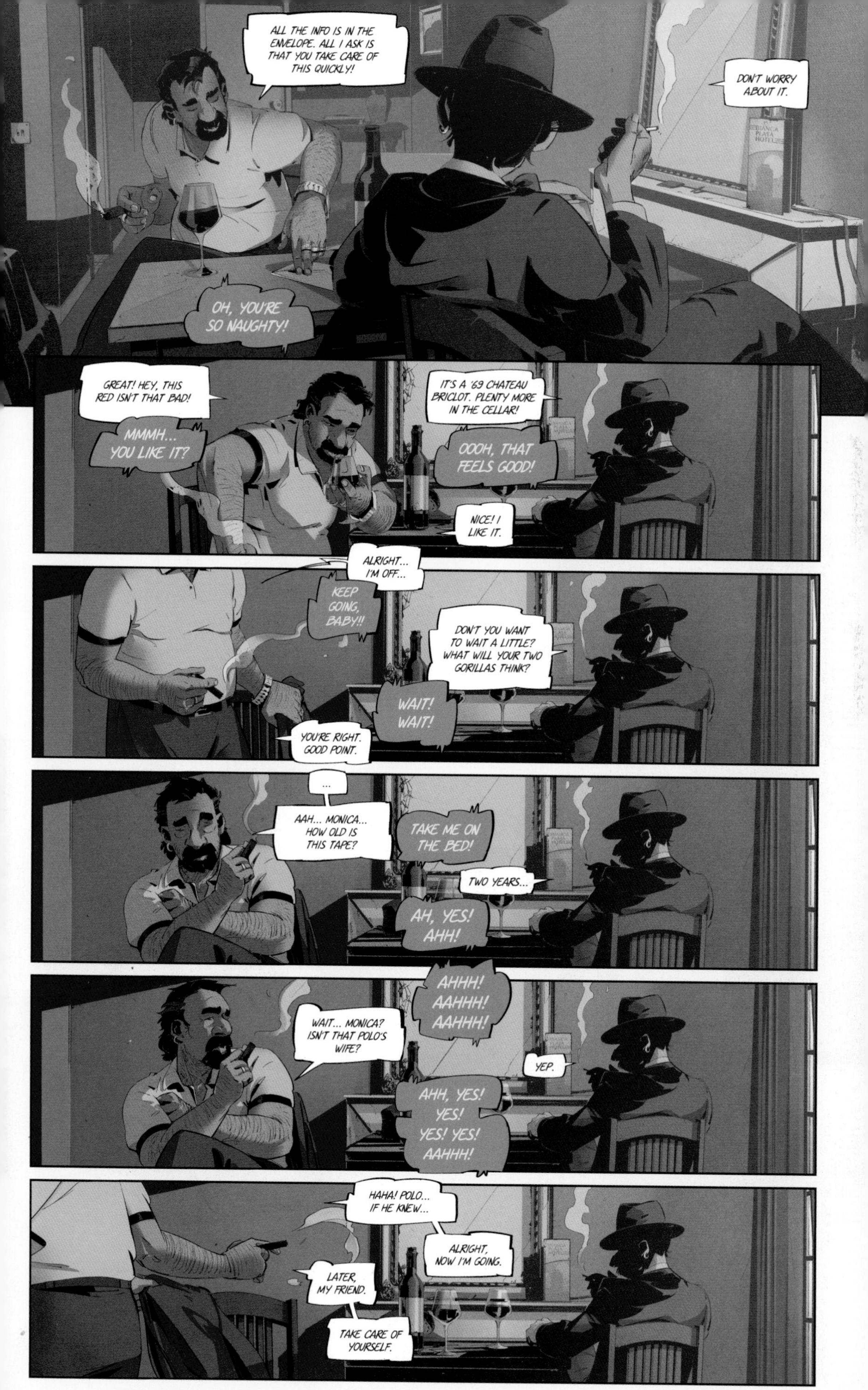

ALL THE INFO IS IN THE ENVELOPE. ALL I ASK IS THAT YOU TAKE CARE OF THIS QUICKLY!
DON'T WORRY ABOUT IT.
OH, YOU'RE SO NAUGHTY!
GREAT! HEY, THIS RED ISN'T THAT BAD!
MMMH... YOU LIKE IT?
IT'S A '69 CHATEAU BRICLOT. PLENTY MORE IN THE CELLAR!
OOOH, THAT FEELS GOOD!
NICE! I LIKE IT.
ALRIGHT... I'M OFF...
KEEP GOING, BABY!!
DON'T YOU WANT TO WAIT A LITTLE? WHAT WILL YOUR TWO GORILLAS THINK?
WAIT! WAIT!
YOU'RE RIGHT. GOOD POINT.
...
AAH... MONICA... HOW OLD IS THIS TAPE?
TAKE ME ON THE BED!
TWO YEARS...
AH, YES! AHH!
AHHH! AAHHH! AAHHH!
WAIT... MONICA? ISN'T THAT POLO'S WIFE?
YEP.
AHH, YES! YES! YES! YES! AAHHH!
HAHA! POLO... IF HE KNEW...
ALRIGHT, NOW I'M GOING.
LATER, MY FRIEND.
TAKE CARE OF YOURSELF.

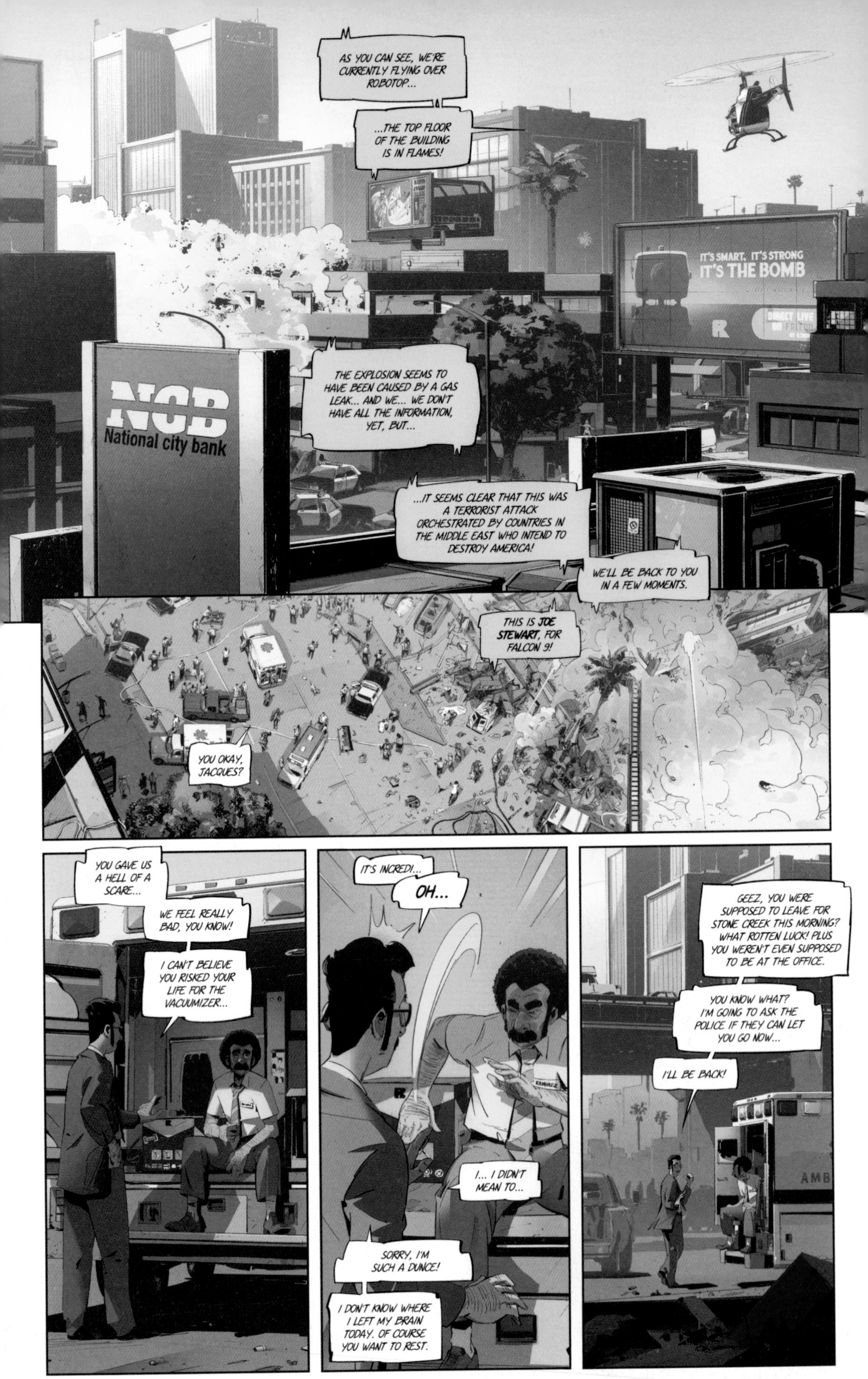
AS YOU CAN SEE, WE'RE CURRENTLY FLYING OVER ROBOTOP...
...THE TOP FLOOR OF THE BUILDING IS IN FLAMES!
IT'S SMART. IT'S STRONG
IT'S THE BOMB
NCB
National city bank
THE EXPLOSION SEEMS TO HAVE BEEN CAUSED BY A GAS LEAK... AND WE... WE DON'T HAVE ALL THE INFORMATION, YET, BUT...
...IT SEEMS CLEAR THAT THIS WAS A TERRORIST ATTACK ORCHESTRATED BY COUNTRIES IN THE MIDDLE EAST WHO INTEND TO DESTROY AMERICA!
WE'LL BE BACK TO YOU IN A FEW MOMENTS.
THIS IS JOE STEWART, FOR FALCON 9!
YOU OKAY, JACQUES?
YOU GAVE US A HELL OF A SCARE...
WE FEEL REALLY BAD, YOU KNOW!
I CAN'T BELIEVE YOU RISKED YOUR LIFE FOR THE VACUUMIZER...
IT'S INCREDI...
OH...
I... I DIDN'T MEAN TO...
SORRY, I'M SUCH A DUNCE!
I DON'T KNOW WHERE I LEFT MY BRAIN TODAY. OF COURSE YOU WANT TO REST.
GEEZ, YOU WERE SUPPOSED TO LEAVE FOR STONE CREEK THIS MORNING? WHAT ROTTEN LUCK! PLUS YOU WEREN'T EVEN SUPPOSED TO BE AT THE OFFICE.
YOU KNOW WHAT? I'M GOING TO ASK THE POLICE IF THEY CAN LET YOU GO NOW...
I'LL BE BACK!
AMB

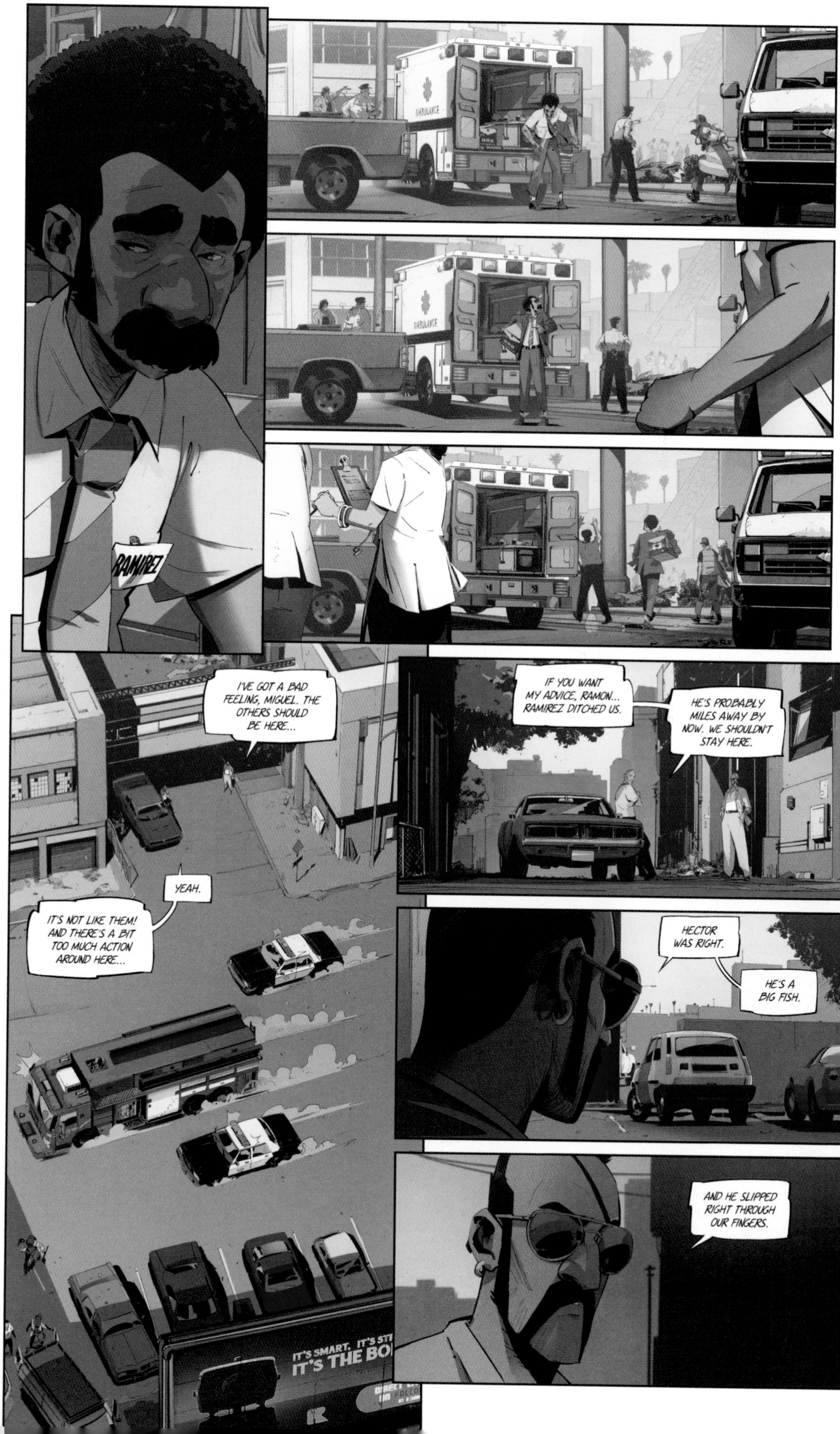
AMBULANCE
RAMIREZ
I'VE GOT A BAD FEELING, MIGUEL. THE OTHERS SHOULD BE HERE...
IT'S NOT LIKE THEM! AND THERE'S A BIT TOO MUCH ACTION AROUND HERE...
YEAH.
IT'S SMART.
IF YOU WANT MY ADVICE, RAMON... RAMIREZ DITCHED US.
HE'S PROBABLY MILES AWAY BY NOW. WE SHOULDN'T STAY HERE.
HECTOR WAS RIGHT.
HE'S A BIG FISH.
AND HE SLIPPED RIGHT THROUGH OUR FINGERS.

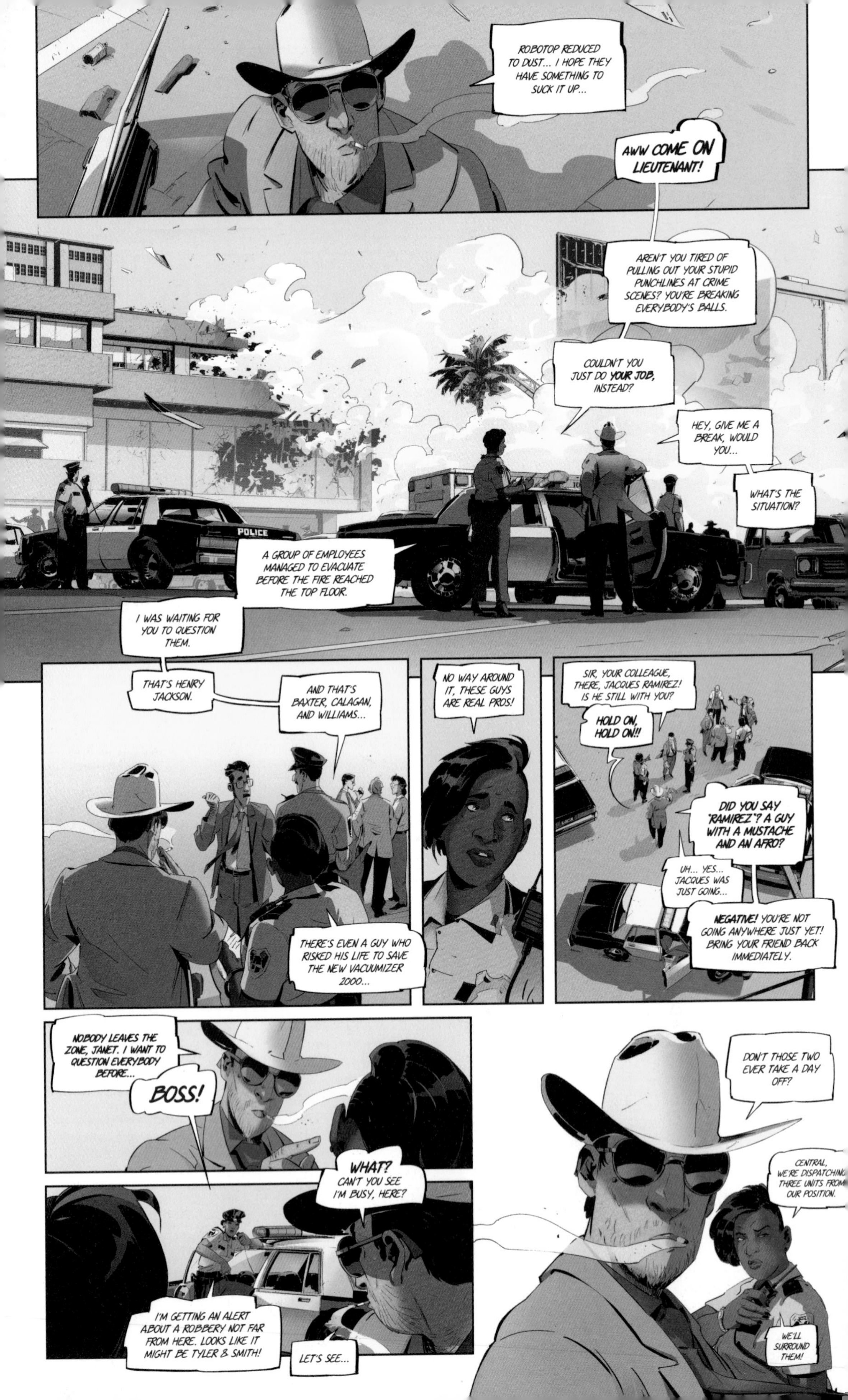
ROBOTOP REDUCED TO DUST... I HOPE THEY HAVE SOMETHING TO SUCK IT UP...
AWW COME ON LIEUTENANT!
AREN'T YOU TIRED OF PULLING OUT YOUR STUPID PUNCHLINES AT CRIME SCENES? YOU'RE BREAKING EVERYBODY'S BALLS.
COULDN'T YOU JUST DO YOUR JOB, INSTEAD?
HEY, GIVE ME A BREAK, WOULD YOU...
WHAT'S THE SITUATION?
POLICE
A GROUP OF EMPLOYEES MANAGED TO EVACUATE BEFORE THE FIRE REACHED THE TOP FLOOR.
I WAS WAITING FOR YOU TO QUESTION THEM.
THAT'S HENRY JACKSON.
AND THAT'S BAXTER, CALAGAN, AND WILLIAMS...
THERE'S EVEN A GUY WHO RISKED HIS LIFE TO SAVE THE NEW VACUUMIZER 2000...
NO WAY AROUND IT, THESE GUYS ARE REAL PROS!
SIR, YOUR COLLEAGUE, THERE, JACQUES RAMIREZ! IS HE STILL WITH YOU?
HOLD ON, HOLD ON!!
DID YOU SAY "RAMIREZ"? A GUY WITH A MUSTACHE AND AN AFRO?
UH... YES... JACQUES WAS JUST GOING...
NEGATIVE! YOU'RE NOT GOING ANYWHERE JUST YET! BRING YOUR FRIEND BACK IMMEDIATELY.
NOBODY LEAVES THE ZONE, JANET. I WANT TO QUESTION EVERYBODY BEFORE...
BOSS!
WHAT? CAN'T YOU SEE I'M BUSY, HERE?
I'M GETTING AN ALERT ABOUT A ROBBERY NOT FAR FROM HERE. LOOKS LIKE IT MIGHT BE TYLER & SMITH!
LET'S SEE...
DON'T THOSE TWO EVER TAKE A DAY OFF?
CENTRAL, WE'RE DISPATCHING THREE UNITS FROM OUR POSITION.
WE'LL SURROUND THEM!

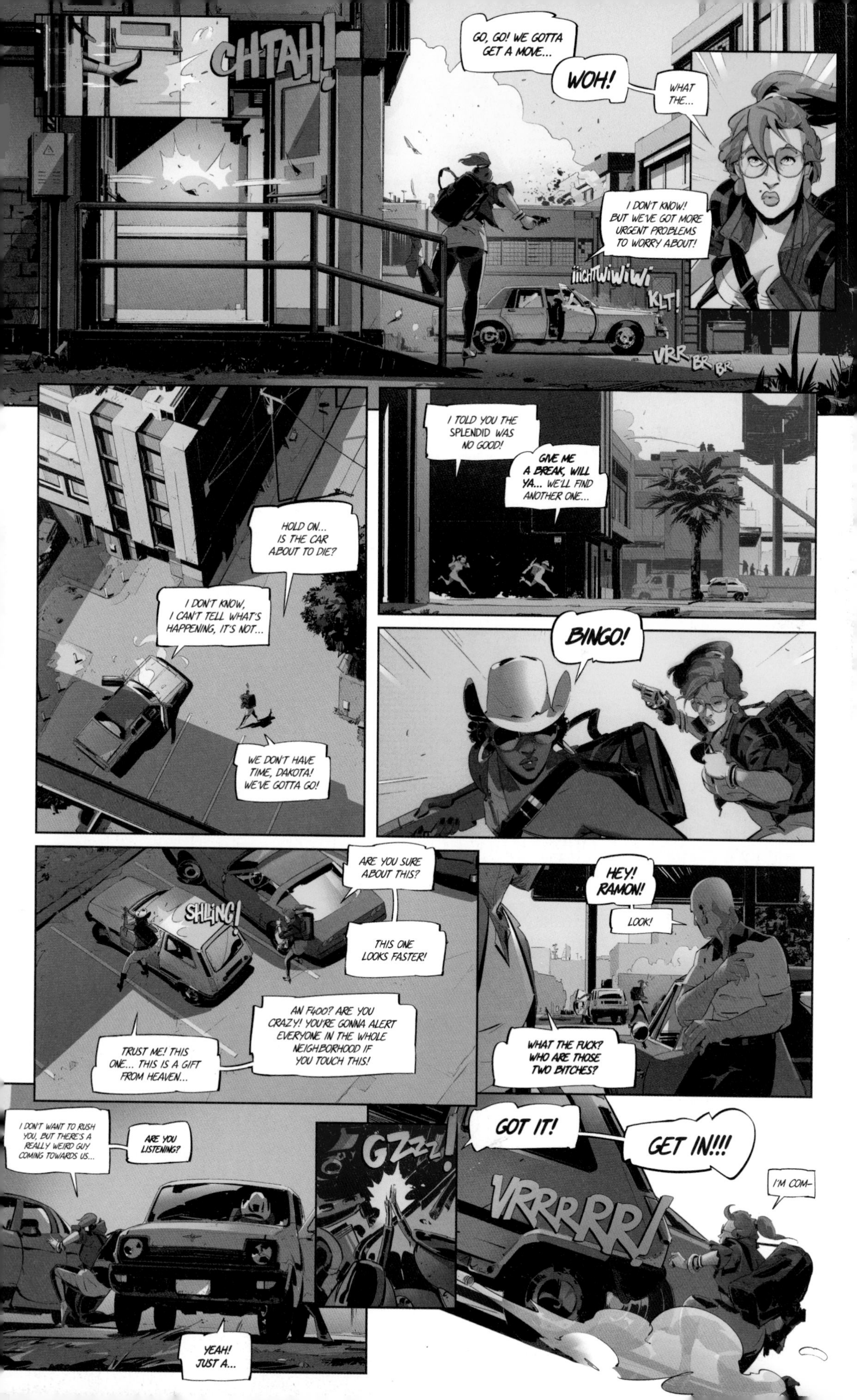
CHTAH!
GO, GO! WE GOTTA GET A MOVE...
WOH!
WHAT THE...
I DON'T KNOW! BUT WE'VE GOT MORE URGENT PROBLEMS TO WORRY ABOUT!
IIICHTWIWIWI
KLT!
VRR BR BR
HOLD ON... IS THE CAR ABOUT TO DIE?
I DON'T KNOW, I CAN'T TELL WHAT'S HAPPENING, IT'S NOT...
WE DON'T HAVE TIME, DAKOTA! WE'VE GOTTA GO!
I TOLD YOU THE SPLENDID WAS NO GOOD!
GIVE ME A BREAK, WILL YA... WE'LL FIND ANOTHER ONE...
BINGO!
ARE YOU SURE ABOUT THIS?
SHLING!
THIS ONE LOOKS FASTER!
AN F400? ARE YOU CRAZY! YOU'RE GONNA ALERT EVERYONE IN THE WHOLE NEIGHBORHOOD IF YOU TOUCH THIS!
TRUST ME! THIS ONE... THIS IS A GIFT FROM HEAVEN...
HEY! RAMON!
LOOK!
WHAT THE FUCK? WHO ARE THOSE TWO BITCHES?
I DON'T WANT TO RUSH YOU, BUT THERE'S A REALLY WEIRD GUY COMING TOWARDS US...
ARE YOU LISTENING?
YEAH! JUST A...
GZzz!
GOT IT!
GET IN!!!
VRRRRR!
I'M COM-

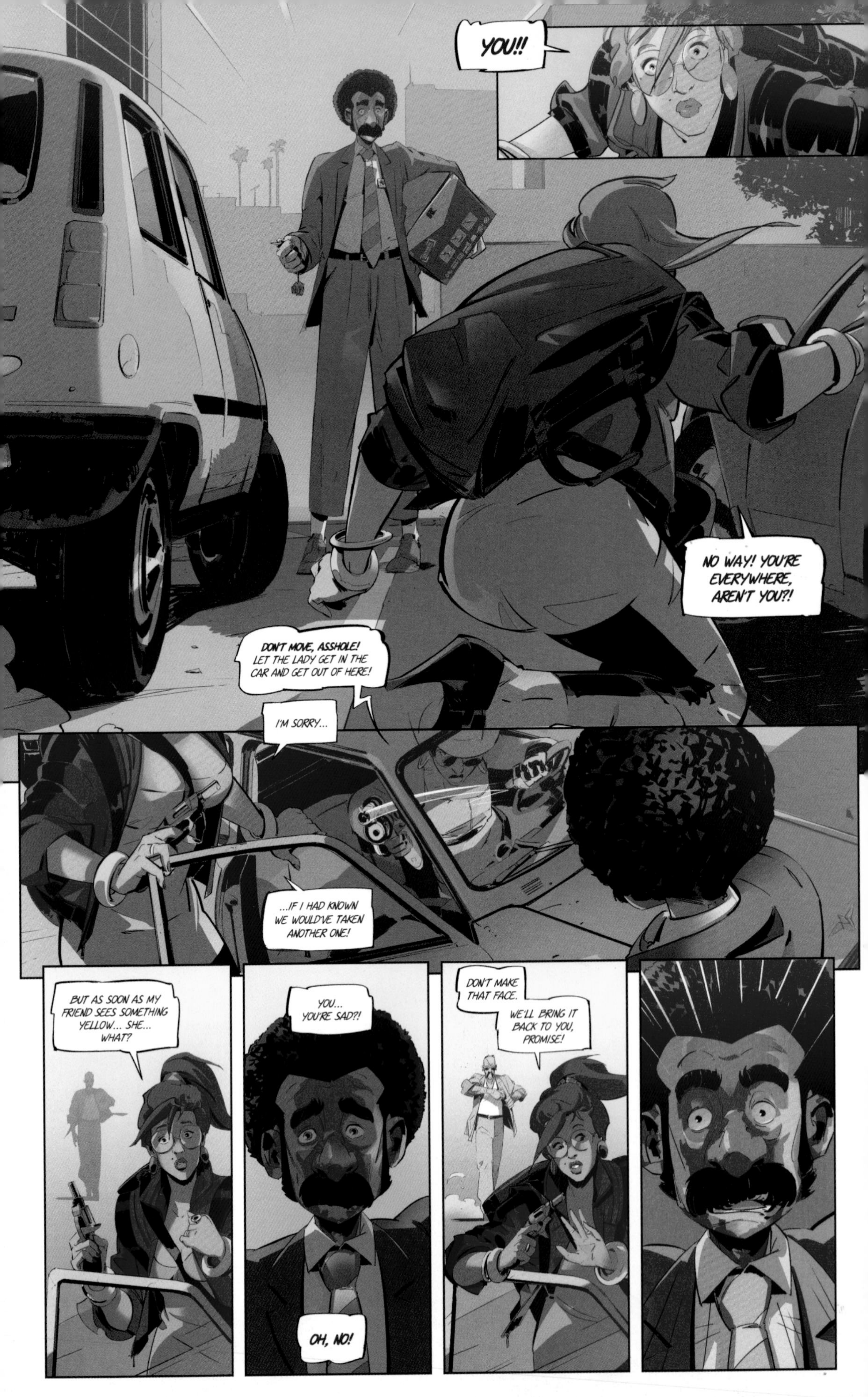
YOU!!
NO WAY! YOU'RE EVERYWHERE, AREN'T YOU?!
DON'T MOVE, ASSHOLE! LET THE LADY GET IN THE CAR AND GET OUT OF HERE!
I'M SORRY...
...IF I HAD KNOWN WE WOULD'VE TAKEN ANOTHER ONE!
BUT AS SOON AS MY FRIEND SEES SOMETHING YELLOW... SHE... WHAT?
YOU... YOU'RE SAD?!
OH, NO!
DON'T MAKE THAT FACE.
WE'LL BRING IT BACK TO YOU, PROMISE!

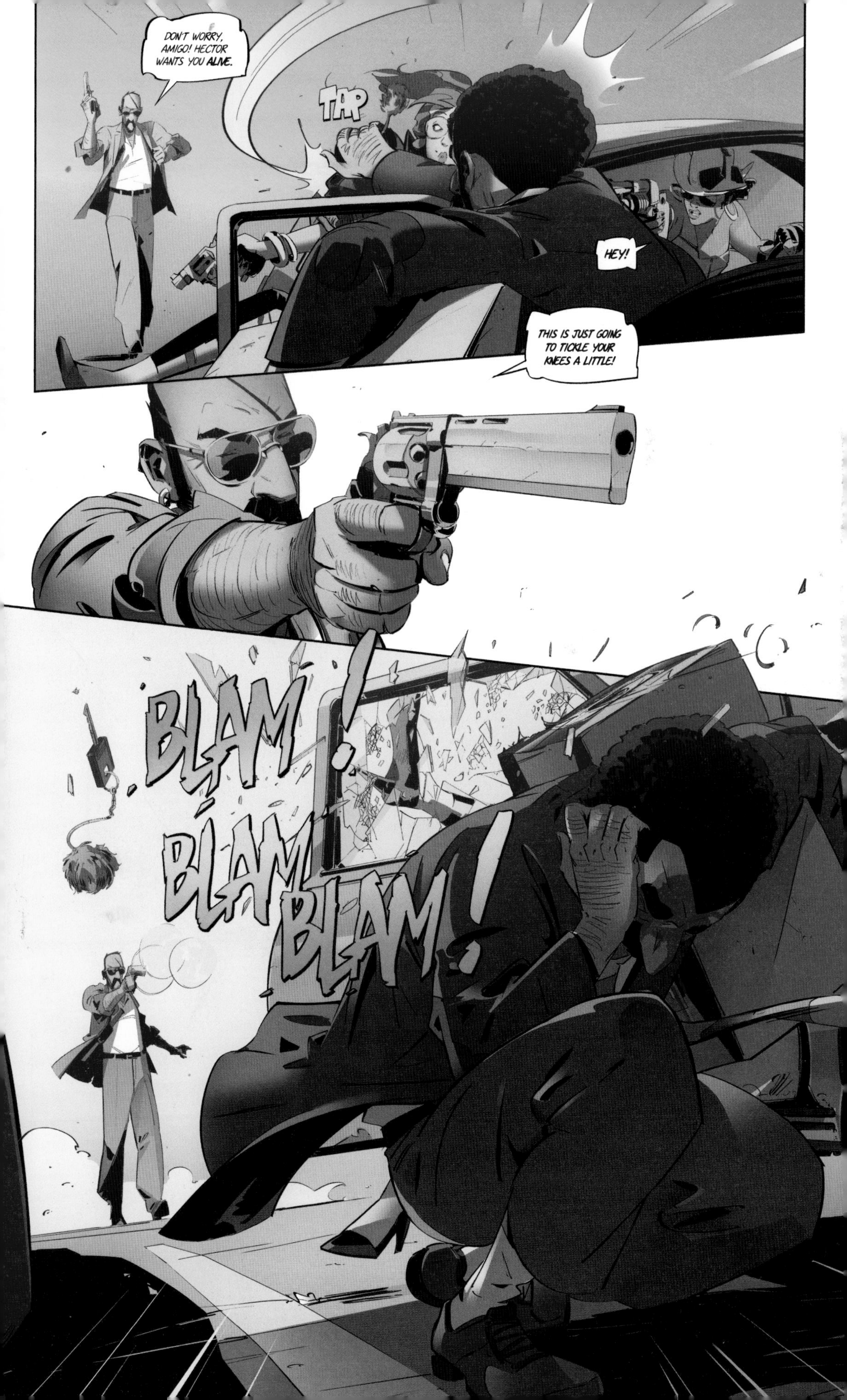
DON'T WORRY, AMIGO! HECTOR WANTS YOU ALIVE.
TAP
HEY!
THIS IS JUST GOING TO TICKLE YOUR KNEES A LITTLE!
BLAM! BLAM! BLAM!

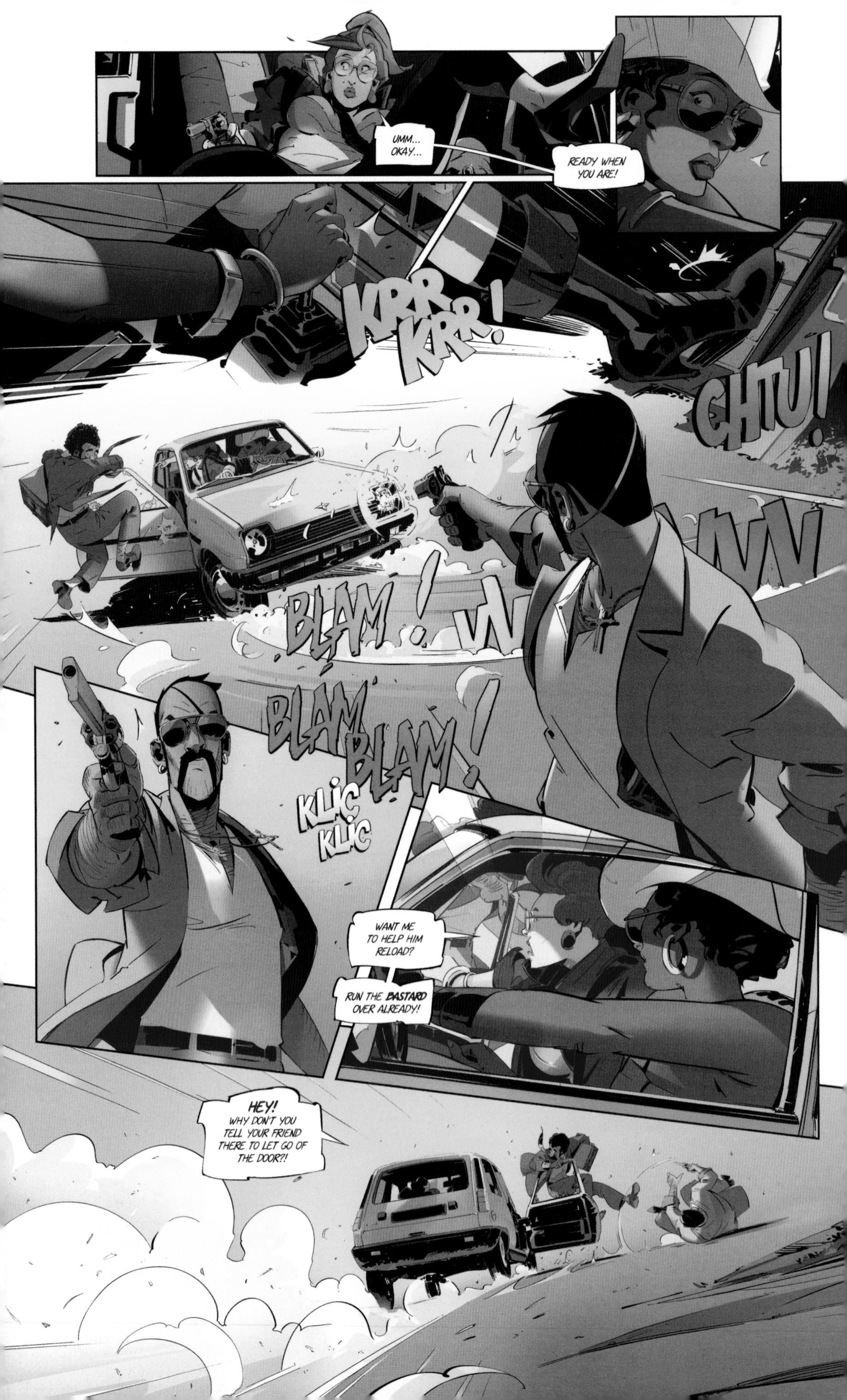
UMM... OKAY...
READY WHEN YOU ARE!
KRR KRR!
CHTU!
VVVVV
BLAM!
BLAM BLAM!
KLIC KLIC
WANT ME TO HELP HIM RELOAD?
RUN THE BASTARD OVER ALREADY!
HEY! WHY DON'T YOU TELL YOUR FRIEND THERE TO LET GO OF THE DOOR?!

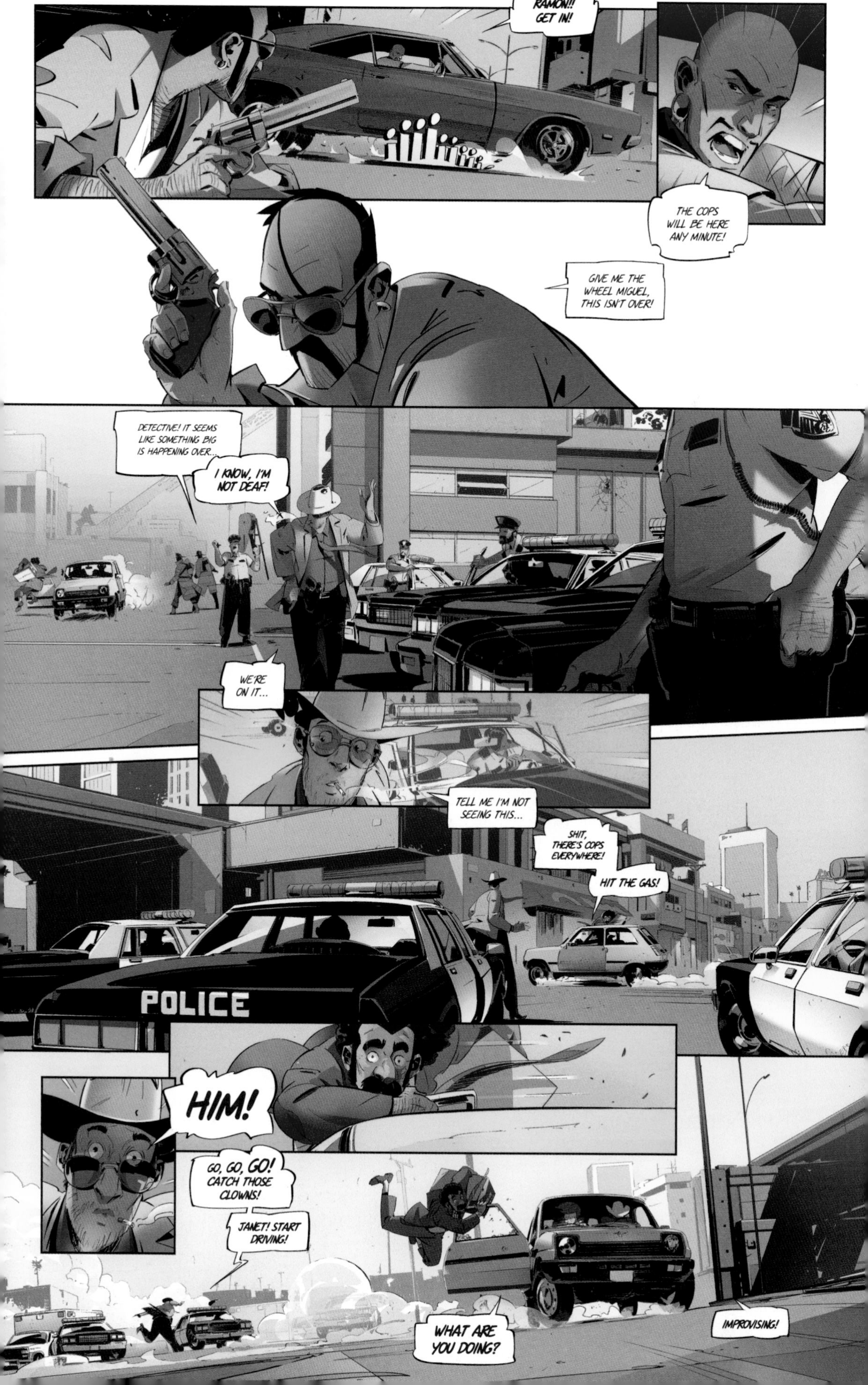
RAMON!! GET IN!
THE COPS WILL BE HERE ANY MINUTE!
GIVE ME THE WHEEL MIGUEL, THIS ISN'T OVER!
DETECTIVE! IT SEEMS LIKE SOMETHING BIG IS HAPPENING OVER...
I KNOW, I'M NOT DEAF!
WE'RE ON IT...
TELL ME I'M NOT SEEING THIS...
SHIT, THERE'S COPS EVERYWHERE!
HIT THE GAS!
POLICE
HIM!
GO, GO, GO! CATCH THOSE CLOWNS!
JANET! START DRIVING!
WHAT ARE YOU DOING?
IMPROVISING!

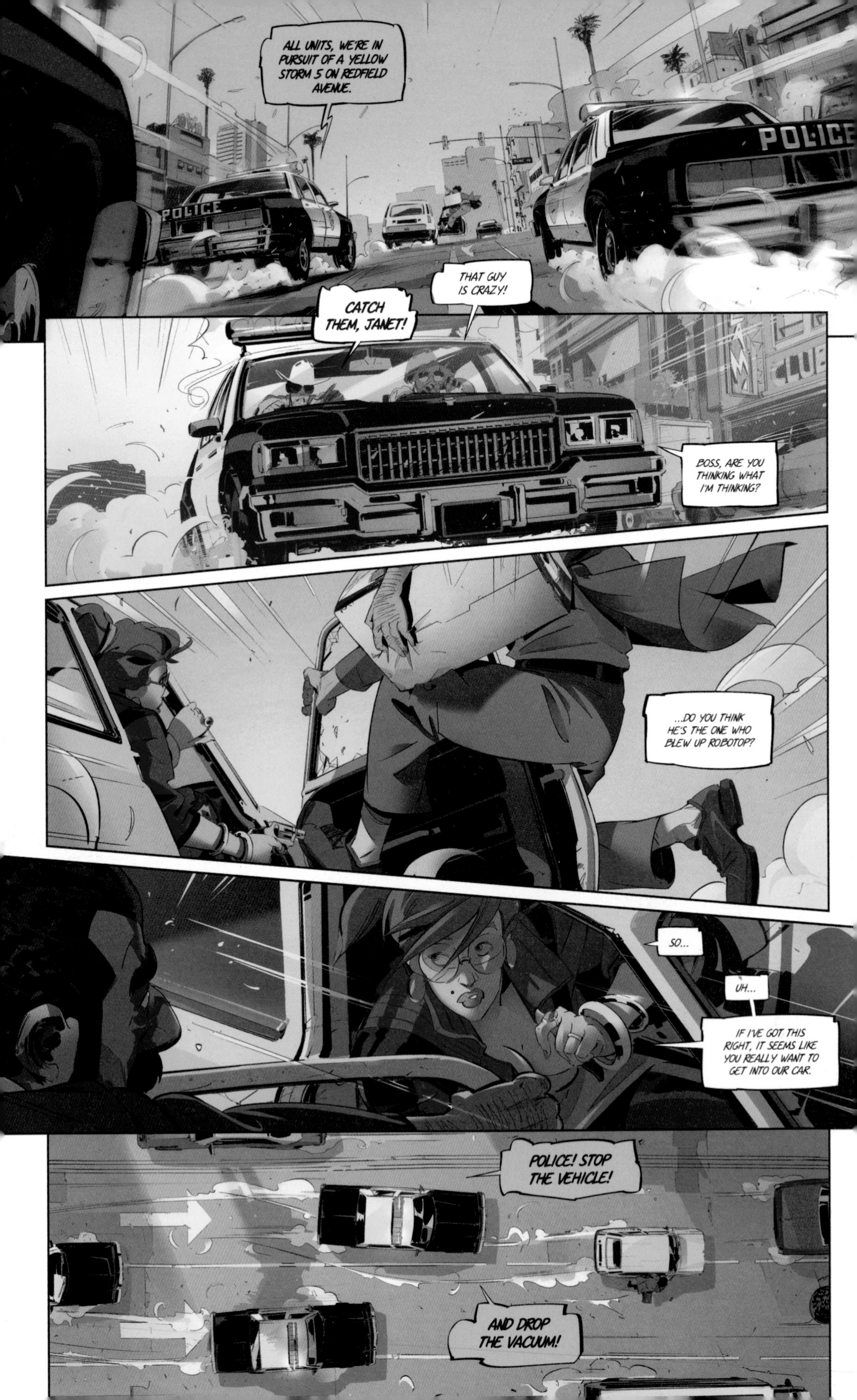

ALL UNITS, WE'RE IN PURSUIT OF A YELLOW STORM 5 ON REDFIELD AVENUE.
POLICE
POLICE
CATCH THEM, JANET!
THAT GUY IS CRAZY!
BOSS, ARE YOU THINKING WHAT I'M THINKING?
...DO YOU THINK HE'S THE ONE WHO BLEW UP ROBOTOP?
SO...
UH...
IF I'VE GOT THIS RIGHT, IT SEEMS LIKE YOU REALLY WANT TO GET INTO OUR CAR.
POLICE! STOP THE VEHICLE!
AND DROP THE VACUUM!

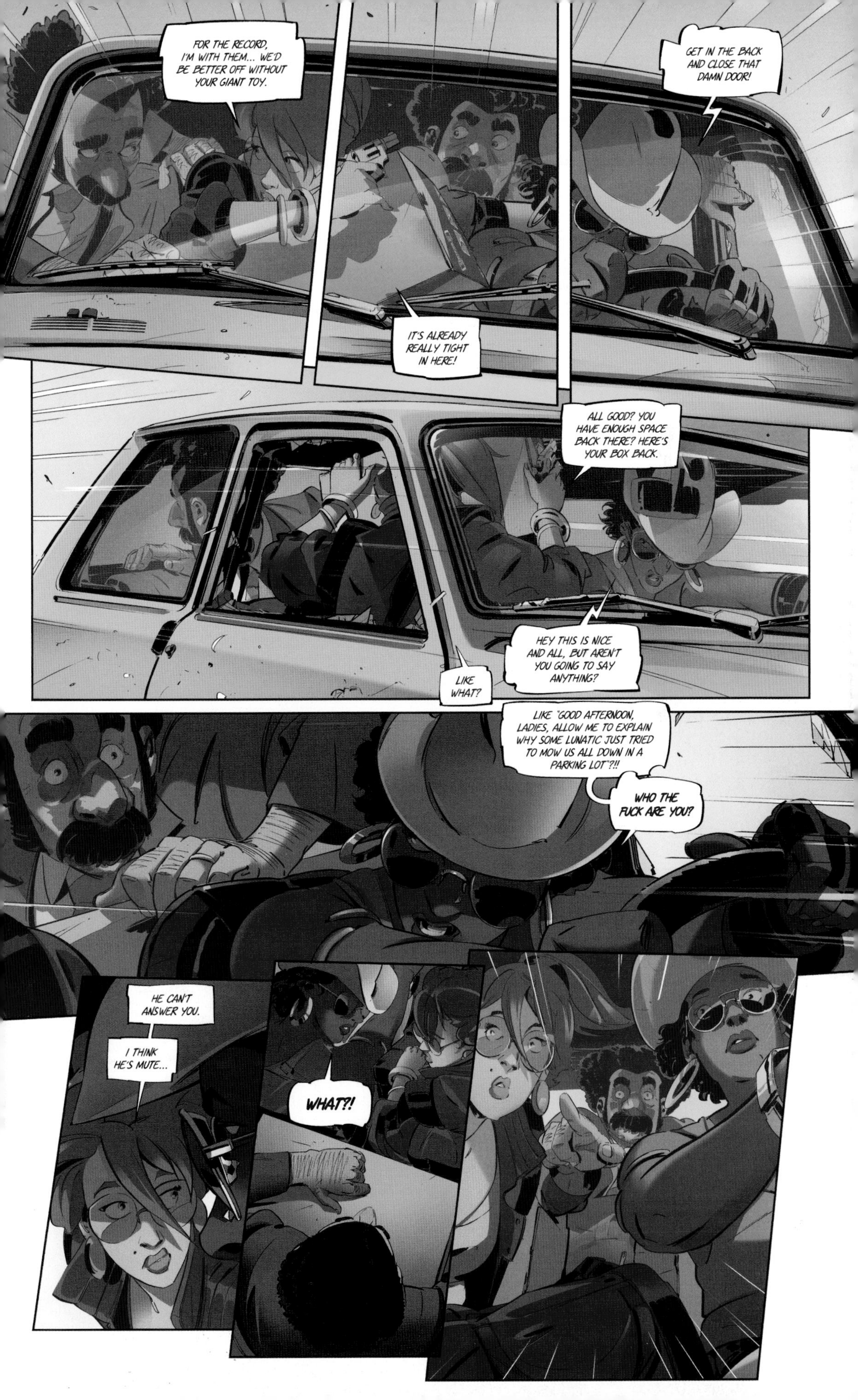
FOR THE RECORD, I'M WITH THEM... WE'D BE BETTER OFF WITHOUT YOUR GIANT TOY.
IT'S ALREADY REALLY TIGHT IN HERE!
GET IN THE BACK AND CLOSE THAT DAMN DOOR!
ALL GOOD? YOU HAVE ENOUGH SPACE BACK THERE? HERE'S YOUR BOX BACK.
HEY THIS IS NICE AND ALL, BUT AREN'T YOU GOING TO SAY ANYTHING?
LIKE WHAT?
LIKE "GOOD AFTERNOON, LADIES, ALLOW ME TO EXPLAIN WHY SOME LUNATIC JUST TRIED TO MOW US ALL DOWN IN A PARKING LOT"?!!
WHO THE FUCK ARE YOU?
HE CAN'T ANSWER YOU.
I THINK HE'S MUTE...
WHAT?!

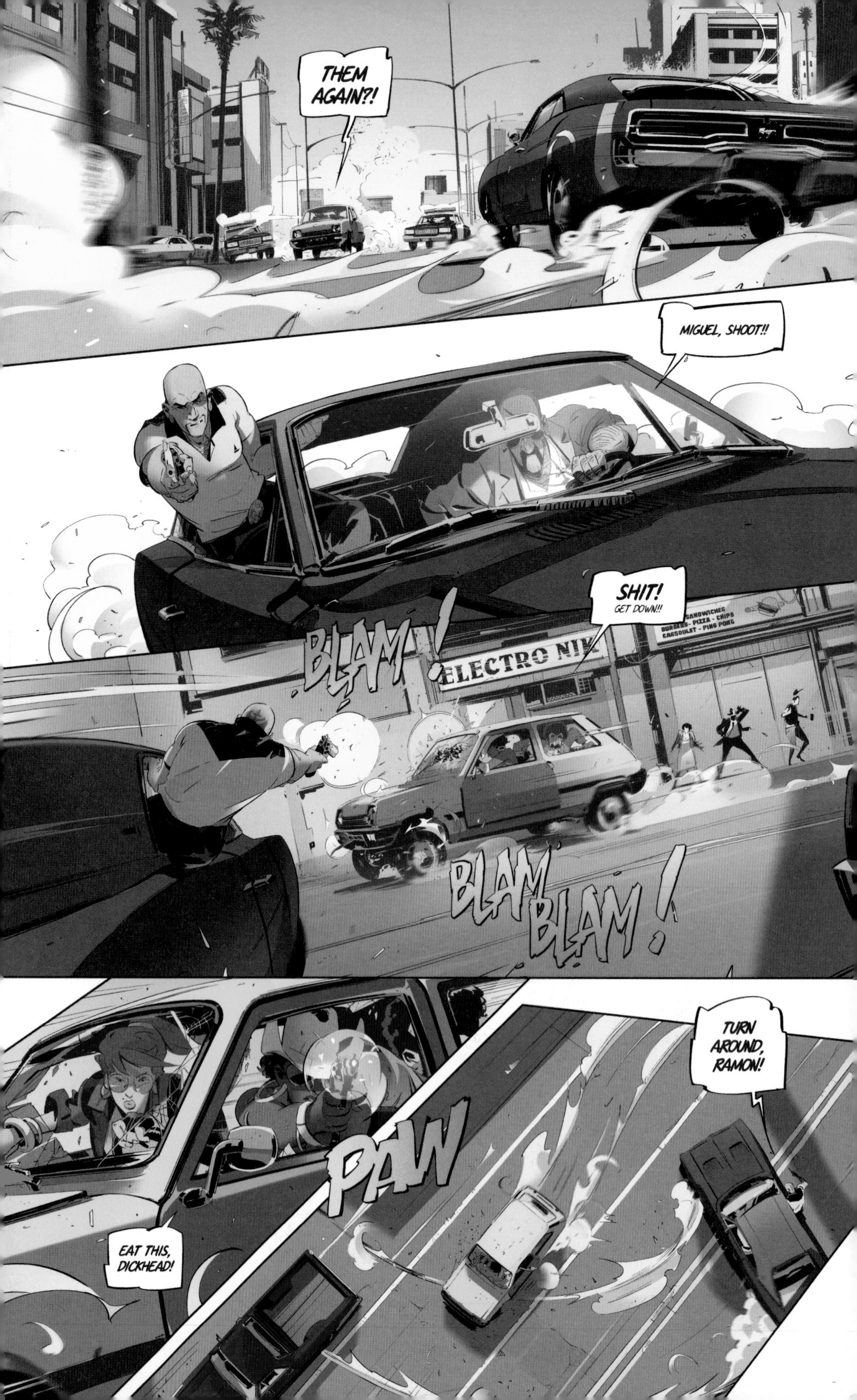
THEM AGAIN?!
MIGUEL, SHOOT!!
SHIT! GET DOWN!!
ELECTRO NIK
SANDWICHES BURGERS - PIZZA - CHIPS CASSOULET - PING PONG
BLAM!
BLAM BLAM!
TURN AROUND, RAMON!
PAW
EAT THIS, DICKHEAD!

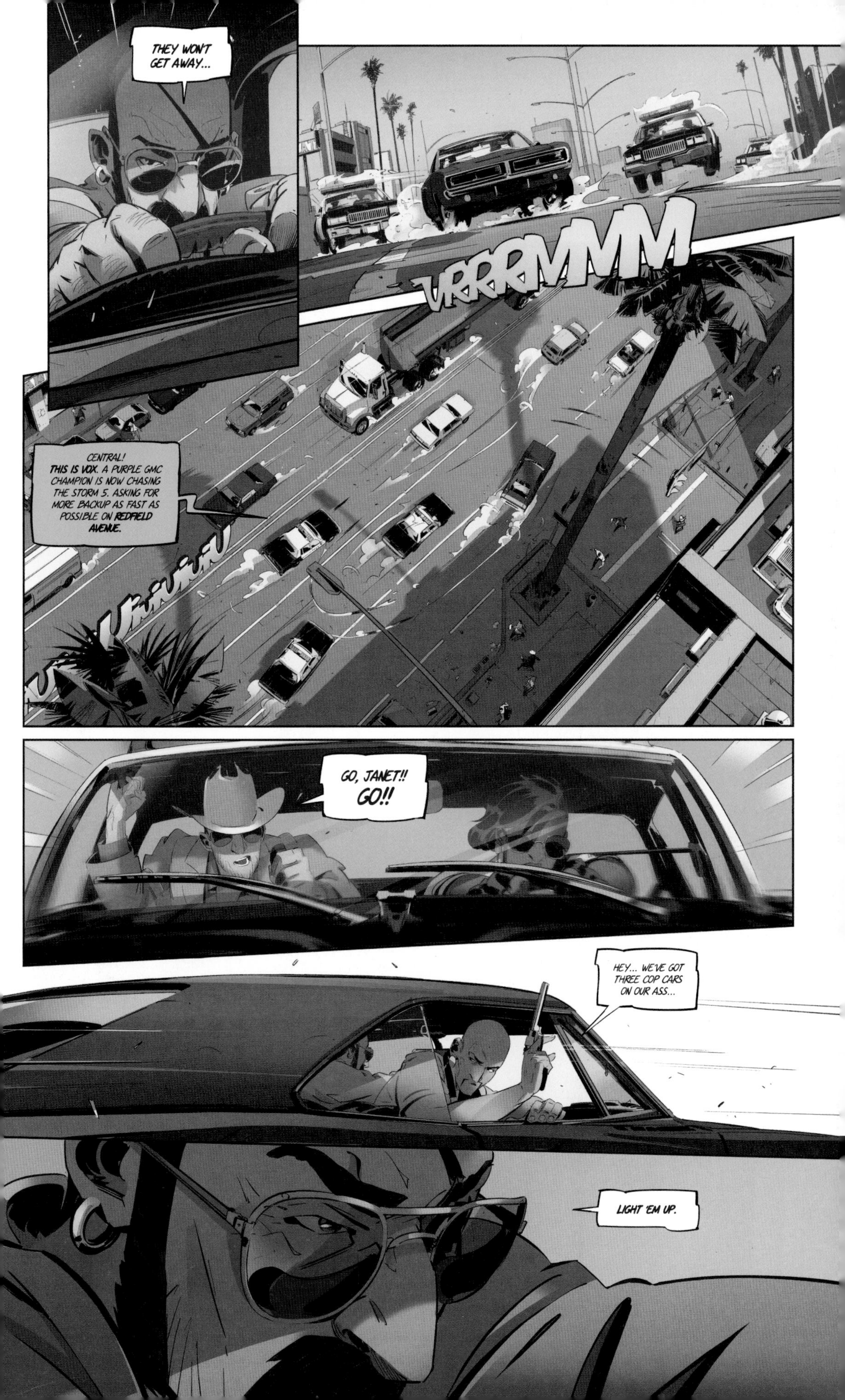
THEY WON'T GET AWAY...
VRRRMMM
CENTRAL!
THIS IS VOX. A PURPLE GMC CHAMPION IS NOW CHASING THE STORM 5. ASKING FOR MORE BACKUP AS FAST AS POSSIBLE ON REDFIELD AVENUE.
GO, JANET!! GO!!
HEY... WE'VE GOT THREE COP CARS ON OUR ASS...
LIGHT 'EM UP.

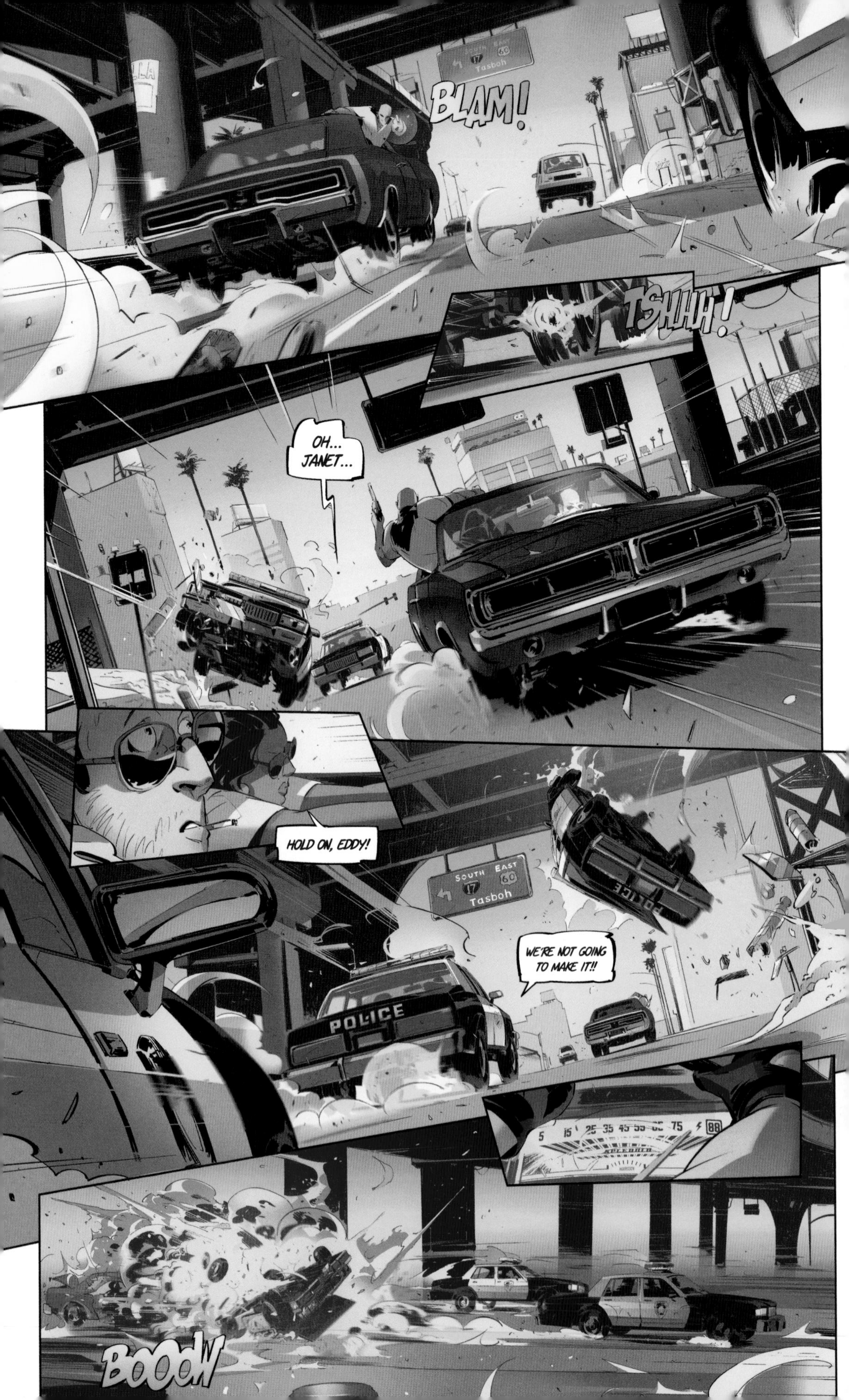
South East
17 60
Tasboh
BLAM!
TSHHHH!
OH... JANET...
HOLD ON, EDDY!
SOUTH EAST
17 60
Tasboh
WE'RE NOT GOING TO MAKE IT!!
POLICE
POLICE
5 15 25 35 45 55 65 75 88
BOOOOM

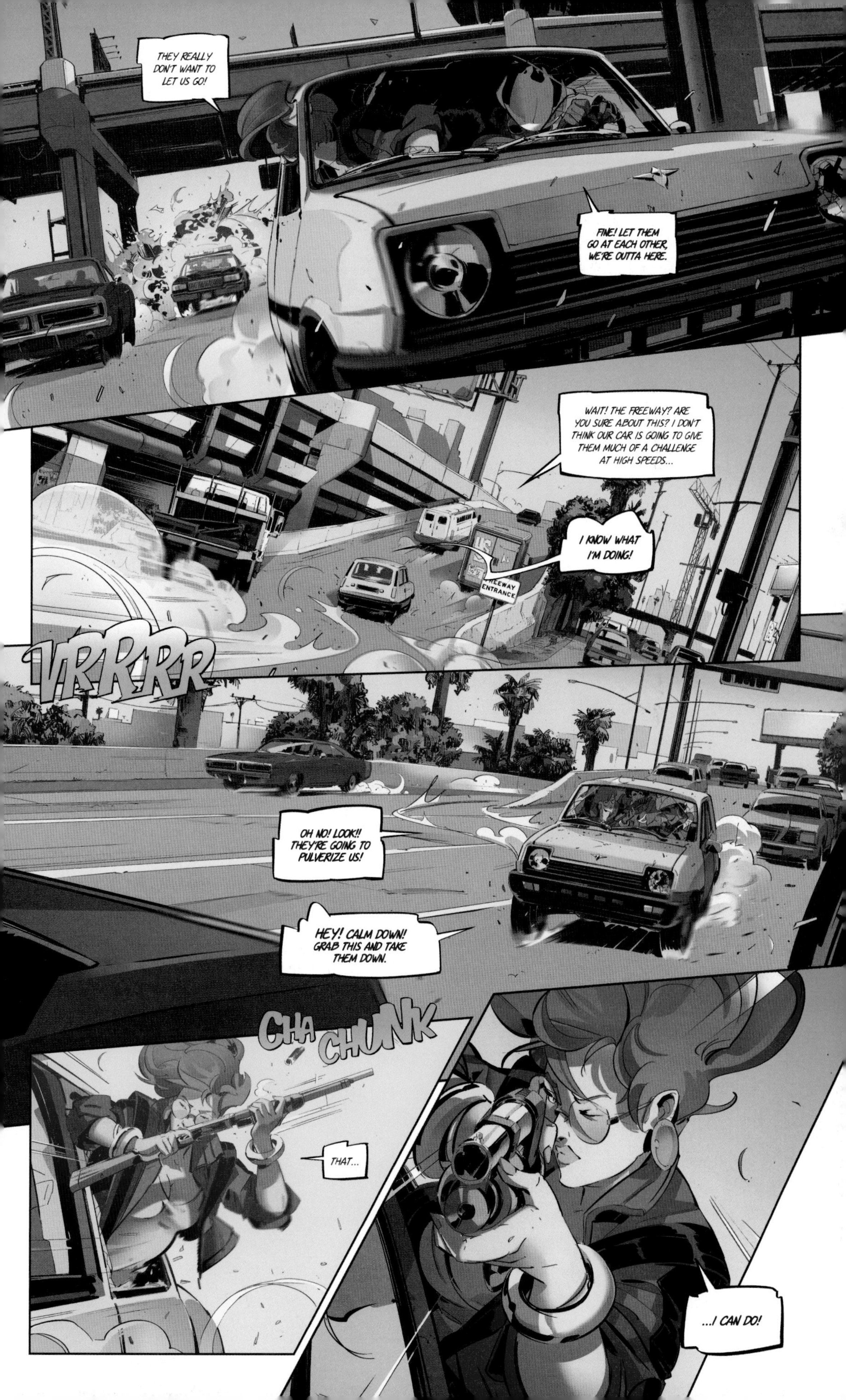
THEY REALLY DON'T WANT TO LET US GO!
FINE! LET THEM GO AT EACH OTHER, WE'RE OUTTA HERE.
WAIT! THE FREEWAY? ARE YOU SURE ABOUT THIS? I DON'T THINK OUR CAR IS GOING TO GIVE THEM MUCH OF A CHALLENGE AT HIGH SPEEDS...
I KNOW WHAT I'M DOING!
FREEWAY ENTRANCE
VRRRR
OH NO! LOOK!! THEY'RE GOING TO PULVERIZE US!
HEY! CALM DOWN! GRAB THIS AND TAKE THEM DOWN.
CHA CHUNK
THAT...
...I CAN DO!

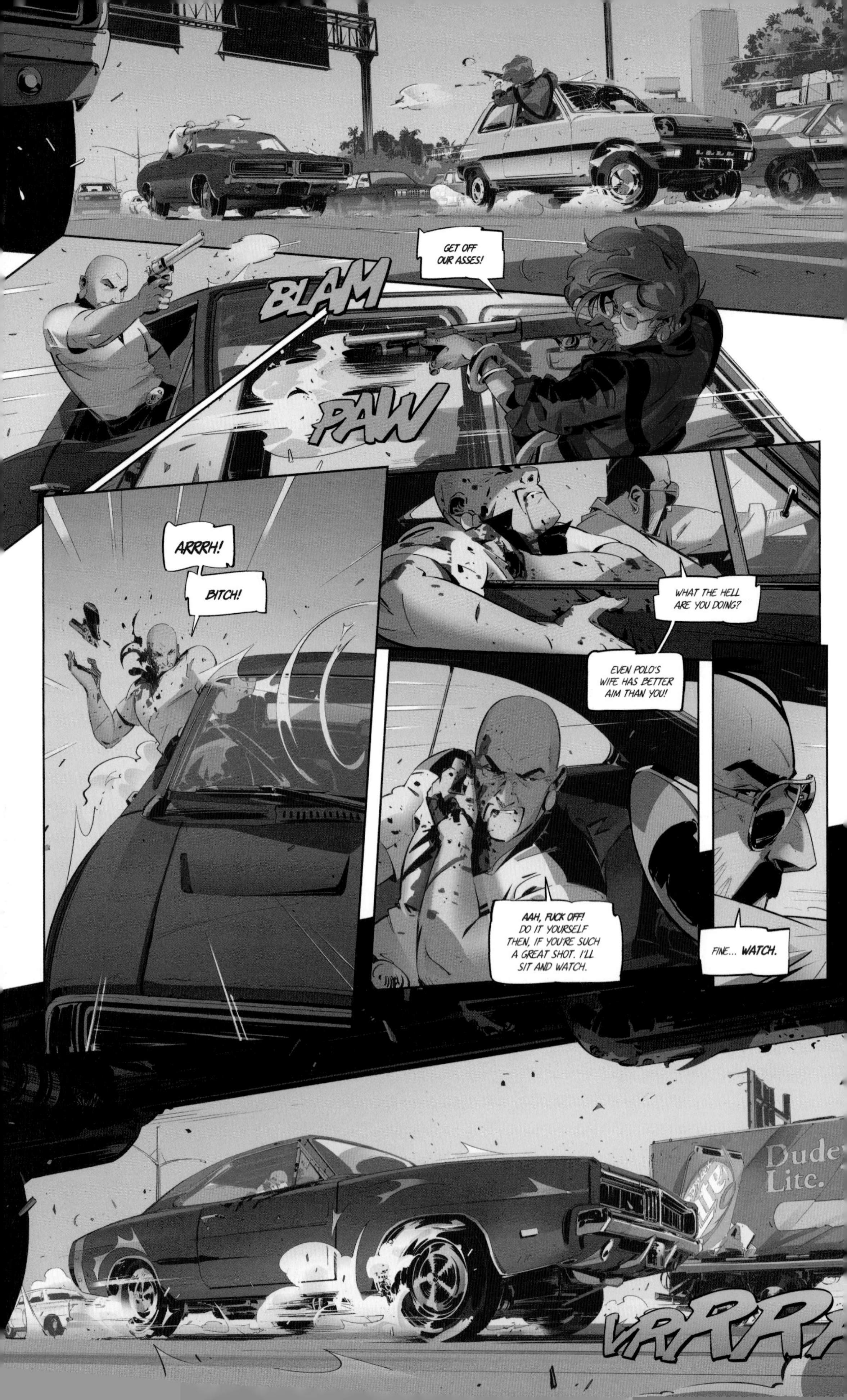
GET OFF OUR ASSES!
BLAM
PAW
ARRRH!
BITCH!
WHAT THE HELL ARE YOU DOING?
EVEN POLO'S WIFE HAS BETTER AIM THAN YOU!
AAH, FUCK OFF! DO IT YOURSELF THEN, IF YOU'RE SUCH A GREAT SHOT. I'LL SIT AND WATCH.
FINE... WATCH.
Dudey Lite.
VRRRR

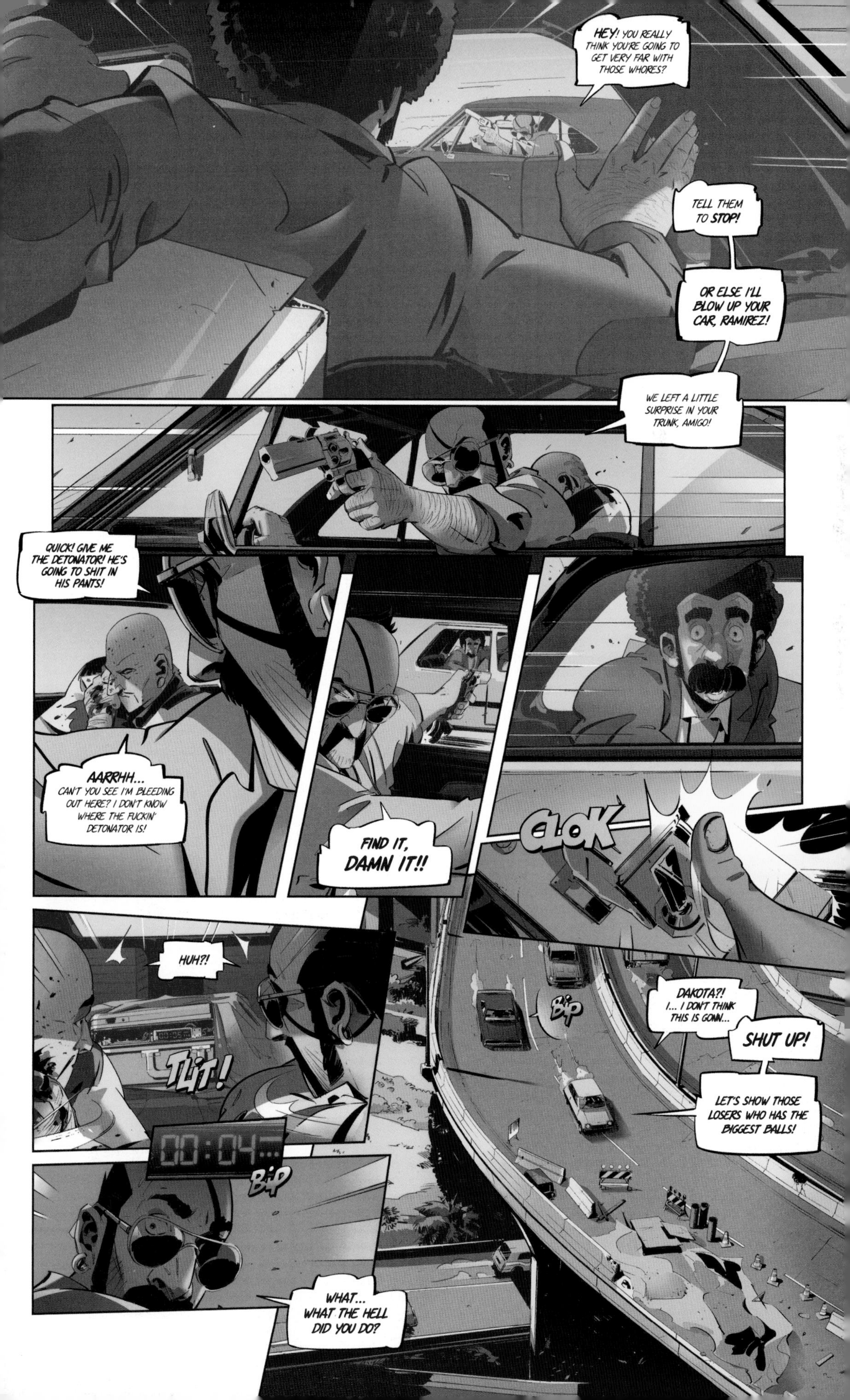
HEY! YOU REALLY THINK YOU'RE GOING TO GET VERY FAR WITH THOSE WHORES?
TELL THEM TO STOP!
OR ELSE I'LL BLOW UP YOUR CAR, RAMIREZ!
WE LEFT A LITTLE SURPRISE IN YOUR TRUNK, AMIGO!
QUICK! GIVE ME THE DETONATOR! HE'S GOING TO SHIT IN HIS PANTS!
AARRHH... CAN'T YOU SEE I'M BLEEDING OUT HERE? I DON'T KNOW WHERE THE FUCKIN' DETONATOR IS!
FIND IT, DAMN IT!!
CLOK
HUH?!
TUIT!
00:04
BIP
BIP
DAKOTA?! I... I DON'T THINK THIS IS GONN...
SHUT UP!
LET'S SHOW THOSE LOSERS WHO HAS THE BIGGEST BALLS!
WHAT... WHAT THE HELL DID YOU DO?

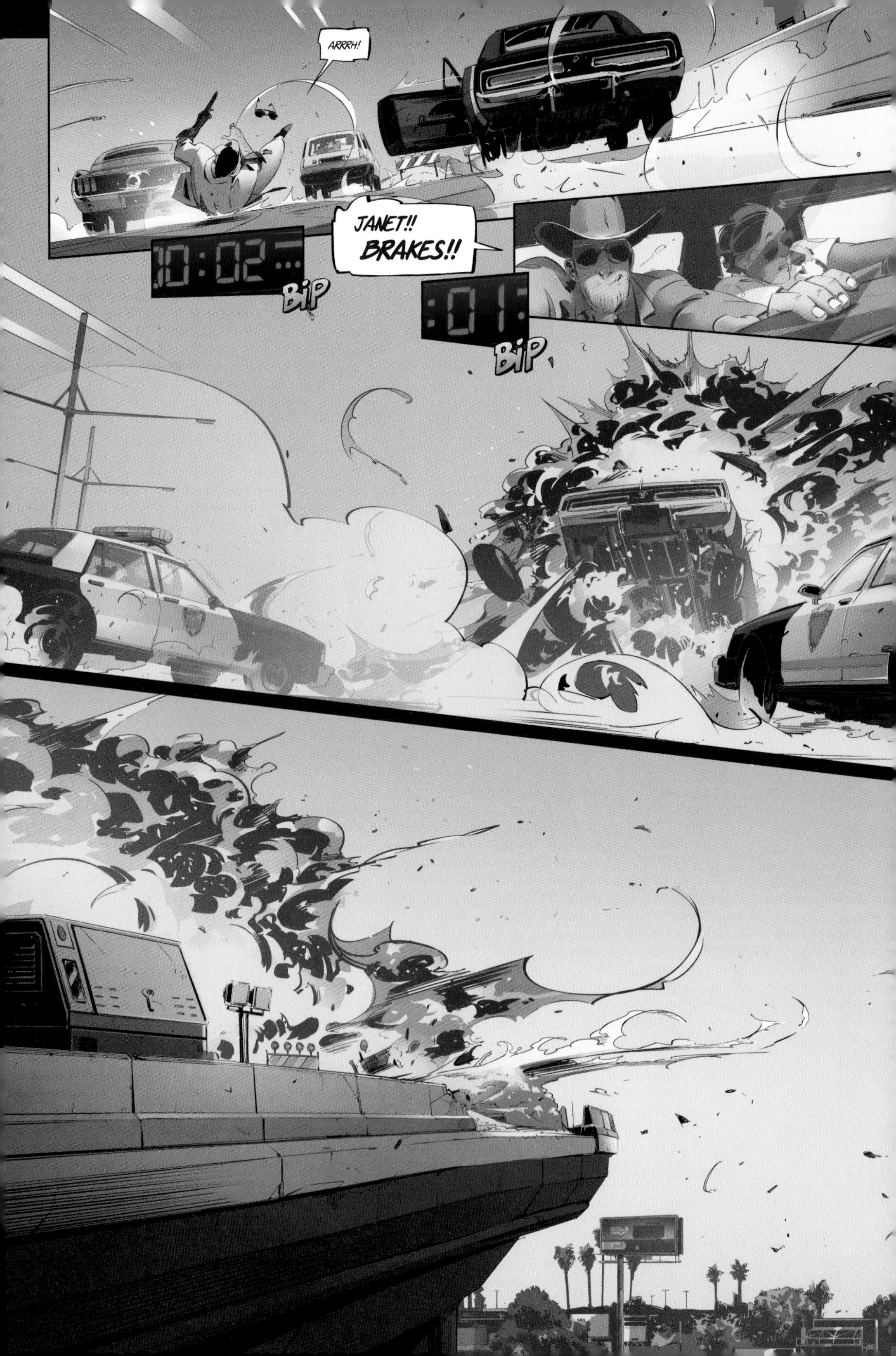
ARRRH!
10:02
BIP
JANET!! BRAKES!!
:01
BIP

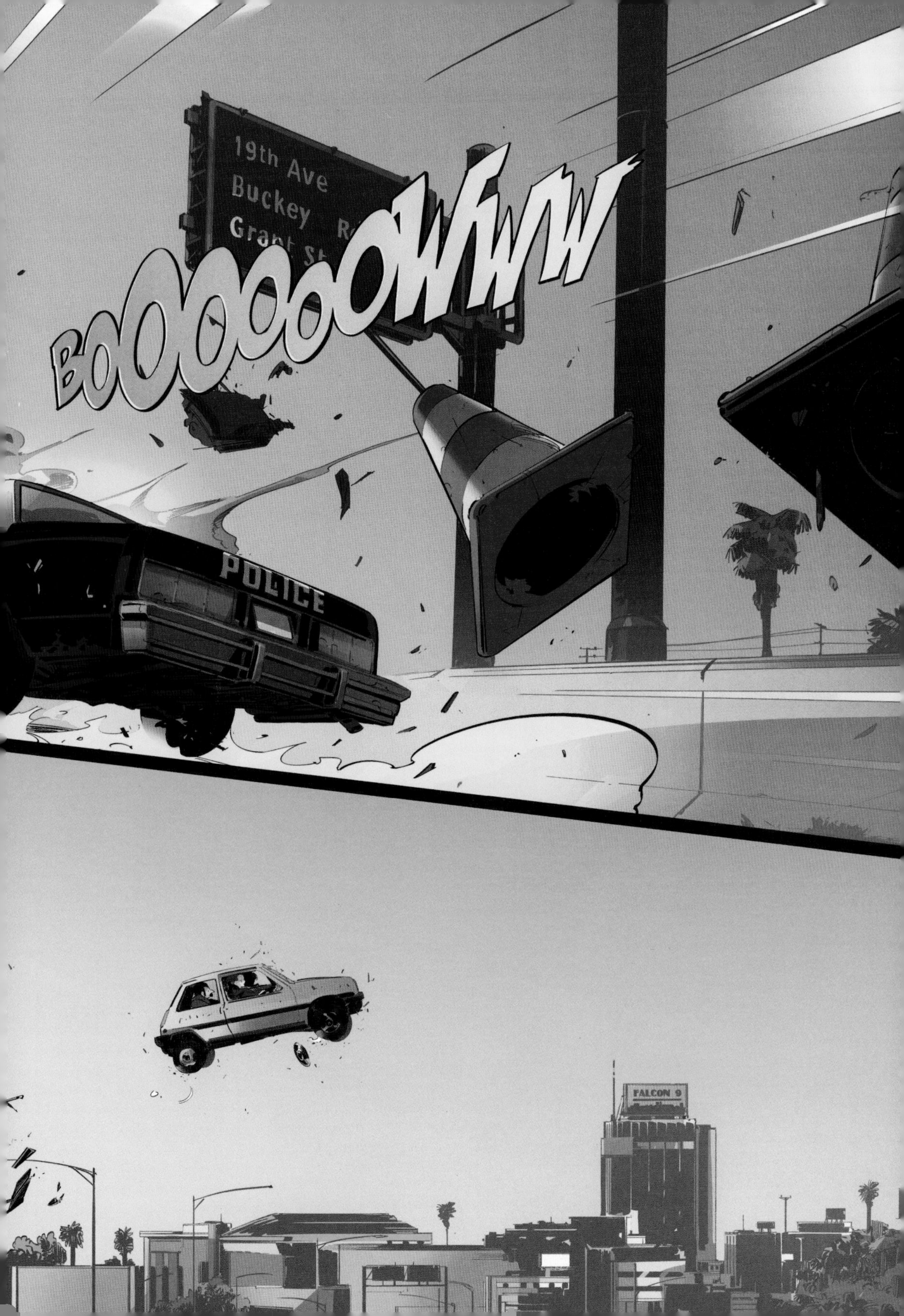
19th Ave
Buckey
BOOOOOOWWW
POLICE
FALCON 9

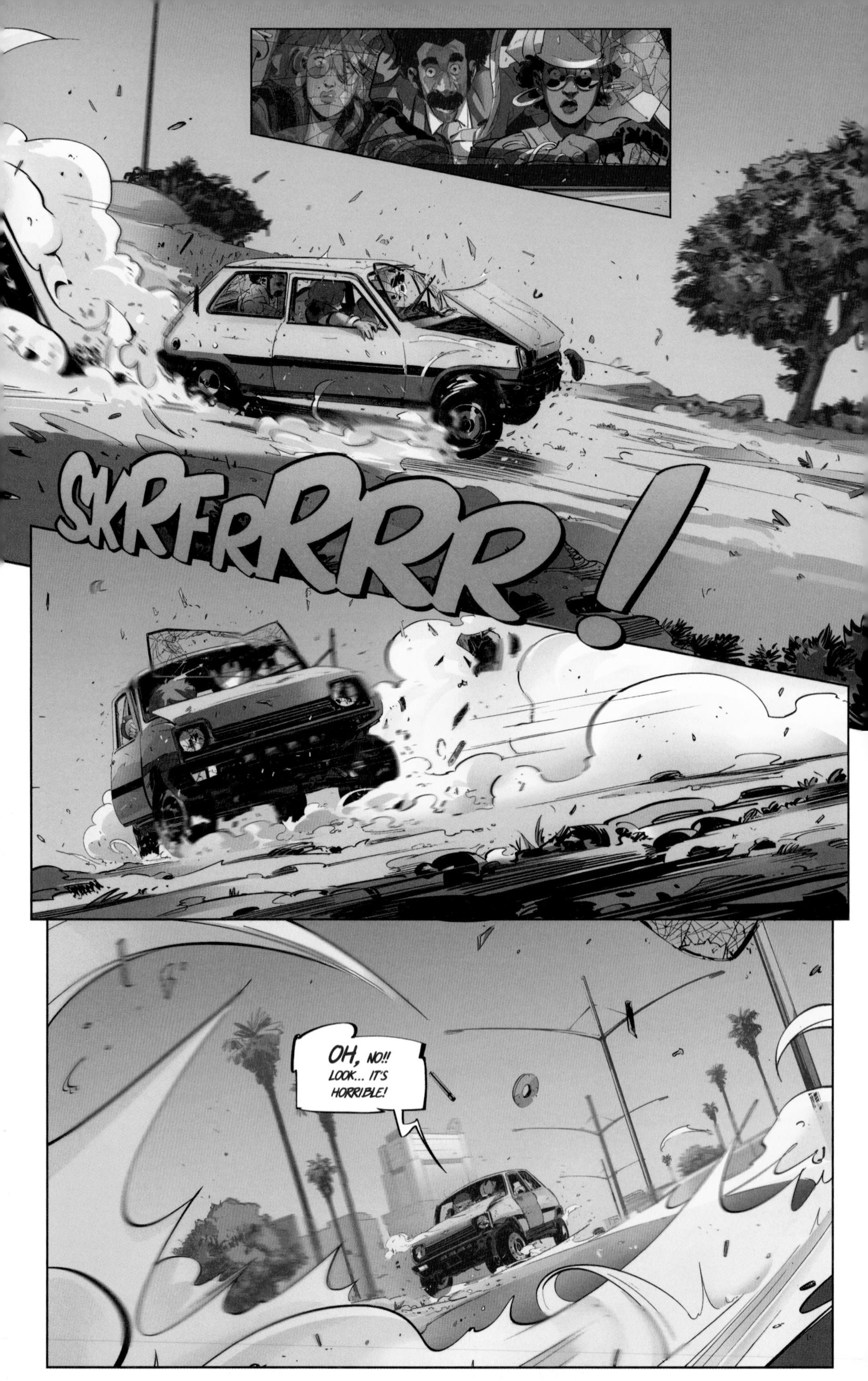
SKRFRRRRR!
OH, NO!! LOOK... IT'S HORRIBLE!

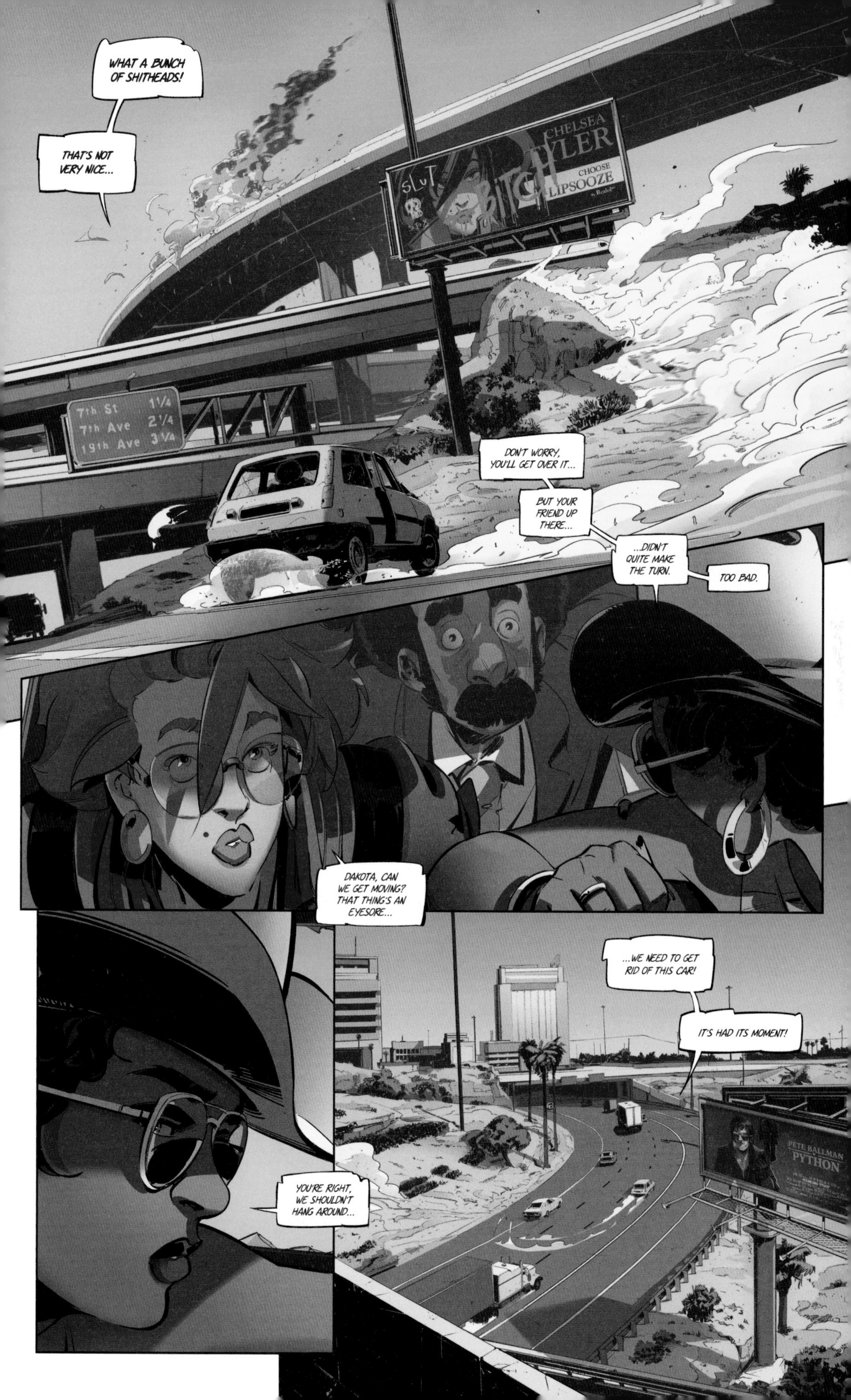
WHAT A BUNCH OF SHITHEADS!
THAT'S NOT VERY NICE...
CHELSEA TYLER
CHOOSE LIPSOOZE
SLUT
BITCH
7th St 1 1/4
7th Ave 2 1/4
19th Ave 3 1/4
DON'T WORRY, YOU'LL GET OVER IT...
BUT YOUR FRIEND UP THERE...
...DIDN'T QUITE MAKE THE TURN.
TOO BAD.
DAKOTA, CAN WE GET MOVING? THAT THING'S AN EYESORE...
YOU'RE RIGHT, WE SHOULDN'T HANG AROUND...
...WE NEED TO GET RID OF THIS CAR!
IT'S HAD ITS MOMENT!
PETE BALLMAN
PYTHON

StormBird
presents

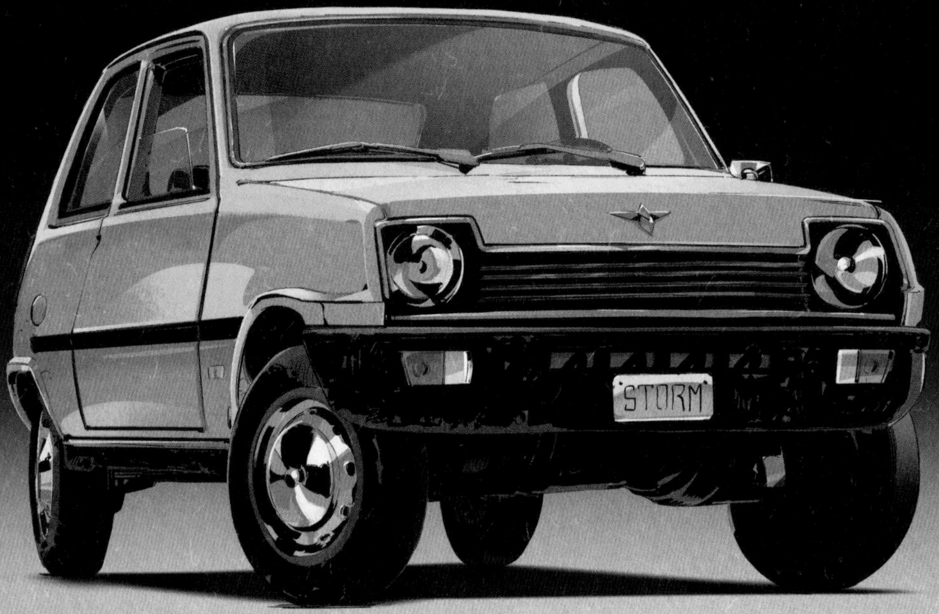
STORM

THE ORIGINAL STORM 5

"Le lil' Hotrod"

Need an escape, or some fresh air? Want to take a break and float through the sky like a butterfly? You're tired, aren't you? Tired of driving your old pick-up truck. It's loud and unwieldy, isn't it? Admit it! You know it's true! You're afraid that people in your neighborhood won't respect you anymore! But let me tell you - you couldn't be more wrong! StormBird® thought long and hard about your problem and, today, offers you an answer that will make everyone you know jealous!

In fact, the new Storm 5™'s motor was specifically developed to give your all-purpose vehicle a motor powerful enough for a high-speed train. Our specialists successfully accomplished this challenge and installed a Gigatronic neutron emitter paired with a three-phase rotation timing belt (that probably won't mean much to you, given that it doesn't mean much to me and I'm the one writing this ridiculous advertisement for this damned dishonest marketing agency. But the people in charge at Stormbird© don't care. They think that if the marketing is complicated enough, you'll believe every word, and you'll go out and buy the car, no questions asked! In reality, the car does boast a decent engine, but don't buy it expecting to win the Formula 1 Grand Prix).

Thanks to its small size, the synergistic circuit allows for a 317% increase in power and will help your small car run like a cheetah in the savannah! (... like a cheetah in the savannah... seriously?! Come on...). Take to the highway behind the wheel of your new Storm 5™ and beat any and all previous speed records for getting to work! Thanks to its 8" wheels you better believe that you're going to feel the road like you never have before! (Well, they're not wrong about that... Your butt will definitely be feeling the road...) So don't hesitate! Buy the latest in the next generation of small cars! (Oh... Apparently, I was just fired...)

Feel the road ! SB

STORMBIRD™

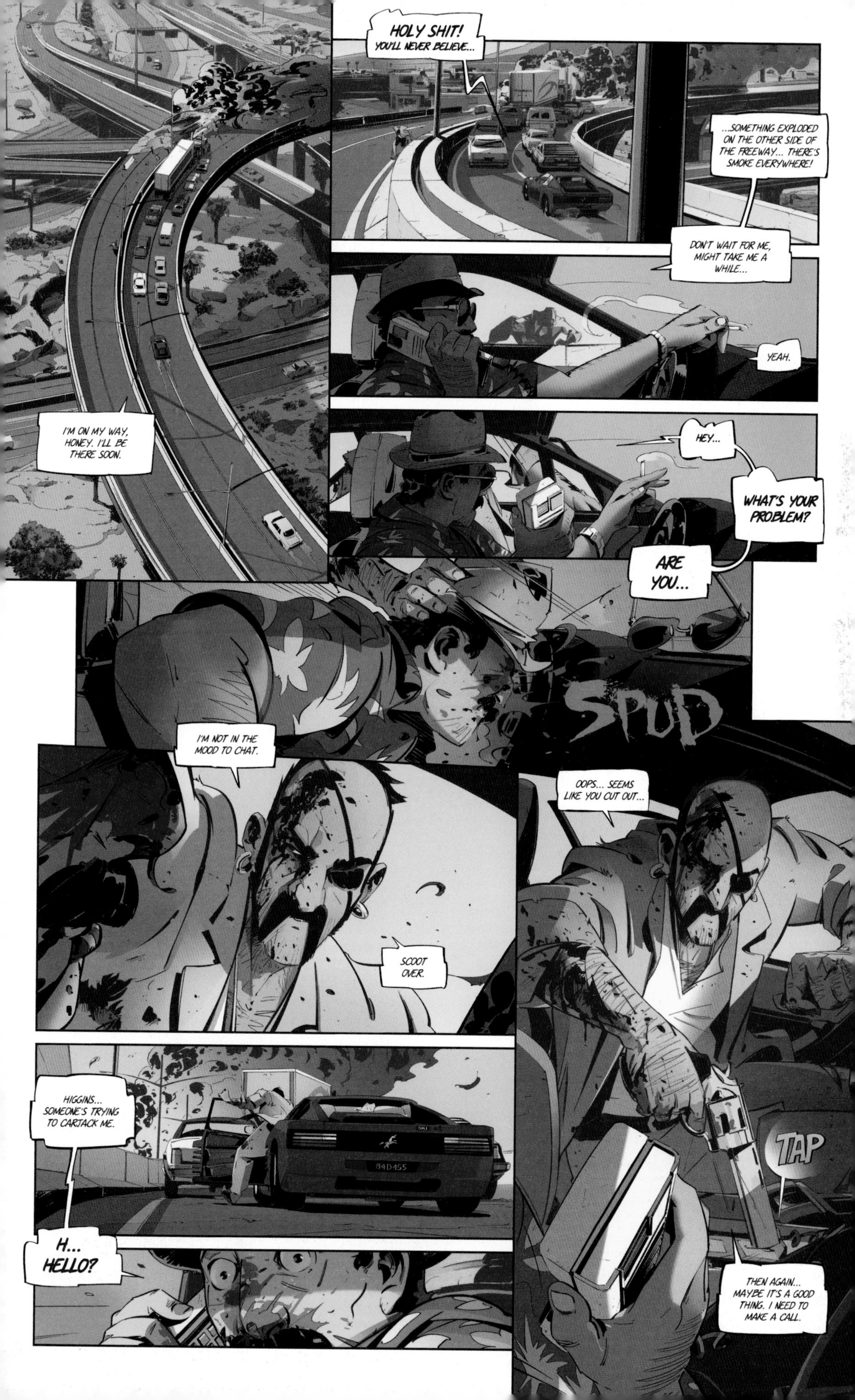
I'M ON MY WAY, HONEY. I'LL BE THERE SOON.
HOLY SHIT! YOU'LL NEVER BELIEVE...
...SOMETHING EXPLODED ON THE OTHER SIDE OF THE FREEWAY... THERE'S SMOKE EVERYWHERE!
DON'T WAIT FOR ME, MIGHT TAKE ME A WHILE...
YEAH.
HEY...
WHAT'S YOUR PROBLEM?
ARE YOU...
SPUD
I'M NOT IN THE MOOD TO CHAT.
SCOOT OVER.
OOPS... SEEMS LIKE YOU CUT OUT...
HIGGINS... SOMEONE'S TRYING TO CARJACK ME.
H... HELLO?
TAP
THEN AGAIN... MAYBE IT'S A GOOD THING. I NEED TO MAKE A CALL.

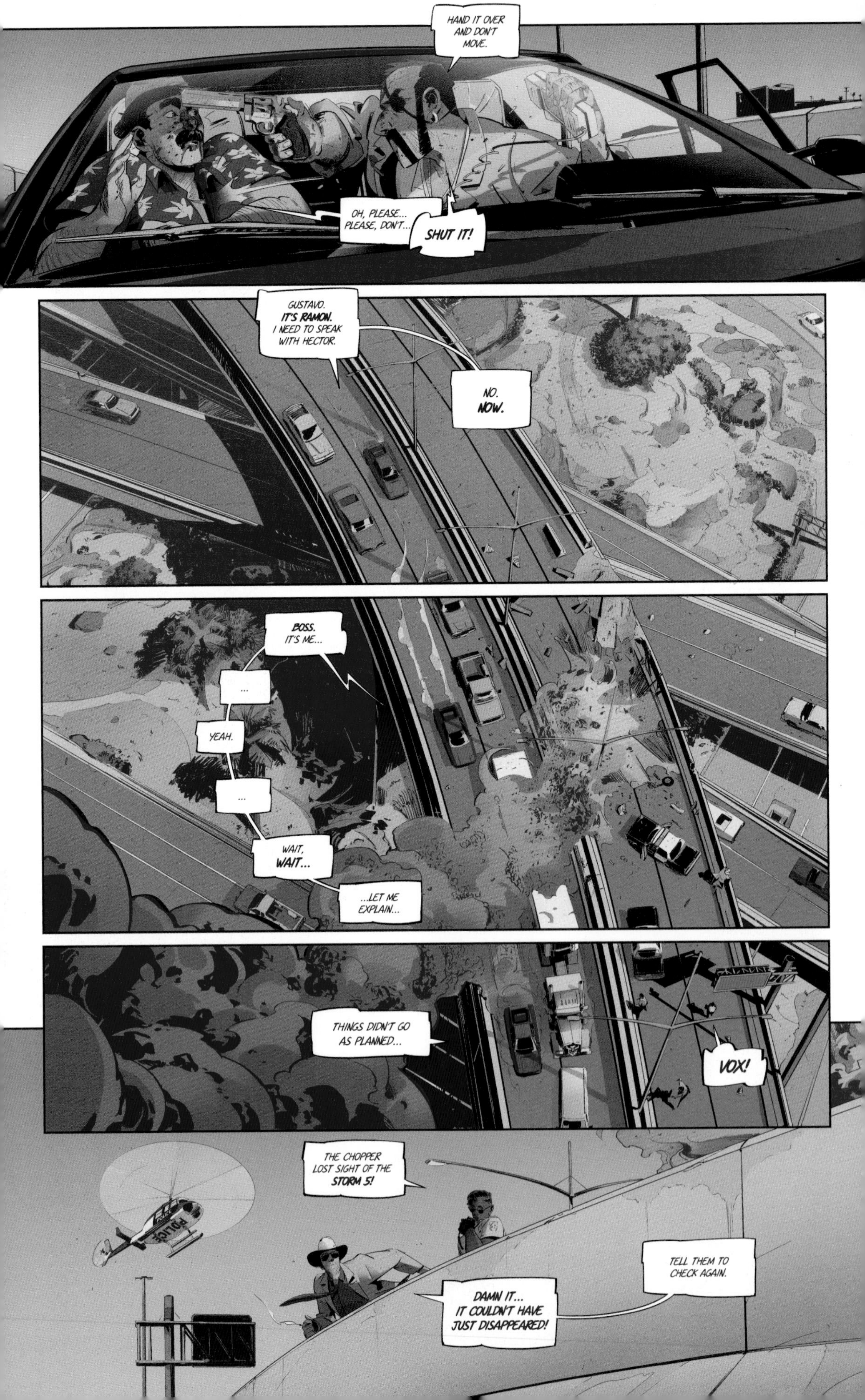
HAND IT OVER AND DON'T MOVE.
OH, PLEASE... PLEASE, DON'T...
SHUT IT!
GUSTAVO. IT'S RAMON. I NEED TO SPEAK WITH HECTOR.
NO. NOW.
BOSS. IT'S ME...
...
YEAH.
...
WAIT, WAIT...
...LET ME EXPLAIN...
THINGS DIDN'T GO AS PLANNED...
VOX!
THE CHOPPER LOST SIGHT OF THE STORM 5!
DAMN IT... IT COULDN'T HAVE JUST DISAPPEARED!
TELL THEM TO CHECK AGAIN.
POLICE

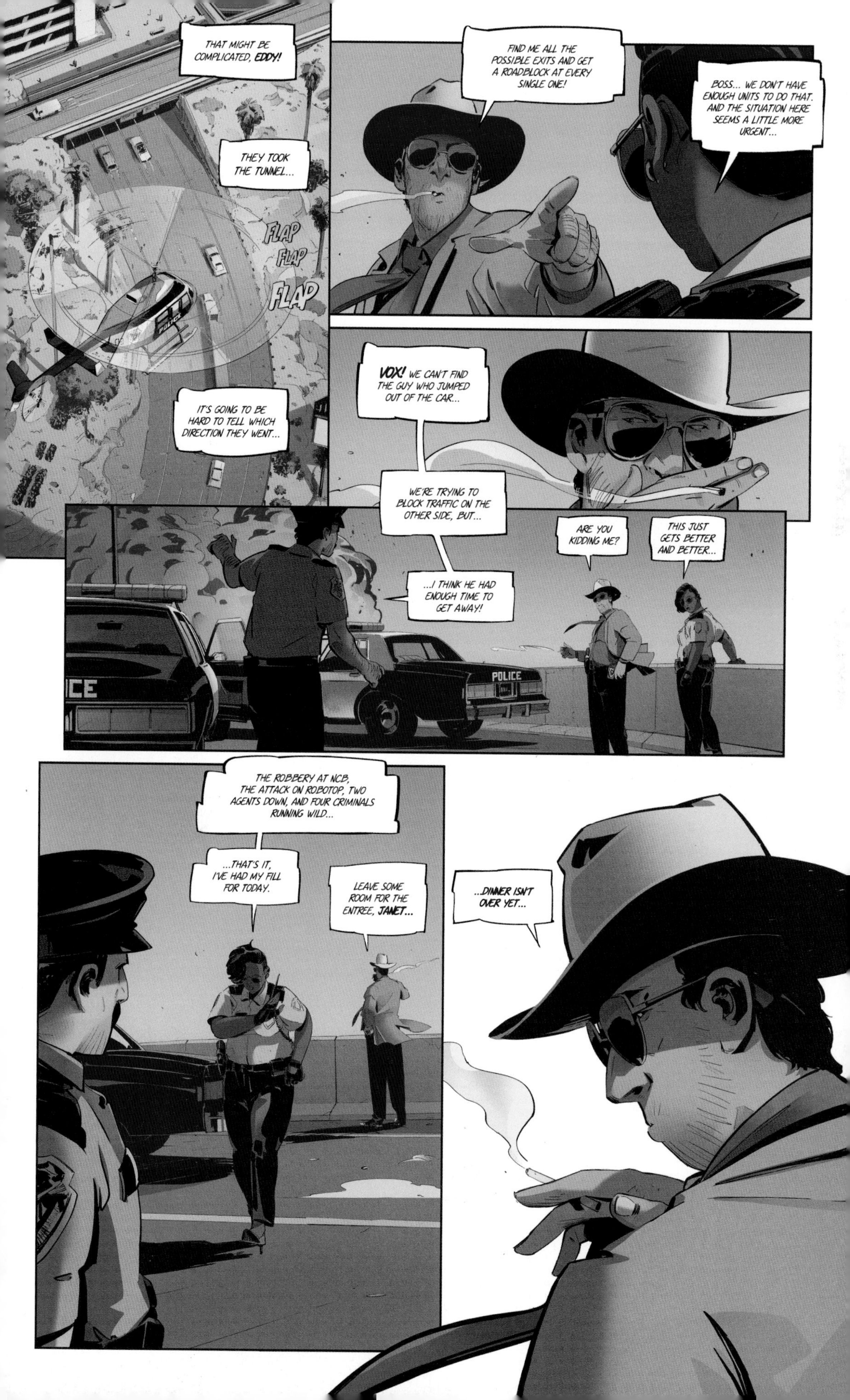
THAT MIGHT BE COMPLICATED, EDDY!
THEY TOOK THE TUNNEL...
FLAP
FLAP
FLAP
IT'S GOING TO BE HARD TO TELL WHICH DIRECTION THEY WENT...
FIND ME ALL THE POSSIBLE EXITS AND GET A ROADBLOCK AT EVERY SINGLE ONE!
BOSS... WE DON'T HAVE ENOUGH UNITS TO DO THAT. AND THE SITUATION HERE SEEMS A LITTLE MORE URGENT...
VOX! WE CAN'T FIND THE GUY WHO JUMPED OUT OF THE CAR...
WE'RE TRYING TO BLOCK TRAFFIC ON THE OTHER SIDE, BUT...
...I THINK HE HAD ENOUGH TIME TO GET AWAY!
ARE YOU KIDDING ME?
THIS JUST GETS BETTER AND BETTER...
POLICE
THE ROBBERY AT NCB, THE ATTACK ON ROBOTOP, TWO AGENTS DOWN, AND FOUR CRIMINALS RUNNING WILD...
...THAT'S IT, I'VE HAD MY FILL FOR TODAY.
LEAVE SOME ROOM FOR THE ENTREE, JANET...
...DINNER ISN'T OVER YET...

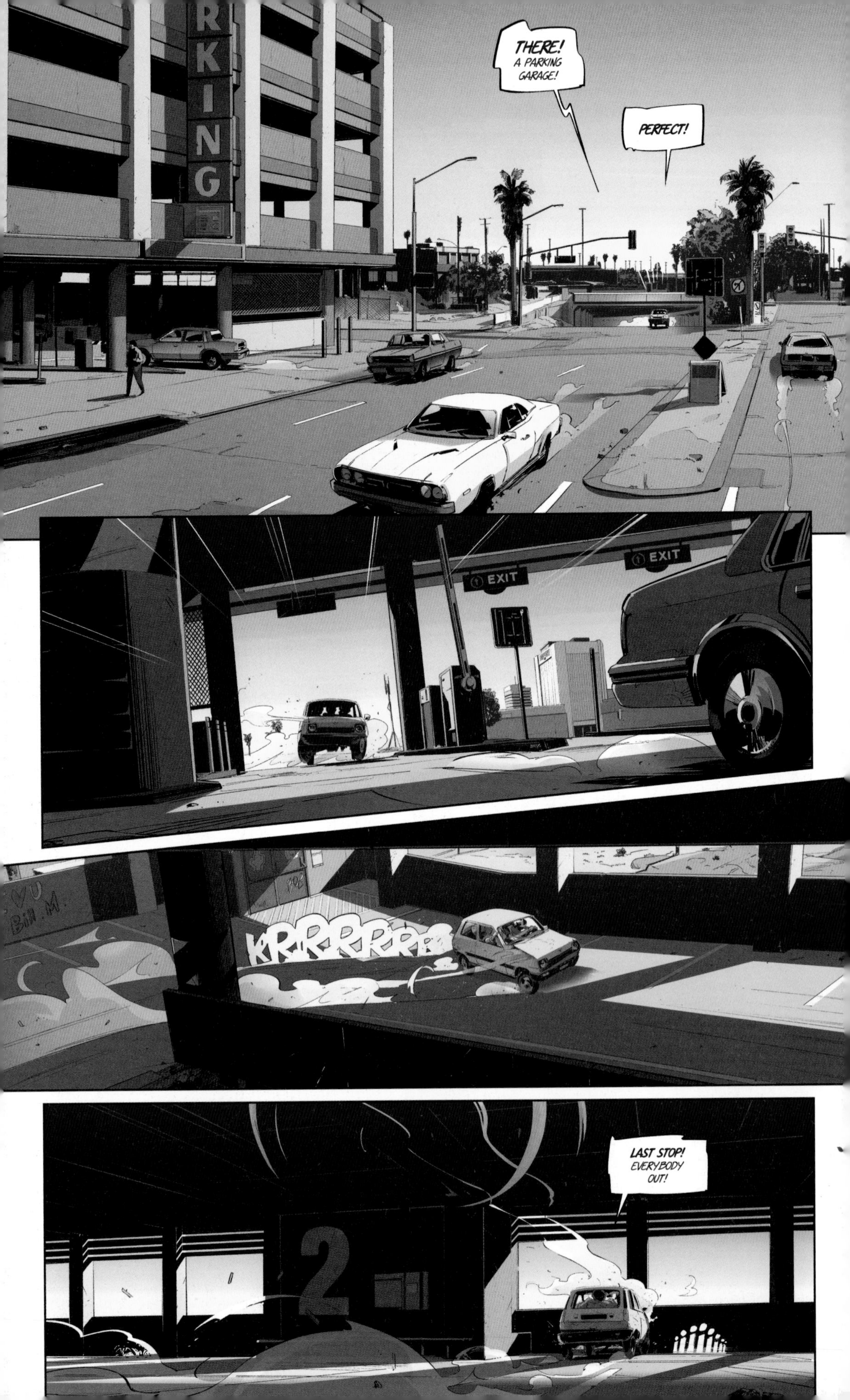
RKING
THERE! A PARKING GARAGE!
PERFECT!
EXIT
EXIT
KRRRRRR
2
LAST STOP! EVERYBODY OUT!

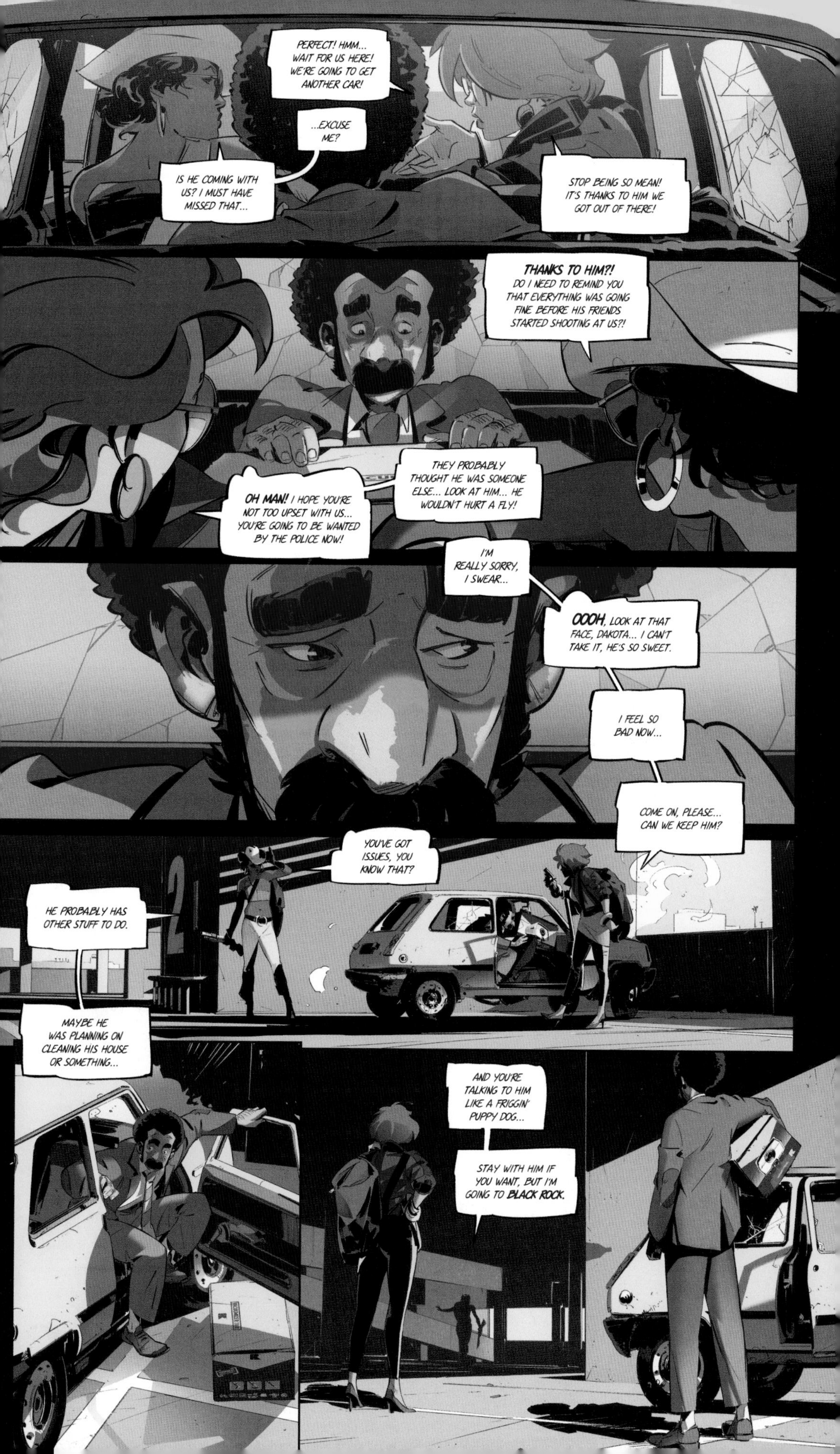

PERFECT! HMM... WAIT FOR US HERE! WE'RE GOING TO GET ANOTHER CAR!
...EXCUSE ME?
IS HE COMING WITH US? I MUST HAVE MISSED THAT...
STOP BEING SO MEAN! IT'S THANKS TO HIM WE GOT OUT OF THERE!
THANKS TO HIM?! DO I NEED TO REMIND YOU THAT EVERYTHING WAS GOING FINE BEFORE HIS FRIENDS STARTED SHOOTING AT US?!
OH MAN! I HOPE YOU'RE NOT TOO UPSET WITH US... YOU'RE GOING TO BE WANTED BY THE POLICE NOW!
THEY PROBABLY THOUGHT HE WAS SOMEONE ELSE... LOOK AT HIM... HE WOULDN'T HURT A FLY!
I'M REALLY SORRY, I SWEAR...
OOOH, LOOK AT THAT FACE, DAKOTA... I CAN'T TAKE IT, HE'S SO SWEET.
I FEEL SO BAD NOW...
COME ON, PLEASE... CAN WE KEEP HIM?
YOU'VE GOT ISSUES, YOU KNOW THAT?
HE PROBABLY HAS OTHER STUFF TO DO.
MAYBE HE WAS PLANNING ON CLEANING HIS HOUSE OR SOMETHING...
AND YOU'RE TALKING TO HIM LIKE A FRIGGIN' PUPPY DOG...
STAY WITH HIM IF YOU WANT, BUT I'M GOING TO BLACK ROCK.

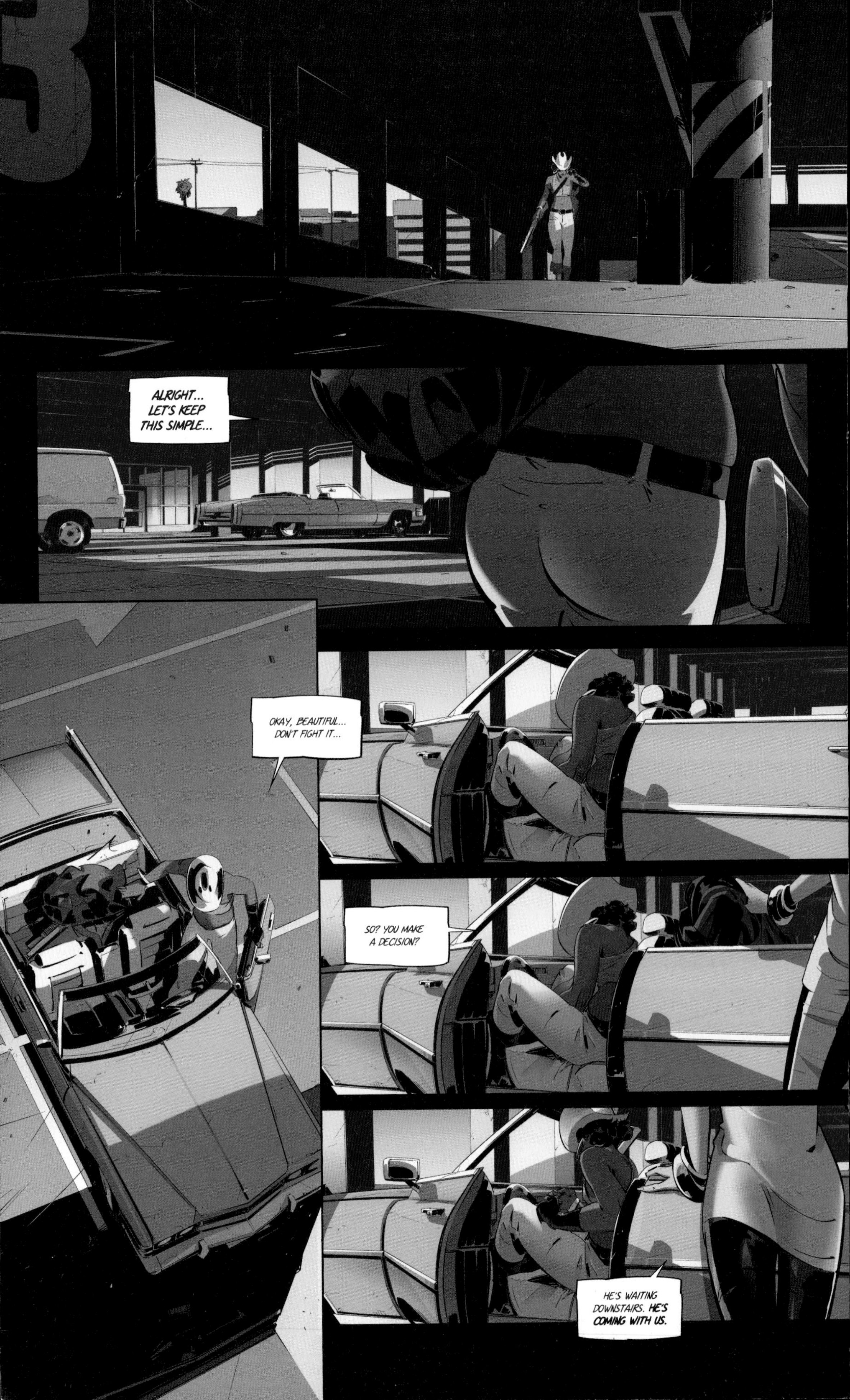
ALRIGHT... LET'S KEEP THIS SIMPLE...
OKAY, BEAUTIFUL... DON'T FIGHT IT...
SO? YOU MAKE A DECISION?
HE'S WAITING DOWNSTAIRS. HE'S COMING WITH US.

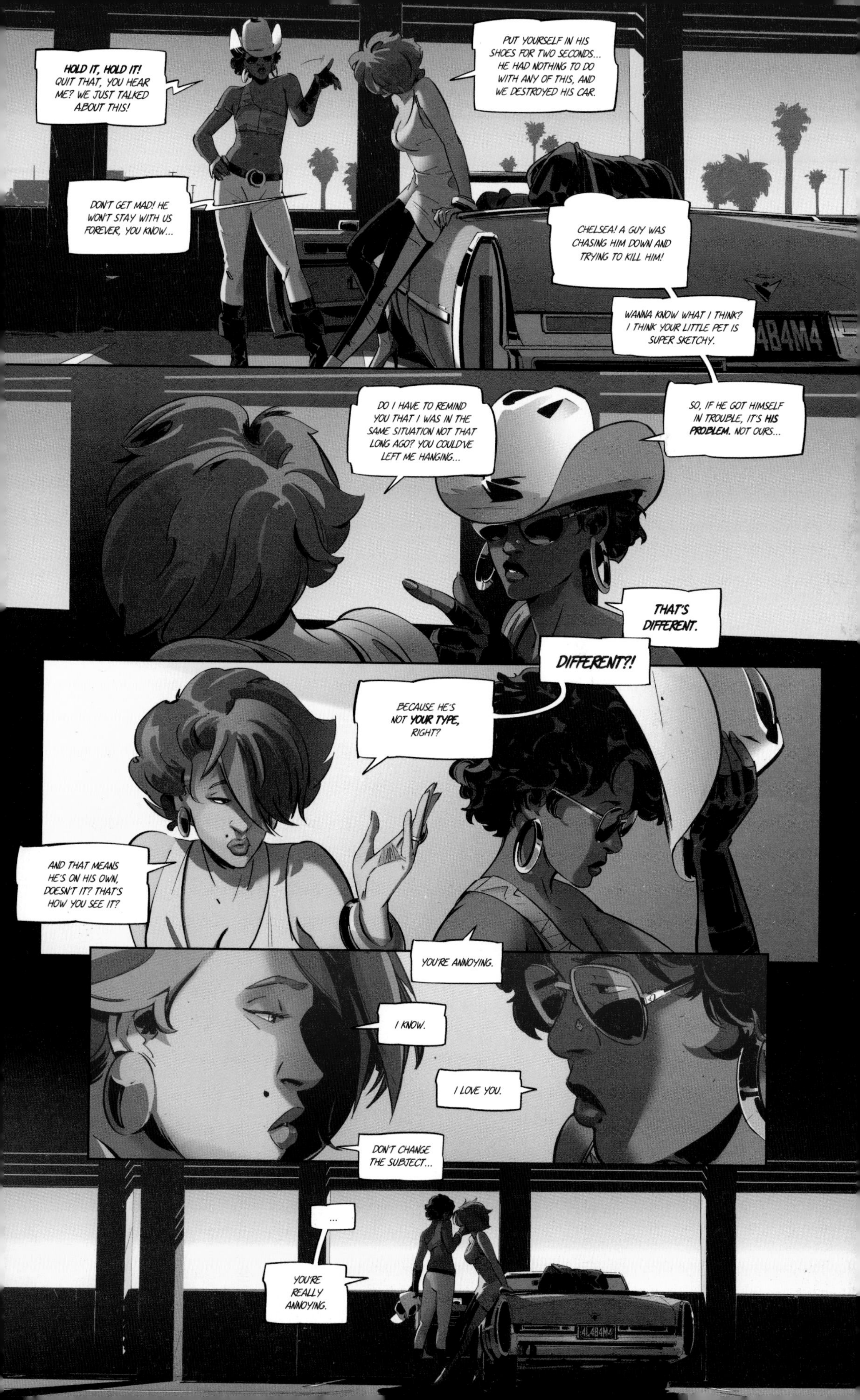
HOLD IT, HOLD IT! QUIT THAT, YOU HEAR ME? WE JUST TALKED ABOUT THIS!
PUT YOURSELF IN HIS SHOES FOR TWO SECONDS... HE HAD NOTHING TO DO WITH ANY OF THIS, AND WE DESTROYED HIS CAR.
DON'T GET MAD! HE WON'T STAY WITH US FOREVER, YOU KNOW...
CHELSEA! A GUY WAS CHASING HIM DOWN AND TRYING TO KILL HIM!
WANNA KNOW WHAT I THINK? I THINK YOUR LITTLE PET IS SUPER SKETCHY.
4B4M4
SO, IF HE GOT HIMSELF IN TROUBLE, IT'S HIS PROBLEM. NOT OURS...
DO I HAVE TO REMIND YOU THAT I WAS IN THE SAME SITUATION NOT THAT LONG AGO? YOU COULD'VE LEFT ME HANGING...
THAT'S DIFFERENT.
DIFFERENT?!
BECAUSE HE'S NOT YOUR TYPE, RIGHT?
AND THAT MEANS HE'S ON HIS OWN, DOESN'T IT? THAT'S HOW YOU SEE IT?
YOU'RE ANNOYING.
I KNOW.
I LOVE YOU.
DON'T CHANGE THE SUBJECT...
...
YOU'RE REALLY ANNOYING.
4L4B4M4

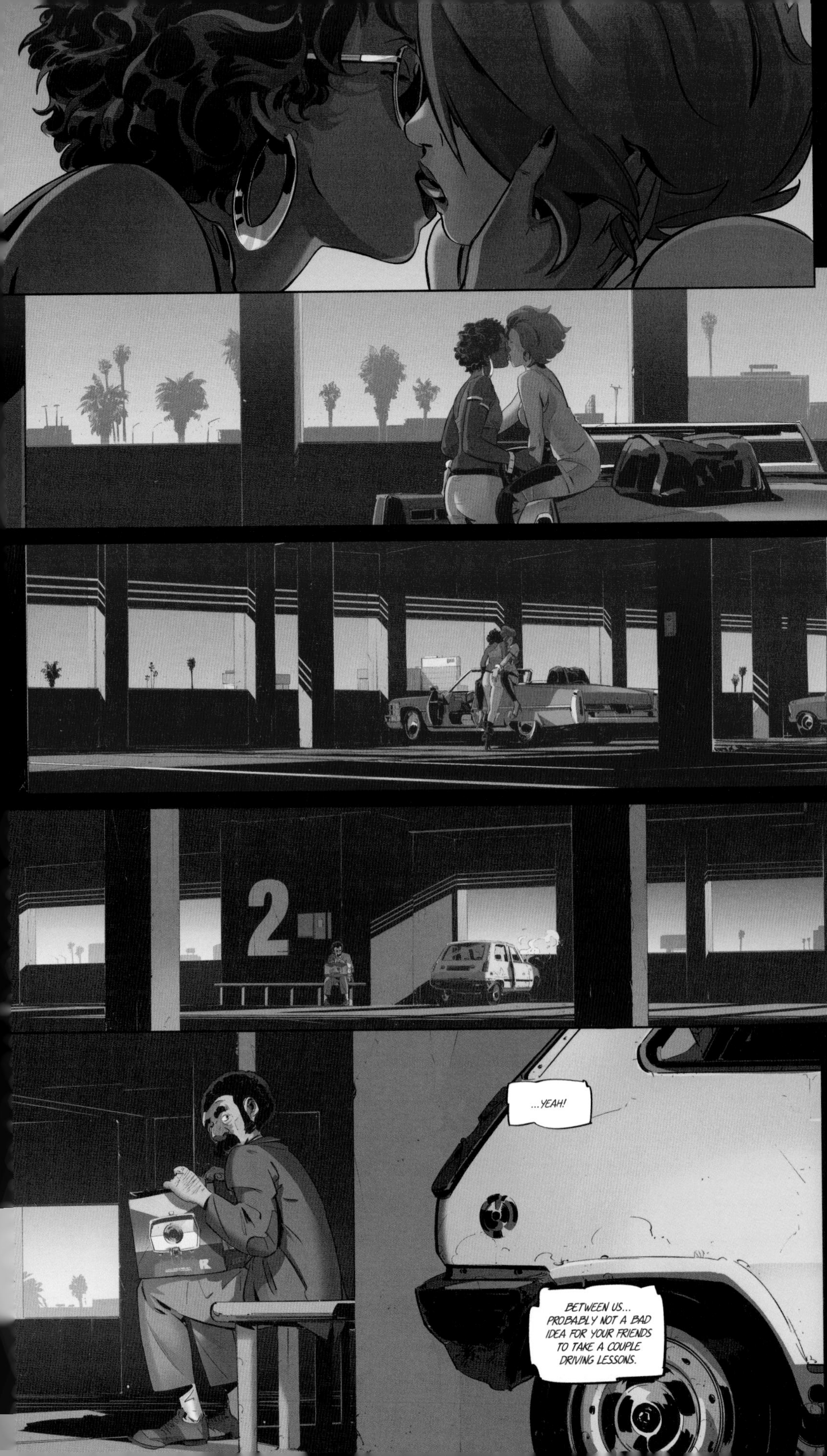

...YEAH!
BETWEEN US... PROBABLY NOT A BAD IDEA FOR YOUR FRIENDS TO TAKE A COUPLE DRIVING LESSONS.

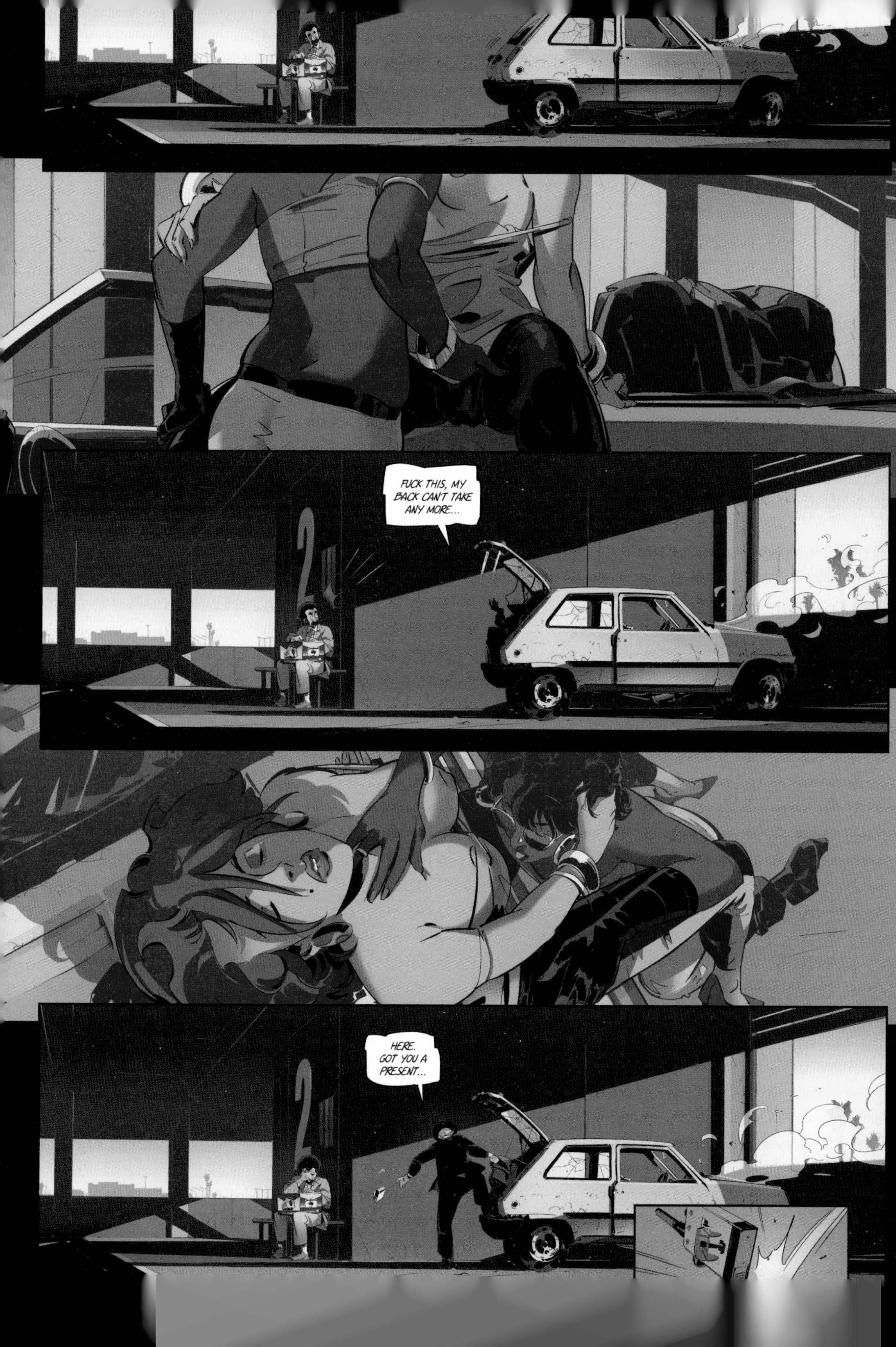
FUCK THIS, MY BACK CAN'T TAKE ANY MORE...
HERE. GOT YOU A PRESENT...

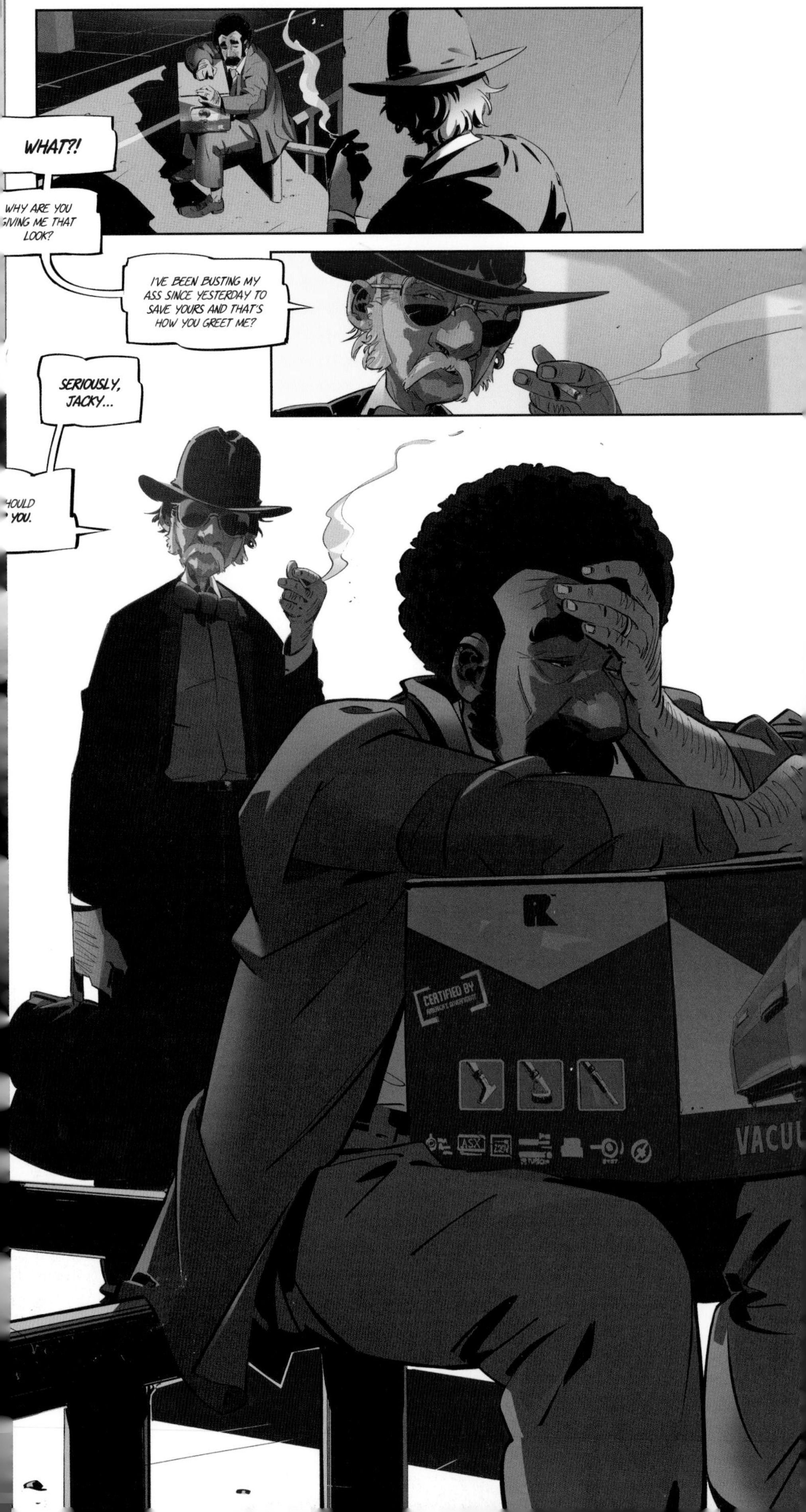
WHAT?!
WHY ARE YOU GIVING ME THAT LOOK?
I'VE BEEN BUSTING MY ASS SINCE YESTERDAY TO SAVE YOURS AND THAT'S HOW YOU GREET ME?
SERIOUSLY, JACKY...
HOULD
YOU.
CERTIFIED BY

R 2000

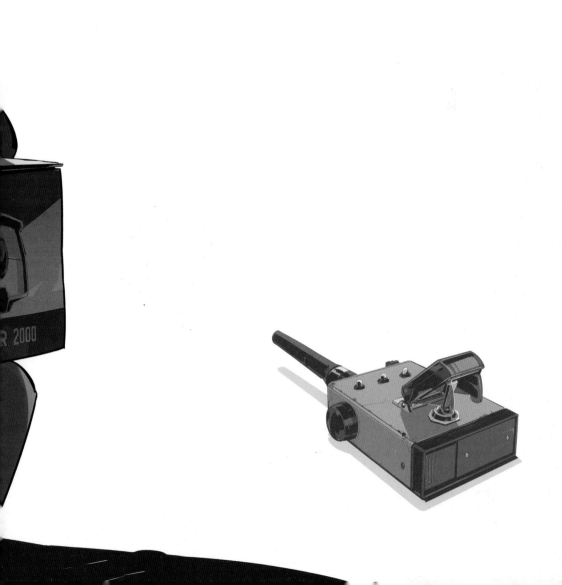

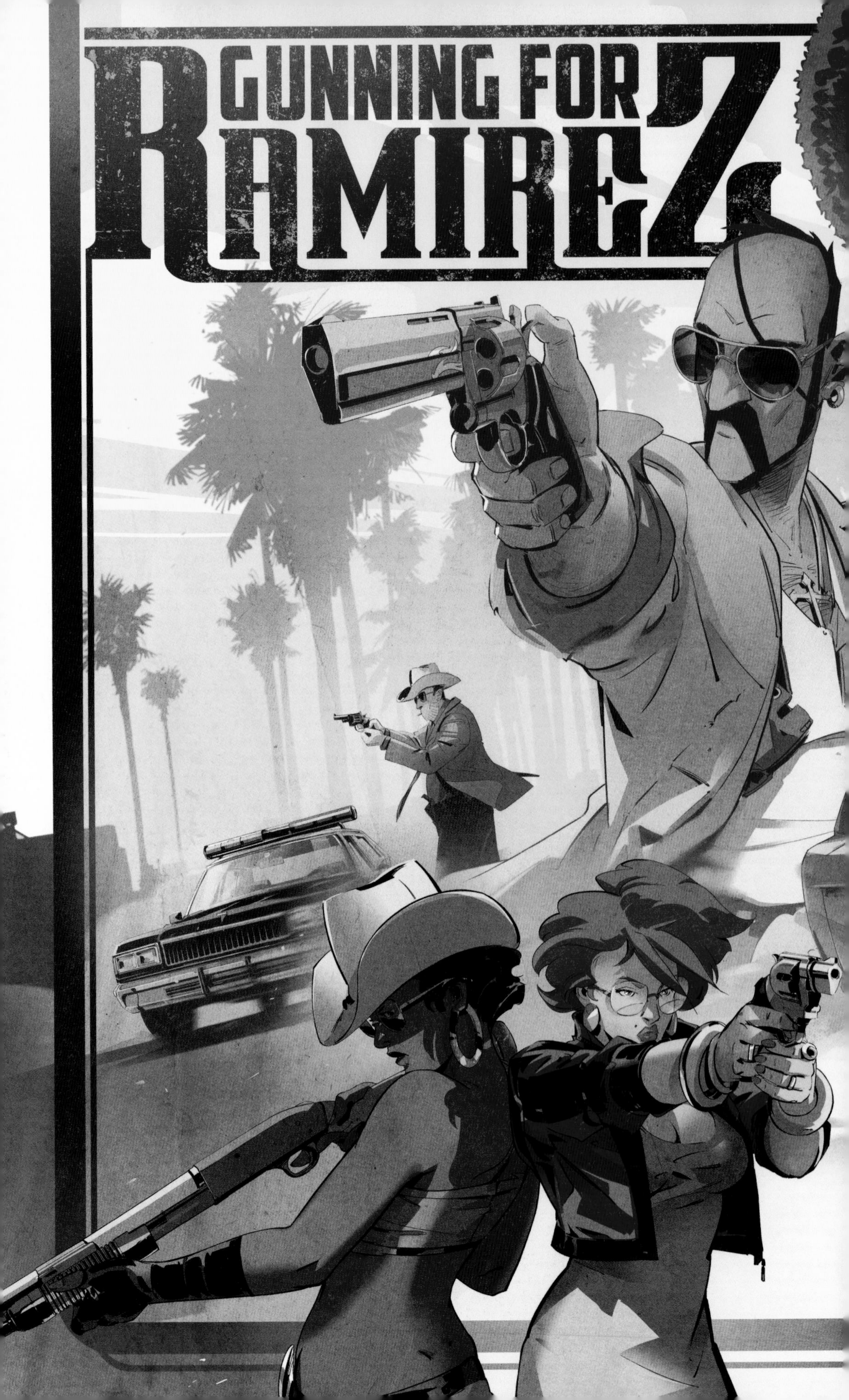

GUNNING FOR
RAMIREZ

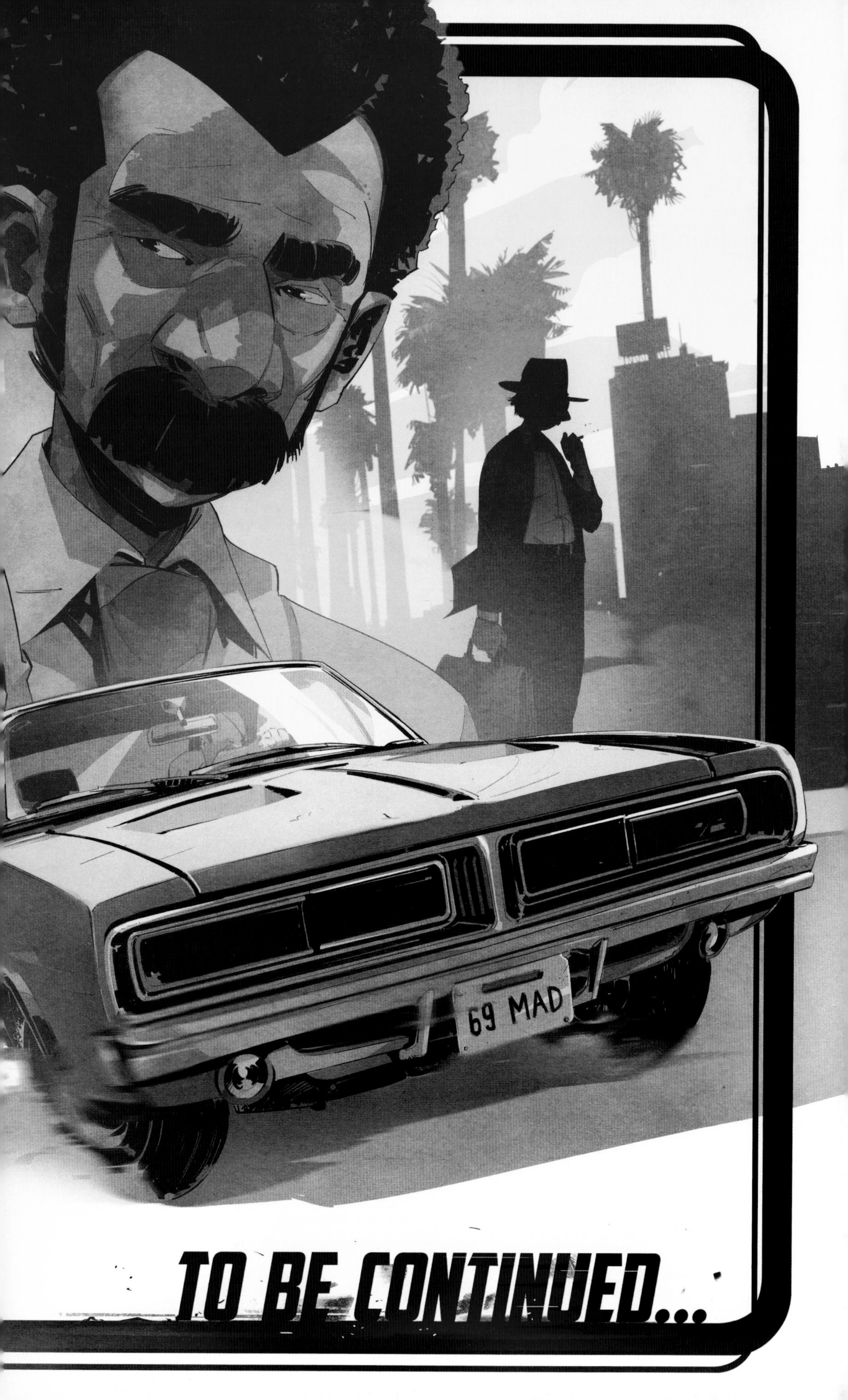
69 MAD
TO BE CONTINUED...

WRITTEN AND DRAWN BY
NICOLAS PETRIMAUX

PROJECT MANAGER **OLIVIER JALABERT**
JULIA SOUCHAL

TRANSLATION **JEREMY MELLOUL**
JOLIE HALE

COLOR ASSISTANT **LÉO SIRET**

QUALITY SERVICE **MATHIEU SALVIA**
AURÉLIE NEYRET
SOPHIAN CHOLET
ALEKSI BRICLOT

BETA-READERS **ARNAUD & VIRGINIE DAVID**
RACHEL TRIBOUT
JULIE ROUVIÈRE

WEB **NICOLAS PETRIMAUX**
ÉLOÏSE DE LA MAISON

IMAGE COMICS CREW **ERIC STEPHENSON**
JEFF BOISON
KAT SALAZAR
TRICIA RAMOS
ERIKA SCHNATZ

FLINGUERRAMIREZ.COM

«TRAILER & VACUUMIZER 2000 COMMERCIAL»

«JIMMY» SANDERS **FABRIZIO DEITOS**
MME JONHSON **MARIE NEYRET**
VOICE OVER **AUGUSTIN JACOB**
AUDIO MIX **ARNAUD DAVID**

SPECIAL THANKS **MORGAN CLÉMENT**
AURÉLIE, GÉRARD & ANNIE NEYRET
CYRIL ET BERNARD ALBRUS
«FRIPES KETCHUP»

MUSIC TRAILER MIDNIGHT KIDS REMIX «QUIT YOU»
(LOST KINGS FEAT. TINASHE) INSTRUMENTAL VERSION
AND OLIVIER DERIVIÈRE

COMMERCIAL MUSIC MITCH MURDER - «KILLER ANGELS»

THE AUTHOR WOULD LIKE TO THANK...

The whole team at Glenat for the enthusiasm they showed during the production of this first volume, in particular, Olivier Jalabert, for his trust, and for giving Nicolas the chance his 11 year old self dreamed of... to tell his own comic book stories.

Thanks to Olivier Peru, Audrey Briclot, Wilfried Lupano and Xavier Dorison for their advice.

To Leo for his help and incredible work on the color preparation for the endings of episode 2 and 3.

And a loving caress to my beautiful Sophian and my dear Aleksi for all the time they gave me and their feedback.

I'd also like to express my gratitude to Mathieu Salvia for his help in writing, editing, rewriting, finishing, reading, analyzing, and finishing my first book that's wholly «mine.» I owe him enormously for his help in every moment. For his expertise, enthusiasm, talent, and, of course, his friendship.

And, finally, thank you to the woman I love for supporting me in this crazy endeavor and making my world that much funnier.

DRAWN ON

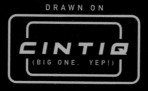

CINTIQ

(BIG ONE, YEP!)

COLOR BY SATURATEK®

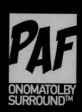

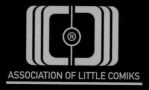

ASSOCIATION OF LITTLE COMIKS

PAF

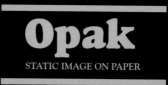

ONOMATOLBY SURROUND™

!! WARNING !!

FOKIEW !

SOME VULGARITY SEQUENCES HAVE BEEN PERFORMED BY PROFESSIONALS. FOR YOUR SAFETY, DON'T TRY TO TALK LIKE THAT TO ANY ONE.

HIGH LEVEL OF VULGARITY

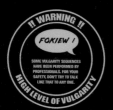

Opak

STATIC IMAGE ON PAPER

No mug (or almost) was mistreated during the realization of this book.

IN THE NEXT EPISODE

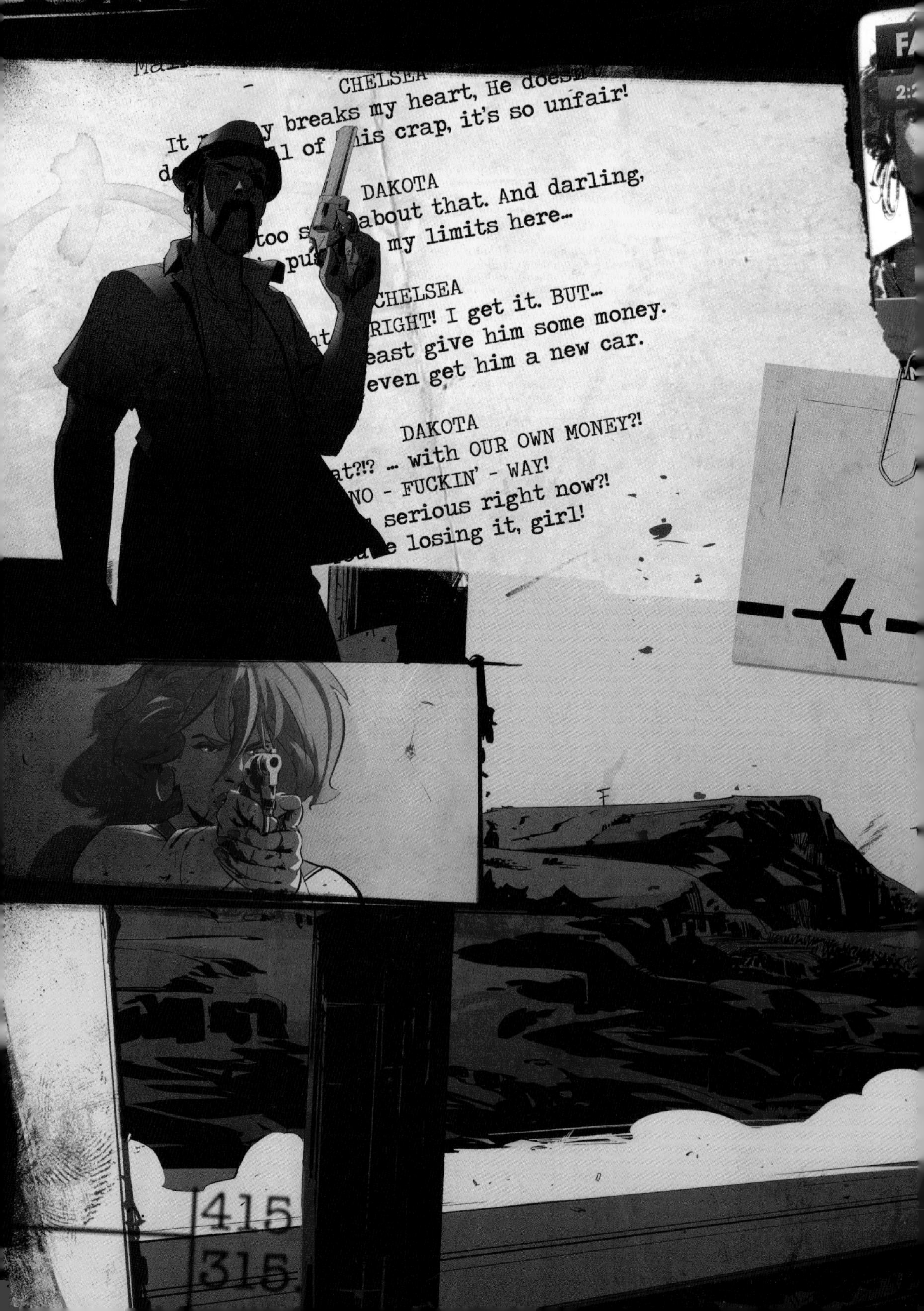
CHELSEA
y breaks my heart, He doesn
is crap, it's so unfair!
DAKOTA
about that. And darling,
my limits here...
CHELSEA
RIGHT! I get it. BUT...
east give him some money.
even get him a new car.
DAKOTA
at?!? ... with OUR OWN MONEY?!
NO - FUCKIN' - WAY!
serious right now?!
e losing it, girl!
415
315

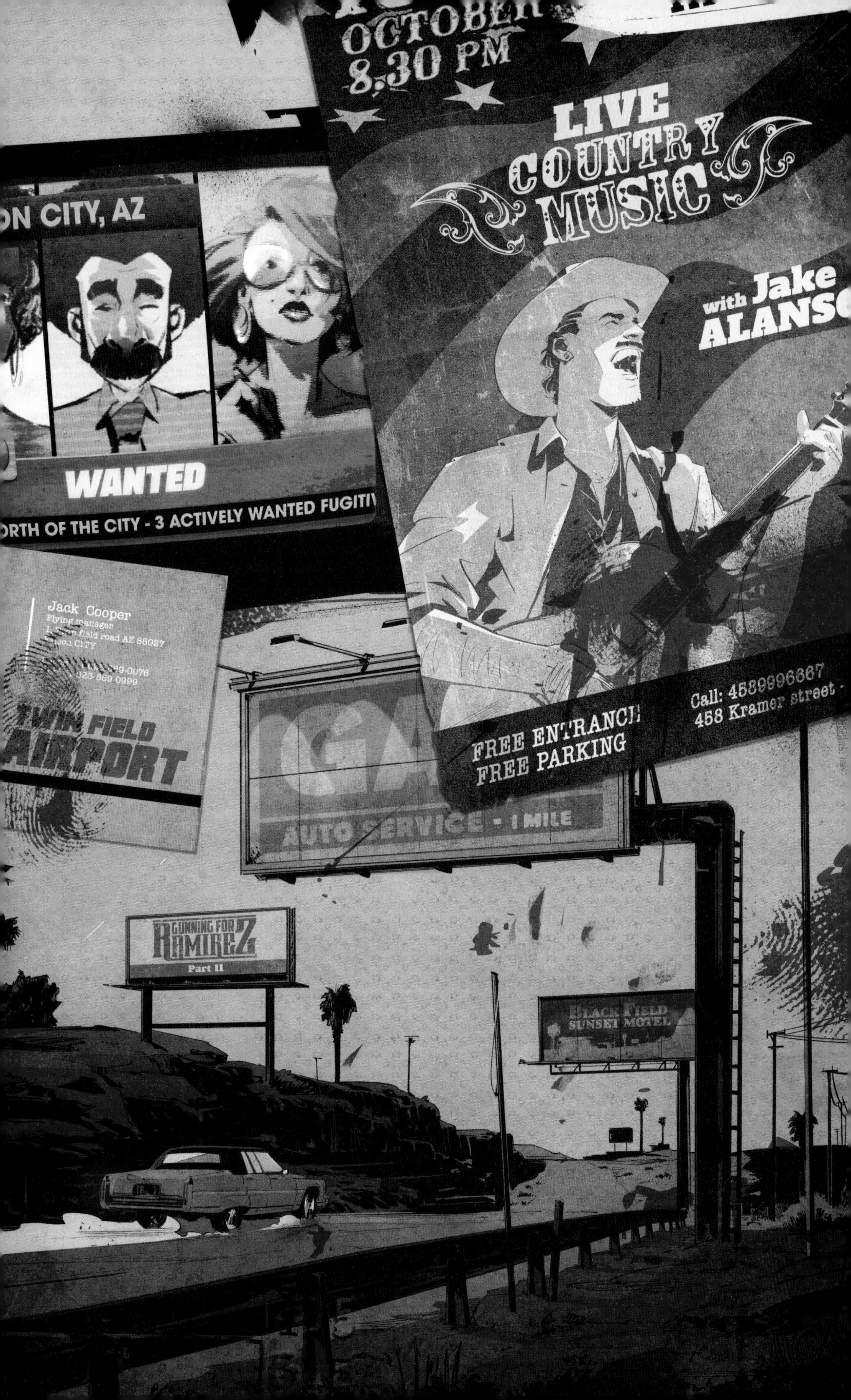
OCTOBER
8.30 PM
LIVE
COUNTRY
MUSIC
with Jake
ALANS
FREE ENTRANCE
FREE PARKING
Call: 4589996367
458 Kramer street -
ON CITY, AZ
WANTED
ORTH OF THE CITY - 3 ACTIVELY WANTED FUGITIV
Jack Cooper
Flying manager
field road AZ 85027
CITY
323-869-0999
FIELD
AIRPORT
AUTO SERVICE - 1 MILE
GUNNING FOR
RAMIREZ
Part II
BLACK FIELD
SUNSET MOTEL

ADDITIONAL INFORMATION

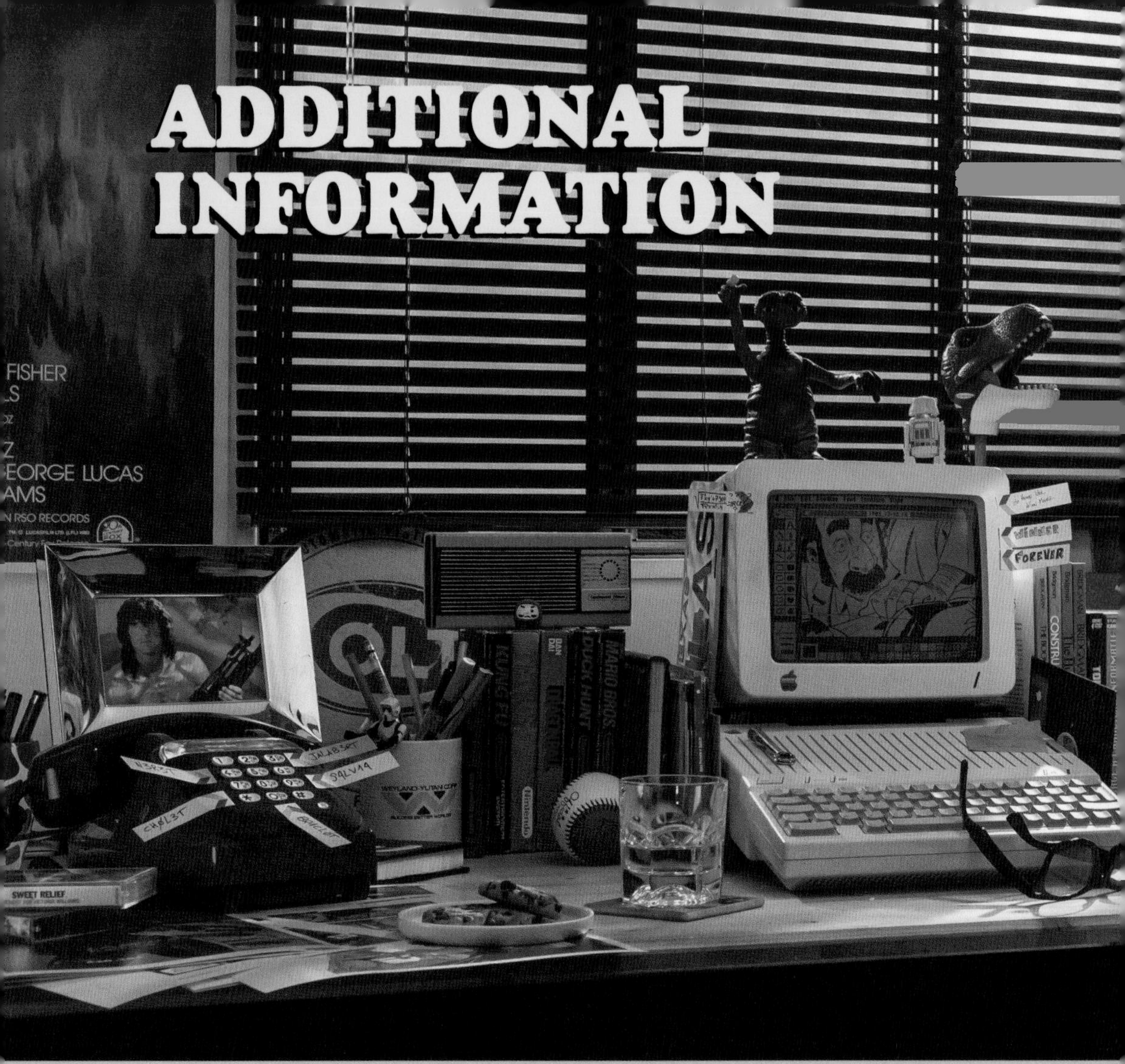
FISHER
EORGE LUCAS
AMS
N RSO RECORDS
KUNG FU
DUCK HUNT
MARIO BROS.
Nintendo
WEYLAND-YUTANI CORP
FOREVER
SWEET RELIEF

Nicolas Petrimaux was born in Normandy and was weighed the first day E.T. came out in movie theaters. Too young to see the masterpiece on the big screen, he waited until he was 7 to see it on television, an experience which gave rise to an American movie addiction and sent him deep into the aisles of the Video Center in his town. He, like all the other little idiots of his generation, devoured movies from the 80s and at the age of 8 years old started working on a remake of Back to the Future using his dad's Rover and strips of paper covered in fuel. After numerous disagreements due to the overly-costly special effects, his parents decided to end the production of the movie.

So, in 1994, in seventh grade, he launches into a remake of Point Break. Like a real hothead, he quickly reimagines his version of the story in a future in which teenagers his age are allowed to be part of the F.B.I. It's not without plot holes from his avant-garde script, but he finishes this first short film and presents it to his class at the end of the year. A few years later, he throws out this first work and destroys all trace of the audiovisual disaster by recording a television version of The Fifth Element over the original copy of his movie. At the end of the 90s, Nicolas puts a hold on his career as an independent filmmaker in order to devote himself to manga. In 2000, after a trying biology class, he manages to convince his professor to give him the points he needs to secure his freedom from school. After obtaining his baccalaureate with an easy grade of 10.01 he begins to study art in Paris.

In 2004, after finishing his four years in Applied Arts, he declares:

"Cool, that took long enough!"

And launches himself into the video game industry, thankful for the community at CSFL.net which, at the time, was a gathering place for actors in the industry. One night, while watching The Fifth Element on television, he realizes how wrong he was to erase the original copy of his first film. Consumed with regret, he decides to try his hand at filmmaking again with a few colleagues, and make a short zombie film shot in the hallways of the company that employed him at the time. In 2005, Nicolas changes jobs and joins a company

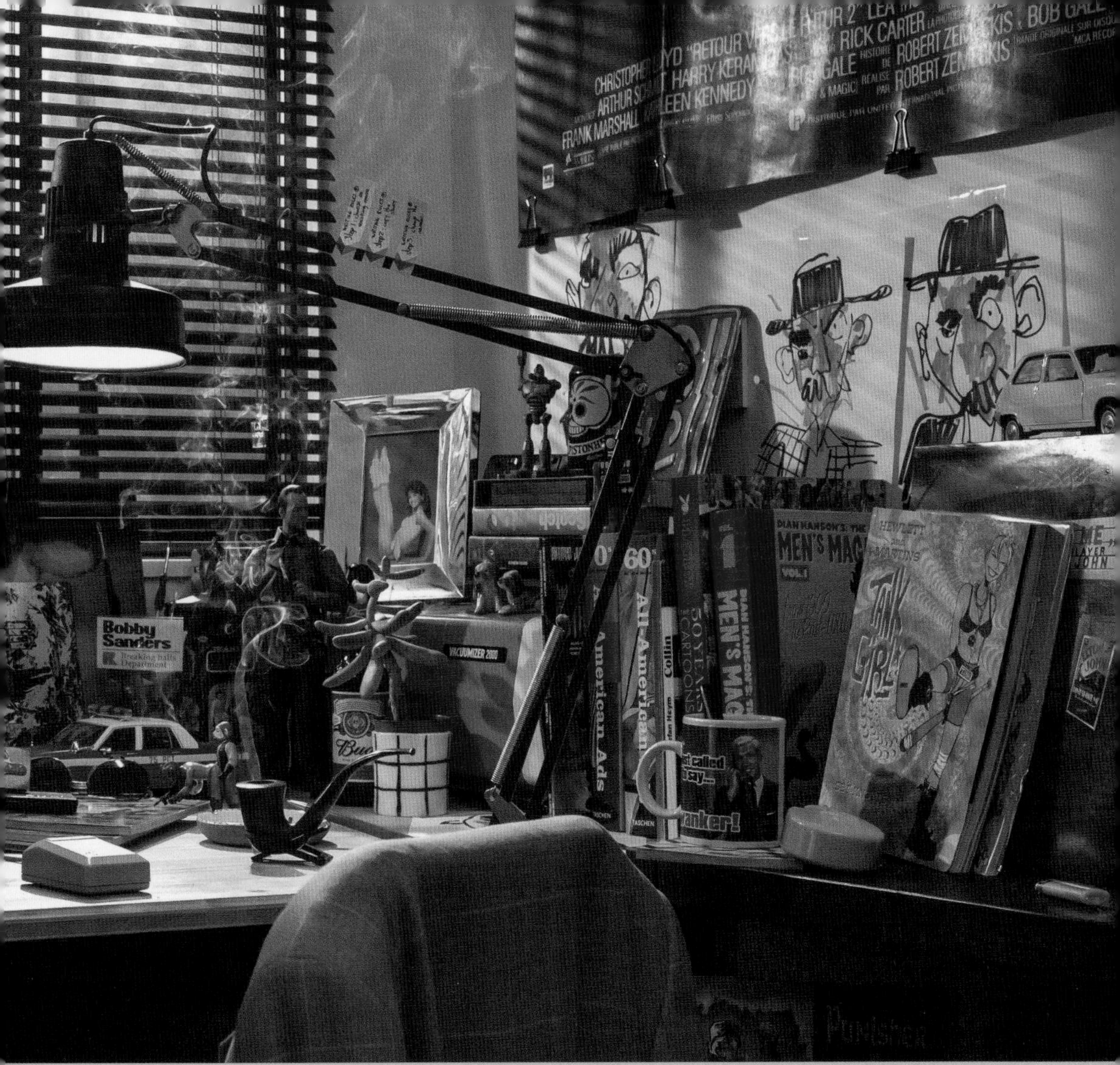
CHRISTOPHER LLOYD
ARTHUR SCHMIDT
FRANK MARSHALL
HARRY KERAMIDAS
KATHLEEN KENNEDY
RICK CARTER
ROBERT ZEMECKIS
BOB GALE
Bobby Sanders
VACUUMIZER 2000
MEN'S MAG
All-American Ads
50 YEARS OF CARTOONS
TASCHEN
TANK GIRL
HEWLETT
Punisher

specializing in special effects post-production. He meets new people and learns a bit about the art of matte painting and compositing with After Effects, allowing him to finish the post-production on his short film Hello Zombie and take home a prize awarded by the magazine Mad Movies, at the French Cinematheque. From 2009 to 2011, he worked on developing CFSL Ink (subsidiary of Ankama), alongside the creators of the website, and continued to work in the entertainment industry on a freelance basis.

"A VEST, A PIPE... A VACUUM!"

In 2012, he starts to focus on comics and video games. He publishes a short story with El Diablo for the DoggyBags collection published by Anakama Editions, along with the first one-shot of the Zombies Nechrnologies series for Soleil Anticipation, with Olivier Peru and Sophian Cholet. Between the comics work, he continues to work in video games and produces storyboards, concept art, illustrations, and animations for Arkane Studios, developing the Dishonored license.

In January of 2015, Nicolas pitches Olivier Jalabert a useless idea called Gunning for Ramirez, and, a few months later, agrees to publish it at Glenat.

P76
E228-QCS

CUSTOMER SERVICE

the customer who submitted the questions has :

- ☐ A HAT?
- ☐ A BEAR? SOME GLASSES?
- ☐ YOU'RE SAM ? (YOU WIN, LET'S PLAY AGAIN!)

ROBOTOP'S SATISFACTION FORM

● ABOUT YOUR PRODUCT:

MODEL:

SERIAL NUMBER:

PURCHASE DATE:

RETAILER:

● AND HOW ARE YOU DOING?

COME ON, TELL US EVERYTHING:

● YOU'RE INCREDIBLE! HEY, YOU GUYS AND US ARE ACTUALLY FRIENDS, IN A WAY.

1 – HOW WOULD YOU DESCRIBE YOUR DEVICE?

- ☐ THE BEST
- ☐ INCREDIBLE
- ☐ AWESOME, DUDE!
- ☐ BIG

IF YES, WHY?

2 – HOW MANY TIMES DO YOU USE IT PER DAY?

- ☐ 2 TIMES MINIMUM
- ☐ 3-6 TIMES PER DAY
- ☐ 7-10 TIMES PER DAY
- ☐ ALWAYS ACTIVATED

3 – HAS IT EVER BROKEN DOWN?

- ☐ NOPE
- ☐ NOT THAT I KNOW OF
- ☐ NEVER
- ☐ DEFINITELY NOPE

● LET'S ADMIT THAT YOUR DEVICE HAS STOPPED WORKING...

DESCRIBE THE PROBLEM YOU'RE HAVING:

DID YOU BRING IT TO OUR CUSTOMER SERVICE?

| YEP | NOPE |

(IF YEP) HOW DID THE SUPPORT EXPERIENCE GO?

- ☐ GREAT
- ☐ QUICK
- ☐ UNFORGIVABLE
- ☐ SIMPLE AND FUNKY
- ☐ FRESH
- ☐ FANTASTIQUE

HOW LONG DID IT TAKE FOR YOU TO GET YOUR DEVICE BACK?

- ☐ LESS THAN 2 HRS
- ☐ LESS THAN 6 HRS
- ☐ LESS THAN 24 H
- ☐ YOU NEVER RETRIEVED YOUR DEVICE

● MAKE US PART OF YOUR WAIT (COMPLETE THE PHRASE)

IT WOULD BE AWESOME IF...

_____

_____

_____

_____

WHO DO YOU RECOMMEND OUR DEVICES TO? (CIRCLE YOUR ANSWERS)

MY MOTHER	MY FRIEND(S)	C.E.O PEOPLE
MY FATHER	MY KID(S)	THE PRESIDENT
MY BROTHER	MY NEIGHBORS	PEOPLE ON THE STREET
MY SISTER	MY WIFE/HUSBAND	WOMEN/MEN

THANK YOU SO MUCH FOR YOUR TRUST. #SEEYOUSOON

CONTACT US

Best way for you to send your beautiful survey to us.

Customer SERVICE Address : ROBOTOP - CS - 1245 Bradford Av., Falcon City, AZ 94556

Don't forget to slide your survey into an envelope, stick the stamp on, and then give your letter to a qualified transporter so they can deliver your statement to us so we can continue to improve our services and products. Except, of course, if they were already perfect.

ADDITIONAL NOTES

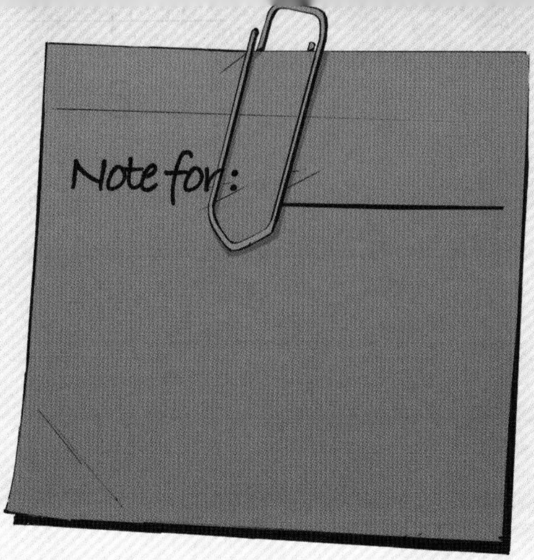
Note for:

IMAGE COMICS, INC. • TODD McFARLANE: PRESIDENT • JIM VALENTINO: VICE PRESIDENT • MARC SILVESTRI: CHIEF EXECUTIVE OFFICER • ERIK LARSEN: CHIEF FINANCIAL OFFICER • ROBERT KIRKMAN: CHIEF OPERATING OFFICER • ERIC STEPHENSON: PUBLISHER / CHIEF CREATIVE OFFICER • SHANNA MATUSZAK: EDITORIAL COORDINATOR • MARLA EIZIK: TALENT LIAISON • NICOLE LAPALME: CONTROLLER • LEANNA CAUNTER: ACCOUNTING ANALYST • SUE KORPELA: ACCOUNTING & HR MANAGER • JEFF BOISON: DIRECTOR OF SALES & PUBLISHING PLANNING • DIRK WOOD: DIRECTOR OF INTERNATIONAL SALES & LICENSING • ALEX COX: DIRECTOR OF DIRECT MARKET & SPECIALITY SALES • CHLOE RAMOS-PETERSON: BOOK MARKET & LIBRARY SALES MANAGER • EMILIO BAUTISTA: DIGITAL SALES COORDINATOR • KAT SALAZAR: DIRECTOR OF PR & MARKETING • DREW FITZGERALD: MARKETING CONTENT ASSOCIATE • HEATHER DOORNINK: PRODUCTION DIRECTOR • DREW GILL: ART DIRECTOR • HILARY DILORETO: PRINT MANAGER • TRICIA RAMOS: TRAFFIC MANAGER • ERIKA SCHNATZ: SENIOR PRODUCTION ARTIST • RYAN BREWER: PRODUCTION ARTIST • DEANNA PHELPS: PRODUCTION ARTIST • IMAGECOMICS.COM

GUNNING FOR RAMIREZ, VOL. 1. FIRST PRINTING. SEPTEMBER 2020. PUBLISHED BY IMAGE COMICS, INC. OFFICE OF PUBLICATION: 2701 NW VAUGHN ST., SUITE 780, PORTLAND, OR 97210. COPYRIGHT © 2020 NICOLAS PETRIMAUX. ALL RIGHTS RESERVED. "GUNNING FOR RAMIREZ," ITS LOGOS, AND THE LIKENESSES OF ALL CHARACTERS HEREIN ARE TRADEMARKS OF NICOLAS PETRIMAUX, UNLESS OTHERWISE NOTED. "IMAGE" AND THE IMAGE COMICS LOGOS ARE REGISTERED TRADEMARKS OF IMAGE COMICS, INC. NO PART OF THIS PUBLICATION MAY BE REPRODUCED OR TRANSMITTED, IN ANY FORM OR BY ANY MEANS (EXCEPT FOR SHORT EXCERPTS FOR JOURNALISTIC OR REVIEW PURPOSES), WITHOUT THE EXPRESS WRITTEN PERMISSION OF NICOLAS PETRIMAUX, OR IMAGE COMICS, INC. ALL NAMES, CHARACTERS, EVENTS, AND LOCALES IN THIS PUBLICATION ARE ENTIRELY FICTIONAL. ANY RESEMBLANCE TO ACTUAL PERSONS (LIVING OR DEAD), EVENTS, OR PLACES, WITHOUT SATIRICAL INTENT, IS COINCIDENTAL. PRINTED IN THE USA. ISBN: 978-1-5343-1697-3.

WWW.FLINGUERRAMIREZ.COM

SD -2 | APPROVED BY **THE FUNNY COMPANY**

SOME SITUATIONS MAY USE THE DEGREE NUMBER TWO